Elvis, Fast Cars, & The Brown Mountain Lights

A Novel by

Gary L Street

Titles Also Available by Gary L Street

Beyond the Majestic

Guarding Buffalo

Cloudland: *Where the Flowers Touch the Sky*

Killing Blackbirds (sequel to Cloudland)

On the Road to Panama

~

Web Site: garystreetmedia.com

Email address: garystreetmedia@gmail.com

Elvis, Fast Cars, & The Brown Mountain Lights

by Gary L Street

A DEDICATION

I would like to dedicate this book to my wife, Nancy, who has been a great part of the lifetimes I have so far lived. I would also dedicate this book to my sons, Ryan and Chris, and their wives, Jennifer Marie and Jennifer Lynn, for being such a wonderful part of many of my lifetimes. Finally, I would like to dedicate this book to my grandchildren, Grant and Victoria, who make a new lifetime so joyful.

Elvis, Fast Cars, & The Brown Mountain Lights

by Gary L Street

ACKNOWLEDGEMENTS

There many people involved when developing a literary work. It always begins with an idea. This work is certainly no different. I'd like to thank my son, Ryan Street for the idea of using the *Brown Mountain Lights* as a part of the background for my story. The idea gave impetus to a great storyline in this saga of the 1950's

I would also like to thank my lovely wife, Nancy, for another wonderful cover for my book. This is the fifth cover she has done for me and they have all given a wonderful visual for what is between all the pages.

Thanks to my son, Chris, who adds his own creative skills to digitally enhance the covers and make them pop as he adds verbiage and highlights to make the details stand out.

Another big thank you to Monica Berry who helps keep me alive in the world of technology. Monica's assistance in putting my work into a format that allows it to be read both electronically in the form of an eBook as well as a nice paperback edition. (Also, a shout out to her daughter, Lorelia, for letting me borrow her Mom!)

A special thank you from the many colorful characters of my stories to my understanding wife who shares me so unselfishly with them.

And thanks to the people who have made this region such a wonderful place to grow up and live. Those who have lived and are still living in this region inspire my characters in their independence, resourcefulness, and genuine interesting lives. You can't tell a good story without the context of authentic and interesting people.

"We experience our life through a variety of lifetimes we live. We see the past reflected in our legacy while we find the present soon becomes our future's memories. Life may appear only linear, but it is actually a merging of our many lifetimes into one life traveled. We then must travel on, keeping these two ideals in mind: We are accountable for all of the lives we live. And in the end, we will discover that how we lived those lives for others is what mattered most."

Gary L Street

Elvis, Fast Cars, and the Brown Mountain Lights

A Novel by
Gary L Street

PROLOGUE

She ran! Her feet barely kept her upright as she fled across the uneven ground. She'd lost one shoe getting out of the car and the other wasn't designed for running. Still, she ran!

There was a roar behind her. It was the motor of the car chasing her. It just as easily could have been the sound of anger coming from her wounded kidnapper. Her head throbbed from the blow he gave her when she stabbed him. Hitting the window with her head addled her even more. Her mind was so muddled she didn't remember opening the door and jumping out. It was all so...wrong.

Still, she ran. Her bare foot cried out in pain as she stepped on rocks and other unyielding objects. Her right ankle painfully twisted as it slid off something slick. She felt dizzy. It may have been from the blow to her head or just from a lack of oxygen. Running was her only hope, so she ran.

A crazy thought crossed her mind. The groceries she'd bought for dinner with her boyfriend would spoil in her car. The thought caused her to scream, expelling precious oxygen. She stumbled, almost pitching forward. Getting her balance, she tried to will herself to run harder...away from the madman chasing her. On she ran, making herself believe she would escape.

The roar of the engine filled her ears. He was still coming! He was right behind her now! *"Please God! Save me! Let me see Ford again! Let me see my Family!"*

She heard the car bouncing on the uneven ground. The sounds of the wheels hitting the rugged sod made her feel like the very ground itself was rising up against her. Her legs were failing her. They screamed in pain. She had to run! Why was this happening? She felt sick. She wanted to vomit. She was losing control. Her legs were so weak. Run…just keep running!

She tried to ignore the noises of the beast that was closing in on her. She sucked in great breaths and kept running! She saw bright spots in her vision. Her ears were shrilly ringing. Run…don't give up!

The car behind her hit a large depression in the ground causing it to land hard and bounce forward. She could feel the heat of the engine. There was a cry from inside the car. She heard it...she knew she did. Maybe there was a chance. Maybe...

Chapter One

~ 1932 ~

"Mara looked deeply into J.J.'s eyes, smiling in her most coy way."

It was one of those beautifully clear September nights that made you forget cold weather was only weeks away. Scenic spots like this were just one of the many perks of living in these mountains. The dark sky was filled with a glorious blanket made up of millions of stars, each twinkling for attention.

Of course, argument could be made that the September days of clear, deep blues and azure skies were just as breath-taking. Whether it was day or night, Mara DeVoti Rawlings felt blessed to live in these mountains with the love of her life, John Jacob Rawlings. Day or night, she considered her new life to be a miracle.

This was indeed a land illustrating so many of nature's beautifully created spectacles. Regardless of the season, Mara basked in the beauty of this land. Each breath reminded her that she was a part of this year-round calendar of fresh, clean air.

Mara anxiously awaited J.J.'s return home from work. She'd taken lunch to him at J.J.'s Motor Pool, the garage they owned. After returning to his parents, Bailey and Ada Rawlings' home, she found she couldn't get him off her mind. She felt the flush of passion that a husband and wife of only two years still experienced. It was palatable at times as they found it difficult to keep their hands off each other. Living with J.J.'s parents made it challenging to calm those fires of passion, even though it did slow them down at times.

J.J. arrived just before six o'clock with a look of hunger in his eyes that had little to do with food. He quickly cleaned up a bit and ate supper with more than a little haste. With barely two-years marriage under their belt, their marital urges could be quite fierce at times. The small house they shared with Bailey and Ada Rawlings lent itself to only the barest sense of privacy. Mara came from a passionate Italian background but that was tempered with modesty when it came to affairs of the bedroom. So, the young couple looked for places they could release their inhibitions without embarrassment to themselves or Bailey and Ada.

The couple found themselves under a starry night, looking out on Brown Mountain. They'd finished two beers each when J.J.'s amorous urges fully kicked in. It was such a beautiful night they left the top down on Mara's Ford Convertible Cabriolet so the stars could be easily seen. The black sky was overwhelming with its thousands and thousands of twinkling specks. The seat of their car was not an ideal substitute as a bedroom. It was just that the tiny bedroom in Mr. and Mrs. Rawlings small house could not contain the sounds of the loud, squeaky springs of their bed or banging of the bedposts against the very thin walls of the Rawlings home.

J.J. tossed his empty beer bottle into the dark night and had Mara in his arms before the container hit the ground. They meant to put the convertible's top up before their passions began but they became overwhelmed so quickly, the need for privacy was forgotten.

Almost immediately, Mara felt the flush of her own passion grow quickly as her husband began rearranging her clothing. She'd decided not to wear undergarments so that everything would go along quickly. It was always a possibility that someone could come along and interrupt them. She felt it important to be prudent with the amount of time given to their passions. She also realized the limited amount of the space inside the car often led to unnecessary entanglements when trying to remove certain articles of clothing in swift manner.

Mara braced herself against the corner of the seat back and the side wall of the interior. The car interior wasn't that roomy and certainly not very comfortable for these types of night moves.

J.J. positioned himself over her as he kissed her deeply and passionately. His hands were always a bit rough due to his work but this made him even more sensual to his wife. As good as his hands were on a speeding car's steering wheel or when putting together a powerful engine, they were still better when giving his wife the passionate pleasures she so enjoyed.

Mara dropped her head back on the edge of the open window, allowing the waves of passion, along with the cool night air, to wash over her. She took a very deep breath as their love making began peaking. Opening her eyes wide, she gazed over toward the distant outline of Brown Mountain. At that moment, bright lights began dancing across the mountain. She gasped, not knowing if it was a result of her passion or the bewildered surprise at seeing the lights so clearly. They appeared to move, suddenly seeming to come toward them.

Her husband, sensing a change in her excitement, amped up his movements. In only seconds they collapsed onto each other, allowing their euphoria to wash over them both as they slowly cooled down.

Mara was the first to say something, "Oh John! That was amazing!". She only referred to her husband as "John" when they were intimate.

J.J. replied, a slight breathiness still in his voice as his heart beat slowly returned to a normal pace. "Baby, you're so good yourself! I love you, baby!"

Mara pushed herself up in the seat as J.J. moved around so he could embrace her. Mara, her eyes still widely excited exclaimed, "No! It was the lights…I mean you're good…no, I mean great! But, I saw the "lights"! They were large, I mean big. They were moving! I think some of them came right to us. Right when, you know, when we were finishing!"

She sat straight up, pointing to where she saw the lights. "They were there…and then there. I don't know where they went. I closed my eyes just a second…you know, right at that moment. Then I opened my eyes and they were gone. It was just like that…really!"

She saw J.J. looking at her strangely so she said, "I didn't mean you weren't good…you're the absolute best. I love you John!" She then kissed her husband passionately, pulling him close to her as he silently wondered what had just happened to his wife.

Mara looked deeply into J.J.'s eyes, smiling in her most coy way. "Those lights were amazing John…I mean especially since we were love making. I mean, I felt like I could touch them…or maybe they touched me. I've never felt anything like this John. It's…I mean, it's…" She couldn't find words to end her sentence.

Then, she looked directly into her husband's eyes, a giant smile crossed her face. She put her hands on each side of his face and softly said, "John…I believe I'm pregnant."

J.J. looked at her with surprise and amusement as he tried to find words to say. Mara cut him off, "The lights…that wasn't an accident! It really happened! You'll see…I know what it means! We're pregnant John! I just know it…"

Chapter Two

~1957~

"One thing Mara DeVoti could do was make a quick decision."

Mara Rawlings enjoyed those quiet times she could sit on her front porch, sip coffee, and let a peaceful day wash over her. She could contemplate, daydream wistfully, or recall the many moments of her two lifetimes.

When she thought of her first lifetime in New Jersey, she could conjure up many fond memories as she grew up. Her parents were typical of most working-class Italian-Americans. They still lived in the rich heritage of their Italian ancestors while embracing the ways of this Country. Life had been good…normal.

Then, just as she reached adulthood, her father died due to an accident where he worked. Her mother, always a frail woman, died only two years later. Some said her heart was broken from the loss of her husband…the Doctors only said her heart could no longer take the stress of a tragically weakened body.

The losses of her parents left Mara with a determination to make her own life and fulfill their dreams. Unfortunately, fate put her in a situation that almost ended her life before it began.

Mara shook her head as she sat on her front porch, not allowing those dark memories to find a foothold in her thoughts. The front porch was a place meant for memories of her current lifetime, for the enjoyment of the beauty that was before her.

Another sip of coffee was followed by a deep breath of the early morning September air. It was just the recipe to forget thoughts of the dark times. Some folks living in these tall, welcoming highlands might take this wonderful place for-granted at times. Mara could only appreciate the beautiful landscapes of the high mountains and wandering valleys. Her appreciation reflected the differences in the environment where she was raised.

Sometimes her memories of the New Jersey shoreline made her a little melancholy. She did so like going to the beach on those lovely June days. Her walks with her father and even her mother when she could manage, were wonderful. When she closed her eyes, she could sometimes still hear the waves break and the gulls call. The air was good along the coast, especially after a cleansing rain storm passed through. But, it was a different type of air than was found in these mountains. She remembered it feeling heavier, salty, with a flavor you could taste at times.

She did not miss the winters in New Jersey. They were rougher there, or at least they were remembered to feel much rawer and last longer. When Mara began thinking too much about New Jersey, she always found a fresh cup of coffee enjoyed on her porch would wash away her thoughts before they got to the really bad parts. She sorely wished she could somehow extinguish the dark part of that past, even if she had to make that entire lifetime disappear.

Solace from those memories could also be found in reminding herself of the events responsible for her living this lifetime. It was her past lifetime that caused her to cross the path of John Jacob Rawlings. Part of that past was filled with danger and fear. Now she was surrounded by these mighty mountains that protected her as well as the strong arms of J.J. Rawlings.

~1930~

It was 1930 when she found herself enjoying a rare night out at the Starfire Club. The club was near her apartment in her new home of Mercerville, New Jersey. She'd only lived there a little over a year after leaving Asbury Park and the nearby sandy beaches. Mercerville was located closely to the Army's Fort Dix, so it was normal seeing soldiers around town. Mara was doing all she could live a quiet life, blending in without notice. Fortunately, she managed making a few new friends from work. They were just enough to keep her from feeling totally isolated and alone.

She was at the Starfire Club on that fateful night, celebrating the recent engagement of one of their group, Darlene Rossi. Everyone thought Darlene would be the last to marry but she fooled them, becoming the first...well, almost.

J.J was at the Starfire Club with some Army buddies, celebrating their last leave before finishing their tour of service. It would only be a short time before they would be rejoining civilian life and their loved ones.

The two of them met at the lone telephone booth in the back of the club. Both needed to make a call but found each other more interesting than any telephone conversation.

The chance meeting resulted in a few awkward sentences being exchanged before they made their way to a table where J.J. ordered drinks. Drinks led to a couple of slow dances where he literally swept her off her feet. This soldier, J.J., as everyone called him, was the most dashing man she'd ever met. His uniform could not hide his strong physique. His cool, southern drawl, along with a chiseled chin, dark hair, and sparkling ebony eyes were just too much to disregard.

The dashing Southern soldier found Mara equally intriguing. He couldn't take his eyes off this beauty with the dark, raven hair and the flashing eyes that danced as she spoke or laughed. All he could think of that night was that each minute he spent with this girl made him want another.

One thing Mara DeVoti could do was make a quick decision. That ability had saved her virtue and possibly her life once before. In fact, it was that event that caused her to leave Asbury Park and the seaside behind.

It was on that night though, as she looked into J.J.'s intense eyes, she made the decision that she wanted him to be it for the rest of her lifetimes.

J.J. was on the first day of a three-day pass when they first met. Before his pass ended, they were married. One of Mara's girlfriends worked at the courthouse and was able to get all the paperwork and red tape expedited. A Priest was located to perform the ceremony as Darlene Rossi and Corporeal Morgan Grant looked on as witnesses.

Suddenly, the life she'd been dealing with began fading far away. A new lifetime was beginning, one she never thought possible. J.J. not only brought overwhelming love into her life but he also offered her the opportunity to start over again.

All she ever hoped for was a person to live a life with, a family to love and cherish, and a world that did not include the ugly nature of violent men. She had never considered it too much to ask, and now that she'd found it, she determined to hold on to her dream life with all her being.

Of course, getting what you want never means it's destined to last forever. In the back of her mind she knew that one day, this peaceful, new life could be shattered by the ugliness she was leaving behind. Because of this, Mara could not help but keep a careful eye on her past.

Mara wasted no time in kicking her old life to the curb and setting her course on the opportunity of the next lifetime. On the day J.J. and his buddies returned to Fort Dix, Mara filled three suitcases and a large shoulder bag, hopping on a bus to begin her trip to

Treemont, North Carolina.

Mr. and Mrs. Bailey Rawlings met Mara at the bus station, immediately welcoming their new daughter-in-law into the Rawlings family. It so easily became the place that the young, New Jersey woman, had always hoped to find. A place she could not only call home but could build her a different life that had nothing to do with her past.

~1957~

Mara's porch musings usually resulted in a salty tear or two by the time she reached this part of her story. The tear was a result of many things. The joy of what had become her life, the tragedies of the past, and the unbelievable happiness she had known in most of her life in North Carolina.

She thought about how long ago 1930 seemed when her second life began. She still felt a fondness for the Rawlings home where she and J.J. spent the first two and a half years of their marriage. Sitting on her own porch of her own home was a feeling she could hardly put into words. She rubbed her hands on the well-worn rocker arms feeling the grain of the wood and the comfortable peace a home brings.

They'd lived with J.J.'s parents longer than she originally anticipated. This didn't cause her unhappiness, only a bit of restlessness. J.J. persuaded Mara they should put most of his savings into opening their own business, J.J.'s Motor Pool. J.J. was such a great mechanic they all knew it had to be a success. So, the business came first and Mara waited and worked patiently toward their own home.

Mara never doubted they'd made a sound decision, but she always yearned for a time when she'd have the privacy of her own home. Each day she awoke with the same thoughts, *"Soon, very soon Mara. You'll have your own home, your own family, and your own...very private life."* And now, looking back from her porch, that dream had been fully realized.

She had immediately felt a kinship with Bailey and Ada. They were very helpful and caring without being intrusive. Not only did they make it a point to welcome her into their home but they saw to it that she quickly found a place in the community. And, she had found it easy to adapt into the community because she discovered a joy of living a simple, country lifestyle.

It made Mara smile as well as chuckle as she remembered those early days spent helping J.J. establish the business. She worked in the office and even crawled under a hood to be schooled on the workings of a gasoline engine. Ada and Bailey patiently spent time with her as they educated her in living a self-sufficient life in these mountains. Mara remembered trying to absorb every detail in her new mountain home so as to be a good wife to J.J. She also found great joy in teaching Ada and Bailey the recipes of good Italian cooking. Having a garden was delightful as it produced so many fresh ingredients for her sauces and dishes. Bailey became so enamored with Italian cuisine he one day proclaimed himself to be at least twenty percent Italian.

Both parents made a good effort to introduce her to the people of the community. For the most part, everyone was open and welcoming to this Yankee with the large, contagious personality. She tried not to stand out in her new home but it was difficult for her to tone down her nature. She was the one most surprised that people took to her buoyant personality and even encouraged it.

As she thought of those nights she and J.J. would slip away for a little intimate time away from the thin walls of the Rawlings' house, she thought of Brown Mountain. And, Brown Mountain made her think of the mystical lights that are given to surprising visits on clear, Fall nights. It was one of those nights that their son, Ford, was conceived. Mara chuckled at how it always embarrassed the now grown man to hear her tell the story.

She looked across the yard at her yellow1932 Ford Cabriolet convertible and found herself revisiting that night and many others when J.J. and her wanted to be alone. Star gazing from the convertible was an enjoyable experience. Looking out at Brown Mountain, anticipating the chance of seeing the mystical Brown Mountain Lights was certainly exciting. Mara could only wonder why she had never seen the lights appear on Brown Mountain since that one special night.

J.J. had told Mara the many stories and legends regarding the mysterious ghost lights. She remembered some of the stories went back to the days when only the Catawba and Cherokee Indians lived in these mountains. The tales of people seeing the glowing orbs on, or just above the mountain sounded like the fantastic stories a person would tell a child to entertain them.

J.J. swore to Mara he had only witnessed the phenomenon once in his life. At first, she accused him of being drunk when he thought he'd seen the lights. Then, she began hearing similar stories from people all around the County. After a while, she found she craved to see these mysterious lights herself. Several times she ventured out into the evening only to be disappointed.

Mara, like many who had never seen them, ended up being purely skeptical of the lights. Bailey and Ada both claimed to have observed them but Mara still felt these "lights" were maybe just a phenomenon with a sketchy history of documentation over the decades.

Some of the tales and legends concerning the lights were outrageous and downright funny. Speculations ranged from Alien visitors, to mysterious gases, to mystical ghosts, and refractions of lights from trains or automobiles. The opinions varied greatly among the local populace. J.J. claimed some of the local moonshiners may have created the lights at times to throw off the Law as they hunted for their stills. Since J.J.'s brother was one of those moonshiners, she wondered if that might be closest to the truth.

Two of the oldest legends spoke of the spirit of an old slave, carrying a lantern around the mountain looking for his master who became lost. Another legend was that the lights were the spirits of Indian maidens from the Catawba or Cherokee Indian tribes searching for their fallen warriors who died in a great battle on the mountain.

After a while, Mara had heard so many tales about the lights that she could not find reason in any of them. The former New Jersey girl was just no longer impressed. She remembered thinking she was just too sophisticated and intelligent to believe in such things.

However, Mara actually did believe in miraculous things. Her marriage to J.J. was a miracle she could not deny. No matter how she tried to deny the existence of the mysterious mountain lights, she always felt there was something there she needed to connect with. She remembered at one time making a great show in denying their existence, while holding on to a deep, inner truth she truly wanted them to exist.

It was in from this grain of belief she formed her own intimate belief in the lights. And, on one beautiful September night, her faith had been rewarded as she, J.J. and the lights created a true miracle. Now, she could only pray daily that they might somehow return…and bring her son with them.

PART ONE

From the Past to the Present

The Next Lifetime Begins

Chapter Three

~1957~

"As Ford and Deputy Lon Shell met on a roadside that early morning, the first of Ford's lifetimes passed away."

Ford Rawlings was driving down a highway that was very familiar. He'd traveled this piece of asphalt a good part of his life. But now…it just seemed almost foreign to him as it led to a place he wasn't sure he wanted to go. The odd thing about this destination was that it was the only place he'd ever called home.

As he got closer to the little North Carolina town called Treemont, his thoughts wandered back to the time he left this pristine mountain paradise. Sadly, because of the tragedy he left behind, he could find little joy in his remembrance of this place…or his return. Time had passed but that only offered brief periods of forgetfulness of the sadness he'd left behind. Some would say he'd never found closure. That may have been accurate because he never understood how to find closure.

Ford cruised down the roadway as his '57 Chevy seemed to control his journey. He was no longer the infamous "Hot Rod Rawlings" people often told raucous stories about. That was laughable to him now. He could still drive with the best of them as well as put together a powerful engine…he just no longer owned these roads.

Every few moments he had a great urge to turn his steering wheel so as to head directly away from these many sad memories. However, he knew he couldn't get rid of them by doing this. His history…his other lifetimes proved that to be true.

Instead of turning around, Ford gritted his teeth and traveled on…rethinking all that happened here. It may have been the millionth time he'd gone over the events that caused him to leave. There were answers here. He knew they were here but still didn't know how to find them. Ford felt…no, he believed, that when the answers were found, they would be in the dark and evil heart of some person…or some people still living their lives here.

Ford promised himself…one more time, *"I'm going to learn the truth! I'll not leave this time until I have the answers…even if it kills me."*

Ford calmed himself as his mind wandered back in time, back to 1951 and his first lifetime…

~ 1951 ~

The small country town of Treemont was located in the midst of the many beautiful Western North Carolina mountains. The primary commerce of the area was farming and mining. Timber was good at times. What was always good was a local endeavor called moonshining.

The area was flush with the elements required for a successful moonshining business. Pristine water and secluded land could always be found. The hardware needed along with the skilled producers required to make a good product were plentiful enough. Demand was always high, keeping the suppliers busy.

The mountains always seemed to have an adequate number of people skilled in producing the illegal product. One other element required was able young men skilled at transporting the moonshine to areas of high retail and wholesale possibilities. And they also needed to be skilled in not getting caught doing it. That was the one reason that Ford "Hot Rod" Rawlings had made such a name for himself.

All these elements made moonshining a good paying, "cottage industry", howbeit, a very illegal and often dangerous endeavor. It was true a careless moonshiner might blow himself up from time to time. There was also a good chance of arrest, which would put you behind the bars of the someplace like the "Old" Craggy Correctional Prison. All in all, there was plenty enough risk in either producing or transporting the product.

Law Enforcement Agencies, Federal, State, and local, would attempt to arrest both the producers and the transporters. Jailing them was the goal but they did not hesitate coming in, guns blazing. The law breakers were usually not shy in defending their enterprises, either. For a significant reward, there were plenty of dangers for both those breaking the law and those trying to stop them.

Ford's specialty was often the most dangerous. Transporting the liquor while avoiding the Law earned Ford the nickname, "Hot Rod Rawlings". Driving the curvy mountain roads at flat-out speeds in the middle of the night was a harrowing enterprise. There were plenty of stories of both the chasers and the chasees ending up rolling and crashing down the side of one of the mountains. Ford Rawlings had never been one of those unfortunates to feel the unforgiving wrath of the mountain roads. He went about his business, almost always delivering his product and bringing home the cash his efforts brought.

While enforcing the Law and catching lawbreakers was first and foremost with most Law Enforcement officers, there were some individuals who had other agendas. A few found it easier to allow the moonshine to run as long as they got their own piece of the action.

Some moonshiners felt that when they heard someone tell them they expected and wanted, "their own piece of the action", it mostly negated the whole idea of a tax-free product controlled by some Federal or State regulations. In fact, some moonshiners, including Jubal "Skillet" Rawlings, found the idea of partnering with someone like Sheriff Royal Albert Majesty to be distinctly distasteful.

In addition to the Law, good or bad, there were those who felt they should be paid for other people's labors, especially when it came to moonshine. These "jack-legged", low-life's, thought it a good idea to steal another man's product so they could sell it with little or no overhead to themselves. This rarely worked out well for the thieves but some still tried. Hard working moonshiners believed a fair price should be provided them for their "white lightning". They were usually loyal and fair to their regular customers. However, those trying to steal a man's livelihood often found themselves bloodied and in need of casket.

It was the trickiest task in the whole process that Ford Rawlings found the most exciting and fun. Getting the product out of the mountains to places where it could be profitably sold got his juices flowing even though it meant flirting with dangers around each and every curve.

Three adjoining States to North Carolina, had very thirsty folks who didn't see the percentages in paying the Government taxes for a good drink of whiskey. Some patrons loved the illegal whiskey because their home Counties allowed no whiskey at all, legal or illegal. Other people just appeared to love and prefer the "white lightning" over all the bonded products.

These thirsty folks needed to be serviced regularly and often. Having the best moonshine whiskey on the planet was of no matter if you couldn't get it to the customer when they wanted it. This was where daring young men like Ford "Hot Rod" Rawlings earned their money…and their fame.

Moonshine was transported mostly by night. This added to the element of danger as many daring car chases occurred on the dark mountain roads. More than a few of those chases involved the young daredevil son of J.J. and Mara Rawlings.

Uncle Jubal "Skillet" Rawlings made sure Ford had plenty of "shine" to run. From the time Ford was big enough to handle one of the heavy, powerful cars with hidden moonshine compartments, he was running the roads.

J.J. and Mara didn't approve, and neither did his lovely and beautiful, Julia. She was the only part of Ford's life that did not involve an engine and four wheels.

However, Ford was a head-strong, willful young man when it came to the allure of cars and driving fast. The truth was, he cared little about the moonshine or even the money he made driving for his Uncle. He just loved to out-drive, out-maneuver, and outrun anyone who thought they could catch him. Many joined in the chase only to end up in a road-side ditch or much worse.

Some thought they could anticipate the moonshine runs and their schedules. Traps were set as Deputies waited in the dark, mountain night to catch the young daredevils, especially the one called "Hot Rod Rawlings". They all wanted to be the one to catch that young 'shine runner.

The truth was, if they were really fortunate they would spend the night waiting on a car that never traveled their way. Those that chased the tail lights of Ford Rawlings never tasted the victory of catching him.

Some claimed they knew when it was Ford they were chasing because he liked to "play" with them. He would allow them to stay close enough to think they just might catch him. Then, just as they were ready to force him off the road, he found another gear and left them chasing fireflies in the dark night. Many who were tasked with catching Ford were just happy to be going home as opposed to climbing out of a wrecked car on the side of a mountain.

But you see, all of that took place in Ford's first lifetime. In fact, that first lifetime ended early one sunny morning as Ford found himself returning from a successful delivery run to Asheville. It had not been an easy run due to a few County Deputies guessing correctly.

Ford had been driving along the curvy stretch of rough asphalt known as Rucksack Road. It was just past one o'clock in the morning. His car was running well on the sketchy piece of rough County road. Uncle Jubal had the Chevy sedan cranking plenty of horsepower to get the heavy load of moonshine down the road. The suspension design was set up well in order haul a full load of whiskey through the demanding mountain roads. Ford found himself enjoying the fast ride on such a beautiful mountain night.

He passed a small cut-out road. Glancing to his rear-view mirror, he noticed two sets of headlights falling in behind him. He wasn't too concerned until he noticed another vehicle joining the procession. This time, it wasn't headlights he saw. Instead, it was tail lights. He guessed the following cars had a two-way radio that allowed them to call ahead to another car.

The lead car slowed, keeping Ford from passing it while the other two cars closed the space between them. Suddenly, a flashing red light came on as did a loud siren. Both chase cars went into full Police mode. Ford looked ahead and saw the passenger in the lead car trying to lean out the window in order to aim what appeared to be a shotgun at his car. Ford thought, *"Well now, if that's the way you want to play, I can sure accommodate you!"*.

Ford shifted gears as his car accelerated quickly. He veered to the left of the lead car only to quickly cut back to the passenger side. The man holding the shotgun had managed to get almost half of his body through the window. Momentarily losing sight of Ford he'd relaxed his aim. When Ford's vehicle veered back to his side he was caught by surprise.

He tried to bring the shotgun up to a firing position just as Ford's front bumper made contact with the rear bumper of the Deputy's car. The crunch of metal on metal resounded loudly. It caused the man with the shotgun to fire prematurely, actually shooting into the fender-well of his own vehicle before he lost his grip on the weapon. The heavy shot tore through the fender of the car and punctured the tire. The shooter was knocked against the window frame as his car swerved.

Ford blew past the sliding car just as shots were fired from the first trailing vehicle. The pistol rounds did not hit their intended target though. Ford cut back across the road ending up in front of the former lead car. The shots from the trailing Deputy's car struck the car Ford had just passed. One round exploded through the car's rear glass while another round hit the exposed Deputy in the shoulder. Ford caught just a glimpse of him react in agony from the gunshot before he pulled swiftly away from all three cars.

Unfortunately, when the Deputy driving the damaged car tried to reach out to his gunshot companion, the rear tire blew completely from the rim. The cars rear-end slid violently to one side as the driver attempted to regain control. The result was a fatal over-correction which took the vehicle off the road, down a steep hillside. The man hanging out of the window was thrown from the car, slamming into the dark ground. The driver rode the car down the embankment where it ended up on its top.

Both chase cars slid to a halt, the rear one almost hitting the lead car in the side. Ford looked in his rear-view mirror just in time to see a belch of flame shoot up from below the road. Ford wondered if the gun shots might have been the reason for the explosion or if the fuel tank ruptured as it rolled down the mountainside.

Whatever the reason, he suddenly realized he might be accused of murder…that is if either one of the Deputies died. He felt remorse for the men even though he knew in his heart he did nothing to cause their injury.

Then he paused, *"The hell I didn't do anything. I didn't pull a gun…never would. But I sure as hell was a part of that accident. If I wasn't running the 'shine, those old boys wouldn't have been chasing me."* As he drove along, he pondered the whole situation. Finally, he came to a conclusion. *"I need to stop this crap. Uncle "Skillet" was going to have to find somebody else. I can't lose everything over something like this. Good lord, I can't lose Julia!*

The rest of the trip was without incident. He slipped into the outskirts of Asheville, delivered the 'shine, and was out of the area by the time the sun was rising. There was no news of the chase or wreck on the Buncombe County radio stations. He'd have to listen to the radio once he got within range of the station in Burke County. Maybe their news would offer some account of the chase. He was doubtful there would be much detail unless someone died.

Ford almost stopped a couple of times to make a telephone call to Uncle Jubal. It would have been a waste of time since his Uncle never talked "business" over the phone. He was a cautious man which was the reason he was one of the most successful moonshine producers in the mountains.

Ford couldn't forget the short-lived glimpse of the fiery crash. It was probably the worst accident anyone had ever experienced while chasing him. He hoped the two men survived and would be okay. There was no intent to hurt them even though they appeared to have every intention of hurting him. Never had anyone shot at him, even the few times someone tried to hijack him. The fellows chasing him appeared to want him harmed more than they wanted him stopped.

The whole thing was confusing. Such violent force wasn't used by lawmen unless someone was first firing at them. He wondered what might have changed. Maybe there would be news once he returned to his Uncle's place. Uncle Jubal always had a way of getting the latest news…at least the news that affected his business. The events of the night before certainly would affect Jubal's business. This might cause Jubal to bring out his infamous skillet to pound across somebody's head.

For the time being, Ford would have to wait to find out if he was a *wanted man.* That had such an unnatural ring to it.

Ford closed his mind to all the disturbing events of the last twenty-four hours as he found himself closer to home. All he wanted to think about was the wonderful evening he planned with his girl, Julia Anne Harmon.

He had money in his pocket for as expensive a dinner as could be bought, at least in these parts. And, he had a beautiful ring to slip on Julia's finger during the dessert course.

After dinner, he was thinking they might slip up to an overlook spot and see if the famous Brown Mountain lights might show up tonight. Three people recently reported seeing them over the past few nights, so he figured his chances were good.

He knew his mother, Mara, would be especially thrilled to know they became engaged and observed the lights in the same night. It would certainly make her happy that another important event in the Rawlings' family came about as the evasive Brown Mountain lights appeared.

Mara often embarrassed Ford by telling people that her son was conceived under a starry night in the presence of those crazy mountain lights. Just as embarrassing was the fact that Mara's Ford convertible was most likely the reason for Ford's name. "*Ford*", he thought, "*Well, at least they weren't sitting in a Packard when it happened!*"

As he drove along, he considered his Dad's story of how the Ford convertible had come into their possession. He chuckled to himself, *"It was after all, a pretty good story."*

~1931~

J.J. surprised Mara, as well as Bailey and Ada, when he drove the Ford Cabriolet up to the Rawlings house. He had come to own it on his way home after being discharged from the Service. He loved telling the story of how he'd won the car in a poker game that took place on a long train ride heading home.

To pass the time, he and four other fellows ended up playing poker in the Club car. They finally reached that one hand where the pile of chips grew and grew. The betting was intense and all of the players felt they had a winning hand, at least at first. As the level of bets increased and the pot grew fatter and fatter, the men, one by one, lost their nerve and folded. Finally, it was down to only J.J. and a young man from Charlotte. The young fellow, Clive Bennet, was the son of Red Bennett, owner of three Ford Dealerships in the North Carolina area.

Clive held a hand of three kings and a pair of Aces. A very strong hand. But J.J. held four threes'. There was no reason for either to back down since neither man believed he could lose.

There'd been a considerable amount of alcohol consumed, especially by Clive. This probably was one reason the pot grew so large in the first place. It was Clive who blinked first as if a sobering thought occurred to him when he realized how much money was laying on the table. He decided to "call" J.J.'s last, very large raise.

Clive opened his small briefcase in order to pull out more funds to cover his last bet. That was when he discovered his stash of cash was gone. It seems a young lady he'd been spending time with prior to the train trip had helped herself to the considerable amount of cash hidden inside the case.

Embarrassed, he showed J.J. the empty compartment, suggesting, "Tell you what I'll do, old sport. I want to be square with you, especially since you just got out the Army. First of all, I want to find a way to assure you I'm good for the money. To that end, I'll give you a signed IOU for the balance acknowledged by these good men. My father is a successful man in Charlotte so I won't be stiffing you. Secondly, for your trust, I'll pay you the cash as soon as we can get to a Bank."

He hesitated as J.J. was looking unsure. Absolutely sure he had the winning hand he decided to sweeten the pot. "Tell you what else I'll do, old sport. If I lose, I'll take you to my Father's car lot and give you any used car you choose, free and clear." He then added, as if he needed to justify himself, "I really did have the money but I guess I let that girl run off with it. Don't seem too smart to let that happen…but she was a looker!" Clive's face reddened a little as the men around the table chuckled at him.

J.J. figured he was mostly playing with everyone else's money by now, so he agreed. Of course, the four threes carried the hand. Now Clive's face turned even redder. He shook his head, "Damn son, you are some fierce poker player.

By now, Clive tried downing another long shot of whiskey only to get choked as he saw J.J. pulling his winnings to his side of the table. The man continued staring at the table as he poured himself another drink.

The next drink steeled Clive, so instead of quitting, he offered, "Now, if you're a real betting man, old son, I'll bet you double or nothing on the cut of this here card deck. If you win, I'll just pay you a lot more cash when we get to Charlotte." Clive was still looking at the pile of money in front of J.J. He noticed J.J. was not looking as if he was going to accept the wager. He took another swallow of whiskey and added. "Tell you what, sport. Take this bet and instead of a used car, if you win, I'll let you have any new car at my Daddy's car dealership in addition to the money. That's all free and clear, you know!"

J.J. couldn't resist such an offer, so they cut the deck. Clive turned up the King of Hearts which left him with a satisfied smirk on his face. He settled back in his chair, pouring himself still another double whiskey. Before he finished his drink, J.J. turned over the Ace of Diamonds.

Two days later, J.J. pulled up to the Rawlings house with a fat wallet and the shiny, brand-new 1931 Ford Cabriolet Convertible as a present for his new bride. As Mara looked at the car in awe, a smiling J.J. said, "Didn't get you much of a wedding ring, so I thought this might make up for it some. Probably didn't need to be gambling, but I was bored and missing you."

~1951~

The trip back from Ashville eased Ford's worries as he recalled his Dad's story of winning the convertible. Even though he and J.J. could find plenty to disagree about, he couldn't think of any man he admired more. He turned his radio on hoping to catch a newscast. That was about the last moment Ford remembered feeling any kind of peace in his life. In fact, the last memory of that day made Ford feel like closing his eyes and driving off the road into whatever oblivion welcomed him.

He recalled the car radio playing *Indian Love Call* by Slim Whitman as he came up on two County Sheriff's cars parked by the road, lights flashing. He recognized one of the Deputy's as Lon Shell, a boy out of his high school class. Lon recently started working for the County Sheriff's Department and Ford felt him a little too proud of his position. Just before Ford passed, he could see some uneven skid marks as the track of tires left a path through the weeds and grass of the field by the road. Lon was by the road as the other Deputy appeared to be looking for something in the field.

He had both the time and the curiosity, so he pulled over to ask Lon what'd happened. Surprisingly, Lon hurried over to intercept Ford as he stepped from the car.

The two never had much in common, in school or afterwards. Still, they'd always managed to stay civil with each other. This was curious, since after all, one was now a lawman and the other, well, a moonshine runner.

Still, Ford never felt it necessary to not be anything but nice to Lon. A part of this was because Lon grew up without a father. His mother, Betty, always was a woman attractive beyond her years, never married. As a beautiful seventeen-year-old, she disappeared from Freemont for about a year and a half, returning with a baby boy whom she raised by herself. Her beauty never faded but she found no suitor that ever gained her interest. She worked as the Court Stenographer at the Burke County Courthouse which apparently provided a decent life for her and Lon.

By Ford and Lon's high school graduation, their lives were already headed in different directions. Lon opted to attend a Law Enforcement Academy given his interest in the becoming a lawman. It appeared the High Sheriff of Burke County was Lon's champion, helping him get into the school. Now, Lon worked for the man himself while Ford transported illegal whiskey through the night for his Uncle.

As Ford and Deputy Lon Shell met on a roadside that early morning, the first of Ford's lifetimes passed away. To Ford's surprise, Lon walked directly to him and grabbed him roughly, holding on.

Ford tried to pull away as he was startled by Lon's grip. Giving Lon a hard look, he heard the Deputy say, "Don't go over there, Ford. You don't want to do that! They've removed the body already. It was Julia!" His voiced quietened, "She was found over there…in the field. She's gone Ford…she was gone when they found her."

Ford was speechless as Lon told him that Julia's body had been found in the field beside the road early that morning, a hit and run victim. Strangely, they'd found her car a few miles away, at Hiller's Gas and Market… her groceries in the trunk. Ford slumped to the ground and sat staring out toward the field. Lon knelt by Ford, telling him all he knew.

Julia's parents had reported her missing the night before. They'd called the Sheriff's Department when it got late, fearing there'd been an automobile accident. Later, someone remembered her saying she was stopping at the market to get a few groceries on her way home. She was planning on fixing Ford a surprise dinner that night. No one at the store paid any notice to her car still being on the property, even after the business closed. It was a mystery that would haunt the community from that day on and a tragedy that would continue to haunt Ford Rawlings in all his waking minutes.

~ 1957 ~

The memories rushed at Ford from the deep recesses of his mind, a place he tried burying them so long ago. As Ford traveled the familiar country roads and small-town streets he felt everything appeared surreal. His eyes misted over at the realness of it all. The scenery looked no different to him than the picture on a post card. He was home but felt like a stranger…a visitor passing through.

Ford was mystified as he thought that it mattered little where you grew up. It didn't matter where you grew up, a place always appeared smaller when you returned from being gone for a long period of time. The calendar had turned well into 1957 since Ford Rawlings last set foot in the tiny town of Treemont. He drove down Main Street, wondering how so many things could have transpired in his life over the last six years.

Chapter Four

"...he could only wonder why he came back...and how could he possibly stay."

In the aftermath of Julia's death, Ford left. Not only did he leave Tremont, but he left everything that was his life. He didn't feel he had many choices at the time...at least not many good ones. He knew that staying would result in him becoming a wanted man which would only end up hurting more innocent people in his life. So, he ended up letting the Army take him.

And when his Army service ended, he still could not see himself going back to his home. Ford found instead, an unexpected place to spend his next lifetime...far away from North Carolina. Looking back, that lifetime suddenly seemed almost as foreign and strange as his presence now in Treemont.

As he drove down the familiar streets seeing familiar buildings and people, he wondered if he could live through yet another lifetime. He wasn't sure if he could even start one here. He kept reminding himself, *"I can always leave again. There's got to be a life somewhere for me."* Ford had so many doubts, wondering if he could find a satisfying life again...anywhere. He guessed if history had shown him anything, it was that the next lifetime started whether you were ready or not.

As he looked down Treemont's Main Street he noticed only a couple of businesses that had changed over the last several years. Most were still operating just as they did when he left.

A new bank building was being built on a corner in the middle of town. The newly placed sign on the building declared, *Brown Mountain Savings and Loan.* It sounded a risky name to Ford. The Brown Mountain Lights certainly didn't paint a picture of dependable security. Maybe his Mother had a voice in naming the institution.

He recalled an old hotel of sorts previously standing where the bank was built. If he remembered correctly, the name of the hotel had been, *The Mountain Laurel Inn.* His mother mentioned in one of her many letters that the old wooden structure burned to the ground on a cold November night a few years back. He never heard any follow-up as to what caused the fire. It was just one of many bits of news Mara reported in her letters that chased him through his Army destinations and beyond.

Ford's mind raced as he drove through town. His memory of leaving Treemont was hazy, a series of blurred images. He was still in shock over Julia's death when he decided to leave. He went into the Army so that the images of her death would be dulled, faded into shadows as he focused on the rigors of Basic training.

To his surprise, the harsh feelings of guilt and anger returned as soon as the all-consuming rigors of Basic Training were completed. All Basic Training accomplished was to take his mind off Julia for only short moments. His best days were the long and exhausting ones that brought a deep, dreamless sleep when he fell into his cot.

It was the same after Basic as he completed specialized training classes for his assignment. It was in one of those classes that he first met a young fellow from New Jersey named Jovanni "Joey" Visconti, the only person who could keep his mind off Julia.

In Joey, Ford realized he'd found a great friendship that could last beyond even his military career. Looking back, it had to have been fate that brought the two young men together. As soon as training ended, Joey was assigned to another base. Then, for reasons Ford never understood, Joey somehow ended up stationed along with him in Heidelberg, Germany. Ford wondered if Joey had connections even in the Army.

The Army was quick to understand and take advantage of Ford's expertise with anything mechanical, especially when it incorporated wheels and an engine. He was just as adept at driving any type of vehicle as he was keeping them running.

Joey seemed to take to the life of being in the Motor Pool and loved the ready availability of transportation. He seemed to always be in possession of a vehicle for transporting an Officer, materials, supplies, or even for his own enjoyment.

Most of Joey and Ford's escapades in Germany involved being somewhere they shouldn't have been in a vehicle that they shouldn't have been driving. Fortunately, for both of them, they had each other to look out for the other. The two young men forged a lasting bond as the fun-loving boy from Jersey and the daredevil from Carolina lived a lifetime in the Army. It was a bond that was destined to last through many lifetimes.

As Ford continued down Main Street, his thoughts were troubled by the lifetime he left behind in New Jersey. He had never planned on leaving that lifetime but it wasn't his choice. The terrible truth was that there was much pain involved leaving that life as there had been in leaving his first. Ford's mind cried out with questions, *"Why would I ever want another life? How could I even deserve one? Could I even survive it? Who else will feel the pain from another life of mine?"*

He stopped as a truck picking up a young woman and her little boy stopped in front of him. He could almost picture Julia and their child climbing in a pickup just like the one in front of him. He forced the image from his mind. Two lifetimes had passed for Ford since he lived here. Still, the painful memories were still just as raw now as they were when Ford left.

Ford forced himself to clear his mind and only focus on what was ahead. He had just the one job to do. It might not bring him peace but it could provide some form of closure. That had to be worth something. This time, even the Sheriff of Burke County would not stop Ford from finding out who killed Julia. This time…he was willing to die if that was what it took to sort the mystery out.

Random thoughts continued intruding on Ford's mind as he drove slowly through Treemont. His new India Ivory and Tropical Turquoise 1957 Chevy Bel Air Sports Coupe caught people's attention but Ford did not notice. His vision was hijacked with the many clouded images of his past. Unfortunately, he saw Julia in each and everything one of those images.

Ordinarily, driving a new car like this would have been enough to keep Ford's mind occupied. He'd picked the Chevy up shortly before leaving his latest past life. Even though he was forced to leave a horrible situation behind, and was finding his destination troublesome, Ford did truly enjoy driving to North Carolina in this fine automobile. The Sport Coupe sported a V-8 Super "Turbo Fire" engine with a four-barrel carburetor. By adding an overdrive unit with a four-speed shifter and limited slip differential, he had brought the 220hp engine up around 270hp. He believed he could put this car on most race tracks today with a high assurance of winning, especially with him behind the wheel.

Many men, and some women in Burke County were pretty good mechanics. Aunt Billie knew as much about engines as most men. She was certainly a partner with Uncle Jubal in all things. Most mountain people used their automobiles, trucks, farm equipment, and any other piece of mechanical equipment until they were completely used up. The same could be said about these hardy mountain people.

Fortunately, there were still folks who still came to *J.J.'s Motor Pool* to get their problems solved. J.J. was one of the best mechanics in all of Western North Carolina. Ford was under a car with is dad before he could ride a bicycle. As he grew older he would go to his dad's garage directly from school. He would always be grateful for the education J.J. imparted to him. He could not imagine who he would be without the smell of oil and gasoline. Ford just hoped now that he was back, his father would welcome his prodigal without judgement.

Ford liked to tell people his first toys were a socket wrench and a screw driver. He took to engines better than most people took to country ham with biscuits and gravy. Not only was he proficient at working on an engine, he soon discovered he had the ability and desire to drive a car or truck like he was racing at the Indianapolis Speedway. It didn't matter whether it was a curvy mountain road or a long straight-away, he could handle it with skill and ease. Of course, those long straightaways were rarely found in these parts.

Ford smiled, wondering who the new hotshots were around Burke County. Would they even know who he was…or even care? He had to admit he loved the day when upstart teenagers to even the "long arm of the law" would have loved to take a run at the infamous Ford "Hot Rod" Rawlings.

J.J.'s Motor Pool became a sanctuary for Ford, heck, it became like his church. By the time Ford hit his mid-teens, he was found "worshipping" at either his Dad's garage or in Uncle Skillet and Aunt Billie's "church". J.J. loved his brother, but his was not exactly the "denomination" he wanted him to join.

Ford could coax more horsepower out of an engine than would seem possible, either as a mechanic or a driver. His blood seemed to run on high octane gasoline. There was only the one person who was ever able to gain any control over the wild young man. It was the same person for whom Ford still grieved, Julia Anne Harmon.

Ford pulled across from Harmon's Mercantile, staring at the building as the Chevy's motor purred like a deep-throated cat. One part of his brain, or maybe it was his heart, was urging him to go inside. He sat staring through the front window, images of the past mingling with the reality of the present. The Harmon's building seemed less diminished than most of the buildings around town. Regardless of his emotions, the place seemed unchanged. However, he knew he could only find a sad emptiness inside that place. What once had been a place he looked forward to visiting, a place filled with anticipation and warm joys, was now a cold and lifeless structure to him.

It was busy inside the store today with people filling one daily need or another. A blue and white striped dress walked in front of the main window, pausing to look at the wares available from a "SALE" table. The girl's head was a glorious tumble of honey-blond, waterfall curls falling across her shoulders. A blue ribbon held her hair in just the perfect way, still allowing it to move a little as the slender figure went about her tasks.

She looked intently at the items on the table, straightening the merchandise and taking care each item was placed just so. Suddenly she stopped and turned to gaze through the clear glass toward the street. Her piercing stare felt as if she was looking directly into Ford's soul.

Ford's heart leapt into his throat, and before he had a chance to think, a word screamed out in his head. *"Julia!"* He tried so hard not to allow that name be intimately entertained by his brain but he failed more often than not.

"Julia!" Ford could almost smell the fragrance she wore. His skin tingled with the remembrance of her gentle touches and the soft skin that was meant to be held. Julia…her piercing green eyes stared through the clear glass…right into Ford's Chevy…or maybe his heart. He felt panicked, cold, and light headed.

With a jerk, Ford sat up straight, realizing a drop of sweat was running down his temple. The girl's look lingered, but Ford was no longer mesmerized. Julia…that wasn't Julia. Julia…that was another life, only a long-ago memory! It was the broken fantasy of a life that never came to be. It was the one thing that Ford could not fix, could not outrun, or could not replace.

He let off the brake, releasing the clutch. Julia was no longer in that building…or any other. Julia was in a hillside cemetery, buried with lost dreams and hopes. Ford pushed the accelerator, causing the Chevy's tires to squeal as he pulled away quickly. Moisture covered his eyes as he could only wonder why he came back…and how could he possibly stay.

Chapter Five

"Three sets of eyes were fixed on the Chevy, waiting to see what the driver was going to do."

Ford decided he'd had enough sight-seeing. He turned down Pine Oaks Avenue and headed east, just past the city limits. It was time to see J.J. and Mara. Really, it was past time. Like everything else, what had been done could not be undone.

The Chevy was still getting looks, none more attentive than the dark pair of eyes that peered through the dirty windshield of a 1954 Plymouth Belvedere. Except this time, the attention given had less to do with the Chevy and more to do with Ford Rawlings. As Ford sped by, the driver of the Plymouth hesitated a minute, pondering just what this meant. Slowly, he pulled out and followed the man who was once called "Hot Rod". The driver wondered if the man in the Chevy was anything like the teenager who earned that nickname? Pondering that question, the man decided on one thing, *"Guess it's going to get interesting around here again."*

Ford's foot fell heavy on the accelerator as he let the powerful engine open up as he hurried down the road. In little time he arrived, allowing the Chevy to glide easily into the parking lot of J.J.'s Motor Pool. Ford did not want a loud, showy arrival. The gravel crunched under the Chevy's High Performance tires as Ford turned the wheel to bring the car around to the back of the building.

"Good lord", he thought, *"it's just like rolling back in time."* Removing his aviator style sunglasses, he sat looking over the building and surrounding area. Some of the cars sitting on the premises were newer, but other than that, it felt and looked like the day he left for the Army.

Three sets of eyes were fixed on the Chevy, waiting to see what the driver was going to do. A smile crossed Ford's face. *"Tom, Gene, and Roy, you old dogs! Just as nosey as ever."*

Ford got out of the car, squinting toward the three observers. He wasn't sure they recognized him at first, so he slowly moved forward waiting to see if their expressions changed. Neither one looked too happy as he approached until he was within about ten feet. A high-pitched whine came from the middle observer, followed by a wagging tail. In another second, the other two tails began wagging as they danced and joined in the whining.

The three full-blooded German Shepard's were all the security J.J.'s Motor Pool ever needed. They were named after three of J.J.'s favorite cowboy actors, Tom Mix, Gene Autry, and Roy Rogers. They stayed in a well-maintained pen behind the garage. Shade was provided by a couple of well-placed trees as well as a covered area that offered shelter from any uncomfortable weather elements. There was a pallet for them to lie on and a large metal tub that held fresh water. A small door allowed access inside the building. Of course, they only came in after-hours as they did not mix well with customers. J.J. kept the door locked to them during the day when customers were present. Inside the garage sat a large, coal-burning furnace that kept the chill off in colder weather.

The dogs were as gentle as any pet, at least toward Ford, Mara, and J.J. himself. They'd never acted aggressively toward Bailey or Ada either, but neither grandparent ever had much to do with the dogs. There was only one other person who'd ever found the dogs to be accepting of their presence. Again, Ford thought of the name he made great efforts to keep from his mind. *"Julia!"*

The dogs allowed her to pet them and feed them by hand. They would lay at her feet as if to protect her when she sat inside the garage, after hours, waiting on Ford to finish the latest tweaking of his car's engine. Ford used to wonder if the dogs sensed Julia was gone…living no more. For some strange reason, he always believed they did.

He walked over to them, watching them become excited as they anticipated his attention. From his jacket pocket, he pulled a bag containing three donuts he liberated from the diner where he'd eaten lunch. He rarely came to the garage without something to give "the boys".

They watched him closely, their tongues hanging out in anticipation. He made them sit by the fence, then one by one, gave them their treat through the fence while rubbing each head. He spoke to each one softly, again feeling like he'd only left a few days ago.

Standing up, he turned back toward his car, stopping suddenly. A figure stood watching him, the sun at his back caused the man's form to be seen with more silhouette than detail. They stood staring at each other for nearly five seconds. When the man spoke, it brought back so many memories.

"So…the dogs not only get to see you first, but you brought them something too. Guess it's easy to see how your priorities run." He broke into a smile, saying, "You look good son. Welcome home.

How about a cold drink?"

Ford was hugging his father in less than three steps. The old man's hair was a touch greyer, but his voice, his feel, and even his smell was just as it was the day Ford left. The two men released the hug but held onto each other, each pair of hands on the other's shoulders.

Ford had not spoken until he said, "How's Mom? Is she still driving that old convertible?"

J.J. laughed out loud, "Sure, I'm fine. Thanks for asking!"

Ford's grin was more embarrassment than anything. "Hey, I know you're fine. Just look at you. You're always fine. You'll be fine fifty years from now."

J. J. grinned, "And your Mother will still be driving that old Ford. Heck, we just may have to bury her in it."

They started walking around the building to the soft drink machine when a dark and dusty Plymouth pulled up beside Ford's Chevy. The driver turned the engine off, checked himself in the rear-view mirror, and stepped out of the car, pulling his tan Stetson with him.

Sitting the hat on his head, a cocky smile crossed his face, "Well sir, I thought that was Mr. Ford "Hot Rod" Rawlings that passed me a while ago. You looked right good driving this very fine Chevrolet. Brand new one, from what I'm seeing. You always did have the best car in five counties. Kinda funny seeing a Ford in a Chevy." He brought his hand toward Ford for a handshake saying, "Good to see you Ford. Wondered when you'd ever come back home."

Ford leisurely placed his sunglasses back on. "Well, I guess it's good to see you too, Lon." He looked closely at the badge on Lon's chest. "Or, should I address you as Deputy Sheriff Lonnie Shell? By the way, how's his Royal Majesty doing?"

Chapter Six

"It was not a difficult desire considering he was after all, a Majesty."

Royal Albert Majesty was the third generation of *Majesty's* to reside in Burke County, North Carolina. His Grandfather, Ezra Buford Majesty, appeared with some mystery around 1830. He brought along his wife, Jasmine, a dark woman of Creole heritage. They claimed to be re-located from the shores and bayous of southern Louisiana due to physical hardships and dangers. Many of his troubles he credited to the horrible storms coming ashore from the Gulf of Mexico.

He identified himself and his usually quiet wife as Pilgrims, seeking a safe mountain home. He then proclaimed he and his wife as being Christian, hardworking, honest, decedents of Cajun royalty, and well-versed in both medical and culinary skills. In reality, parts of all his claims were a bit exaggerated.

People were reluctant at first to welcome the couple. After steady effort by the Majesty's, more and more were won over. As time went on, some of those wondered if accepting them was a mistake.

In less than three years, they were the owners and operators of two businesses and held deed on three other properties. People became reluctant to do business with the sharp couple who always seemed to take advantage every chance they could. Some quietly spoke of the Majesty's being involved in voodoo or other wicked supernatural associations. Others thought they just used the aura of the mysterious to hold advantage over any business contact.

Mrs. Majesty gave birth to one daughter, China Blue, who returned to Louisiana on her eighteenth birthday for a pre-arranged marriage. One which some felt brought a sizable dowry into the Majesty treasury. China Blue never returned to the mountains and neither was she ever mentioned again by her parents.

Their son, Morgan Reginald, followed in the family's business interests, becoming a powerful man in the County. While never an elected official, he appeared to control office holders in three or four surrounding Counties. Morgan held sway in all the Majesty's fortunes through the remaining years of the century. The Majesty holdings grew under Reginald. Property and business holdings spilled over into Caldwell and Mitchell County.

Morgan married a local girl from an old family in the County. As it turned out, the girl, Sally Bernice Powell, was barren. But, being the sole heir to her family's fortune, she was still held in her husband's good graces…at least until her inheritance was fully received.

First, her Mother fell ill from a mysterious illness, dying soon after. The tongue-wagers pointed to Morgan's Mother who they still believed to be some sort of voodoo witch. A year after Mrs. Powell's death, her husband died suddenly from an apparent heart attack.

Within a month, Morgan and his wife had full possession of all the Powell's fortunes. Another six months passed and Sally was suddenly sent to a health asylum in another State. She supposedly had a full break-down of her mental and emotional capacities. No reason was ever given as to what may have caused this tragedy.

Another six months passed and word was sent around the community that Sally had sadly hung herself when inadvertently left unattended at the facility. People were truly amazed at how quickly a local family vanished from the community. It was also interesting to see how quickly Morgan used the assets of his late wife's family to increase his own personal wealth.

However, Morgan was left without a wife or an heir. This did not last very long as a much younger, dark-haired beauty accompanied him home from a trip to Louisiana. He announced that the woman, Beatrice Sadè Majesty, was his new wife.

People were impressed with the new Mrs. Majesty's beauty and grace, but became just as leery of Morgan as they were his parents. By the time their first year of marriage was completed, Morgan had the heir he so desired. Royal Albert Majesty became the heir-apparent to the throne of his father. Another son, Ezra, followed. A third child, a daughter, was stillborn.

On his way to the Majesty throne, Royal decided he wanted to be the High Sheriff of Burke County, North Carolina. It was not a difficult desire to accomplish considering he was after all, a Majesty.

Royal's younger brother, Ezra Morgan Majesty's destiny came to be to watch over the family's holdings and assets. While it might appear that he ruled over the family fortunes, it was actually Royal who made the major decisions.

Ezra was a smaller man than his big brother, due in-part to him having a "club" foot. No expense had been spared to correct Ezra's infirmity. In fact, he had responded as well as possible after a great many surgeries and therapies. He used an ebony cane crested with a silver handle shaped like a great snake's head with ruby stones inserted for the eyes.

Royal could be very personable when it pleased him, all-the-while planning to "stab" the person in the back. Ezra, on the other hand, was a person with a much colder nature. He took an almost sadistic pleasure in finding ways to financially hurt someone, telling them to their face he was going to do it. In fact, one reason he carried his evil looking cane was to protect himself from a physical attack by someone he ruined. With just a flick of his wrist, a lethal ten inch finely honed knife blade was produced.

One thing the two had been taught from their earliest days was that they were to take the name "Majesty" very seriously. Their legacy was to be expanding the family's wealth and holdings, keeping the Majesty name a powerful force.

Ford and his parents held Ezra in little regard. However, when it came to Royal, each one of the Rawlings family had their own reason to wish him harm.

Chapter Seven

"Hello good looking! Want a date? Change ur oil!"

Lon looked at Ford, his forehead creased with wrinkles. "Now Ford, you know he don't like being referred to that way." A grin slowly crossed his face, "But, I'd have to say, *his* Majesty is doing fine I'd reckon…since you're asking. He's still married to that beauty he brought out of Baton Rouge, Angelica Grace. Guess he took after his daddy by going back to Louisiana to get a bride. She's still a very fine looking woman. Believe it or not, she seems mostly happy with Royal and appears at home in these mountains. Kinda hard to believe, huh!"

All three men found a slight grin crossing their faces, each probably for a different reason. A moments silence was needed before any conversation would continue.

Ford put his hand to his chin, asking, "Children?"

J.J. entered the conversation, "Royal's keeping her busy, that's for sure. This County's will have Majesty's around for a long time. Course, that's probably Royals plan."

Lon chuckled before containing himself. "Uh, she had a daughter first, then twin boys. Then another boy. Can't say having four kids has hurt her looks at all. Looks as pretty as the first day she stepped foot in these mountains. Some folks wonder if she'll get pregnant again, but I'm not so sure myself."

J.J. offered, "Yeah, appears Royal is going to assure himself a large legacy around here. But, hey, he's got plenty of money to have a whole batch of young'uns if he wants them. I just hope they all take after their mother and I don't just mean their looks."

Lon looked around as if someone might be listening. "I'll tell you one thing fellows. Angelica Grace is a whole lot more woman than a lot of people might give her credit. She's one person that will not let Royal get away with very much. I've seen her stare him down on more than one occasion. Even ole Ezra gives her a wide berth."

J.J. unconsciously spat at the mention of Ezra's name. "Yeah, guess Ezra still has that little Cajun girl he calls his wife locked up in his big house. Is Raven's sister still with them?"

Lon scoffed, "Now J.J., you know she ain't locked up. She doesn't get out much but I don't think she likes living in the mountains as much as Angelica Grace. And you know, just because Raven's small don't mean she's not a grown woman. She may look like a young girl in the right light but she ain't nothing less than a full-grown, terrifying woman. Her sister, Serafina, is the same way. They're pretty girls but one is just as scary as the other. I don't care to be in a room when both of them are there, especially without Ezra. They can give a fellow the "willies". I won't be surprised if they don't take Ezra out one night, tie him up to a tree, and skin him. They know the voodoo, I'm sure of that."

J.J. smiled at Lon's comments. "I think it's their dark skin that hides their age so well. They're far from white but they don't look a bit like a Negro. They may be scary but they are truly beautiful women…too pretty for Ezra."

"The wife was with Ezra a while back when he stopped by to pay a bill. She sat in the car the whole time, staring off in the distance. When Ezra started to pull out, she looked over at me and flashed a crazy-like smile. Made me hope I never ran into her on a dark night."

Lon added, "Some say her great-granddaddy was a Turkish pirate and her great-grannie was some sort of Cajun priestess. You never know about those stories but that'd be one way to add to the Majesty legacy. Heck, even Royal claims his grandmother was some sort of Cajun royalty…whatever that means?"

He went on about Ezra's wife. "Let me tell you something boys, don't even speak to that woman if you ever meet up with her away from home. Believe me when I tell you, she'd cut you quicker than Ezra. Carries a straight-out skinning knife with her at all times. Her sister does the same. I'd bet you that either one would be fairly proficient with a blade."

"Hell, I won't even go near their house unless I just have to. Been there about six times and I won't even let her see me look at her. Sometimes her and the sister will stand on either side of you to see if you'll look directly at one or the other. Damn, don' know how Ezra lives with them." Lon began rubbing the sleeve of his right arm to calm the chill bumps created by talking about the women.

J.J. added, "Guess the legacy of the whole Majesty family is mostly creepy, huh! So, what you think, the sister there to stay?"

Lon lit a cigarette as if he needed it to just speak of Raven and Serafina. "That, I couldn't tell you. She don't appear to be leaving anytime soon. Who knows? Personally, I think she's even prettier than Raven…just scary as hell!"

Ford smiled, "Maybe she's looking for a husband, Lon. I bet she likes the look of a man in uniform."

Lon was drawing on his cigarette which brought about a fit of coughing. He gained control to hear J.J. saying with laughter in his voice. "Don't do that to our fine Deputy Sheriff, Son. He's one of the few Lawmen around here you can depend on."

The three men fell silent as they looked for another subject. Finally, Lon offered, "Hey, I've got to get going. Got something strange to check on. A call came in when I was coming over here. I've got to check on a wreck over on Brown Mountain on Rucksack Road. A highway crew found a car sitting in that old "stink" pond out that way. Seems the crew was out there working on widening that bad curve by the pond. You know the place. It's that nasty old curve right before you pass the pond. Ford, you've slid sideways around it a few times if memory serves."

Ford gave Lon a hard look but he decided not to bite on the implication.

Lon went on, "Anyways, Claude and Retha Kelley's boy got killed in that curve about a year back. He was driving too fast, lost control, and flipped his car. Ended up on its' top, right at the edge of that pool of stinking water." Lon paused a second before adding, "Think it broke the boy's neck. Don't think he knew how to handle the road or his car. Hated it for the family. He was their only."

J.J. looked away at the mention of the boy's death as Ford brought up a mental image of the bad piece of road.

Lon went on, "Well, it seems his Daddy's brother is some sort of State Legislator over near Greensboro. Guess he's got some say-so with the State Highway Department. Anyways, it ain't going to do that boy any good now. One of the guys working on widening that part of the road caught a glimpse of some chrome shining through that muddy water and reported it. Phil Sizemore's got his wrecker over there pulling it out. Guess I need to go take a look."

Lon realized he'd been rattling on and acted a little embarrassed. "Anyways Ford, let me know if I can help you in any way. Let's get dinner sometime soon…I mean after you settle in a bit. I'll look you up." He tipped his Stetson toward J.J. saying, "Mr. Rawlings, always good to see you. I'm sure you're staying busy." He turned to leave but looked back to say, "Your Dad's a hell of a mechanic, Ford. Heard you kept the Army running all by yourself over in Germany. I guess you've done well. I know you learned from the best."

With that, Deputy Sheriff Lon Shell jumped in the Plymouth, turning on the red bubble light on top as well as the fender lights of red and blue. He quickly pulled out, throwing gravels behind him as he hit the blacktop. J.J. watched the Plymouth find the highway and speed away.

"I'd watch that fellow there. He acts all friendly most times, but there could always be an agenda under that cowboy hat of his. Pretty loyal to the Majesty's…course he would be since Royal made him Deputy Sheriff as young as he is. Their relationship goes all the way back to when Lon was a little boy, I'd guess. I think Royal has been a help to him and his mother over the years. Go figure. Hey, how's about that cold drink now?"

The two men walked around the building to the main garage door where a sign proclaimed, "Cold Drinks". It was the old chest type dispenser with the metal rack that formed a labyrinth the bottle had to be worked through to get it out.

While J.J. pulled two RC Colas from the box, Ford nodded to the three old fellows sitting in weather-worn ladder-back chairs, spitting tobacco juice and whittling on sharp pointed sticks. All three were squinting at Ford, trying to discern who this young man was.

Harv Coleridge spoke up, a smile showing a mouth-full of badly stained teeth. "Well, lordy goodness! Ford Rawlings, you finally come back home. How you doing son?" Before Ford could answer, all three men were standing, shaking his hand and patting him on the shoulder.

Harv was always the most outspoken of the group. The other two, Trace Clinger and Wallace Terrell were constant sidekicks. J.J. called them the *"Three wise men"*, since they seemed to know something about everything. Trace was the more cynical of the three and Wallace, the wittiest. Their presence around J.J.'s Motor Pool was as dependable as an old hound dog sunning himself on a front porch.

J.J. handed Ford his drink, nodding to his three regulars. Warm days found them outside on the porch while cooler days brought them inside around the coal furnace. Some cold days would find them surrounding the old "pot-belly" stove that sat in the middle of Calvin's Seed and Grain store. J.J. often wondered if they'd brought their own chairs to that establishment like they'd done at the garage.

Ford was answering questions about Germany, the Army, and where he'd been since. The answers were pretty non-specific, knowing that whatever he said would be all over town by the time the sun set. None of them mentioned the tragedy that caused Ford to leave in the first place which was appreciated and kept him in a congenial mood.

With tobacco juice flying as fast as the questions, Wallace spoke up, "Guess you haven't had a chance to meet your new brother yet? You haven't, have you Ford? He looks a lot like you with that "Elvis" haircut…pretty good singing voice too. You-all may want to think about doing a show down at the Armory one weekend."

Everyone became silent as they waited for Ford's reaction. J.J. rolled his eyes saying, "Oh, lord!" He slid his empty bottle into the bottle rack and walked into the garage mumbling something about "old fools" that had too much time on their hands.

Ford stared at Wallace while the other two tried to hide their emotions. Now Wallace was a black gentleman who'd lived all his life in Burke County. He'd been a blacksmith, a carpenter, raised horses, and sired many children.

Every time Wallace was asked how many children and grandchildren he had, he would look to the sky replying, "Well, lordy, let's see how many I'm up to now. He'd mumble some numbers out loud and then he'd say something like, *Oh, you're right Lord. Can't forget Missy and her two, and I'd better count Wilma and her brood even though they ain't all mine."*

This would go on for a minute or two until he'd conclude, "Too many! Just can't seem to quit making them…but they're all sweet, sweet children. I love them all and they love me…most loved person in three Counties I'd recon."

Ford knew Wallace was "pulling his leg". He also knew that J.J. and Mara were never able to have another child after he was born. They'd tried, even seeking medical advice both in Asheville and Charlotte. It just wasn't to be.

Mara swore she'd only gotten pregnant with Ford because of the "lights" on Brown Mountain. She'd seen them that one time, swearing they were the reason she became pregnant. J.J. wouldn't entertain such a thought, usually leaving the room if she ever brought it up.

Harv spoke up, "Ain't you wanting to meet your little brother, Ford. He stays mostly in the office there…when he comes in to work with J.J. Everybody likes him, especially the girls. I've heard he gets a little "fresh" with the ladies but they seem to like that kind of thing. You know how the kids are these days…loose morals and all."

Ford's curiosity was peaked as he knew the three wouldn't leave him alone until he went in to meet this new "brother" of his. He sat his bottle in the rack as he walked through the office door, the three loafers following a few steps behind. A bell jingled loudly when he opened the door as he stepped inside.

The room was dimly lit with only the light from a puny desk lamp sitting on J.J.'s messy desk. The counter was in its usual jumbled state. A massive parts book held down one end while a variety of small advertising displays and sundry papers covered the remaining surfaces.

As with everything else, this room looked almost the same as the day he left. The only noticeable change was the calendar that hung over the desk. Instead of a scenic country picture over the current month there was one of a pretty girl in a tight blouse and tight shorts holding a can of engine oil.

The smell of the garage was inside the office. It was old oil and grease with a strong hint of sweat and grime, just as Ford remembered. He noticed the front window, which he doubted had seen much if any cleaning since he'd left. It seemed to absorb most of the natural light trying to come in. A decent collection of dead flies and other insects littered the window sill. Ford thought once again, *"Just like I never left."*

Ford stood there, continuing to look over the unchanged office, wondering where this new brother was. He walked to the counter, leaning forward so he could see if his "sibling" was on the other side. Seeing no one, he turned to the men with a shrug. Just then, a voice spoke to him, *"Hello good looking! Want a date? Change ur oil!"*

Chapter Eight

"...besides, he threw a monkey turd at her when she tried to play with him."

Ford slowly turned back to the counter, truly puzzled. "I'm sorry, what did you say…uh, I mean, who said that?" The three on-lookers snickered in the background, obviously having a jolly time at Ford's expense.

"Hey baby! Elvis loves you, baby!" The odd voice seemed to be coming from over near the desk. The strange voice sounded again, *"Hey baby! Elvis all shook up!"*

Ford had a bearing now and walked behind the counter, "Alright, who's doing that?"

"You're a hound dog."

Ford stopped suddenly, dropped his head and began laughing until his body shook. He stared at an old, but decorative, bird cage sitting in the shadowy corner. The cage had a cover partially draped over it with the one side open for light. "Oh man, where in the world did you come from?" He turned to the three-man audience, "All right…okay, you guys got me! But where in the world did this guy come from?"

A new voice entered the room, "I see you met Elvis." Ford looked over at a smiling J.J. "He came to live with us about two years ago. Mara usually has him with her, but she drove over to Morganton this morning. He gets lonely if he's left by himself very long, so I bring him down here. People sometimes stop by just to see if he's here. He really likes the ladies."

Ford walked over to the desk, leaning against the end of the beat-up piece of furniture. He stood there staring at his new-found *brother*. "What's your name? What do they call you?" The answer came quickly, *"Elvis, baby...all shook up."*

By now the audience of three had to exit the office for needing to both laugh out loud and spit out some built up tobacco juice. J.J. walked over to Elvis and gave him some type of nut that appeared to make the little fellow happy. Elvis saw the nut coming and responded, *"Thank you! Thank you very much."* Ford was mesmerized.

J.J. lightly rubbed the exaggerated pompadour styled head as the beautiful grey, white, and yellow Cockatiel worked away on the nut.

"Fellow came through Treemont a couple years ago…well, he tried, until his car broke down. Had three birds, a boa constrictor, and a mangy looking monkey traveling with him. Said he was trying to catch up with a traveling Carnival of some sort."

J.J. appeared to be trying to pull all of the memory back into his mind. He nodded, "Seems he left the Carnival to go to his Daddy's funeral. He was trying to catch up the Carnival folks before they headed to Florida. He already owned the birds, but the snake and the monkey was his Daddy's. Anyways, his car broke down and he didn't have all the money he needed to pay for the repair. Unfortunately, Mara was here when he offered one of his animals to cover part of the repair cost. Before I could say no, your Mother already had Elvis here on one hand while she fed him with her other."

J.J. sat on a stool laughing, "Before I could say anything, she'd ask his name and was saying, "*We'll just take Elvis here to cover the balance. Now, what all does he eat?""*

Ford continued looking at Elvis, "I'm surprised she didn't want the monkey."

J.J. gave Elvis another nut as he shook his head, "She said she wouldn't have that nasty, foul smelling animal around here…besides, he threw a monkey turd at her when she tried to play with him."

Ford continued watching the bird, trying to tease more words and phrases from him. It was fascinating watching the feathers on the bird's head rise up as if they were part of an exaggerated, living hair-style. He pranced around on the perch in the large cage like he was some sort of rock and roll star.

J.J. offered, "The fellow said he was about five years old then, but would probably live another thirty years if he's taken care of correctly. Of course, Mara makes sure that happens. He's really quite friendly…even affectionate at times.

"So, Mom didn't name him Elvis?", Ford asked as he gave the bird another small nut, trying to make friends. "I'm surprised, because she does have this strange thing about names…as I know all too well."

"Nope, wasn't your Mother this time. Fellow we got him from, I guess. I'm thinking it's because of those crest feathers. They always rise up when he gets excited, kinda like Elvis' hairstyle. Mara says that little beak of his makes her think of the way Elvis curls his lip when he says something to make the girls all hot and bothered."

Ford found it funny to hear his Dad talk about Elvis and his attributes. He turned serious as he considered his Mom, "How's she been doing? Did she get real mad at me for leaving? I know I got a lot of letters from her over the years. There was a time, at first, she seemed to get pretty dark. I never got the feeling she was mad at me, at least I hope she never felt that way."

J.J. walked to the counter, gripping at its edge. "Truth be told, I don't think I ever knew all that went on in her head. She was…like you say, in a dark place for a while. Then, one day, she just announced she needed to go to Asheville for the weekend. Didn't say why…just told me to trust her. Said there was a Doctor she needed to see and a couple of things she wanted to look into."

"What do you think it was, Dad? Was it because I left? Was she sick?"

J.J. looked steadily into his son's eyes. "She was just sad to see you go, but the other…no, it wasn't you. I never knew her to be sick. You know, she just loved that girl…it hurt her so badly…as bad as anyone I think. She understood you leaving…maybe better than any of us."

Ford noted that it seemed even J.J. found it difficult to say Julia's name out loud.

J.J. added, "She was a sweet girl. You know, we all loved her, we really did."

Ford was in a conversation he didn't mean to happen. At least not now…not this soon. "What happened in Asheville?"

J.J. walked toward the garage when he stopped to lean against the door frame. "Don't really know. She left on Thursday and was back early Sunday morning. Never said a lot about what happened but her whole demeanor gradually improved. I mean, she was acting nervous and jumpy for about a week but she settled down and has been okay ever since."

J.J. appeared lost in thought. "I'm thinking that was a little over a year after you left. Right around that time was when Holly began dropping by regularly. Seemed to be healing for both of them. I think your mother has developed a real fondness for her…sorta like a daughter she never had. It's been good for both of them."

Ford found something re-assuring as well as unsettling in his father's words. "You know, that sounds about the time I felt her letters started sounding more like herself…more upbeat. She indicated she'd finally been able to start putting the whole thing behind her and was going to focus on what was ahead of her. Said she hoped I could do the same."

J.J. asked, "How's that going for you, son?"

Ford turned back to Elvis, "I'm working on it, Dad."

The conversation was interrupted by the sound of Phil Sizemore's wrecker pulling into the garage's lot. He was pulling a Glen Green Buick four-door Deluxe Sedan. J.J. and Ford were immediately curious since Lon Shell said Phil was over near Brown Mountain. The Buick did not appear to be a car pulled out of a swampy hole. Without hardly a look at Phil's wrecker, J.J. recognized this car and it wasn't the car Deputy Sheriff Lon Shell was in such a hurry to see.

Chapter Nine

"Who was the other dead body, Phil?"

J.J. walked over to Phil who was already unhooking the Buick. "What you got there, Phil. I thought you were over on Rucksack Road helping the Sheriff's boys pull some old car out of the muck."

Phil took his cap off, wiping sweat with a bandana that looked as dirty as the overhauls he was wearing. "I was. Feels like I been chasing chickens all day. Can't get anything accomplished today. This here is old Miz Watkins' car. Don't know what she does to this old beauty, but I usually have to pick it up three or four times a year and bring it over here. Most of the time, she just wants you to give it some attention and me to give her a little of the same. Always asks about my Mother and then gives me a jar of homemade jam or jelly."

Phil blew his nose in his banana. Shaking his head, he added, "Don't know why she just don't drive it into the garage herself and save the tow. But, hey, money in my pocket. She says for you to call her when you see what it needs."

J.J. laughed, "Think she just likes you, Phil. You know, if you'd get past the age difference, she'd treat you well." Phil spat some tobacco juice, "Shoot J.J., she's older than my mother. And I sure don't need another mother! Mine's just got plain ornery the last few years. Can't please her and can't shoot her… Aw, I didn't mean that, she's just got a lot of pains and takes it out on me when I'm around."

J.J. felt a little bad for kidding him, but not so bad he regretted it.

Ford walked over to see what was going on. "What about that other car, Phil?"

Phil squinted and then his face lit up. "Boy, howdy! Ford Rawlings. When in God's time did you get back home?" He grabbed Ford in a big hug, then pushed him back to look him over. Dang son, you filled out…in a good way, I mean. You know, you kinda look like that ole "Hound Dog Man", ole Elvis dad-burn Presley. I mean, you're not skinny like him, but you got the looks."

Ford winced from the reference. He'd heard that reference so many times. Starting in Germany and everywhere since then, he was compared to the rock and roll musician. Before he could evade Phil, he found himself the recipient of another powerful hug from the big fellow.

It seemed the Elvis reference was destined to follow Ford. It was his looks as well as the smooth, polite Southern voice. The image was magnified by the confident way he moved and carried himself. He even sounded a lot like Elvis Presley when he sang, which didn't happen very often. His dark hair resembled the rock and roll singer once he let it grow out of the Army crew cut.

As the popularity of Elvis grew, so did the notice of Ford's physical qualities. By now, he was mostly accepted the unwanted attention unless someone was just plain rude about it. The last one to be taught a lesson about considering their behavior was a mostly drunken truck drive in New Jersey. He wanted to prove he could best "Elvis" in a fight. Ford left him on the barroom floor minus a couple teeth.

The nickname first began when he served in the Army. An Army Drill Sargent was the first to use it as he tried to get into Ford's head. Then, there were guys in his motor pool who would kid him in a good-natured way about his resemblance to Elvis Presley.

After the Army, he worked for Visconti Transport. It wasn't long before the nickname caught up with him again. A fellow named Mikey Falcone, who worked for the New Jersey trucking company hung the "Elvis" nickname on Ford. Mikey loved Elvis as much as any New Jersey boy could. He was twenty and would have loved to imitate Elvis himself. The only trouble was that Mikey was short, stocky, and couldn't sing a lick. So, he christened Ford with the nickname and went about spreading the news.

Ford understood it really wasn't much of a stretch to compare his looks to the rock and roll singer. In truth, he really did resemble the singer from Memphis. When he was talked into singing, the audiences took great notice of both his appearance and his singing. He was always applauded for his efforts wherever he sang. Since the singing took place after a little too much to drink, Ford tried his best to limit his alcohol intake.

Over time, he'd learned to just not say anything when he was called "Elvis". After all, it was easier to laugh it off or just ignore the jokester. His biggest concern was that someone would push it too far at the wrong time. The wrong time being one of his dark days when the face of Julia would not leave his mind.

J.J. walked over to the Buick, taking the keys from Phil as he walked by. "So, tell us about the other car, Phil? What happened to the one you pulled out of that swampy pond? Any idea as to who it belonged to?"

Phil pulled his cap off again, lowering his voice, "Well, I tell you boys something, but don't be saying anything. See, they told me to leave it there by that pond and come back in a couple of hours… seein' how I was so busy anyways. They said they needed time to look over the car before it was towed to the Sheriff's compound. I tell you what, it was a mess. It would've taken them more than a couple hours to go through that car. I just think they didn't want me around for a while."

Phil paused to wipe the sweat from his head and neck again. He looked around like someone was watching, which of course they weren't. "Keep this to yourself boys, but there were two bodies in that old car. Both of them shot!"

Phil looked around again while his audience tried to wait patiently. "Okay, here's the thing. One of the bodies looks to be Harris DePaul. You remember that ole scoundrel, J.J. They pulled his wallet and found ID. I was standing there when they opened the wallet. The Deputy saw me looking so he told me to get back to the wrecker. Oh yeah, they matched the car tags to him. I heard that over the two-way radio. I tell you, some of those Deputies are plain sloppy.

"I tell you something else, boys. That body looked pretty rough from laying at the bottom of that stinking pond. It was pretty evident the old boy had a bullet hole right between his eyes!"

J.J. and Ford looked hard at each other. Harris had not been seen by anyone in four years or more. Just seemed to vanish one day. Some people figured he'd left for greener pastures. He had in fact, told a couple of fellows he needed to get away from Burke County. Considering how he was always chasing women, most figured he either had gotten a girl "knocked up" or was scared off by a jealous husband. I guess it looks as if he found himself on the wrong side of the greener pastures.

Harris was indeed a slick dresser who liked women, honky-tonks, whiskey, and an easy way to make a buck. He had only a few friends and was hardly missed from the day he disappeared. In fact, had it not been for an appointment or two he missed, people may not have known he was gone. His closest acquaintances were some of the more shady and unbecoming people in the County. He hung out with a few drinking buddies, random women of loose morals, or a few people he tried to do business with. No one else appeared to have that much to do with him.

Ford asked, "Well, who was the other body, Phil?"

Phil shook his head, "Strangest thing. It was a big ole dog. Black one I think, but you know, had all sorts of crud on the body and it'd been in that soup a long time. No collar, so no identification. It was shot too, maybe more than once."

Phil took time to wipe sweat again and chuckled, "Funny thing, they found that ole dog in the driver's seat while Harris was laying in the back. And get this, when they opened the trunk, it was loaded with moonshine. Some of the containers were broken, but most were still intact. Don't know who the spirits belonged to, but I'm guessing Harris was on a delivery run. Never knew him to run moonshine. I mean, he drank plenty of it but didn't appear to have enough ambition to go into delivery. Funny that whoever shot him left the 'shine."

They all puzzled on Phil's last statement, knowing about how much a trunk load of moonshine could bring. J.J. thanked Phil for getting the Watkin's car over to him and indicated he needed to get back to work.

Phil said he was going to get some food before he headed back over toward Brown Mountain. "Let's get a beer sometime, Ford. I'm sure you got some dandy stories to tell. Meet any good-looking women in Germany?"

He immediately regretted the last statement, but Ford let it slide. *"This won't be the first time it's going to be awkward, he thought."*

Phil hopped in the wrecker as the other two began looking over the Buick.

Suddenly, the air was filled with the blasting of a car horn. Loose gravels began flying through the parking lot as the roar of an engine came off the highway. Brakes were applied hard to the four speeding tires causing more mayhem. Ford looked back, immediately thinking, *"Here's when it starts getting good!"*

Chapter Ten

"Ford found himself a little white-knuckled as Mara sped down the highway..."

Before the car came to a full, skidding halt, Mara Rawlings was opening the door. In fact, she needed to lean back in and apply the hand brake to assure the car stayed put. Still, the dust that was kicked up from her exaggerated arrival wasn't nearly settled by the time she'd ran to Ford, jumping in his awaiting arms. Her delightful squeal brought Harv, Trace, and Wallace to their feet from their weathered chairs.

Mara lunged into Ford's arms so fiercely that he ended up swinging her around in circles to shift the momentum that would have otherwise knocked him to the ground. As he slowed their rotation, Mara planted a kiss on each cheek, squeezing him in such a bear hug he thought he heard vertebrae pop. She excitedly started speaking as Ford returned her to steady footing on the ground.

"Why didn't you let me know you were coming home?" With that, she punched him hard in the front of his shoulder.

"You better tell me you just got in, or I'll be slapping you sideways silly! Where's your car? You're going to stay a while, aren't you?"

With that, she grabbed him and pulled him tightly into another bear hug.

After several long hugs, she finally let loose of him long enough to holler over at her husband, "J.J.! Look, it's Ford! He's back!"

Immediately, she felt a little foolish, recognizing that Ford and J.J. had already been together for a while. So, she hit him again in the shoulder! "Darn your hide! I could have had you a good meal cooked if I'd known you were coming."

She gazed into his face and took a step back. "Son, you've filled out some since the last picture you sent me. My, my, don't you look sturdy. And you let your hair get longer. That looks good…you look just like…" Ford reached out to keep her before she said, Elvis. But, she grabbed his hand, saying, "My goodness, you sure remind me of your Daddy when we first met. He just took my breath away."

By this time, J.J. was beside them, hoping to give Ford some support. Mara was saying, "I'd a never gone to Morganton this morning if I knew you were here. When did you get in? I need to get

Elvis and take you both to the house…"

J.J. was doing a count-down with his fingers from five as Mara rattled on. "Oh, wait. You don't know about Elvis! He is just the neatest little guy. Wait till you hear him speak. Makes me laugh all the time!"

By this time, Ford and J.J had Mara maneuvered into the office. The "three wise men" tipped their hats as she went by, her mouth running as fast as she could get the words out. She greeted each one by name as she walked by. This put a grin on each of their faces. They were getting an insane kick out of her rapid-fire speech. As she went inside she called back with a smile in her voice, "Hey Wallace, got any new babies lately?" Wallace was caught off guard as he fumbled a "No Mam…got two new great grandbabies is all." Mara smiled and ducked inside.

As she made her way to the counter, an excited voice called out, *"Hey good looking! Gotta go…gotta go? Change ur oil…need a tune-up?"*

By now, Mara's adrenalin had waned a bit. She walked over to Elvis' cage, pulling the cover off. She gave him a treat and stroked his crest, "Look who's home, Elvis. Ford's here…have you met Ford? You're going to like having him around…I know I am."

She turned back to Ford, almost whispering, "You are staying…aren't you? I mean, even if it's just for a while."

Her eyes hopefully pleaded as Ford replied, "Yeah, I'm staying a while…I'll give it a try."

J.J. gave Mara a hug and a light kiss, "Why don't you take him to the house, Mara. I've got work to finish here. Take Elvis and let Ford follow you. I'll be along later." He turned to Ford, and with a wink said, "I'll try and get home before she changes your mailing address to Treemont."

Ford took care of getting Elvis ready for travel with guidance and advise from Mara. As he took care of Elvis, she made a couple of quick telephone calls using the phone on J.J.'s desk.

"Who'd you call, Mom? It's too late to plan a surprise party for me." Ford was teasing, but at the same time he was always a little suspicious of Mara's intentions.

"Oh Ford, now don't go getting all paranoid on me. I'm not getting any kind of party together. My goodness! I was just cancelling an appointment with my friend Francis Potter and I called to see if Raymond Lake has any good steaks down at the Butcher's shop."

Then her eyes brightened, "It doesn't matter…I've just decided, I'm going to fix you my homemade spaghetti, sausages, and meatballs, just like from the "old country". I've got fresh ground meat and sausages in the fridge. I bet it's been a long time since you had a good Italian meal. My goodness, I even baked a fresh loaf of Italian bread this morning. How's that sound?" Mara didn't wait for an answer or notice Ford roll his eyes at her last statement.

Ford thought to himself, *"Guess she's forgotten where I've lived the last several years."*

As soon as Mara spotted Ford's new Chevy, she insisted on taking a ride. She was thoroughly impressed with the rush of horsepower, squealing in delight in almost child-like glee. This was one of her personality traits Ford loved about his mother. She always was just a little more than a "nudge" on the carefree, spontaneous side of life. Before they headed back to the garage, Mara convinced Ford to allow her to drive.

There were very few people Ford would allow behind the wheel of his car, especially females. But, he just couldn't find it in his heart to say no to his mother. Ford found himself a little white-knuckled as Mara sped down the highway, actually passing a couple of old farm trucks along the way. The Chevy had a lot more horsepower than Mara's four-cylinder Ford convertible. To Ford's surprise, she was handling the powerful car pretty well.

Her laughter challenged the sound of the powerful engine. He tried to take comfort that she was actually a very competent driver. She liked to kid that she was the "wheel man" for a gang of bank robbers back in New Jersey. *"Better than Bonnie Parker because the cops never caught up with me or shot me down!",* was her favorite line.

Pulling onto the garage property, he noticed "the Three Wise Men" and J.J. standing by the large garage door watching Mara pull up to the door. They wore smiles, close to laughter, across their faces. J.J. carried the bird cage containing Elvis out to the Ford Convertible and secured it. He then put the top up and handed Mara her set of keys. "Be home in about three hours, darlin'. Don't be giving the boy any grief." She looked back over her shoulder, sticking her tongue out at her husband as she got in the car. "I think you need to get us a Chevy like Ford's…except a convertible. That is one fine ride!"

"You wanting to sell your old Ford? That what you're saying?" Mara stuck her tongue out at J.J. again, laughing as she gunned her convertible in reverse.

They left…Ford cruising along behind Mara. The drive was pleasant and he felt satisfied just letting the afternoon pass over him. It wasn't so bad, being back home after several years. It truly was a beautiful area, offering a fellow space and freedom. Most of the people weren't unreasonably difficult to get along with and he still was acquainted with probably the majority of the County. He could help his dad some at the garage so he wouldn't feel like a free-loader.

Ford felt it'd sure be a lot more peaceful here than the end of his last lifetime. Of that, he was certain. He'd made good money in New Jersey and along the upper East Coast. Then it turned ugly and he wanted no more of life in New Jersey. Maybe, he could make this work out for a while. Even if he ended up moving on, Mara and J.J. wouldn't feel so abandoned.

A dark cloud of a thought overcame Ford's mind. *"I'm still going to find out what happened to Julia. I'll not be run off this time. I don't even care who I have to hurt to find the answers!"*

Ford felt a twinge of nostalgia as he pulled up to the two-story white house with green shutters and multiple flower gardens across the yard. It too had not changed much over the years he'd been gone. The yard looked and felt familiar. Mara's colorful pinwheels blew in the breeze and a bevy of blue, glass bottles hung from tree limbs. They added a fantasy-like element to the yard.

Over to his right was the family "pet cemetery" with all his childhood pets buried in a nice row. J.J. built Mara a small, white wooden fence to surround the plots. He'd crafted wooden headstones with their names and Mara made sure the area was kept pristine, filled with perennial flowers of all colors.

Gazing across the yard, he couldn't help but imagine Mara at work in the flowers. To his dismay, he also could see Julia, working hand and hand with his mother. They both loved the flower gardens as both possessed a creative "green-thumb". *"Just get ahold of yourself Ford. You're going to have to learn to deal with this very thing…she'll be everywhere you go around here."*

He noticed he was gripping the steering wheel very tightly as he looked across the colorful yard. Mara was already out of her car, waving at him…except he wasn't the one she was actually waving at.

Ford turned his head to see a blue and white, '55 Pontiac 2-door Chieftain slowly pulling into the driveway. The car eased on down the driveway, past the maple trees on either side. Ford recognized it was the '55 model with the newest V-8 engine that topped out around 180hp. It was a good, solid ride, and this one still looked brand new.

The car came to a full stop in the drive. That was when Ford stopped noticing the car, looking only at the driver as she gazed at her reflection in her rear-view mirror. Her delicate hands were brushing a lock of honey-blonde, waterfall curls from her face.

Chapter Eleven

"It appears we have a mysterious crime to solve"

"Now you look here, Melvin. I'm telling you, this is going to be done just like I say! I don't give a flying flip what you believe. I don't care what the Whitehead family might believe. I'm the law around here and I'm ordering you to do it! Do you understand me, Melvin?"

Deputy Sheriff Lon Shell was more upset than he should've been. It was just that he didn't feel like arguing any longer with the hearse driver, Melvin Taylor. Maybe the Whitehead's, of Whitehead Mortuary and Funeral Home, would not want to hear that the body of a long-deceased dog was transported in their very fine funeral hearse. It was evidence in a murder case even though it was a long-dead dog. Lon wondered if you could call the carcass of a mud-covered hound, evidence…but it was, just like the other body of what looked to be the late Harris DePaul. That body was already bagged and in the hearse.

Melvin walked over to wrap the dog cadaver in a sheeting material so the inside of the hearse wouldn't be soiled. He was cursing under his breath, just loud enough for Lon to catch a few words. Lon was trying to tell one of his Deputies just how to write up the initial report when he heard a few of Melvin's words.

Suddenly, he turned on Melvin. Getting right in his face, he spat words. "Listen here you-sawed-off moron! You better shut your big mouth, get these victims secured, and worry about making me happy. If this doesn't get done in the next five minutes, I swear…I'm putting cuffs on you and have one of my Deputies throw you under the damn jail! Understand!"

Since Melvin was looking directly at the handcuffs in Lon's hand, he turned a fine shade of pale and began scrambling to get both corpses secured. He meekly said in a very low voice to no one in particular, "You don't have to cuss at me, I was getting it done."

Heads turned as a fine, shiny black 1956 Cadillac sedan pulled off the road at the scene. A lone figure sat in the back seat. The driver, a lean, stoic figure known as Ferrell, got out to open the door for his passenger. The man unfolded himself from the sedan, looking around to survey the entire scene. His noticeable presence included a frame measuring 6'2", a head of shiny black hair with greyish sideburns and a muscular, lean torso. An off-white Stetson hat was handed to him by the driver which he placed squarely on his head. Shiny leather boots peeked out from the pants of his light tan suit. His piercing grey eyes once again took in the surrounding scene. A newly lit cigarette hung from his mouth, just underneath a finely waxed moustache.

Sheriff Royal Albert Majesty looked nothing like what you might expect to be the High Sheriff of Burke County. There was most assuredly no Sheriff of any Western North Carolina County that matched his style.

He walked with a casual grace, allowing those around him to pay appropriate homage as if some royal personage had just entered their world. The Deputies, along with other personnel, stopped to show quiet respect as he entered the scene. Ferrell allowed him a few steps before closing the door and falling in behind the Sheriff.

The shiny Cadillac was left glistening in the early September sunshine. An impressive car like that stood out in everywhere it traveled. There were plenty of fine automobiles around, but this was probably the only Cadillac to be seen with the words "High Sheriff of Burke County" affixed to each front door. A large, red bubble light was added to the roof and a chrome siren was attached to one fender, near the door. The driver left the engine running, filling the air with a very deep, resonance of sound.

Royal walked toward the salvaged car, stopping a few feet away. An ornate badge indicating the wearer as the High Sheriff was on his vest. At his side was an ivory handled, nickel plated, .357 caliber Colt Python. It was a lot of pistol, but Royal considered himself a lot of man.

It was widely known that Royal was an excellent shot with both revolver and rifle. Rumors floated about that his beautiful wife, Angelica Grace Majesty, carried a .38 Smith and Wesson Chief's Special in either her purse or secured to her thigh by a garter holster. The rumors did not indicate whether the pistol was meant for defense against an assailant or her husband. Suitable arguments had been offered either way.

Lon approached the Sheriff as the man looked across the dark, murky pond from which the car had been removed. He stood silently as Royal took off his dark glasses, tapping them against his thigh as he stared intently at the scene. It was as if he was visualizing the actual events resulting in Harris DePaul's demise and placement into the murky waters.

"Deputy Sheriff Shell", the Sheriff addressed his Deputy without looking at him. "It appears we have a mysterious crime to solve. What are the early indications and actualizations of the crime scene?"

Lon began explaining how the sunken car came to be discovered and the protocol he followed in bringing the car to the surface, early examinations of the two bodies, and initial examinations of the car itself.

Royal spoke, still not looking directly at his Chief Deputy. "You say there are two bodies? Do you know the identities of the deceased?"

Lon squinted at the Sheriff realizing he'd not heard about the deceased dog found in the front seat. "Yes sir, Sheriff Majesty. The one body appears to be a Mr. Harris DePaul. But the other one, well, you see, it wasn't a person. It was a dog…but it too was shot. Mr. DePaul was in the back-seat area and the dog was in the front seat, behind the steering wheel."

The Sheriff finally turned to look at Lon, an incredulous look on his face. His deep, greyish eyes looked as if they were trying to look into Lon's mind as he said, "That's rather incredible, don't you think. Do you have any thoughts? Could the animal and the victim have exchanged places as they rested in the water all this time?"

Lon chose his words carefully when speaking with the Sheriff about details of a crime or investigation, "I'm not sure about the dog, but Mr. Harris' body was most likely dumped into the back of the car before it was pushed into the water. So far, there's little evidence concerning the dog, one way or the other. Several of the Deputies knew of Mr. Harris but none remember him having a dog."

Then, he added in a very professional voice, "Whatever the connection, we'll find it. I already have Deputy Burns contacting known acquaintances. The victim disappeared about three and a half to four years ago. Operated on the wrong side of the Law most all his life. Didn't have any relatives, at least none around here. We'll be checking."

The Sheriff appeared to be pondering the information. "You say the man appears to be Harris DePaul? We need to be sure of that identity. We haven't heard anything concerning him in quite some time." He took a long draw from his cigarette and flipped the remainder toward the pond with little care of any contamination of the crime scene.

"Well then, please make sure we know whether the bullets pulled from the victims' match. Also, I understand there was moonshine in the trunk. Do you recall ever dealing with Mr. Harris in such matters? It can be a bad business if you deal with the wrong people."

Lon himself now turned away, looking at the pond. "No sir, don't believe he ever looked into setting up any arrangements regarding moonshine. No recollection of him doing anything much more than drinking it."

Royal did not bite at the slightly sarcastic remark.

Lon continued, "In all likely-hood, he was involved in some type of thievery of merchandise and paid a dear price."

Royal turned, nodding to Ferrell, who also wore a uniform of the Burke County Sheriff's Department. "It is curious that they left the liquor, Deputy?" Royal and his man walked toward the Cadillac with Ferrell closely eyeing anyone in their path.

The Sheriff spoke one more time to Lon, "There'll be plenty of gossip over something like this. You need to keep any information within the confines on this Department. Give nothing of any detail to the newspaper. Let's not allow this to get …complicated. We need to know exactly who was involved with this before too much information gets out. I want daily reports on anything going on and do not hesitate to call on my private line if something urgent comes up. Standard codes on the radio if I'm not in the office. Don't let me down, Deputy Sheriff."

Lon nodded his head, saying, "Yes sir. I will not."

Sheriff Majesty turned toward his waiting car, the driver already at the rear door when Lon spoke up, "Sir! One more thing you'll want to know. Not about this case, but I know you'll be interested."

Sheriff Royal stopped, taking off his dark glasses again and waited for the information.

"I just thought you'd like to know that Ford Rawlings is back in town. Saw him at his Daddy's garage on the way over here. Think he may be planning on staying awhile."

The Sheriff seemed to smirk slightly, "No law against that Deputy. However, there are enough laws about plenty of other things. We'll just see how the boy does. Keep an eye on him." He started to turn back but something seemed to cross his mind. "Oh, and thank you for that information. I expect I'll be seeing "Hot Rod" Rawlings soon enough."

Chapter Twelve

"Ford found himself frozen, not only in place, but also in time."

Ford was about to do a "slow burn" as he watched the pretty girl in the blue and white striped dress get out of the car. She looked so familiar, and yet so different. The nervous look on her face betrayed her as she moved toward Mara with some uncertainty. Ford watched her as he tried to decide whether to leave his car and join them or just drive through the nearest flower garden and hit the road. Mara couldn't even let him put one foot on the old home property before trying to meddle.

He was about to drive away when the girl, or as he should say, young lady, looked his way and smiled. Rebecca Holly Harmon looked so different from the young girl he'd last seen at her sister Julia's funeral. As his eyes fell on her face he could see both the young girl of memory and the transformation to a stunning young woman before him.

She still had those piercing green eyes that captured your attention. The honey-blond curls highlighted her smooth skin and slender face as it fell onto her shoulders. She still held that compelling presence that made her appear accessible.

As he looked at her closely, he couldn't deny a similar aura that so resembled Julia. Perhaps it was more noticeable now because she was older, more mature. They were sisters after all. But there was a mannerism, a countenance that was more like Julia than he remembered. Ford found himself frozen, not only in place, but also in time.

With one hand on the door knob and one hand still on the steering wheel, Ford's mind became torn as which to use. Mara broke the spell, calling out, "Ford, honey! Get over here and say hello to Holly! She's dropped by for a visit. I've talked her into staying for supper. Come on now!"

Ford inhaled deeply, closing his eyes for just a moment. *"Don't act like a clown, Ford. This had to be done...sometime. You can handle it...you've handled a lot more than this."*

Ford knew it was a set up by Mara. Probably one of her telephone calls from the garage. Looking at Holly he believed her to feel just as awkward as he did. He decided to just get it over with. He patted the steering wheel before leaving the car and walking directly to Holly. She stood holding both hands in front of her, her eyes never wavered as he approached. *"A good sign he thought."* Maybe it wouldn't be too awkward. Maybe he could just let this be natural.

He stopped just in front of her, pausing to look into those sparkling green eyes. They neither wavered or blinked as they watched him. "Hello Holly…you still answering to the name of a prickly bush?" It was an old joke of theirs.

"Well, hello Mr. Ford Rawlings…you still going by the name of that second-rate car? I see you've at least stepped up to driving a Chevy. As you can see, I'm a Pontiac girl myself."

Ford grinned, in spite of himself. He could see a smile crossing Holly's face. She reached her hand out to shake his. To everyone's surprise, including Ford, he stepped forward and gave her a warm, welcoming hug.

It felt right to Ford, even though he suddenly had a flash of a memory when he'd last held Julia. The hug felt so natural, a familiar fragrance of life, a tug of oneness of the soul.

He forced himself not to let that memory affect his outward composure. Holding on to Holly's hands, he said, "My goodness girl! What a difference five years makes. You've grown into quite a young woman!" Ford noticed Mara's big smile, causing him to release Holly's hands and step back.

"I guess you've been pulled into my Mother's web of intrigue today. Mara won't be denied a little drama at all times."

Mara flushed, "Now don't go on like that Ford. Holly is just like family to us and I think it's wonderful she can take part in our little home-coming here. Now you two catch up while I go and start supper. I'll bring some lemonade."

Holly called out to help Mara, but was turned down in hand and ordered to the front porch to await the lemonade. She looked at Ford, shrugging, "I believe Miz Mara has spoken."

Ford took her by the arm, "There's never been a time that Miz Mara has not spoken." They climbed the three steps to the front porch where Holly sat on the swing as Ford settled into a wide wicker chair. Neither one could find a starting point, so silence filled the porch for a moment.

Ford finally asked about her parents, then their store, and what she was doing now. It was pleasant, polite conversation…but that was about all.

Holly answered his questions in general. She asked if he was going to stay for a while and then how he liked Germany. This banal banter continued for several minutes until Mara reappeared with a pitcher of iced lemonade. "Now you two help yourselves and for goodness sakes just take some time to get reacquainted. You've got plenty of time to just talk to each other. I'm fixing my Mama's authentic Italian spaghetti dinner for tonight. It'll be Ford's homecoming dinner!"

She laid her hand on Holly's shoulder, "Holly, you being here will just make it even the more special."

Holly again asked if she could help, which caused Mara to lean over and give the girl a hug.

"You're so sweet Holly, just like your whole family! You've got just the sweetest parents. William and Jeanette Harmon are two treasures! They've always been so kind to me from the time I first came to live in Treemont."

She straightened and smoothed her apron, "No, you sit out here with Ford. You two have to have some catching up to do. I've made this dinner so many times it almost makes itself. Besides, I bet you've already put in a full day's work at the store. You all just sit and visit. It's such a nice day…it really is."

Mara realized she was gushing, so she stepped back, only to rattle on further, "Really, this supper will truly make itself. Thanks for the offer. I baked a big loaf of good, thick Italian bread early this morning. My sauce is easy and I'll have the sausages and meatballs cooking shortly."

Ford offered without thought, "I have missed your sauce Mother."

She walked over, gently laying a hand on his shoulder. Taking the opportunity to brag, she added, "Ford does love my sauce. Nothing from a can. My Momma would've clobbered me if I even thought about that. It's an old recipe handed down from my great-grandmother I guess. There's two types of tomatoes along with chopped peppers, mushrooms, and onions from the garden. I'll add basil and bay leaves, then I throw in some good sausage with a couple of chicken necks. You just can't beat the taste."

She lovingly laid her other hand on Ford's neck and then brightened. "Oh, and I've got an antipasto that's ravishing. Grew most of it here. I have to go to Asheville for the olives and oil, but it's worth the trip. Helps a lot that there's a Greek community there."

She stopped, studying to see if she'd left anything out, and then brightened again. "Now, let me tell you about something special. Your father brought home two big jugs of Uncle Jubal's homemade red wine. Old "Skillet" says he don't like to drink the stuff, but he sure makes some mighty tasty wine. I sampled it the other day when I was using some on a roast I cooked. The wine made that meat so tender and so delicious…and, well, the glass I drank was awfully good too. It's going to be really tasty with the pasta. I may even sneak a little in the sauce."

She lowered her voice as if sharing a secret. "I hope my Mamma don't get wind of it. She would never change that recipe at all. She might just send one of the Angels from over on the mountain to have a talk with me."

Mara often teased about Angels stopping to rest on Brown Mountain before they ascended back to Heaven. She felt they needed a little time after going about the earthly chores they were tasked to do. As Ford well knew, she wasn't always teasing about the Angels. Ford learned long ago to not respond in any way when Mara spoke of the mountain or her "angels".

Mara stopped at the door. "Holly honey, you don't have to drink any wine if you'd prefer not…I've got plenty of sweet tea."

She then smiled at Holly saying, "But Holly…you gotta try this wine. It's not like what they make in Italy, but it is delicious!"

As she walked through the door, she gave Ford that coy smile of hers, "Ford, darlin'…how'd you like some of your Momma's homemade cannoli's? I must have had a premonition yesterday morning when I just decided to make some. You may recall, I have a mighty taste for them at times." She stepped back, looking closely at Ford and Holly as if she felt mighty pleased with herself.

Looking at the two of them, she knew there was still a distance between them. She wanted to get back to the kitchen but there just seemed to be more words to say. Before she knew it, she walked back outside and stood between them.

She first took hold of Ford's hand and then Holly's. "You both have a very dear connection. Julia was just so lovely, and Holly, you are ever-bit the lovely person that your sister was…maybe even more, I think. You two have a connection and you need to use it to get closer, not further away. I'm not trying to match-make, I'm just trying…well, to give you a chance to be "family". It's okay to be "family". You both need family. You really can help each other…you'll figure it out, if you'll just try."

With that, she threw up her hands saying she needed to get to work on the meatballs and finish her sauce. Neither Ford or Holly saw how Mara's eyes had almost turned liquid. She left the porch quickly leaving Ford and Holly feeling a little overwhelmed. Ford stared after his mother, wondering if she had gone a bit insane. All Holly could do was stare down at her hands, looking as if she had just been told some intimate secret.

Ford measured the young woman sitting cross from him. He knew her but then again, he didn't. "You and Mara seemed to have gotten pretty close since I've been gone."

"Yeah, I guess we have. She's been so kind to me and my family. She's special."

"I guess that's been a good thing…for both of you. Having Julia in common helped, I'm sure. Those two were close."

"She helped me with some things…things we both needed to deal with. When everything seemed to be at a standstill, she stepped up. She included me…didn't pass me by like I was still a kid. She wouldn't leave it alone. She stayed with…" Her voice trailed off and her face flushed.

"You're right. She stayed and I didn't. I made a choice and I've been haunted by it every day since. I'm glad you at least had her…as well as your parents."

Now Ford appeared to fall in to an emotional hole.

For a few seconds, they continued in silence. Holly spoke first, looking back at Ford with those piercing green eyes. "I guess I've really missed you Ford. It was like you disappeared from our life just like Julia. I don't want you to feel bad but I'm okay talking about Julia, or anything else, I guess. I just…well, I looked up to you…I believed you were someone I could always count on and someone who could protect me too. Then you were gone…not like Julia, but the same."

Ford jumped up from his chair, emotion washing across his face. He paced away and then back to Holly, obviously torn in what to say. Looking into those green eyes, he softened just a bit, "I couldn't protect Julia…how do you think I could protect you? That eats at me every day I wake up and breathe. I think it's obvious I can't protect anyone. Let me tell you…I've proved that on other occasions as well."

He stopped, letting his emotions slow before continuing, "Okay, I'm sure I'm not saying this way I should. You were…still are, I guess, family to me. But when I see you, I see Julia. It doesn't feel right…and yet, it feels "too" right. Look, I loved your sister. I wanted to marry her and take care of her and let her take care of me. I just wanted us to be together. Listen, I wanted you to be my sister…my family. Then it all changed!"

He paused again to try and slow his emotions. "Julia's gone and I'm still here. I still don't feel right about that. I feel guilty! It's been all these years and I still don't know what to do about it." Ford walked to the porch steps, pausing to grip the top of the railing and wondering again if all this was just one big mistake.

Holly walked over to him, gently laying her hand on his back. "Ford, I still want you to be my big brother…or my friend…my family and my friend."

She leaned against the railing, facing Ford. "I think Mara just wants us to stay close because she knows we do have a bond. You may think it's only because of Julia, but I'm not so sure that's the only bond we have. I think I need you to help me get past losing Julia…at least as much as I can. I need you to know who I am and challenge me to be more. Maybe I can help you too. I know I've grown up a lot and I'm sure you have you too. I'm not going to say it's the way Julia would have wanted it…because she didn't want to die. But I know she loved you and wanted you to always be happy."

Ford's body felt like it was going to collapse. *"Maybe she's right. It actually feels right. Maybe the rawness of living in the face of pain, is what gets you through it."*

Ford wrapped his arm around Holly's waist and gave her a little tug. "Okay! I'll try and be your big brother, but I'm not sharing my Christmas presents with you…or my desserts!" Holly gave him a light punch in the ribs with her elbow, saying, "You don't have to worry about giving me anything "big brother" …I take what I want."

Mara's ears were tuned into the conversation on the porch and a large smile was drawn across her face. It was just then her telephone rang. She answered and to her surprise a person with a very familiar accent spoke to her, "Yeah, I'm lookin' for Ford Rawlings. Sometimes people call him "Elvis", you know, cause he sorta looks like the guy. *Youse* have any idea where I might find him? It's real important, ya see. What yah say, lady?"

Chapter Thirteen

"I've told them no before...I just need to tell them again!"

Mara noticed her hand was clinching the hand-piece of the telephone with too much force. Her mind raced as she tried to think of any and all the scenarios that this call could represent. It was difficult to think of any good ones.

What surprised Mara the most was not the voice on the other end but the fact that they were asking for Ford and not her. She always knew that one day she'd get a call like this or even worse, an unannounced and unwelcomed visit. Her heart raced as she tried to consider why this person on the other end of the line was asking for Ford. Too many lifetimes had passed for this to happen.

Just then, Ford walked inside from the porch. A genuine smile crossed his face as he carried the empty lemonade pitcher inside. Holly followed behind with two empty glasses. They'd obviously found some happy, middle ground as Holly jabbed at Ford's ribs with one of the empty glasses.

Mara could hear the voice on the other end saying, "Hello? Hello? You still there, lady?"

She answered, "Just a moment." Looking at Ford, she raised her index finger to her lips to quiet him, then motioned for him to come to the phone. When he reached her, she held the phone in her hand so they both could listen.

She gave him the quiet sign again, then spoke, "I'm sorry...had to take my spaghetti sauce off the eye. Now, who you lookin' for, buddy?"

The voice on the other end seemed to respond a bit to the change of attitude in her voice. "Look lady, I just wanted to know if youse heard of a Ford Rawlings? This is the Rawlings house ain't it?"

Mara's eyes flashed as she tried to read Ford. "Hey buddy! You called me. How about showin' a little respect! And yeah...I know of a Ford Rawlings, but he don't live here. What is it you want?"

There was silence on the other end as the man spoke to someone in the background. He answered back with a much smoother tone, "Sorry to bother you Miz Rawlings. I'm calling for a business acquaintance of Mr. Ford Rawlings. He just needs to speak to him is all."

Ford reached for the receiver, but Mara's grip was strong. "Okay, I can give him a message if I see him. I got to tell you now, he ain't been around here in a long time. But, I'll make sure I remember to give him the message if I see him sometime. So, tell me. Who's this message from. I'm writing this stuff down in case it's a while before I see him."

Again, there was hesitancy on the other end as a few muffled words were exchanged. "*Youse* just write this down. Tell him Vincent DiPoli needs to speak with him. Yeah, ya see, Mr. DiPoli wants to know if he needs any work. I mean, he's got work for him and wants to speak with him about it…the work I mean. Got that?"

There was another pause as Mara didn't answer. The voice came on again, "Tell him, Mr. DiPoli will be at Mary's Diner in the morning from nine *toose* ten o'clock. Tell him it would be *advantageous* for him make *dis* meetin'. But, if *youse* speaks to him and he wants, he can locate Mr. DiPoli at the local hotel or whatever it is. It's called the Alpine Inn. Tell him it's very important that he speaks with Mr. DiPoli, as the gentleman in question will not be satisfied until he sees him."

Then he closed by saying, "Got all that lady?"

When Mara said "Sure, why wouldn't I?", the caller said, "*Tanks*…tell Ford we'll be seein' him, soon."

The line went dead, but Mara still held on to the handset. As she hung up, she saw a blank look on Ford's face as he was obviously in deep thought. "Ford, Darlin'. What was that about? Who is that?"

This brought Ford out of his thoughts. "Aw, just a guy from back in Jersey, I guess. I worked for somebody he knew. This guy works for a guy who thinks I owe him something. Just a pain-in-the-…behind, type of guy. Guess he followed after me…to Carolina, I mean. I've told them *no* before…I just need to tell them again! These people just don't seem to understand the word *No,* unless they're the ones saying it."

Mara grabbed ahold of Ford's arm, staring hard into his eyes. They looked at each other as if daring the other to blink. Holly, feeling very uncomfortable with the situation, moved back to the porch. She was obviously in an awkward spot, in an awkward family type situation. She moved out and sat in the swing, wondering if it was better she just snuck away.

Mara noticed Holly move to the porch. While still holding Ford's gaze, she called out, "Holly, honey! Now don't you be leaving. We'll just be a minute. It was just an odd telephone call. Ford will be back out in just a minute. Sorry for the interruption. It's just one of those Yankee fellows, bless their hearts, you have to look over them for their rudeness."

Mara heard Holly respond, "It's all right, Mara. I'll just wait here and enjoy the view…and the nice breezes."

Mara turned back to Ford, her eyes locking onto his as she whispered, "These people that don't understand the word *No*…are they also known as "The Mob"?

Chapter Fourteen

"I may just starve to death before I get another chance at a good meal."

Beppe Carbone was a hard working "soldier" for an Under Boss, one, Demetrio Silvestri. Mr. Silvestri sent Beppe to be a part of Vincent DiPoli's organization. Beppe was a small mountain of a man which was why DiPoli liked to have him close by.

DiPoli's lieutenant was a man named, Dino Bellini. Dino was trying to be to be an "up-and-comer" in the Silvestri organization. He was actually little more than a knee-breaker, a hard case that was trying to become a "made" man in the *Family.* He seemed to love the physical part of his job which made him a good *enforcer.* Beatings or even worse got his juices flowing. Vincent used Dino accordingly but was wary of the younger man. DiPoli knew the man had visions of taking over his job. That was one of the reasons Beppe was a handy man to have watching his back.

The *Family* was becoming more and more wary of DiPoli's decisions. He had made several decisions of late that had cost the *Family* money or brought too much attention their way. The most recent being a hijacking that resulted in the loss of several of their men, either dead or incarcerated. They were sure the Feds were putting the "screws" to those men to "rat" out anyone of their bosses. Vincent had given the go ahead and Bellini had supervised the debacle. It only illustrated their concerns about the two men and their judgement.

They were becoming a dangerous pair that could expose the *Family* in critical ways. The Feds were getting better at bringing some of the top men in the organization down. Several were already spending time in prison and those still leading the organization wanted no part of that life. It was because of these concerns they'd sent Beppe to work for DiPoli, keeping a close eye on him and Dino.

Beppe knocked on the door of room 321 of the Alpine Inn, waiting impatiently for an answer. He needed to know if there were any additional instructions for him from either Dino or Mr. DiPoli. The whole idea of chasing a "redneck" truck driver all the way to the mountains of North Carolina made little sense. He figured Vincent must be following orders from above but he also knew Dino wanted to hurt this kid in the worst way. This kid had cost the *Family* both money and men. Costing the *Family* anything was an unpardonable sin, costing them money was even worse. Dino's losses at the hijacking fiasco had both *family* and personal implications. Several men were lost, several directly under Dino. Dino himself ended up with an injured shoulder and a cut on his head due to being in a car that Ford ran off the road. Of course, the worst injury to Dino was a large dose of damaged pride. Beppe knew this whole thing was mostly personal to Dino.

The whole fiasco should've been handled in Jersey was Beppe's thoughts. Also, Beppe figured it never should have gotten so bloody. The Caputo's, Vincent, and Dino could see no other way than going at the trucks hard and bloody. Well, a lot of people paid a dear price because of that decision.

"Break a leg…an arm, maybe both and the right message would've been sent." That way, it would have been back to normal business and a good Italian boy like Beppe wouldn't be stuck in these rough mountains eating country *vittles*.

Maybe there was more to it than Beppe knew. The frown on his face indicated he probably knew the most of it. This was more about ego, about *fierezza* or *egocentrico* going on here than anything else. It was a very rare moment when someone stood up to the organization. Of course, there was still the money…the mostly easy money that could have been had. DiPoli should have never promised to deliver the shipment before they actually had possession of it.

Vincent probably had already spent more on this little venture into North Carolina than was lost because of Ford Rawlings. This "field trip" was going to be a waste of time and money. Vincent DiPoli did not like looking bad to his bosses and he didn't want them to think he'd allow a "hayseed" like Rawlings show disrespect to the *Family*.

Beppe saw the need for revenge in Dino's beady little hate-filled eyes. He'd heard his mouth go on and on to the bosses how he would never allow some redneck hillbilly get away with such disrespect. His declarations were probably the main reason that Mr. DiPoli felt obligated to arrange this trip down to the North Carolina mountains.

Beppe knew Vincent better make good on this trip. If it didn't work out…well, he best be finding himself a good hiding place deep in the mountains.

Beppe wondered, "*How much money could they have lost in one shipment of medical drugs? I mean, the kid was honest about the whole thing from the beginning. The Visconti Brothers too. They had good reasons not to go along. It wasn't anybody's fault but that damnable Caputo family anyways. It was probably the best thing anyone could have done for the 'Family' by getting them out of the way!"*

Beppe continued to muse, *"The kid was a good driver...and, as it turned out, a good fighter. That's why they wanted to bring him into the organization. If he didn't go for it in New Jersey, he simply was not going to be interested now. Dino and Vincent thought they'd make a name for themselves by running the kid down. Seems they should have already found out that the moonshine runners from these parts are a lot better than you'd know."*

Anyways, the truth was the organization didn't accept any kind of loss. Beppe's brow creased again. He knew the loss of profits looked bad. Losing the men in New Jersey was unacceptable, even if they were all *stupidi teppisti*. Beppe had known the Caputo's for a long time. They were little more than stupid thugs who only used thugs far more stupid. The whole group found out the hard way that they were no match for Ford or the Visconti Brothers. *"That was all on the Caputo's and Vincent. They made the mistakes."*

Beppe shrugged, *"They're all mostly dead now so what should it matter?"* Unfortunately, he knew all too well that it did matter. It always seemed to matter when too much pride was involved.

Beppe knew Vincent DiPoli had some very hard men to answer to. Dino, on the other hand was just wrapped up in his ego and his craving for power and notice. For some reason, he didn't realize his neck was on the line too.

Dino didn't feel he was moving up the ladder fast enough and saw this as an opening. Beppe smiled as he thought of how surprised Dino would be when he found out he'd also take the hit if this didn't work out. He might not even make it back to Jersey…not in one piece, anyway. Beppe's smile grew…that would not bother him at all!

Dino's whole ruse of trying to get the kid to work for the organization as a driver was hardly even a little clever. They planned on making him promises that he could pay back the debt and make some money for himself. He knew that would not fool the kid. The kid would find it laughable when they offered a promise of a position with the organization as long as he wanted it.

Beppe's ten-year-old daughter could see through a story that flimsy. Hell, Dino even tried selling similar lies to him and the boys. He always treated the men that worked for him like they were dopes.

The more he thought about this whole mess the more his stomach growled and the madder he became. *"Like they'd go to all this trouble to secure another driver for hauling stolen and illegal goods up and down the East Coast! Bull!"*

The idea that neither Vincent or Dino acted like they could trust Beppe with even the smallest of tasks made the big man furious. *"It's like I can't be trusted to know stuff. I can be trusted plenty. I'm a loyal guy."* He straightened his tie and knocked harder this time to show he was a man up to any task and didn't want to be kept waiting.

Dino appeared at the door, looking at Beppe as if he was surprised. He stuck his head into the hall and looked both ways, "Yeah? You got something' for me?"

Beppe stepped back, "No, I ain't got nothin' for *youse.* Youse said, "Come up later to see if *youse* would be needin' me for anyting else."

Dino blinked like he was startled, but then, he always blinked, more than was necessary. It was an unfortunate tic. He had a nickname only certain people were allowed to use, "Blinks". Blinks Bellini was what he was called. He didn't mind it, but it wasn't his idea, so he was selective as to who could use it.

"Naw, ain't got *nuttin'* now. *Jus'* wait on us in the lobby. We'll be down to go over to that Diner so we can get a feel for the place. Marco already checked it out, right?" Before Beppe could answer, he added, "Keep your eyes open and let us know if anything looks suspicious." Dino shut the door in Beppe's face leaving him looking foolish standing there.

Beppe shook his head, talking to himself as he walked down the steps, *"Only thing suspicious around here is some of that food over at that Mary's Diner. Who ever heard of something called chicken-fried steak?"*

He remembered the Rawlings woman talking about fixing pasta and sauce. This made his stomach growl in a loud roar. The thought of some good homemade pasta and gravy made him hungry for his wife's home cooking. His wife, his mother, or anyone of his Aunts could put a feast on the table that'd make a grown man weep. Beppe felt his stomach turn over again with a low rumble. *"I may just starve to death before I get another chance at a good meal."*

Beppe Carbone settled into a well-worn seat near the window of the small lobby of the Alpine Inn. If he noticed the shiny black

Cadillac sitting down the street, he didn't let on. Inside the black machine sat Sheriff Royal Majesty having a discourse with his Chief Deputy, Lon Shell.

It seems the local information hotline had been buzzing ever since the three cars from New Jersey appeared in the town of Treemont. Word actually reached the Sheriff's office not too long after the three black Buick Roadmaster's crossed the County line.

Lon was saying, "We're checking the New York license plates as we speak. The names on the hotel registry too. I doubt either one will provide us any real information. Most likely the plates are bogus or stolen. These guys use a lot of traveling aliases."

Royal wasn't looking at Lon as his Deputy spoke, but began smiling as Lon explained his assumptions. "Tell me Deputy, by *these guys*…do you believe them to be "wise guys"? I assume you know that organized crime resides in many places besides New York and New Jersey."

Lon never appreciated Sheriff Majesty's belittling and sarcastic tone of voice. He was doing his job correctly and he didn't like being lectured or spoken down to when reporting information.

Lon tightened his jaw, continuing, "They're keeping one or two guys around the cars at all times. A couple more inside. One is usually upstairs in the hall and one downstairs in the lobby. Big brutes, both of them, especially that guy over in the lobby right now. From the bulges in in their coats, I'm sure they're carrying armament."

Royal continued looking out the window, "Pistols…I assume you are speaking of pistols, Deputy?"

Lon began biting into his cheek. "Yes sir. Since they aren't wearing long coats, I would assume they are pistols. They could be revolvers or automatics. Also, they might have knives, truncheons, garrotes, brass knuckles, grenades, "billy-clubs" or a knitting needle on their person…but we're thinking mostly guns and knives."

Silence hung inside the car as the driver discretely looked in the rear-view mirror. Lon shook his head, "One too many I'm guessing…eh, Sheriff."

Royal looked at Lon for the first time in moments. "Yeah, I'd say at least one…but I understand."

Sheriff Royal Albert Majesty and Deputy Sheriff Lonny Shell had a most complicated working relationship. The Deputy Sheriff could get away with things others couldn't but at the same time, he was held to a higher level of responsibility. Royal sometimes pushed Lon in unusual ways and Lon would at times "bite" back as if speaking to a contemporary. The Department was waiting for one or the other to explode.

There was a top secret "pool" going around the Department as to which one was going to explode first. The side bets ranged from how long it'd be before that happened to if Lon would still be a part of the Department when it happened. There was even a separate bet as to who would throw the first punch.

The Office "pools" were a popular diversion in a Department that was usually quiet and uneventful. Car wrecks, breaking up a moonshine stills, or chasing a moonshine runner were the most exciting things they handled. Civil disputes were the most common occurrence. In fact, if it wasn't for the occasional encounter with the moonshiners, most days could get terribly boring. Considering the number of Officers in the Department, a person would think it would be just the opposite. It was what the Sheriff wanted however, so it was what he got.

Royal rolled down one of the rear windows and lit a cigarette. Lon added, "I looked through their rooms when they went out to lunch. Just a light look-over. Nothing of any consequence. May try it again when they go to supper, unless they leave a guard." Royal mused, "If they don't leave a guard, there's nothing they're worried about anyone finding. But I agree...look anyway. People get careless."

"Well, they're not careless with their cars. They have them under close watch at all times. If they hang around here very long, I'll find a reason to get inside them." Lon waited for Royal's reaction.

"I know you will Deputy. They're not just stopping by for a meal and a powder. They think they have some business here...but I'm of another opinion. Still, I would like to know what they consider their business to be."

Lon exited the car and moved across the street to his own squad car. Royal flipped the cigarette out the window, raising the window slowly as he looked at the large, dark man in the lobby of the Alpine Inn. "Take me to the office, Ferrell. I need to make some calls to Charlotte and Raleigh. These old boys don't realize it yet, but they're in Majesty territory now."

Chapter Fifteen

"But, instead of calling the men to the table, she walked over and took Holly's hand."

Ford sat on his parent's front porch, having another unwanted conversation. J.J. had only been home long enough to clean up and change clothes. He sat opposite Ford, trying his best to find that fine line between Father and friend, sounding board and source of sound reason.

Ford, at first, had been doing a pretty fair job talking around the reality of what the telephone call meant. But his story kept falling apart as he went from first dismissing the call to admitting he didn't leave New Jersey without leaving some issues behind. Finally, he admitted some unpleasant people became involved in his job just prior to his leaving.

The men's discussion continued on the porch as Mara and Holly tried to catch some pieces of the conversation as they sat the table. Holly was obviously more confused about the whole thing than Mara. The matriarch appeared to have a certain understanding even though she lacked details.

The younger woman felt as if she was intruding on an intimate family situation, but could find more reasons to stay than to leave. Ever since the first moment she was once again in Ford's presence, she knew she'd do anything she could to help him stay in Treemont…his home.

Mara was so interested in the conversation on the porch she paid little attention to Holly. Looking over the table, she appeared satisfied with the spread laid out. Instead of calling the men to the table, she walked over and took Holly's hand. "Holly, I can tell you wonder if you should be part of this. Let me say something to you, and it's not that I'm trying to scare you or put you off."

A look of determination crossed Holly's face, "Don't worry, I want to be…for Julia's sake, and to help Ford have a chance to find his home again."

Mara smiled, "I like grit and I know you've got grit. Lordy girl, I've seen your grit. I've watched you since Julia passed and you have grown into your own woman. I'm proud of you and I know your sister would be proud."

"I've just got to tell you, Holly. This situation that's come up could become dangerous. Not just to Ford, either. To any of us. I just don't want you caught up in something that could get bloody."

Holly set her jaw, "Mara, I know you've seen what I can do…you've been there and seen the *grit* I've got. I've had to use it more than once since Julia's death. I've had to do a few things…well, that I never expected. I'm not ashamed of what's been done and I'm not ashamed of my part in what's been done…and I won't hesitate to do more."

Mara looked into Holly's eyes, seeing the same determination she'd noticed on other occasions. Looking through the window, she eyed the men on the porch, saying, "Okay, here's what I think, but remember, it's not what I exactly know. Trust me when I say that I do actually know a few things about these people who called…and here's the thing, it ain't none of it good."

They talked only a few moments, stopping when the men walked in from the porch. J.J. walked passed Mara, leaving a light kiss on her cheek. "My, oh-my! Don't I love it when you cook Italian like your *Madre*."

Mara stopped him, "Just remember my darling, I am Italian, so anything I cook is Italian…and you are one lucky man!"

Elvis chimed in, "*A lucky man. Kiss the cook!*"

J.J. offered a cringed look at the bird. "All I know is the aroma coming out of this house has been starving me to death. My mouth was watering clean out on the porch."

He moved to his chair but before he could sit, a voice called out, *"Starved to death. Starved to death. Elvis all shook up. Feed me, baby!"*

Holly laughed loudly at the animation of the Cockatiel. Ford grinned but it wasn't clear if it was from the bird's outburst or Holly's cheery laughter. Mara walked over to her pet, holding out her arm. The bird jumped from inside his cage and landed on her wrist. He made chirping sounds, raising his crest as he and Mara snuggled their heads together. He called out, *"Oh baby! Elvis all shook up. Nuthin' but a hound dog!"*

J.J. shook his head saying, "You people can listen to the bird or you can join me in this fine meal cause I'm about to start eating."

Mara gave Elvis something to keep him occupied and moved him back to his cage. Holly and Ford sat and passed a large dish of antipasto consisting of pickled eggplant, roasted peppers, cheese, thinly sliced ham similar to *prosciutto,* and olives. It didn't take long before they began passing the steaming bowls of pasta, sauce, and hot bread. J.J. downed a glass of Uncle Jubal's red wine, refilling it before he even had pasta on his plate. "I tell you what, that "Skillet" makes a fine wine…don't know why he doesn't drink it his self? Guess his palate's been burnt away by all the hard stuff he's concocted over the years."

The plates filled up with pasta and antipasto and a heartfelt prayer of grace was offered before the hearty eating began. The volume of food looked to be more than four people could consume. They all ate heartily since it didn't seem proper if anything was left in the bowls. Mara passed a bowl with grated parmesan cheese which was heartily added to, well, almost everything. The conversation was guarded and light-hearted as no one wanted to spoil the meal or the mood.

Finally, the chewing slowed to a standstill. It was hard to determine if everyone was absolutely stuffed or had just worn themselves out eating so heartily. Mara excused herself to the kitchen as Elvis squawked out in his way of singing, "*Since my baby left me, "awk" …found a new place to dwell!*"

J.J. made a face, "I don't mind that crazy bird at all but I hate it when he sings."

Mara returned at that moment, caring a tray with small plates and a platter filled with cannoli's. "Well now J.J., I think Elvis has a beautiful singing voice…and he's not crazy. Birds can't be crazy! Maybe exotic, eccentric, or even occasionally contrary…but not crazy! That's why we get along so, isn't it Elvis?"

Elvis responded, "*Oh, baby!*" causing Mara to smile and Holly to laugh out loud. Mara was still smiling when she said, "Okay, let's eat up these cannoli's. I've got fresh coffee too."

The feast began again with everyone approving of the Italian desert. Mara indicated it providence that she had the inclination to make the tasty desert the day before. "I must have known my baby was coming home!"

Before the last bites were swallowed, Mara broke the pleasant mood. "Okay, before anyone moves from their chair, I want you to tell us what's going on Ford… and be straight, tell us the truth. I've been a good mother to you. Never once gave you grief about running off to the Army and didn't even harp on and on about the fact you stayed away so long after getting out of Service. Don't even need to remind you that all I had for the last few years was a Post Office box as your address in New Jersey. Why I couldn't even come to visit you since I didn't know where to go." Even your phone calls were brief…the few that there were…" Her words hung in the air.

Mara changed her direction slightly. "We're your family, Ford. Even sweet Holly here is family. The time has come when we need to all come together as a family. We'll not meddle but we need to know you're safe and we need to know if we can help you in any way. I can't tolerate any more running away or secrets. So, let's talk…let's all of us talk!"

There was an uneasy silence as everyone gave Ford a determined look. Even Holly appeared to be unmovable in this instance. J.J., who'd already heard a part of Ford's story, put his elbows on the table and nodded toward Ford.

After a beat or two, Ford gave up, saying, "The only way to explain any of this is to start at the beginning. It was a fine meal, Mother. I don't know if what I'm going to say will help with the digestion. I doubt I can give you all the details cause I've got a couple of lifetimes to cover. Let me say this, I can't give you a short version because that might not make sense. I'll start from the day I left Treemont. Get comfortable cause this will take some telling."

Chapter Sixteen

"Mara spoke up, using her silky Carolina voice. Ford honey, just tell the story."

Before Ford could begin his story, J.J. said he needed to "hit the head. Almost immediately Elvis squawked, *"Hit the head! J.J. hit the head!"*

Holly let out another loud laugh as the others chuckled. This time her outburst seemed to embarrass her just a bit as her face flushed a bit.

J.J. responded, "I may have to hit that bird in the head one of these days." Then he grinned and shook his head. "Anyway, this sounds as if it just may get pretty involved and I'd rather not be thinking of a full bladder."

Ford looked at Holly wondering if that sounded a bit too course for her. The flush on her face from her hardy laugh had gone away and she hardly seemed to even consider J.J. speaking of his bladder. Mara, on the other hand, didn't appear too happy for the interruption. She began clearing the table with Holly's assistance.

Ford moved over to the telephone and after referring to the telephone book made a quick call. He'd just hung up from the second one when J.J. walked back into the room and returned to his seat at the table. Mara walked in followed by Holly. She'd obviously noticed Ford make the calls and wondered who he would be calling. She eyed him closely, but said nothing.

Everyone returned to the table, waiting for Ford's story to begin. Mara returned with a fresh pot of coffee just to give everyone something to do as her son told his story. Ford mumbled to himself in a low voice, "Oh man, how should I begin…" He rubbed the back of his head saying, "You know, it's harder to start than I thought."

Mara spoke up, using her silky, Carolina accent, "Ford honey, just tell us the story. It doesn't need to be a speech. Just tell your family what needs to be told."

Ford nodded, saying, "Just finding it hard to get started. Guess the bus ride is the closest to the beginning. Okay, here it is, mostly all of it…like it or not."

The bus ride to Charlotte was tedious, long, and boring. It didn't help that Ford's mind was still reeling from the loss of his beloved Julia. The days following Julia's death were just one long, dark period. The fact that she died so mysteriously, so uselessly, was devastating. Ford wanted to join in the hunt for the vile piece of humanity that would do such a thing. On more than one occasion the Sheriff's Department had told him bluntly to butt out.

Sheriff Majesty made it a point to have Ford brought in to the jail on two occasions. The first was to question his where bouts on the night of the crime. He was told they needed to see his car and got quite angry when he told them he was driving a different car and he couldn't produce it for inspection.

The interrogation lasted several long ours, only ending when the loud, angry voices of Mara and J.J. could be heard throughout the Police Station. It was very fortunate that both of them didn't end up spending the night behind bars instead of Ford.

The fact that he'd been on a moonshine run made his alibi awkward at the very least. The fact that Ford showed up at the crime scene that morning seemed to bring up more questions than answers.

J.J. had opinioned that the Sheriff was more interested in confirming Ford was running moonshine than he was in finding Julia's killer.

The truth was that Sheriff Majesty did have a big problem with Skillet Rawlings, Ford's Uncle. Jubal was the only moonshiner for whom Ford transported moonshine. Skillet was also one of the few moonshiners who wouldn't pay a "tribute" to Sheriff Royal Majesty.

The Sheriff was determined to either catch Skillet processing his liquor or catch one of his "runners" and make him turn on the old moonshiner. He was either going to shut Skillet down and put him in jail, or they would somehow come to an agreement in meeting Majesty's terms.

There were other factors involved which included the Majesty pride. Sheriff Majesty never was one to accept someone not following his orders. He felt disrespected when anyone even disagreed with him a little. When money for the Sheriff's pocketbook was affected he became obsessed with getting his way.

In Ford's case, the Sheriff's Department had so far paid for major repairs to a total of five Deputy's cars that tried to give chase. There was also another car that was totally destroyed as its final resting place was on its side in a deep mountain creek. Sheriff Majesty was sure that Ford was the one driving the moonshine car in each chase.

To make matters worse for Ford, Majesty was sure Ford was running moonshine the night of Julia's death. The Sheriff was livid over the loss of another car and the serious injuries to two of his Deputies. He had not told his men to try and shoot the moonshine runner down. But then, he had come down very hard on his Deputies about the lack of success in stopping certain runners.

As it turned out, the excessive force turned out to be a bad decision on their part. The injuries and damages were hard to take. If they'd shot the runner down…well that could have been another "can of worms". Many of the runners paid Majesty so they could have safe passage. They realized he had to show arrests from time to time. Shooting down a runner, any runner, could have started a little "moonshine war" in parts of Burke County which would certainly have affected the Majesty purse.

The Deputies who were injured the night of Julia's death were in rough condition. They would not be returning to duty any time soon. Prior accidents had only resulted in a myriad of cuts, bruises, and one broken wrist. Usually the cars ended up with the worst of the damage while the Deputies were only left feeling angry and foolish. At the end of any night they tried chasing the elusive "Hot Rod" Rawlings, they were left with only the fact they'd made a mistake.

Ford's Uncle Jubal could build as good a moonshine running vehicle as he could make premium moonshine. Jubal's wife, Billie, was just as good a mechanic as her counterpart and was the one who came up with many of the elements in Jubal's whiskey recipes. They were a team in every way…right down to a stubbornness in the running of their business as they saw fit.

Jubal's cars didn't look like much on the outside and the interiors were mostly stripped out. However, underneath the hood they had engines that would make a racecar driver envious. Some of his cars had specially build secret tanks to handle moonshine hauling in bulk. More often than not, the cars had specially built compartments to handle bottled moonshine.

Yes, Sheriff Royal Majesty had more than a few reasons to dislike Ford, but his issues with Jubal "Skillet" Rawlings were monumental and ran deep into his psyche.

Ford knew the first interrogation was more about moonshine than finding Julia's killer. It appeared that the Sheriff was leading up to offering Ford a deal. A deal which Ford would be guaranteed that no murder charge would be placed concerning Julia. But by confessing to the moonshine running, he would then give up Jubal Rawlings. However, Ford was smart enough to know a confession would put him in jeopardy for charges concerning the damage done on the night before including the injuries to the Deputies.

Majesty got right in Ford's face with all the possibility of charges during the interrogation. He was pushing really hard, sensing he had a great opportunity to get to Jubal. Two things happened just before Ford had a chance to come out of his chair and rearrange Royal's face.

One thing was the reaction of Deputy Lon Shell, who sensed what was about to happen. He moved close to Ford and placed a steadying hand on the young man's shoulder. The other was the crescendo of voices coming from J.J. and Mara Rawlings as they demanded to see their son.

It gave Ford a moment to calm and really think of his position. He was sure the investigation of Julia's death was going to be secondary to the Sheriff's main agenda. He also knew that what he was about to do to Royal Majesty would have put him behind bars the rest of his days if not in a coffin. Still, at that moment, all he wanted was to put his hands around the throat of the pompous, self-serving man.

Lon made sure Ford stayed under control long enough for J.J. and Mara to get their son out of the Burke County Sheriff's office. No charges were placed…at least for the moment. Everyone knew the Sheriff was not finished.

A couple of days passed before Ford was called in for another interview. This time the interview was given by Deputy Lon Shell and Ford was accompanied by the Honorable James T. Myers, Attorney at Law. The meeting was brief and the only topics covered had to do with the murder of Julia Harmon. Ford left the meeting feeling that at least Lon Shell would actually investigate Julia's murder.

After that, Ford tried to keep himself busy. He did his best to involve himself in solving the mystery of her death. Again, and again, he asked questions of anyone who might know anything concerning Julia. It was frustrating as he felt he was getting further and further away from any answer. The Sheriff's Department appeared to be having the same amount of success, at least that was the public face they presented.

Ford knew the Sheriff was still more interested in getting leverage against Jubal. As the days passed with no answers, Ford's dislike for Sheriff Royal Albert Majesty grew from dislike to actual hated. *"This is not going to end well!"* was Ford's foremost thoughts. This was most likely as truthful a statement as could be said. The lingering question was who was going to be the recipient of the bad ending.

The Harmon family, much to the displeasure of Sheriff Majesty, called in two separate Private Detective Agencies. They appeared to work with proper fervor but in the end showed no results. Ford offered to do leg work with the Detective Agencies but again was rebuked. To everyone involved in the hunt, it appeared that whomever had killed Julia had vanished into the same night that took the lovely young woman.

~

It was not long after the Detective Agencies failure in finding any clues concerning the murder that Ford found himself on a transport bus. According to scuttlebutt, the Sheriff was saying he wasn't through with "Hot Rod" Rawlings just yet.

Not long after, Ford found himself on the bus headed to Charlotte. He knew if he joined the Army it would prevent him from getting mad one day and going after Royal Majesty. Even as the bus bumped down the highway, Ford still only had two things on his mind...Julia's killer was still on the loose and he still harbored a great desire to do serious damage to Sheriff Royal Majesty.

PART TWO

The Next Lifetime…

Chapter Seventeen

~ Ford's Story: The second lifetime ~

~1952~

"Loves hard, man!" He looked over at Ford, "You gotta girl?"

Ford knew he'd made a wise choice in leaving Treemont. He managed to wait till just after New Year's Day for his new life to start. His parents were saddened but seemed to understand. They loved Julia as they'd loved him. It was hard seeing them grieve over her loss. He knew the Harmon family felt very close to him, never judging him for working for his uncle. They didn't know all that he did but they didn't let on about what they did know.

Yes, Julia's parents were always very kind to him and her sister Holly had become Ford's second favorite person outside his parents. It was evident that she looked up to Ford just as she did Julia. However, her feelings didn't seem an infatuation with Ford as much as it was the deep feeling of family.

Ford knew down deep that staying in Treemont would end in disaster. Sooner or later, the rage that was the loss of Julia would spill over…and there would be more grieving by people he loved.

The bus moved on toward Ford's next lifetime. He'd drifted off to sleep but was jarred awake when the bus braked hard for a car that pulled out in its path. Ford noticed he had gained a seat partner since he'd fallen asleep. The fellow looked over, smiling at Ford. "Hello. Drew's my name. Drew Alford…from Cold Springs. Hope you don't mind me joining you."

Ford stretched, glancing out the window to see where they might be. "Naw, it's fine. I just drifted off. You join, or drafted?"

Drew looked puzzled at first, "Uh, drafted. You join?"

Ford stared out the window yawning, "Little of both, I guess."

Silence carried them a mile when Drew spoke up. "I didn't want to come. Didn't have a choice you know. Wanted to get married to my girl. Her name's Betsy…I call her my *Bonny Betsy.*" Drew was smiling as he continued, "She said she wouldn't marry me until I got through with the Army…or I guess, it got through with me."

Drew appeared he might get choked up, but he continued, "I almost didn't come anyway. You know, just thought I'd get her to run off with me somewhere and get married. I guess she wouldn't have come with me like that, and they'd surely have come after me. Love's hard, man!" He looked over at Ford, "You got a girl?"

The question rocked Ford. He took a deeper breath, unnoticed by Drew. "Yeah, well, not anymore. She…had to leave." With that, Ford wadded his jacket up for a pillow and laid up against the glass, closing his eyes and hoping Drew would take a hint.

After many body-numbing miles, the bus pulled over for fuel and to offer the riders a chance to eat and take a bathroom break. There was a small café attached to the gas station.

Ford went inside where he ordered coffee and a BLT. Drew sat down beside him ordering pie and coffee. The food came and Ford attacked the sandwich while Drew picked at his pie.

His fidgeting continued until he finally stood up. "I don't feel so well…going out back to the toilet. He laid some coins on the counter and left. Ford noticed him looking over his shoulder as he exited the café.

Ford took a long drink from his coffee cup, got up and walked outside after leaving some money on the counter himself. Instead of walking toward the bus he walked around the back of the café knowing what he'd find.

There was no sign of Drew but Ford knew he was close by. He walked around a storage shed spotting Drew at the edge of the woods behind the building. Ford called out in a steady voice, "It's a long way home from that direction. You think *Bonny Betsy* will marry a deserter, or worse yet, a convict? Not much reward to a fellow's reputation in being called a traitor and a coward. I only say that because you'll be all of those things, or worse, especially to your gal. I mean, she'll never look at you the same. And neither will her family and friends. You going to do that to your girl?"

Drew turned, his eyes wide and full of moisture. His mouth opened, but he couldn't speak.

Ford closed the gap between them, "Drew, the only way you'll ever get Betsy to marry you is to become the best soldier you can be. Show her you'll be a reliable man who can stand tall in any circumstance. Heck, she'll be asking you to marrying her when you get back."

Drew meekly said, "What if she won't wait for me?"

Ford shook his head, "Well, if she won't wait, she'll never be worthy of marrying you anyway. Let her be somebody else's problem." Ford stared at Drew who looked hurt at his last words. He then turned to walk away, calling back, "Do what you want Drew, the bus is leaving shortly and I'll be on it. Choose your life."

Ford walked to the bus, getting a hard look from the Sargent who was supervising the transport. He spoke to Ford, "You take a nature hike, boy?"

Before Ford could answer, a voice spoke up behind him, "Sorry Sargent, he was checking on me. I got a little sick…bad pie I think." Both men climbed on the bus, as the Sargent watched them all the way to their seats.

When they both were seated, Ford wadded his jacket again as he said, "Good choice. Make sure you work your butt off in Basic, be the guy that won't quit. It'll go faster and you'll be proud of yourself when you get through it…and so will that girl of yours."

Drew reached out his hand to shake Ford's, "Thank you Ford. You may have just saved my life."

Ford looked over at him, "Well, that's something I haven't been too good at so far."

Drew looked puzzled. He said, "Well…I sure appreciate you. That girl that left you behind sure made a bad decision."

Ford rolled over on his makeshift pillow saying, "Yeah, well, she didn't have much of choice."

Ford entered Fort Jackson, South Carolina with very little thought. There were boys there from all walks of life. Some were filled with bravado, feeling they were on one great adventure and maybe they were. Others were quiet, almost timid in their new adventure. Ford, on the other hand, was just there…front and center.

He stayed to himself when he could. He kept his mind set on following each and every order as quickly and completely as he could. Soon, his life became a series of long, strenuous drills, lectures that involved much barking and screaming, and a constant reminder that his life was now owned by the Army. It was in all this constant indoctrination of the "Army Way" that Ford found a degree of solace. Pure exhaustion fatigued his mind to the point that he could actually fall asleep when he collapsed into his bunk at night.

Ford began receiving letters from his Mother from the beginning. She tried writing in non-upsetting lines about neutral topics. It didn't matter, Ford kept them in his locker without reading the first one until two weeks before his graduation of Boot Camp.

Ford took the packet of letters to a place he could be alone. He wasn't going to read them though, he was going to burn them. Seeing his Mother's flowing script on the envelopes gave him pause. Before he knew it, he was reading one after another.

Ford had written his Mother a few genetic letters because he was required to. After reading all her letters, he knew he could no longer shut his parents out of his life. So, he began to write home, at least once a week, every week.

With Boot Camp winding down, Ford was anxious to get on to the specialized training classes each soldier was required to complete in order to perform their function in the Military. Ford, like his Father before him, showed great capacity for working with things mechanical, especially engines. So, it was of little surprise when he was assigned to a school of technical training in all types of military vehicles.

Ford received three letters just as he getting ready to transfer to his first assignment after Boot Camp. Two were from his Mother, and one was from Pfc. Drew Alford. That letter was very short. Ford read, *"Ford, I wanted you to know I made it. You were right. I feel proud to get through Boot Camp and my Betsy does too. It seems a picture of a man in uniform really gets to her. We're getting married next year sometime. Thank you! Hope I can return the favor sometime! Pfc. Drew Alford"*

For the first time in a very long time, Ford smiled. He picked up his gear and left the barracks, headed to the beginning of the next phase of this new lifetime.

Chapter Eighteen

~ 1952 ~

Heidelberg, Germany

USAG Heidelberg Army Base

"Before the next half-hour passed, Joey Visconti and Ford Rawlings were on their way to becoming the best of friends."

Some friends are found and some find you. Whichever was the case, Ford found a friend in Jovanni "Joey" Visconti. They first met in an advance training class State side. After that ended they were shipped out to different bases for their assignments. However, a short time later Jovanni Visconti turned up at Heidelberg Army Base. He found himself standing in of all places, the chow line, right behind Ford Rawlings.

Joey was about three inches shorter than Ford, black hair, dark complexion, a grin that appeared to reach from ear to ear, and dark, dancing eyes. He was jovial without being boisterous. He had focus in his work but appeared carefree in the way he looked at life. Ford found him to be one of the most self-assured people he'd ever met…except for the times he descended into his dark, brooding self. Fortunately, that didn't happen often and a long road trip would bring him out of it.

Joey hailed from Trenton, New Jersey where he was a part of a large Italian family. The family owned a successful trucking firm, *Visconti Brother's Transport.* It was run by his father, Dario, and his Uncle Brizio. Growing up around the trucking business made Joey a natural to work in the Motor Pool Division. In fact, he did everything he could, outside of bribery, to become a part of this "outfit" as he called it.

Joey's three older brothers, Leone, Ilario, and Giapaola (Gio), worked in the family business as did Brizio's sons, Nino and Gasparo. Each brother had two daughters. Dario's daughters were Fabrizia and Edda while Brizio's daughters were Gioia and Jemma. There were other relatives involved in the family business too numerous for Ford to account for.

It was, as they say, the *American Dream* that his Grandpop, Abramo Visconti, came to America to find. With sacrifice and hard work, he made the dream a reality for his family. Abramo's two sons never served in the military or earned a high degree through a college or university. Of the six sons the two brothers sired, Joey was the only one to show interest in the Military, and the only one to serve. He was also the only child to earn a college degree. The other brothers and cousins went directly to work for the trucking Company, some, even before they were out of High School.

Jovanni, or Joey, as everyone called him, was a different sort of fellow than his brothers and cousins. They were smart, he was smarter with a clear head for business. Working hard became natural as did his mechanical skills with the trucking fleet. He was as much American as he was Italian. He was also known to be very high spirited and a little reckless. Dario and Uncle Brizio recognized the boy needed some influences in his life that would ground him. College provided a good education but not the stability his father and uncle sought. When Joey mentioned he was interested in the Army, they both did all they could to encourage him to try living the military experience.

One thing Joey found fascinating from the very beginning was the potential of having so much equipment available to him at any given time. It was obvious to anyone who'd met Joey Visconti that his military career was going to be an interesting one.

Ford soon realized Joey to be a hand-full. Just going through the chow line with him could be an ordeal. The young man constantly berated the line servers about not having good Italian food in the Army.

Actually, their first meeting in the chow line cemented their relationship. Ford had moved from amusement to annoyance having to listen to Joey go on and on about the food. Ford leaned over to Joey, saying, "You should try to get decent biscuits and gravy here…holy mother, worst stuff you ever tried to convince your mouth to eat."

Distracted by Ford's talk of food, Joey asked him, "Tell me again… where're you from, and what the hell is biscuits and gravy?"

Before the next half-hour passed, Joey Visconti and Ford Rawlings were on their way to becoming the best of friends. The common language of motors and the vehicles they powered made each feel immediately comfortable with the other.

It didn't take any time before Ford knew almost as much about *Visconti Brother's Transport* as any of the Company's employees by way of Joey's stories. On the other hand, Joey loved to hear Ford talk about the mountains, the moonshining, and the transport of *white lightning* over the crooked mountain roads. Ford's stories of avoiding both the Law and hijackers fascinated Joey Visconti to no end. If Ford couldn't think of a new story he'd just re-tell one, captivating Joey as if he'd just heard it for the first time.

In regard to more current matters, Joey took little time becoming familiar with the availability of any and all vehicles not currently in use. At least once or twice a week he'd show up just as Ford was getting off duty. He might be driving a jeep, truck, or other military conveyance. Sometimes Joey just wanted to drive around to shed his occasional dark mood. He didn't care if it was through the city of Heidelberg or into the German countryside.

The trick for Joey and Ford was not getting away from the base but getting back on it with few questions being asked or someone discovering they shouldn't have left in the first place.

Occasionally Joey would get bored and ask Ford for driving tips. He would speak of the truck engines of his family's trucking company and quiz Ford on how to get more horsepower and performance. Joey loved to push the vehicles he commandeered using the skills Ford taught him.

There were times Joey would find a couple of girls who wanted to tag along for fun. He'd pick up Ford and away they'd go for dinner and drinks, dancing and drinks, or sometimes just drinks and whatever might follow. Joey always had money and insisted on picking up the tab wherever they went and whatever they did.

However, Joey had a problem holding his alcohol. He did fine with wine or beer but the hard stuff could get him drunk in a hurry. When drunk, he tended to be even more foolhardy and less likely to listen to any sound judgement or reasonable thought. In those instances, it fell to Ford to get them back to the Base, get them inside while making Joey look sober, and finally, returning the vehicle which usually shouldn't have left the Base in the first place.

As time went on, Joey's antics became bolder and bolder. Late one night the two had a Major's car out for a "test run" around the city. Their trip included a stop at a lively tavern serving good German food as well as music and dancing. This was accompanied by far too much beer and alcohol.

Ford mostly carried the boy back to the car, propping him up in the back seat just in case he became sick and needed to vomit. As he closed the car door he noticed Joey did not have any shoes on. Ford shook his head as he returned to the tavern to located the boy's footwear.

Because it had taken so long to find the shoes, Ford needed to hurry back to the Base due to the lateness of the hour and the fact that Joey was fading fast. With much effort, he made good time to the gate and managed to get inside with no hard questions asked. This was partly due to the guards having to deal with another drunk who'd been dropped off by a taxi. Ford hustled the sedan around to the building where they were housed. Joey had sounded restless in the dark back seat all the way to the Base. Ford figured Joey would never last long enough to walk back from the Motor Pool.

Before dragging Joey out of the backseat of the car he thought it best to check inside the building, making sure he could get the drunken soldier inside without questions being asked. The coast was clear so he returned to the car to get the boy inside. Ford began calling out for Joey in a staged whisper. A giggle was heard from the back of the sedan. Ford opened the back door to see what Joey was doing.

Behind the front seats was a heavy blanket. He'd remember seeing it when they first left the base. Only now, it wasn't lying flat on the floor of the car. In fact, it was moving around quite a bit. More noises came from underneath it. Ford pulled the blanket back to see Joey lying on the floorboard with a half-naked German lady on top of him.

Of course, the lady knew little English and found herself quite busy keeping Joey's hands from removing more of her clothing. Once she got a clear look at Ford, her eyes lit up as she said in broken English, "Oh, hello handsome American! My name is Ingrid."

She moved her shoulders from side to side, accentuating her bosom as she was immediately attracted to Ford's good looks. He reached to pull her out of the car and was immediately surprised as she clamped on to his forearm and pulled him into the car, on top of her.

By this time, Joey had dozed off for a moment. He was located underneath the other two. Ford was frantically trying to get up as the woman began kissing his face and neck while keeping him pulled on top of her. This continued for a few frantic seconds as Ford kept trying to get a grip on something that wasn't Joey or Ingrid.

As he struggled, Joey revived a bit and decided it a good time to grab ahold of Ingrid's available bottom. She began squealing as his hand found purchase beneath her exposed underwear. He began laughing as she was now scrambling for release.

With a surge of movement, she escaped Joey by switching positions with Ford, putting him between her and the laughing Italian. Joey grabbed again at Ingrid's bottom, only to find himself ahold of Ford's rear. Ford shouted out, "Hey! Let go of me, you drunken *dago.* I'm going to punch your lights out."

At this, Joey found the situation even funnier, slurring out the words, "You can't do that Ford. You're driving and we got to have lights!"

Now Ford started laughing. In fact, the two friends became so involved with the hilarity of the situation they forgot about poor Ingrid. She removed herself from the sedan, leaving the two soldiers alone in their own drunken company. She called out a German insult or two before staggering shoeless down the street while trying her best to put her clothes back together in the correct order.

A little later, Ford managed to get Joey inside and into bed. Joey was barely conscious but was still able to ask Ford, who he thought to be Ingrid, if she'd like to join him in his bunk. Ford grinned at his hilarious comrade. He then returned the car and soon collapsed into his own bed, falling immediately asleep.

The next day came soon enough, finding both men with a tremendous headache and swearing never to do that again. As for Ingrid, she was found passed out on the porch of a one-star General's residence. She was sleeping off her night of partying in the General's porch lounger. Fortunately for the boys, she had no distinct recollection of how she got there or even how she came to be on the Base. When asked who brought her there, her only description of the two was, *"The handsome American soldier and the cute little "grabby-hands" soldier who laughed too much."* She also wanted to know if the General knew where her shoes were!

And so, Ford's lifetime in Germany passed in daily succession. He worked hard, both learning the equipment he was charged with and teaching men like his good friend Joey how to care for that same equipment.

Still, every couple of weeks or so, Ford found himself caught up with Joey in some ridiculous adventure. Joey, when sober, swore he'd never put them in jeopardy again. And to his credit, he'd put his head down and work like the best kind of soldier, but for only so long. Inevitably, the day would come around again with Joey driving away with some type of vehicle and bringing Ford along for either a long drive in the country or another adventure of wine, women, and avoiding the MP's. Ford was often a little surprised at which choice was on Joey's agenda.

Chapter Nineteen

~ 1953 ~

Heidelberg Army Base

"This was evidently not her first rodeo."

By the time their overseas tour of duty was nearing an end, Ford and Joey's experiences had met or surpassed almost anything two daring soldiers could experience in peace-time. A combination of luck, daring, and cunning allowed them to avoid serious run-ins with both Military and Civilian Law Enforcement. Their escapades were becoming legendary among the regular "Joes" of the base.

Each man had an understanding of why he took the risks but had no idea as to why the other one did. It wasn't a competition and didn't appear to have anything to do with disobeying authority. Each one had a need to do risky things as if to plug a hole in their life.

On one hand, Ford and Joey received a number of commendations regarding their outstanding work in the Motor Pool. On the other hand, they'd accumulated enough citations for their non-military activities that they were lucky to still be a part of this man's Army.

Ford finally made it to the rank of Corporeal, while Joey was happy he still held the rank of Private First Class. Ford was feeling almost satisfied they were going to make it out of Germany without spending time in the brig or the local jail. Lately, Joey remained focused on his job. He did appear to be getting a little antsy regarding going home. Army life was winding down and all they had to do was complete each day's work and lay low for just a little longer. It was looking very promising until Joey nearly destroyed all the good their hard work had accomplished. In one afternoon, it nearly fell apart on a Heidelberg street, just a few miles from the Base.

Ford had been working all week getting several vehicles, as well as the whole motor pool, in shape for an upcoming inspection. He'd been told how important a good review was to Captain Hammonds, the CO over the Motor Pool. The Captain was padding his resume in order to achieve a promotion in the new year. Ford's immediate superior was Sargent Arnie Barnes, a pretty understanding guy. He'd looked the other way on several occasions as Ford and Joey returned to work with a hangover and the keys to something they should not have been driving.

Arnie reminded them several times how important this upcoming inspection would be to the Captain. He was obviously trying to avoid the very real possibility that one or both of the boys would screw up at the worst time. The term "Court Marshall" was used morning, noon, and night to emphasis just how important this was to the Captain.

The inspection was only two days away when Joey found himself left to his own devises. This was always a bad idea.

Ford was just finishing the last of his have-to-do list causing him to feel pretty pleased with himself. Before he could leave the shop, the telephone rang. Ford would later regret answering it.

Joey was calling in a panic. He was stuck off the Base at a nearby Beer Hall. It was getting late and he had driven an unauthorized vehicle off Base. The darn thing wouldn't start and he was going to get in serious trouble if he didn't return the vehicle before it was missed. Ford asked his friend what he was driving only to be told in frantic terms to get to him "asap" or he'd be facing a firing squad by morning.

Joey pleaded for help with more desperation than Ford had ever heard in his friend's voice. Joey was on the phone begging for help in his deliverance and making wild and random promises. At first, Ford told him he didn't have the time right then to come after him. Finally, an already worn out Ford gave in to Joey. Promises of a lifetime of indebtedness to Ford actually concerned him.

Joey gave him an address and promised him he would do anything to repay Ford for this one last saving moment. Ford grabbed a tool bag and headed out. He figured he could get away easy enough but wasn't sure how easy his reentry to the Base might be.

Ford managed to get off the Base in the Motor Pool jeep to which he'd added more tools as he tried to think of any scenario why the vehicle was stalled. Joey was a more than adequate mechanic which made Ford wonder what the boy had done.

By the time Ford turned down the last street, he was getting concerned it was more than a simple stalled engine. He arrived to the address in little time only to find something he could never had prepared for. As soon as he drove half way down the long street, Ford realized what Joey had done…he just didn't know how or why.

Ford saw Joey right away. He was smoking a cigarette and pacing in front of a M41 Walker Bulldog tank. Ford almost kept driving. In fact, he probably would have passed by had Joey not run in front of Ford's jeep upon spotting his friend.

Ford got out of the jeep, an amazed look on his face. He walked the length of the tank as Joey walked along side trying to explain what seemed to go wrong with the tank. Ford exploded, "What went wrong! Are you kidding me? What went wrong is they let an idiot like you in the Army in the first place! You're going to be in a Military Prison until you're an old man! I'm leaving!"

Ford stopped, grabbing Joey by each shoulder, "How in the hell did you ever get this thing off the Base and through the streets without getting arrested!"

Joey smiled back, "Guess I had the biggest guns."

Ford almost slugged his friend, letting out a howl instead. It was all he could do to contain his urge for violence against his friend.

Just then, a soft, Southern voice floated down from the turret of the tank. "Corporal! Oh Corporal! Thank you for coming to our rescue. You are a darling boy for doing this. I just don't know what we were thinking or what we were going to do. I just couldn't leave our dear friend Joey stuck here. You are an angel!"

That was when she leaned forward on the turret, batting her long eyelashes as the spaghetti strap of her dress fell off her shoulder, "My oh my, you are one handsome man Corporal Angel. You should be in the movies. You're even better looking than that Elvis fellow."

Ford couldn't close his wide-open mouth. He looked up to see Captain Hammond's wife situated inside the turret. She was dressed in a deep blue gown of sorts. Her hair and make-up were just a little askew but she still looked the beautiful woman she was. Setting aside his amazement, he turned to Joey, "Tell me Joey, how in the world did you get this off the Base?"

Joey looked a bit embarrassed as he looked up at the lady, "She wanted to go for a ride. Said she'd never ridden in one of these." He lowered his voice as he leaned in close to Ford, "I don't think this type of thing is her first rodeo, if you get my drift. I think she's pretty used to getting her way."

Joey looked up at the lady, his eyes began dancing as he said loudly, "Let's get this vehicle started up Corporal! Mrs. Hammonds has an early dinner event to attend and we can't delay the lady!"

Then he lowered his voice again, saying, "She refuses to leave me and get a taxi back to the base. This chick is crazy from the neck up."

Then he grinned and added, "And she has a really "crazy" body from the neck down, if you know what I mean."

Ford's mouth fell open again, "You don't mean…you and her…in the tank!"

Joey's grin was radiant, "Hey man, like I said, she's a strong-willed woman…and very…flexible. You understand flexible…don't you?"

Ford was doing a slow burn that had almost run out of fuse. Before he let Joey have it, he decided to just grab some tools and frantically began working at getting the tank running again. By some miracle, he had the engine running in about twenty minutes.

In the meantime, Mrs. Hammonds had managed to exit the tank without damaging her evening dress. She gave Ford a hard kiss on the cheek to thank him for his gallant and timely rescue. Turning to Joey, she also kissed him on the cheek, saying, "Joey honey, you just show a girl the most lively of times."

Just as they were about to begin their parade back to the Base, a Military Police jeep pulled up. Two very serious looking MP's slowly exited the jeep as they looked over the situation.

They spotted Joey first and one of them sided up to him, asking, "Soldier, are you responsible for this tank being here and why is that so?" Joey began sputtering trying to form an answer.

Ford walked around to the trio and was met by the other MP, blocking his way. Before Ford could say a word, the MP spoke some surprising words, "Well, hello…Corporal Ford Rawlings! Didn't expect to be running into to you outside of North Carolina. Looks as if you're having a day!"

Before he could think, Ford's jaw dropped for at least the third time in the last hour. Standing before him was none other than Drew Alford…now, Sargent Drew Alford, MP, United States Army!

Ford felt like grabbing the soldier and giving him a big hug. He started praying that Drew would lend a kind hand to this delicate situation. In a low tone, he asked Sargent Alford if they could speak in private. They walked away from the tank as Ford gave Drew a quick explanation with only the slightest mention of Mrs. Hammond who now stood near Ford's jeep, powdering her nose.

In spite of himself, Sargent Alford ended up grinning at the explanation. “Boy oh boy, Corporal Rawlings, you could say you boys have stepped in it and it don’t smell good at all.” He looked past Ford toward the other MP, “I’m not one to forget a favor…and I owe you a big one. I’ll speak to my partner. Be back in a sec.”

Sargent Alfred pulled the other MP aside, speaking with him for almost five minutes. Ford and Joey were getting anxious but Mrs. Hammonds was looking very bored. She lit her third cigarette since Ford arrived.”

Sargent Alfred walked back to the trio as his buddy climbed back in their jeep. “Why don’t we see if we can get this “visual aid” off the streets and back home…put it to bed as they say. How’s that sound…okay?”

Ford could not believe his luck. Joey wanted to ask questions, but Ford pushed him toward the tank, saying “Later!”

He walked over to Mrs. Hammonds and explained the turn of events as quickly as he could to let her know this would be a great time to go back to the Base.

At that, she held out her hand for Ford to assist her into his jeep as Joey climbed back into the tank. With an escort of the Military Police and Mrs. Captain Jacob Hammonds leading the way, they managed to return the tank with only a few questions asked by Base security. As Joey had said earlier, *“This was evidently not her first rodeo.”*

Chapter Twenty

~ New Jersey, 1953 ~

"Ford old buddy, that's one of the saddest stories I've ever been told."

Ford was given one last surprise before he re-entered civilian life. He was standing outside enjoying a sunny morning while awaiting a tardy Joey. All that was left was their final "processing out". It was like a surreal daydream as he stood still, imagining what it would be like to be out of the Army. The time had passed faster than he could imagine. He'd considered more than once the idea of re-upping for another tour. Each time he came to the conclusion that he couldn't do it. He was ready for another lifetime to start. What that lifetime would be was anybody's guess.

Joey walked into his line of sight sporting a silly grin on his face. He held two envelopes in his hand. Walking up, he handed Ford the unopened envelope and strangely kissed the other one. "What a woman! It was worth almost getting thrown in the brig and maybe shot at dawn for one afternoon with her."

Ford thought his friend either drunk or finally out of his mind. He grinned thinking it would be hard to determine which applied considering it was Joey. Ford looked at the inscription on the envelope. The address was postmarked, Germany. The last name, *Hammonds*, was inscribed in a flowing script. Ford glanced back at Joey whose face was still consumed with that silly grin.

"Open it up, Ford. Let's see what the Lady has to say to you." He then voluntarily began reading his letter out loud.

Dearest Joey,

I do hope you get this letter before returning to your life in New Jersey. You are just the sweetest boy! I can't tell you just how much I loved our little drive in the tank. It's something I will always remember. You were as gallant as you were amorous. If you hadn't left Germany I do believe I might have persuaded you to take another tank ride. Have the best life! Keep your life and your love as sweet as it is now!

Love you dear Joey, M.H.

"Now that is some woman! What did she write you, Ford?"

Ford knew he might as well read it out loud since Joey would pester him until he did. Ford slit the envelope with a knife, not wanting to tear the paper, an old habit of his. He read.

My dear, handsome Ford,

I just had to thank you one more time for coming to my rescue. You were just as much a gentleman as you were an excellent mechanic. I don't have to tell you how awkward it could have become. I will owe you a favor anytime you need one. Let me just say that Captain Hammonds will be coming back State-side in the next year or so. Guess he's getting his promotion.

You may think I am a bad person with my flirtations with your friend. Not to make excuses, I have found myself quite lonely and ignored these past few years. I met my husband at the University of Tennessee and found him a dashing and reliable man. He has stayed the love of my life but I am not sure I am the love of his life anymore. At least not his first love. His career path has consumed him and I find myself only along for the ride. I consider this my circumstance and I will continue to deal with it as I am able.

Ford honey, I'm a former Tennessee girl, born and bred. You Western North Carolina boys are just like cousins to us Tennessee girls. My Family still lives in Kingsport, so who knows, I might be in your nick of the woods one day. In the meantime, if I can ever help you, just look me up and I'll come to your rescue. I'd really love to do that for you, you very handsome man. I really meant it when I said you were better looking than Elvis. I heard you could sing too. Maybe I'll get to hear that voice one of these days. In the meantime, I hope all your sunsets are glorious and all your sunrises are met with a beautiful woman in your arms.

Always grateful my love, M.H.

Ford looked over at Joey. The big grin was gone, replaced by something between surprise and a frown. Ford couldn't help but smile. "She sure is some woman. Real nice of her to remember to thank us again. I didn't know she was from around my "neck of the woods".

Ford could tell Joey was upset at the content of Ford's letter. He wadded his envelope into his pants pocket saying, "Took her long enough just to say thank you. Don't know why she had to go on and on. Some women don't know when to stop." He looked around like he was expecting someone before saying, "Well, let's not stand around here all morning. I'm ready to go somewhere that don't require a fellow to wear a uniform."

And before Ford knew it, he was looking at the Army in his rearview mirror.

Two things were evident after Ford and Joey's enlistment ended. Joey had a life and a job to return to…Ford did not. The idea of returning to North Carolina left Ford with a ragged, raw set of emotions. Mara and J.J. certainly expected their son to return home and re-start his life. However, Ford was still faced with dealing with the horror of the unsolved murder. With this on his mind, what kind of life could he re-start. He knew he couldn't go home to begin anything new until the old business was finished. To make matters worse, he still harbored his disgust toward Sheriff Royal Majesty for his incompetent handling of Julia's death.

Joey insisted on Ford taking one last road trip with him in his new, 1953 Cadillac Eldorado Convertible. The car was as slick as anything in Ford's traveling experience. It was Alpine White with a 331cubic inch V-8 engine that moved down the road in a hurry. Joey drove it like a kid with the most exciting toy ever built.

The road trip was Joey's idea of a last great hurrah before settling in to the responsibilities of the family's trucking business. Ford had no immediate plans so he was ready to hit the road with his friend. Fortunately, their last assignment at Fort Dix had been short and uneventful. Joey's diligent behavior both surprised Ford and came as a great relief. The old demons were back in Ford's mind and he didn't have time to fool with any of Joey's erratic behavior.

No sooner had their discharge been finalized when the duo found themselves in the Cadillac traveling to places like New York City, Atlantic Beach, and Philadelphia. The men were like two school boys on their first road trip without their parents.

Ford kept successfully dodging the attempts by Joey to discuss his friend's immediate future. It was the night before they were to head back to Joey's home in Trenton, that Ford began talking. For the first time, he told Joey all about Julia's death and the troubles he'd experienced with the County Sheriff because of it. In no small detail, Ford spoke of Sheriff Royal Majesty and his contempt for the man. He still had a great desire to tie the contemptable man to the rear bumper of one of his Uncle's moonshine runners and drag him across the County, possibly to the ocean.

Joey listened patiently, something that rarely came easily for him. When Ford finished, the room was filled with a silence that could be felt. Joey stood up, walking to the hotel room's dresser where a half-empty bottle of whiskey stood. He poured a long double in two glasses before looking at his friend. "Ford, old buddy, that's one of the saddest stories I've ever been told. Listen to me, I want to say something that comes from my heart…I really want you to consider it, okay?"

Ford was quiet, only partially interested in hearing what Joey had to say. Joey sat the drinks on a coffee table without offering one to Ford.

Joey's face indicated how serious he felt. "Ford, you are the best mechanic, best driver I've ever seen. Plus, you're no doubt the best friend a fellow could ever have. I know I've given you reason to shoot me on several occasions. It's taken a great amount of effort to keep me out of the brig or some local jail…more times that I can remember. I know I've been a pain, but you stayed my friend. It's hard to say where I'd be if you hadn't been around for me. I owe you man."

With that being said, he picked up the glasses of whiskey and added, "You say the word, and you'll be working for *Visconti Brothers Transport*, like yesterday. Mechanic, driver…hell, we'll give you an office and let you help run the place. Some of my cousin's ain't that smart, if you know what I mean. Hell, even my brothers won't mind. They got plenty on their plates as it is. My father and my uncle already know a lot about you from my letters and calls. They'd gladly be on board."

Ford stood up, walking directly in front of his friend to give him a long eyeball to eyeball stare. Several seconds passed when he held out his hand to shake Joey's. "If you're serious Joey, well then, I guess New Jersey has a new resident." Joey gave Ford a glass while grasping his friend's other hand. They both smiled as Joey said, "Salute!"

PART THREE

Another Lifetime and Then Some

Chapter Twenty-One

~ 1953-1954 ~

"Before he knew it, Ford was being drawn back into the fulfilling elements of home and Family"

Trenton, New Jersey was as busy a place as Ford had ever lived. Yeah, he'd visited New York, Philadelphia, and a few metropolitan cities in Europe. However, he'd never lived in any of them.

Of course, the Base in Heidelberg was a beehive of activity. Its population made it as sizable as some cities but at least it slowed down at night. However, a great many of the populace of Trenton seemed to never take time to sit still or ever slow down. There was activity all through the night in certain areas in and around the City. On any given day, the anxious activity started before the sun was up and lasted hours past the time the last rays faded. Even the Sundays appeared to slow only a few degrees.

In comparison, Ford had to chuckle to himself when he thought of his home in little bitty Treemont. That little bit of a town looked like a pimple on a gnat's butt compared to this place.

And even though Treemont could never be as significant as the large metropolitan cities Ford had seen, the people living there worked just as hard, living and dying just as importantly. Even though the people living in small towns like Treemont were never recognized by those in the fast-paced world, they left their own personal mark on their world. Their lives were lived with an equal amount of importance, especially in the way they affected others.

Ford was often reminded of something his Dad would say, *"Don't ever get too excited about how big or grand a place is. Don't be fooled into being impressed by the number of folks who make an effort to live together in some large area. Just remember, it's the quality of the people that matter. It's the opportunities offered by the goodness of the land, the water, and the air that is shared. These are the things that make a place special and worthwhile."*

No one would consider J.J. Rawlings a philosopher. He just had a wealth of "country wisdom" that was as practical as it was simple. J.J. claimed much of his "wisdom" came from his father and grandfather, both modest and smart mountain men. J.J. was often heard passing his country wisdom on to others, especially his son.

Ford now credited much of his own good, common sense to be garnered from those same three men. Now, more than ever, he understood the simple truths imparted to him. Not that he had always followed the wisdom of past generations. At least he had their wisdom to eventually bring balance to his life.

Ford could still remember laughing at his Grandfather saying things like, *"Why burn up all your wood just to admire a great blaze. You can stay plenty warm with just one good log and have the rest saved for another long cold night."* At some point in his life, sayings like that meant more to him than he would have ever imagined.

Ford felt that setting a good ole boy from a small North Carolina town down in Trenton was as foolish as planting a daisy in a hurricane. At first glance, he wasn't so sure he was meant to thrive in such an environment.

What Ford Rawlings came to discover was that he was just too grounded and self-assured to allow a new place or group of people perplex him. Just like in his Army years, he tended to flourish mostly because he meant to. The biggest obstacle in his life was always the memory of Julia and her unsettled murder. The Army kept him so busy that his mind couldn't dwell on the past very often. Now, he hoped Trenton could do the same thing for him. If it didn't, then his life was about to become very bleak.

The Visconti Family welcomed Ford into their home in the same manner they did their own son. The house and business were located in a suburb called Chambersburg. Located south of the main city of Trenton, the Chambersburg community was home to a large number of Italian communities, all filled with a myriad of Italian-American owned businesses, Catholic churches, as well as the marriage of traditions, both Italian and American.

The year of 1953 was coming to a conclusion. Thanksgiving would be celebrated in only a few days. All around the 128,000-strong community were signs of the upcoming Holiday season. There were even some early snow flurries finding their way into the cooling air that surrounded them. It seemed to help put people in a good mood rather than reminding them of the cold, gloomy days of winter that were ahead.

Thanksgiving and Christmas were an especially difficult time for Ford. He did miss his family and felt guilty for not going home to see them. The reality that Julia would not be there to welcome him was still too much. Ford wondered if he'd ever again get past the emptiness in his life that Julia always filled. I was difficult finding joy in the holidays because Julia so enjoyed the holiday season. Her joy caused everyone in her life to be uplifted and recognize the things that were special.

It wasn't just in the grandness of the season that Ford felt Julia's presence. He was constantly amazed at how many times he was reminded of Julia in the small, subtle things that made up Christmas or even a winter day for that matter. When it occurred, it was never just a simple memory. It was if he was transported back into time for an intimate visit with Julia in a particular moment. That glorious moment was fleeting as it quickly turned into a bleak, hurtful sadness. The reality that it wasn't Julia there and that it would never be Julia there, cut him deeply.

Ford knew this would be hard. The Military offered him a shelter that cloaked him from the things he missed most, especially this time of year. But right now, he would have to resist the pull of Julia's memory in every Christmas song he heard or every twinkling light that caught his eye. Even the sight of a young woman dressed in a bright red winter's coat, black scarf and knitted cap gave him pause. In the still of the cold air, he seemed to catch the fresh fragrance from her honey-blonde, waterfall curls that cascaded around the soft silhouette of her glowing face. That simple memory alone would cause Ford's breath to catch, leaving him frozen in a moment of the past.

He determined he would not be drawn into the "family" scene as he met Joey's family. It would be better to stay away from the closeness and drama of family. That idea lasted hardly a long moment as the Visconti family overwhelmed him with their warm embraces, good cheer, and hardy words of welcome. Before he knew it, Ford was being drawn back into the fulfilling elements of home-life and family. In a guilty moment, he almost felt like he was *"home"*.

Chapter Twenty-Two

~ Trenton: 1954 ~

"Of course, he'd still catch her discretely "crossing" herself when she thought he wasn't looking."

Ford made himself at home in the Visconti Brother's garage. Their fleet was made up of relatively new, *White Motors* trucks. Even though they were being maintained sufficiently, Ford showed even the seasoned mechanics a trick or two. Most of the mechanics were older than him but took to the easy-going mountain boy. Perhaps it was Ford's likable disposition or the fact that Joey's family seemed to have adopted the boy that caused his co-workers to readily accept him. The addition of a Southern boy was at first a novelty. However, in very little time he'd become a respected part of the shop.

Most of Ford's day was spent in truck repair or providing needed maintenance. He enjoyed the intensity of the work as well as the fine vehicles that were his charges. One thing he found to be even more to his liking was working on the family's cars. Even Joey's father and uncle allowed this newcomer the opportunity to climb under the hood of their prized autos.

There were a variety of cars owned by the rather large Visconti family. All of them had one thing in common, horsepower. In fact, the whole family was into powerful machines. Ford knew how to tweak the already powerful engines in such a way as to improve their performance as well as their sheer power. He liked to make sure they were safe as he spent time checking brakes and suspensions as well as transmissions. The family as a whole found themselves relying on Ford for any number of car related issues. He was even known to take some of the younger cousins out for driving lessons. It seemed the young, former moonshine runner always had some kind of impressive information to offer.

The streets around Visconti Brother's Transport was often filled with the squeal of tires as Ford showed the young men of the Visconti family how to handle their cars in tight places as well as the open highway. They were all enthralled by the young man's driving skills. Plus, they absolutely loved hearing him tell of the adventures he'd experienced as he ran moonshine. Being chased by the law or some rascal wanting to steal the load of whiskey made Ford seem a lot like a Robin Hood figure to the Visconti clan.

Another thing they loved about Ford was his recounting stories about Joey and himself in the Army. Even Joey loved to join in as their escapades were told and re-told. Ford discovered he felt at ease reliving stories of their adventures. He enjoyed telling the entertaining stories as he discovered many of the guys in the shop appeared starved for entertainment. The one thing Ford avoided discussing was the personal details of his life and those who shared it. Especially, Julia.

It wasn't until the third month of Ford's employment with Visconti Brother's Transport that his hated nickname resurfaced. It was started by Joey's cousin, Michael, or as he was called by almost everyone, Mikey. The christening of Ford with the nickname, "Elvis", seemed to take off immediately.

Ford was well into an engine overhaul from one of the older trucks. He was alone, in the back of the shop, with only the company of a radio sitting on a shelf above a workbench. Elvis Presley's voice was coming out of the radio singing, *That's All Right*. Ford was concentrating on the engine valves, hardly realizing he was singing along with Elvis. It wasn't just that he was singing, but he was singing with gusto…almost as if performing.

Mikey, a big Elvis fan, stood watching Ford sing the whole song. Of course, Ford had no clue anyone was watching him. He turned to retrieve a tool from a large tool box only to find Mikey standing there, a big smile across his face. Mikey eyed him up and down, his smile never diminishing. Ford waited, expecting a question.

Mikey's response was unexpected. "Damn son! You got the stuff…you're a natural. And hell, you even look like "the man" himself! The chicks around here are really going to dig you, son. Gonna start calling you, "Elvis"!"

Ford offered an awkward grin, thinking that would be the end of it. But to Ford's chagrin, the nickname stuck, and before long, everyone was using it. Joey found it a little funny but refrained from using the nickname himself. Neither would either Visconti brother or their wives. Mamma Visconti said it was charming but she refused to call anyone by a nickname. However, Joey's siblings and cousins, along with most of the employees of the trucking concern took up the nickname readily. Before long, it seemed to spread throughout the neighbor to boot.

Ford found out too late that nicknames were more difficult to shed than a pair of water-soaked denim jeans. Mamma Visconti at first thought "Ford" was a nickname. She would frown and say, "What kind of name is "Ford"? You're much too handsome to be called by the name of an automobile."

Ford kept insisting that this was his only name. Finally, with Joey's fervent admonishments that "Ford" was his actual name, Mamma Visconti finally accepted it.

Still, she did not let Ford get off too easily. This was because she kept asking questions about the origin of his name. For some reason, she had come to believe that he must be related to Henry Ford. She was so stubborn about that theory that Ford finally shared the whole story of why he came by the name. In the telling, he also swore her to secrecy.

Mamma Visconti crossed herself, kissing her crucifix and muttered something in Italian, or maybe it was Latin, for all Ford knew. Joey found the whole thing hilarious. He spent a long time convincing his mother that Ford was not born under a "bad sign" because of the lights of the Brown Mountain.

As time went on, the Italian matriarch would often use "my darling" in front of "Ford" or "Ford, my darling boy". It was like the additional words offered a buffer against any potential evil presence. Of course, he'd still catch her discretely "crossing" herself when she thought he wasn't looking.

Chapter Twenty-Three

~ Trenton: 1954 ~

"One evening when Joey and Ford found themselves too far into a bottle of Crown Royal..."

Ford surprised even himself at the ease he slid into this next lifetime. The Visconti family went out of their way to make the Southern boy feel at home. Ford realized that many of the stories about saving Joey's butt from jail meant a lot to the whole family. He was already considered a real *paesano* before he'd ever set foot back in the States.

Ford learned that both Joey's Father and Uncle had encouraged the boy to become a soldier. They felt he might learn some needed discipline which would safe-guard him from the bad influences around Trenton. However, as they learned of Joey's journey in the military, they realized being in the Army offered its own temptations. There were plenty of demons wherever you went that would cause a young man to find trouble. This was one reason they were so grateful to Ford Rawlings for watching over their worrisome boy. And now, they all wanted to do something to help the young man from North Carolina find a home as well as the certainty of being loved.

It wasn't long before things began changing in Ford's New Jersey life. He began being noticed wherever he went. In fact, he was becoming quite well-known around the neighborhood. His good looks and smooth accent made him very noticeable to the young women of the local Chambersburg area.

Because of his good standing with the Visconti family, the young Italian girls felt him to be approachable as well as a good catch. Even some of the mothers of the many Italian daughters in and around the neighborhood were found inquiring about the handsome young man with the looks of Elvis Presley. Joey's sisters and cousins were falling under the "spell" of the newest "member" of their family. Ford's mystique and closeness to the Visconti females caused their friends to constantly ask questions concerning him, mostly about his availability.

As Ford and Joey ventured into the nightlife around Trenton he noticed the type of appeal he had with the local women. Not only did they admire his good looks but took to the nickname of "Elvis".

This caused him to be even more intriguing to the locals, both female and male.

Many assumed he could sing due to is nickname. The fact that he had that "Elvis look" added to the fantasy that he was the man himself. In little time, he found he was being asked to take the microphone in some of the Night Clubs Joey visited. Unless too much alcohol had been consumed, Ford turned down all offers to sing. If the level of intoxication caused him to let down his inhibition, he could sing a ballad with a very pleasing voice. But in doing so, he added credibility to the miserable nickname he wanted to avoid.

One evening, Joey and Ford found themselves too far into a bottle of Crown Royal to account for their actions. Ford ended up front and center as Joey all but dragged him onstage to accompany him as he sang a love ballad to a raven-haired beauty he'd been talking with. Joey's stage presence didn't last very long as the alcohol suddenly took its toll, causing him to hastily head to the wings as well as the bathroom.

Ford continued the song, taking over the stage. Not only did he finish the one song but surprised everyone with another song and then one more. As he finished the last song, a loud round of applause exploded along with calls for another encore.

The encore never took place. Instead, Ford ended up putting Joey into a cab home while he found himself climbing into the car of the raven-haired beauty. The very attractive young woman planned on finishing with Ford what she'd started with Joey. As they drove away, one set of eyes noticed Ford's exit from the Club with the girl. It was immediately reported by a telephone call from the bar.

Monday mornings were usually hectic around the garage of Visconti Brother's Transport. Trucks were being dispatched for destinations near and far. The garage was busy sending out newly repaired or serviced trucks as well as processing trucks that'd come in at the end of the week. Ford found the surge of activity to be stimulating.

With a cup of steaming hot coffee in his hand, he walked out to the back lot to pull one of the older White tractors around for service. As he started to climb in the cab a voice called out from behind him. "Hey! Hey you! You the one they call Elvis?" Ford turned around to see who this wise guy was that was trying to spoil his morning. Walking toward him were three young guys, each trying to look tougher than the other.

Ford waited for the trio to get closer, not responding to their words. The lead guy walked a couple of steps closer to Ford, an angry look on his oily face. Ford took notice of the guy's oily face because it rivaled the sheen of whatever substance the guy used on his dark hair. Ford took a small sip of the steaming coffee as he waited to see what these guys wanted.

The lead guy looked at Ford as if waiting for some response. When none came, he spat on the ground, then menacingly said, "You deaf? You're the one they call Elvis ain't you?" Ford still resisted reply, wondering just what these jokers had on their minds. He couldn't recall ever seeing either of the fellows but for some reason they believed they had an issue with him.

The guy on Ford's right growled, "What's your problem? Answer the man." Ford looked at each one of the guys as they attempted to puff themselves up in stature, obviously trying to intimidate.

Ford then answered, rather dismissively. "If you boys have business with the Visconti's, you're talking to the wrong fellow. If you don't, you're taking up my time and I've got a busy enough day already." He let the words hang in the air, noticing they only agitated the three.

Finally, the lead guy took another step toward Ford. He lit a cigarette, blowing smoke as he spoke. "I'm told you put on a show down at *The Jersey Moon* on Friday night." Ford rolled his eyes at this as the guy continued, "I'm also told you left the Club with my girlfriend." Ford rolled his eyes again and shook his head just a little.

He thought to himself, *"Monday morning idiots! Just what I need!"*

By now, the lead guy was visibly agitated, his face clouding over as his voice rose. "Adalina Bucci! Ring a bell? Are you acting like you're stupid or are you actually this stupid? I'm losing my patience with you, hillbilly!"

Ford remained calm. As far as being called a hillbilly, it was not even close to the first time. As far as the slang name itself and the history behind it, Ford considered it to be more of a compliment than an insult anyway. So, it neither insulted or intimidated him.

As the guy tried to stare him down, Ford actually smiled at the fellow. "Well, a couple of things come to mind…I'm sorry, don't know your name."

The guy was obviously confused at Ford's nonchalant attitude. "You want to know my name smart guy? Tony Fentilucci's my name. You'd be wise to remember that name, Elvis what-ever the hell your name is."

Ford grinned at the man, causing him even more confusion. "Well, I'll tell you old son, my name's not Elvis and I'm not acquainted with your girlfriend…what did you call her, Adalina? So, how's about moving on and let me get to work."

All three men moved closer to Ford with the two goons moving more to the side of Ford. All three faces were creased with hateful looks. Tony spat, "You're lying. You was seen leaving the Club with Adalina!"

Ford's face betrayed nothing as he stated, "If you're talking about a girl named Angel, well then, you've got me there, old son. She told me her name was Angel, and yeah, I jumped in her car for a ride. She didn't tell me she had a boyfriend and to be honest she didn't act like she had one."

The guy on the left took an aggressive step toward Ford at this statement, but Tony grabbed the guy's arm.

Ford continued, "All we did was ride around for a while. In fact, I got behind the wheel for most of it. She was a lot drunker than I'd imagined. In fact, I was far closer to sober than her. So I took over driving to get her home safely. She did mention she was very upset with some guy…actually I think she did call him Tony. Called him a few other names to boot. Most of the time though, she talked to me, well, about me. Seemed grateful I was getting her home safe and sound. She even called me a cab from her place. Nice girl, I thought."

Before Tony could say anything, Ford continued, "You know pal, she needs to take her Pontiac to a good mechanic. Her valves are making some noise."

At that, Tony exploded. "You're a real smart-mouthed guy ain't you? I'm through wasting time on you. Me and the boys wasted enough time here. I'm going teach you a lesson about climbing into cars with somebody's girl."

He started to take a step as Ford said, "Tell you what old son, you better have a talk with your girl about inviting guys into her car. While you're at it you might want to start treating her better if you really like her. I just didn't get the impression she's very impressed with you."

At that, the guy on the right pulled a short pipe from under his jacket and lunged toward Ford. Before the pipe could hardly be raised, Ford threw the still hot coffee in his face. He screamed out just as Ford spun him around…just in time to receive a blow from a similar pipe wielded by the other fellow.

As the one fellow fell out of Ford's grip, the other looked shocked that he'd just slugged his buddy. His eyes followed the fellow to the ground, only looking up in time to catch Ford's right fist, flush on his nose. The guy went down in a heap, laid out cold beside his buddy.

Tony reacted just a beat too slow, trying to pull something from inside his coat. Ford grabbed Tony's arm and spun him around as he forced the arm up behind the man's back. A slight cracking sound was heard as he screamed out in pain. Ford then kicked the man's leg out from under him, sending him to the ground. Tony cried out again in pain followed by a string of curses.

Ford looked down at the man, "Look pal. I just drove your girl home the other night. She was too drunk and too horny for her own good. All that happened was that I got her home safe and she thanked me by calling a cab. You need to get your story straight before you go acting all tough-guy. She's a sweet girl…if you let her be. Now get your sorry butt out of here, I got work to do."

To Ford's surprise, Tony jumped quickly back to his feet, pulling a revolver from inside his coat. The gun had barely cleared Tony's coat when a loud shot rang out just beyond where they stood.

Up walked Dario Visconti carrying a smoking shotgun. Beside him were two of his son's, Joey and Ilario, and three other Visconti employees. "I've got one more barrel for your head Fentilucci. You better drop that weapon or you'll be sleeping in the marshes tonight."

Tony froze as the Visconti employees quickly surrounded the scene. Dario ordered, "Take those two slugs and throw them in their car." He turned to Tony, "Listen here Fentilucci, you got no business on this property. You get off and stay off!"

Tony started to protest, "Hey old man! You know who I work for! You better mind your…" Before Tony could finish, Dario walked up to him, roughly sticking the barrel of the shotgun just under his chin. "You *jamoka*…your mouth and your temper are going to get you real dead…real young and real soon, Fentilucci. Don't you start throwing your bosses' name around too loosely. I know the man, and I know he won't like your nonsense. You don't want to make both him and me angry with you at the same time. Get out of here and take that tough-guy bull with you. Don't be bothering us, or Ford, ever again...*capiche*?"

At the mention of Ford's name, Tony shot a hard look in his direction. He turned and spat in the direction of Dario. Before he could say another word, Ford landed a very hard right fist on Tony's jaw. For the second time in minutes, Tony landed hard on the ground. This time, he wouldn't regain consciousness for some time.

Chapter Twenty-Four

~ Trenton: 1955 ~

"In fact, they appeared to be so interested in staring into each other's eyes that no words were needed."

Ford's "meeting" with Tony and his boys caused more than a little gossip around the shop. There were muted conversations that quietened when Ford approached. There were other conversations that pulled Ford into the discussion. The Visconti brothers told Ford not to worry about it for now. He knew if they sensed a problem they'd be sure and give him any information he needed. Joey's take on Tony and his two goons was that they were low level punks involved loosely with some larger criminal concerns.

Dario came to Ford, telling him not to worry about the incident but to be watchful anytime he was away from the Trucking Company. "You'll be alright, for sure. Do not worry about those *chooches*…just be on guard. If they start something, they'll have more than me to deal with, *capiche*? Trust me, Ford. You handled those punks just fine. They'll leave you alone. You're doing okay."

The sentiment was appreciated and Ford did consider himself fine with the whole incident. He wasn't sure he understood all Dario was telling him but he figured he understood enough. It did seem that Dario was going overboard assuring him he was fine. In fact, that was the one thing that made the whole episode a little worrisome.

As time went forward into a new year, Ford mostly forgot about the incident. He found he naturally became much more careful if he was out with friends. He cut back on his drinking as well as his availability to strangers. Especially female strangers.

Ford's Trenton days fell into a rhythm of work at the garage and easing into the New Jersey lifestyle. The Visconti families reached out to him making him always feel at home. Joey kept him occupied on most weekends and he found every holiday was a family affair. Ford noticed that Joey's wild-side had diminished greatly since he was back home and a working man. There were occasional trips to Atlantic City, Philadelphia, and New York City. Sometimes Joey would still hijack Ford and they would start driving in any direction without any idea of a destination. It seemed the open road and a different local soothed his troubled mind.

Ford never understood why Joey needed the occasional, random drives. There were times he just found himself in a darker, more pensive mood. The drives always improved his attitude, putting him back into his usual laid-back, carefree mood. They also brought back memories of their trips around Germany. Those trips were filled with sight-seeing and relaxing banter as well as the occasional drinking and reverie. Fortunately, none of their current road trips put them at risk of spending time in jail.

Most of 1955 was spent with nothing out of the ordinary happening. Ford was getting accustomed to the occasional female being put in his path. Those who were related in some way to the Visconti family had to be handled carefully. He didn't want any hard feeling created in the family because of him.

He wrote and called home on a regular schedule. His parents did not completely understand why he never came home. Ford couldn't completely understand it himself. He truly wanted to see them but was afraid of the terrible pain that a visit might bring up. He would go back one day…he just had no idea when.

There were plenty of ladies who wished to give Ford a reason to stay in New Jersey. However, Ford had never found a woman that really stirred him. Maybe the ideal that was represented by his memory of Julia would never allow him to find another woman that interested him.

However, there was one young lady that not only caught Ford's notice but did stir him in ways he had long ago forgotten. She was an attractive Secretary who worked in the Company's shipping office. He'd noticed her on many occasions but didn't get to know her until late one freezing afternoon in early December. Her car failed to start after a late workday. She came into the garage to find Ford the only person still there. He parked her shivering body next to a large heater, grabbed a heavy coat and proceeded to spend about forty minutes working on the frozen car.

Ford pulled the car into the garage in order for it to run a bit and get it out of the freezing cold. The attractive brunette met him with a large mug of freshly made, steaming hot coffee. Her name was Felisa Gervasè. Ford took the cup, sipping tentatively to avoid burning his freezing lips. He stared into Felisa's deep, dark eyes that always appeared as if they twinkled.

"Thanks for the coffee, Felisa. It feels good just to hold it and breathe the steam."

She smiled an acknowledgement, saying, "It's my place to thank you. You saved me a long and freezing walk home or the wasted effort of trying to find a cab in this weather."

Ford wondered why she would have to walk instead of calling for someone to bring help or a ride. "Glad I was here. It may be your fuel pump or fuel line. Bring it to me one day this week and I'll take a closer look at it. Don't want you getting stuck again and I wouldn't want you getting stranded when I'm not around." He immediately felt sorry for his attempt at a slick statement. He rallied by saying, "What does Felisa mean?"

Felisa giggled at his question before answering, "Well, you may find this hard to believe, it means "lucky"."

Ford let this information sink in before a big smile crossed his face. "Yeah well, there's luck and then there's luck I guess." He again felt a little foolish in his response.

Felisa laid a hand on his arm and spoke intimately, "But don't you see. I was very lucky tonight. You were here to rescue me from the freezing cold. You got my car to running. My Mother's in the hospital from having gall bladder surgery. No one is with her. There was no one to come for me. Uncle Joe is away, so I couldn't call him. No, I was very lucky! How many girls can say that Elvis rescued them on a freezing night?"

Her smile brightened as she could see her teasing brought a response from Ford. It was the first time she'd ever used the unwelcomed nickname that'd been pinned on him. Ford shook his head, letting her have her moment.

"Well then, I may just have to walk over there and stop that fuel line right back up. Shame you don't have boots to wear in this snow."

She grinned at his attempt at playful banter. "But, in the movies, Elvis is the hero and the hero always rescues the girl. Sometimes he rescues her and then sings to her too. You've got a reputation to live up to, *Elvis*. When are you going to sing to me?"

Ford was sipping a hot swallow of coffee when she asked the question. He nearly lost the coffee before he could recover. "All right, you got me. Just please don't start calling me Elvis. I get enough of that around here, and lately everywhere else I go. I sure wish that Elvis guy had just kept driving trucks instead of becoming so famous."

There was an awkward moment when both of them felt a loss for words. In fact, they appeared to be so interested in staring into each other's eyes that no words were needed.

Felisa broke the spell, "I guess I should be going. I need to go by the hospital…Mama will be worried.

Ford walked over, picking up her coat and helping her put it on. "Be careful out there. Those streets are icy." Felisa held out her hand to shake Ford's. "Hey, I'm a Jersey girl, I can handle this weather…at least as long as my car starts."

Ford walked over and pulled open the garage door. There was a loud squeaking noise as the metal resisted being moved. Felisa peeked out the door and proclaimed, "I should have known! This explains so much."

Ford was curious. "What are you saying? You should have known what?"

Felisa's smile was radiant in the moonlight. "My Grandmother told my Mother a lot of stories when she was a young girl. One of them had to do with the full moon…one just like we have tonight."

Ford glanced upward a couple of times, trying to find something in the bright yellow orb hanging in the black, frosty sky. "Yeah, that's a pretty bright moon. What'd your Grandmother say about it?"

Felisa was buttoning her coat as she answered. "She called it a…*indovinare luna.* It means a divining moon. She said that nights like tonight are when both angels or devils come out to play with an unsuspecting person. Because devils sometimes disguise themselves as angles, God hangs a bright moon in the sky so that the person can identify who they are dealing with."

Ford laughed, not knowing just how to respond. With little else coming to his mind, he responded. "I like that story. Sounds like a tale my Mother would tell. Now, she's got a dandy story she tells about the "Brown Mountain Lights". That's a mountain back home…there's mysterious ghost lights that are seen on or over the mountain. No one really knows what they are. Mara, my Mother, says Brown Mountain is where Angels come to rest after their tasks on earth are completed. She's convinced the lights are Angels and they need to rest before they return to Heaven. I think she's the only person I've ever heard who believes such a thing."

Felisa turned her head a little, obviously not fully understanding.

"I'll tell you more on that story another time. It's a doozy!" He looked into her deep eyes and lovely face. "You know, you haven't told me if it was an angel or a devil that came out to play tonight. Which is it?"

Felisa pursed her lips. She feigned trying to look as if she was trying to make a hard decision as she allowed her tongue to slightly slip between those full, sensuous lips before speaking. Her response was a bit coy…playful even. "I'm not quite sure Mr. Ford "Elvis" Rawlings…I'll let you know when you tell me the rest of that story."

A big smile crossed her face and her dark eyes danced. She stepped closer and leaned into him, giving him a soft kiss on the cheek. "Thank you, Ford. I'm glad you found a home here. Come up and see me in the office sometime. I'll treat you to a warm coffee and some pastry. We always have something sweet to eat. I have to watch my figure, but you…you could use a pound or two. Thank you again!"

The soft, last thank you, almost sounded sensual. At least it had an effect on Ford. Of course, the kiss on the cheek had its own affect. He held her door and then closed it once she was ready. He stood by the garage door, as she gave him a wave and the warmest of smiles. Her eyes still twinkled as she took turns looking in the rearview mirror and glancing back at Ford. In an instant, she was gone, leaving the slightest scent of her perfume to linger along with the warmth from her kiss still on Ford's cheek.

Chapter Twenty-Five

"It was easily the best line of the night..."

Felisa Gervasé was the type of young woman that most any young man would be attracted to. Ford Rawlings was no different in that regard. His interest, at first, fell more into the realms of companionship rather than romance. At least that was the way Ford approached it.

Ford appeared to find plenty of excuses to wander through the main office each day. Felisa would seem to magically just be in-between tasks so that there was always time for them to chat briefly.

True to her word, Ford's visits were rewarded with a pastry and a fresh cup of coffee. Some people began kidding him about always carrying an empty cup when going to the office. It must have touched a nerve because began using a different ploy.

Instead of carrying an empty cup to the office, Ford used the disposable paper cups kept by the coffee pot. Felisa began feeling sorry for him saying he should have a proper cup to drink his coffee. So, a clean mug sat on her desk which he took advantage of with each visit. As it usually went among a group of people who enjoyed a good joke, the change of coffee cups did not stymy them. New jokes quickly came about to tease the couple. Since both young people knew the jokes to be good-natured, they returned the jests with smiles and winks.

"Goin' up for a full-cup-of-coffee, Ford?", became almost a routine with some of employees of Visconti Brother's Trucking. The *"full-cup-of coffee"* became the company code for Felisa Gervasé.

At first, Ford felt the line to be insulting. He was afraid they were referring to some physical attribute of Felisa and was concerned it would be hurtful to her. However, she laughed it off after he mentioned his concerns. "Don't worry so much about these folks. They are really my friends. I trust them. This is a family here, even in our disagreements."

She went on to explain, "You won't hear any teasing unless they like you. Why do you think they call you Elvis? You've become a special friend to the people here. You should have heard the fine things they said about you when they found out you rescued me on that terribly cold night. They all were proud of you for standing up to that street thug. They're okay. They like you and think you're okay. Okay?"

That was the first-time Ford kissed Felisa. He didn't know what possessed him to be so bold. The kiss lingered more than a few heartbeats with Felisa never offering to stop. When Ford did stop, he found himself a little breathless, his heart racing.

Felisa took his hand in both of hers as she said in a sweet, delicate voice said, "That was nice. You know, I'm Catholic and Italian …so now you have to marry me!"

Ford dropped her hands as his eyes widened. He began sputtering unintelligible words. In fact, he only stopped when Felisa began laughing loudly. "See, I tease you because I like you. Besides, you're a pretty good kisser for a country boy!"

It wasn't long before the pair gained notice from most folks at Visconti Brother's Transport. She was a dark-haired beauty that matched up well with Ford's dark-hair and good looks. Some of the ladies in the office began discussing how beautiful their babies would be. Other ladies, the younger ones, found themselves a bit jealous that Ford was spending his time with Felisa.

Joey marveled at the connection between Ford and Felisa. He grew up with Felisa so he knew both the story of Ford's losing Julia and the truth behind Felisa's ambivalence toward men. He also knew that down deep, Ford still mourned Julia. Felisa's story, however, was much different.

Felisa Gervasè was in love with a young man of the community. It was a given they would become betrothed. Before a formal announcement could be made, another announcement shattered Felisa's dreams. It seems that her fiancé, Davide Romano, had been found to be unfaithful to her. Her best friend, Francesca Riva, was pregnant with Davide's baby.

Davide made the grand gesture of marrying the girl even though he still professed his love for Felisa. The wedding took place quickly with Felisa even offering her blessings. The new bride and groom were troubled from the beginning of their marriage since neither actually loved the other. Troubling fights were common. There were reports concerning the couple from their neighbors.

The baby was born to parents that wanted little to do with each other. As the arguments continued, the stories began to circulate that the couple had become violent to each other. Francesca was seen with a badly bruised face once. Around that same time, Davide was seen sporting a cloth bandage wrapped around his forehead covering a nasty cut from crockery Francesca had used to hit him.

The families decided a change of scenery might best suit the couple. This was especially true since gossip around the neighborhood continued to increase causing more problems. Finally, it reached the point that people began taking sides. Sadly, the couple seemed to feed off the tongue-wagers instead of attempting to reconcile their differences.

So, instead of an arranged marriage, the couple was shipped off to Cleveland, Ohio for an arranged re-settlement. Both had family there to help them get settled and Davide was set up with a union job in a factory. The only thing left for the families to do was to offer prayers that they'd settle in and make a family before one killed the other.

Felisa had become the forgotten victim in the drama. Those closest to her took turns trying to comfort her while setting her up with their brother, cousin, or friend. Felisa, always the polite young lady, thanked them but said no thank you. Even fellows who ventured their luck at charming the beautiful girl were politely turned away. Felisa seemed content doing her job, taking care of her mother as well as regularly looking in on her favorite "Uncle", Joe Moretti.

All of this began to change when Ford entered the picture. They gave each other warm looks and were heard having pleasant conversations about many things. Theirs was not a conventional type of courtship, if it was a courtship at all. Felisa introduced Ford to her mother and a few cousins. She told Ford her Mother's approval was important but he also had to get her "Uncle Joe's" approval. Friends and family gave Ford a hearty welcome finding it was easy to become close to him. It was almost as if they'd adopted him as a long-lost nephew of sorts.

To illustrate how comfortable the family was with Ford, they never once pushed Felisa about their relationship. It appeared they all had come to an agreement about Ford. They seemed to trust him and his intentions implicitly.

Joey became the only one soured over the relationship. That was mainly because Ford's desire to spend time around Felisa and her family took time away from his old Army buddy.

It was Felisa who came up with the idea that eased the tension. She invited a cousin, Natale Ricci, to join them for a dinner one night at a local restaurant known as *Carlo's.* It was an upscale place with spotless white linen tablecloths, a good band, and an extensive wine list. To cover their intentions, they only offered a small degree of enthusiasm when they invited Joey to join them. It was important to make it sound very low key so as not to spook the boy.

Joey never liked blind dates or set-ups. He preferred to be the hunter, seeking his own prey. The biggest problem with Joey's usual approach was that he often set out on his excursion with too much alcohol ingested and too few brain cells functioning.

To Joey's credit, he arrived at the restaurant a little early. By the time Ford, Felisa, and Natale arrived, the table was already served with a large platter of antipasto consisting of *Creminelli Tartufo salami,* olives, whole milk mozzarella, roasted red peppers, tomatoes, and dark bread. A bottle of bubbly wine sat in a silver chiller filled with ice. Sitting beside the gleaming stand was a sharply dressed Jovanni Visconti. Joey rose to his feet, a genuine smile on his face as Felisa introduced Natale. Ford noted his friend's expression quickly changed from an expression of coolness to a warm expression of delight. Joey seemed immediately smitten with the lovely Natale.

The usual slick-tongued Joey spoke with Natale in a hushed, almost reverent tone. It was if he was afraid of saying the wrong word or speaking in an inappropriate tone which might cause the young beauty to disappear before his eyes.

Later, Joey told Ford that for the first time in his life he felt *thunderstruck.* The funniest thing to come from the evening was when Natale told Felisa that Joey seemed very sweet but was a bit too quiet and reserved for her liking. It was easily the best line of the night considering Joey's usual exaggerated behavior.

In spite of Natale's initial reaction to Joey, he soon began to win her over. His good looks were obvious but it was his genuine charm and witty patter that began to turn Natale around. He could be so compelling without showing off or becoming loud and boisterous. The fact that the manners his mother taught him as a boy were always present in the company of a lady. Heck, they were even present if the Lady wasn't so much a lady. All the boy really had to do to get a lady's attention was to just be himself.

It wasn't long before the foursome was seen together on a regular basis. Joey regained his charming and funny side around Natale who ended up becoming quite taken with the young man. Ford noticed for the first time since knowing Joey that he wasn't as prone to the bouts of melancholy he sometime felt. In fact, Joey had not asked Ford to go along with him on one of his long drives to nowhere and back for a long time.

Ford found himself happy in his relationship with Felisa. At least he was as happy as he would allow himself to be. He'd forgotten how complete and natural it was to have a closeness with a woman. With Felisa, there wasn't all the same feelings he'd had for Julia. Still, he felt very comfortable in the natural warmth of their relationship.

Joey, on the other hand, was a different matter. He seemed to hold all the feelings for Natale that Ford once felt for Julia, plus more. He seemed ready to explode with the feelings he felt for Natale. In turn, she became nearly as animated toward Joey causing all around them to wonder if a permanent match had been made.

The whole future of these four seemed to be in front of them. Everyone who knew the couples could already see weddings in their future. Maybe even a double wedding. What they couldn't see was how the lives of all four would be drastically changed in such a short period of time.

Chapter Twenty-Six

"Joseph's dream had come true as his was now, a living legacy."

Joseph "Papa Joe" Moretti was known by nearly everyone in the very large neighborhood that was home to thousands of Italian-Americans. A few special people knew him as "Uncle Joe". Most called him Papa Joe which he responded to with a beaming smile.

He was first generation Italian. His two brothers accompanied him to the land of the Statue of Liberty from a small Italian city called Piombino on the coast of Tuscany. Together, they barely had enough possessions to fill one small cloth bag. Joseph was the oldest at sixteen. The brothers, Orso at fourteen and Savio at thirteen, looked to Joseph to lead them into this new land.

They left very little behind them mostly because they had so little to leave. Their parents were deceased and there were only a few cousins and one elderly aunt scattered around to call family. Most of the money for passage was garnered from begging, doing hard tasks for merchants and farmers, and occasionally liberating an item or two that they could sell.

Their only living Aunt, an elderly lady who wanted the boys to have a chance at a better life, was a big help. She gave Joseph a family heirloom to sell. It was a silver signet ring and silver necklace of fine workmanship. This, along with their savings, gave them enough money to finally buy passage on a cargo ship. The boys were still left with enough silver coins to buy a little food for their trip and help get a start in America. Joseph was so happy to board the ship he would not leave the railing until land was far from sight.

It was Joseph's dream to come to America. He'd heard many stories from his father about this land with so much opportunity. Joseph memorized each story word for word. It wasn't long before he had his brothers reciting each story precisely.

Upon arrival in America, they were set loose in the massive city of New York. This did not make Joseph hesitate one minute. They lied about coming to live with family. Joseph was able to coerce a fellow on the ship to swear he was their Uncle by paying him what amounted to a dollar.

It wasn't long before he and his brothers had a small gang of other boys just like themselves. They worked, they begged, and they stole. The goal of each boy was to first get money for food, then get money for necessities, and lastly to get money for their future. Every day, Joseph pounded into their heads that this was America, a place where one day they all could become somebody. He also told them that before they could be somebody, they would need money to pay the costs involved in making that happen.

Joseph was a persuasive leader making them all believe in both his plans and their futures. He became their banker as he kept running totals of their shares of the bank, all in his head. He would not trust putting the information on paper lest someone know all that he knew. He made a blood oath that he would guard the money with his life. This was an oath that none of his gang doubted for one moment. None of the gang, except Orso and Savio, even knew where the money was safely kept.

At the beginning of each month, Joseph would tell each member what their share was that had been added to their "bank" and what their current total had grown too. The boys marveled at the amounts as they increased. They never questioned how the money was divided up or any of Joseph's accounting. Joseph was held in high esteem by all his "men" so much that they would not consider him willing to cheat them. The fact that they were extremely poor in math skills seemed to also prohibit them from many questions.

They were happy and content living each day under the guidance of Joseph. It was the first time most of them had anyone to look out for their interests. They looked up to Joseph and his brothers as the only people who'd ever tried to help them and look out for their well-being. Theirs became a family, one which they felt would continue on for the longest of times. Of course, it was really a life that could not continue but a short time. In fact, it fell apart much sooner than anyone could have imagined.

Besides the daily toils of providing for their needs, the other equally important part of each day involved not getting caught by the *Coppers.* They were always trying to interfere with their plans. The Law seemed to only have the intention of catching them and sending them to a reformatory. As if this wasn't enough of a problem to deal with, their growing notoriety became another. The more violent, older gangs that operated in the area expected Joseph and his boys to either join them or pay a heavy tribute. Joseph could not see the percentages of doing either one. It became a dangerous cat and mouse game dodging both the Coppers and the older gangs.

The first causalities of Joseph's gang were a boy called "Little" Elia along with Joseph's brother, Savio. They were jumped by an older and bigger gang one night as they returned from breaking into a Mercantile near the Five Points. Both boys were loaded down with heavy bags of kitchen cookware and hand tools. All in all, an exceptional night's work.

Another boy, Benny "Beans", was also along as a lookout. They all ran when confronted by the rival gang. Benny was without a load to carry so he made a clean get-away. The other two weren't as lucky. Burdened with the loot from the robbery they were easily cornered. Benny later said if Savio and Elia would have just dropped their bags, they'd have gotten away clean. However, neither boy would give up what was in the bags.

It took little time before the two were herded into an alley...a dead-end alley. Benny snuck back but all he could do was witness the final confrontation.

Benny tearfully told Joseph that Savio stood tall, saying they wouldn't give up their sacks and they were through running. There were four much larger boys against Savio and Little Elia. The two put up a hard fight at first, drawing blood from a couple of the gang members. Even at this, the two were still outnumbered and backed further into the alley. The final result came violently.

The fact that they fought so hard seemed to make the older boys furious. In their rage, they beat the boys down and continued to beat them until they were badly bloodied...and then dead. The attackers were all breathing heavily as two of them picked up the bags and walked away from the two lifeless bodies. The leader howled loudly, shouting out to no one, *"Let that be a lesson to anyone who wants to mess with the Beastly Boys!"*

Joseph broke down upon hearing the news. It was obvious he was heartbroken. Before the others had a chance to offer condolences, Joseph walked to the window of the rundown building where they were living. He stood staring for a few moments, his shoulders shaking from his emotions. Then he turned to face his men, a look of resolve crossed his face as he vowed to make those who were responsible pay dearly for Savio's and Elia's death. Each member walked up to Joseph, pledging their life in helping make this retribution take place.

About five months later those responsible received their punishment for Elia and Savio's murders. The gang members were caught in a clever trap set up by Joseph and Franco Esposito, the leader of another gang. They worked together for two months finding who for certain was responsible. Leaking information that a shipment of furs might be available to be "picked up" just outside a warehouse on a certain day was all it took.

Franco had reasons to hate the *Beastly Boys* as did the others. They had ambushed his own gang members more than once. Franco went outside his gang to gathered some additional tough men who were hardened by many street fights and could get rid of the bodies.

They waited with Joseph and Franco for the *Beastly Boys* to show up. The fight lasted only minutes. The bodies of those involved in the murders of Savio and "Little" Elia were never found. Those of the *Beastly Boys* not involved in the beating deaths were roughed up and released with the threat of sure death if they ever came back in the neighborhood or if they were found to tell anyone what happened.

A memorial of sorts for Savio and "Little" Elia was found on the walls of the alley where they died. Painted in red were the words, *VENGENCE IS SERVED!*

Joseph became such a smooth talker that he was able to keep him and his brother from being taken into any of the "organized crime groups". They ran their own operation as they wanted but began paying a tribute to a middle-man of one of the New York *Families*. Joseph, the businessman, earned the respect of the Mafioso who assured the boys they would be left alone. It even seemed to help keep the *Coppers* from causing the boys problems. The tribute was okay by Joseph for now as he did not want to lose any more men. Having the Mafioso as a protector was the only way he felt he could be assured of his groups safety. And besides, the idea of *respect* was something Joseph understood from the *Old Country.*

Joseph's goal was not to become a crime boss or continue being a criminal of sorts. He just wanted to one day own his own business and have the life of his dreams in America.

A second tragedy gave Joseph another hard blow. Orso grew into a bull of a man. His great flaw was that when he drank he came an angry bull. One night he was arrested after he'd got into a drunken fight with two Irishmen at a bar. The room was a wreck as were the Irishmen. Orso was left standing but was bloodied from a hard blow to the back of his head from a heavy chair swung by one of the Irishmen.

The *Coppers* caught Orso after he sat down for another whiskey or two and fell asleep from the alcohol and the damaging blow to his head. He was thrown in a drunk tank with the serious head wound after the jailers roughed him up a bit. The Irish jailers would not give Orso even the slightest medical attention. Being an

Italian *immigrant* brought him no respect or concern.

Orso crawled into a corner of the cell and went to sleep. A day and a half passed before Joseph located his brother. By that time, it was discovered the young man had died from an internal brain hemorrhage due to his head wound. He was found still curled in the nasty corner of the cell. It was Orso's death that nearly broke Joseph.

As Joseph slowly recovered from the death of his second brother he experienced an epiphany. Steeling himself, he became even more determined to make his way in this Country. One night, Joseph had a dream of him and his brothers standing on the streets near the docks of Piombino. They were looking for a ship to take them to America. He awoke in a cold sweat. It was then he told himself, *"I did not come all this way to end up in an unmarked grave in a foreign land. I will succeed! I will not be defeated!"*

The obsession to do great things increased from that day on. He would do it for his brother's sake. He would succeed so his family would have their legacy in this new world. It was his "blood promise", not only for his brothers but to all the nameless multitudes of immigrants who came to America seeking their dreams.

Joseph decided he might not be able to survive the constant hardness of the streets of New York. He gave the members of his gang their split of the bank, taking only the money he and his brothers earned over the years. Gathering his new wife and their few possessions, they moved to Trenton, New Jersey. This would be the fertile ground in which his American Dream would grow.

Of course, many years passed before Ford met Joseph "Papa Joe" Moretti. The old man now owned a nice neighborhood store in the middle of Chambersburg. He was the owner of several properties and legitimate businesses. His sons, as well as his sons-in-law, all worked for him in one way or another. He and his wife resided on the third floor above the market. The second floor was the residences of two of his children. Joseph's dream had come true and it was now, a living legacy.

However, Joseph never forgot the great costs that came with his successes. An important part of seeing his dreams become reality was that he recognized his responsibility to others, especially those less fortunate. The rawness of living on the streets of Piombino, New York, and finally Trenton, would never be forgotten.

These were the driving forces motivating the old man each day. He offered services to those he admired and loved. Even on those occasions when he felt he had to offer a service to those he only tolerated, he did it so that he might continue his way of life.

Joseph gave a service to those people with connections as long as they asked respectfully and as long as it did no harm to others. In this, he gained his own due respect. He might help someone whose business was not fully legal, but he would not enter into illegal businesses himself. The same was true for those who worked for him. If they were so inclined, then they were free to find their employment elsewhere.

Joseph managed to walk that fine line, staying legitimate but having discreet ties to a few people who operated opposite the laws of the day. He managed to do this because he was determined in both his ideals of morality and his desire to control his own destiny. It was most likely his favor in the large Italian community that made even those of questionable reputations see the value in his "friendship".

Joseph never asked for return favors from those individuals who were involved in a *Family* business. He knew that was a road that was littered with many a pitfall. However, he knew he could call on those in power for small incidentals...especially if they were for someone else. The small tokens were generally given as a good-will gesture. They had nothing to do with anyone's business interests and made no difference in how a business succeeded. Joseph Moretti did not come this far, sacrificing so much, to lose control of his life to those who chose a hoodlum's life.

As fate would have it though, Ford found one of Papa Joe's small incidentals resulted in the beginning of the end of Ford's *lifetime* in New Jersey.

Chapter Twenty-Seven

"You will always have my trust unless you disappoint me greatly. Capiche!"

Papa Joe immediately took to Ford. He knew and respected the Visconti family so he knew they would not let a young man such as Ford into their business without feeling him to be respectable. Joe had heard many of the stories concerning the friendship of Jovanni and Ford. Many of those stories had a reoccurring theme of Ford looking out for young Jovanni in some way.

It was a known fact that the Moretti's and the Visconti's had been a help to each other on many occasions throughout the years. One of Dario's sons, Amadeo, was married to Joseph's daughter, Celia. Both families grew in size as one generation grew into the next. Along the way, there were more unions and connections made until they began to consider themselves all "blood related".

Ford found Joe Moretti an especially interesting character. It wasn't long after they met that Joe looked for occasions to spend time with the younger Southern boy. They swapped stories about their different and difficult adventures. Joe kept asking Ford about the recipe his Uncle Jubal used to make his exceptional white lightning. All Ford could offer was that he'd see about getting some of the whiskey delivered to Joe. He didn't want to disappoint the old man but he couldn't promise that Jubal would give up his recipe.

Just to "stir the pot", Ford was constantly begging for Joe's recipe for his famous pasta sauce. He didn't expect to actually get the recipe but he thoroughly enjoyed listening to the old man's excuses denying Ford the ingredients. Sometimes he would share his secret recipe only to change it the next time they discussed the same matter.

In fact, it was over a pot of simmering tomato sauce that Papa Joe brought Ford into a very personal conversation. It was the first-time Joe began to discreetly share intimate details of what Ford could expect in his relationships with the Visconti's, Felisa, and even himself.

There was a full kitchen in the back of Joe's business where many tasty foods were made. Joe loved to cook. He had many delicious recipes which he swore originated in the "old country".

Instead of heating up the oven in his third-floor residence he liked to cook in the large downstairs kitchen. Joe had a friend who was a construction whiz. He rigged a dumbwaiter that quickly carried the food upstairs. There were times his children and grandchildren living in the second-floor residences would try and hijack Joe's dishes as they passed by the door for their apartment. Joe loved to tease his grandchildren as he called them "bandits". He would put stale bread or over-ripe fruit on a covered platter and send it upward slowly if he knew they were going to hijack him. It was a grand game they played. After they were caught, he would gather them up and take them upstairs to share in his grand meal.

Ford found himself in a conversation with Joe over the meaning of a very personal word to both men. The rather amusing conversation concerned the term "gravy".

"Listen Joe, you have to let me make you some sausage gravy over buttermilk biscuits. That's the kind of gravy I'm used to eating. The stuff you're making is what we call pasta sauce."

Joe had a wonderful laugh that would fill the room. "Ford, I don't believe you understand what "gravy" means. Gravy is the "life-blood" of my people. We live with the vigor our "gravy" gives us."

Joe moved to drop another ingredient into the steaming pot along with a heavy sprinkle of ground up seasonings. He tasted from a large wooden spoon, a pleased smile crossing his face. "*Maronna mia!*" He handed the spoon to Ford. "Taste my friend. My gravy is the best." As Ford tasted, his mouth exploded with the zesty flavor.

"Wonderful, is it not?" Ford nodded a smile while Joe emptied a plate of sausage into the simmering pot. "See! Did I not tell you? You start eating this sauce and you will become one hundred percent Italian before you know it!"

Ford tried to hand the spoon back to Joe. "It is wonderful Joe. Just so you know, I'm already fifty percent Italian by my mother. Her sauce is great and your sauce is every bit as good as my Mother's. Please, don't be insulted because that's a great compliment!"

Joe motioned for Ford to stir as he looked at him quizzically. "Your Mother. She's from the North Carolina?"

Ford stirred the sauce slowly, just as his Mother taught him. "No…she isn't a native. Born and raised in New Jersey as a matter of fact. She's from Mercerville but lived most of her life along the ocean…a place called Asbury Park. She was living in Mercerville when she met my Dad. Her maiden name is DeVoti. She doesn't have any close family left in New Jersey. At least none that I know. Never has come back to visit anyone in Jersey and I've never heard her speak of anyone. I think her parents died a long time ago. She's just always kept that part of her life to herself. As far as I know, my Father doesn't even know that much. Of course, my old man can be pretty tight lipped too."

Ford snuck another taste of the sauce. He returned to stirring and speaking of his mother. "She's one hundred percent Italian to be sure. It really shows when she gets mad and wants to make her point known. I still don't understand all the words that come out of her mouth but you get the drift when she explodes." Ford chuckled but noticed Joe appeared to be in deep thought.

Ford stirred for a few more seconds as they stood in silence. Joe appeared to be working something out in his head. He reached over to turn the heat down. Checking the fresh bread in a warming oven he leaned toward Ford, speaking lowly. The low tone caused Ford to lean toward Joe, listening carefully so he could understand what the man was saying. It was a good technique when you wished to make a point and be sure the listener was all ears.

"Ford, let me say this to you. You are greatly respected by the Visconti family. I know you have been a good and loyal friend to Jovanni. His family, including his Uncle, believe the boy has the brains and ability to lead their Company into the future. He has learned the ways of this America and he has at the same time managed to maintain the traditions of the old country."

Joe turned the heat down again as he sprinkled a little more seasoning into the sauce. Then he went on. "Jovanni is smart and he knows how to work hard. That being said, he finds too many distractions in the wrong elements of life."

Ford was listening and wondering what this was about. He found that he'd almost stopped stirring as he waited for Joe to continue.

"Listen Ford. The Visconti's appreciate what you did for Jovanni in Germany. They know you kept him from making many mistakes. They also know you bailed him out of the ones he did make. They will be forever grateful to you."

Ford felt a little embarrassed as Joe went on. "You were offered a job at Visconti Trucking because of what you did for Jovanni and for what you can do with the trucks. In the process, you have become like family as well as a good friend to all."

A smile appeared on his face. "We all know what you did before the Army. No one judges. You are like the heroic bandit of legend. Many men have made their livelihood providing those things that add *color* to the lives of others. The government wants to control such things and take a share for doing this. Most of us have little regard for a government like that."

Joe looked back over his shoulder to see if anyone had come into his little kitchen. "I tell you all of this to say that you may one day have to use your old skills and guile as a service to the Visconti family. This may come as a surprise to you. You are a brave and gifted young man. You will do fine. Just remember, you won't be alone in what you may be called on to do."

Now Ford was extremely confused. "I don't understand. What do you mean I'll be asked for a service?"

The question hung a moment before Joe answered. "Ford, I know things. I've been around a long time. I know lots of people. Many are good…a few, not so much. I hear things from people both good and bad. I usually know things that will be happening long before the time comes for those things to happen. This is one reason I am such a good businessman."

Joe stared at Ford to see if he had at least some understanding of his words. Not really sure, he took a deep breath and continued, "These people who choose a more sordid way of life are very greedy…selfish. They see others doing well. It doesn't matter to them that they do well because they have worked hard and steady…maybe for a lifetime. These low-life's who want to live high from the sweat of others are no more than *brigante*…scoundrels."

Ford was mesmerized by the sound of Joe's voice. The old man leaned over, taking a deep breath of the simmering sauce. He appeared satisfied and continued. "These *brigante*...they want a percentage of what other's hard labors have produced. They take a little and then a little more. The more they get, the more they want. They did not earn the "fruits" by their own "labors" but they want the fruit anyway."

Ford nodded his head, "Yeah, we have some fellows like that where I come from too. I've put my share of them down the side of a mountain or in a ditch when they tried to chase me down. Some people may not think highly of moonshiners or moonshine runners but thieves are worse. I tell you this, and it may just surprise you, but the biggest thief in my County is none other than our own Sheriff. The man is as you say…a *brigante!*"

Joe smiled at this. Ford had completely forgotten to stir so Joe took the spoon away from him, gracefully caressing the sauce as he took deep breaths of the steaming recipe. He broke off a piece of crusty bread and dipped it into the sauce. Breaking the bread in half, he shared it with Ford. A pleased look crossed his whiskered face. "Almost perfection."

Handing the spoon back to Ford, he said, "Stir…lightly. Caress it like you would the delicate skin of a woman".

Then, in a serious tone, he added, "Two things you must know about times to come. You will not think them related, but pay attention, for they are. You will see the relation one day."

Ford readied himself, not knowing what to expect.

"First of all, Felisa and her Mother are very close to me. Dorotea is like a daughter to me. Her husband died tragically when Felisa was very young. It was a senseless death but that is not important. Dying is something you cannot undo. Dorotea has always been very strong. She determined she would go on with her life dependent on no one. She struggled greatly at first. Then I helped her…I helped her help herself. She was worthy of my assistance."

He took the spoon from Ford and turned the heat off. Placing a lid on the pot he said, "Felisa is a lovely young woman. She is my Granddaughter in all but blood. She calls me "Uncle" but trust me, no man has ever had any more wonderful a Granddaughter. I never want to see her hurt. I cannot always protect her from everything but I will never allow her to be hurt if I can help it. I pray for Dorotea and Felisa every morning and every night. My saintly wife understands and prays with me. So, if anyone ever tries to hurt either of those women, then I will not be their friend…that will not be a good thing for that person."

Ford was a little surprised, but it made sense. Joe went on, "Felisa is very fond of you, Ford. More than anyone I have ever seen. She has very discerning taste. I believe she trusts you. The Visconti family trusts you and be assured, Ford…I too trust you. You will always have my trust unless you disappoint me greatly. *Capiche?"*

Ford stared straight into Joe's eye's. Neither blinked. Ford stated matter-of-factly. "Mr. Moretti, I give you my word I will never intentionally hurt or harm Felisa or her mother. I must tell something, though."

Joe raised his bushy eyebrows waiting to hear the boy speak. Ford gave him a hard but hopeless look. "I have learned from personal experience that bad things can happen to someone you care about…things that no one person can stop…or even see coming. That happened in my life and left me feeling a failure. It is something I don't believe I can ever forget."

Joe put his hand on Ford's shoulder, "I believe you carry a burden, Ford. I sense it in you. Believe me when I say I have also suffered losses that weigh on my heart…losses I wish I could have prevented. It is the type of burden only carried by the pure of heart. Just remember this, it is not for you to have complete responsibility for Felisa or even for your employer for that matter. In all things, I will be your champion if necessary. You have me to share in your burdens and responsibilities."

Joe's strong hand squeezed into Ford's shoulder. The old man was emphasizing his message. "What you have said, may have just made my second point…at least the heart of it."

Ford was feeling a little uncomfortable with this cryptic conversation. *"Why couldn't people just say what they mean?"* Ford was reminded of his Father and Uncle Jubal who were two of the straightest talking people he'd ever known. This conversation with Joe Moretti reminded him how refreshing the straight truth was.

Joe watched the young man as he stood pondering his last few words. Ford smiled but Joe wasn't finished. "Before we go upstairs, I need to make my words more understandable to you. It is not for me to speak of what the Visconti's may ask of you. That is their business. I know what I know. Because of the way this world works, I believe they will one day speak to you about a need to protect their business."

Ford put his hand of Joe's arm as he said, "Listen Joe, I don't have the first idea of what you mean. Nothing has ever been said about protecting their business or any reason it needs protecting."

Joe laid his hand atop Fords. "This is the second thing that I mentioned. There are people who want the Visconti's to do their bidding…bring them into the shadows of a business the Visconti's want no part of. It can never happen because the Visconti's will face death before dishonoring their families."

Ford shrunk back a little, fearing what was still to be said. Joe shook his head, disgust written on his face. "This service you may be asked to do will affect your employer as well as your own life. When I say your "life", I mean your safety. I know you are a capable man as are many who work for the Visconti's. It will not be unlike these *disgraziat'*...uh, dirtballs as you say, to threaten those that are loved and cared for. They have no regard for what is moral. They are *schifozz'*...a disgusting thing."

Joe took a deep breath. "What I want to tell you is this. When the time comes...be always on guard. Do this for yourself and for those you care about. This is nothing that will happen tomorrow...but I'm afraid it is becoming unavoidable."

Joe put the warm bread in a basket, carefully covering it with a tightly woven cloth. He sent it, along with a couple of side dishes up to his third-floor home on the dumbwaiter. Next, he pushed a button which sent an electric signal to a buzzer in is home on the third floor so it would be picked up.

He then turned his attention to the pasta. "You are a man who has had to take care of himself in hard circumstances. The people you may have to deal with won't be like the *brigante* you've seen in North Carolina. These are a different kind of animal. Trust me Ford, I have every confidence in your abilities, as do the Visconti's. If it was not so, they would never put you in any danger. Be assured, you will be given an opportunity to turn their request down. They will only ask because they may not have a choice."

Ford was about to speak but Joe held up his hand. "I will not tell you anything else except to say once more, watch out for yourself and those you care about. I do not know how this will come out on the other side but I believe you will make a difference. Besides, you will have the Visconti family behind you along with their friends. And be assured, just as importantly, you will have me on your side."

Joe began filling a very large bowl with the finished sauce. As he did so, a crooked smile came on his face. "By the way Ford, most people call me "Papa Joe", but you can call me "Uncle Joe" if you wish.

Ford looked at the man as he wondered just what his ominous message meant and who Joseph Moretti really was. Joe emptied the pasta noodles into another pot filled with boiling water. He added a little more salt and then turned up the heat slightly. He turned to Ford, "Do you know what the term *al dente* means?"

Ford shrugged, saying, "I believe it means, "to the tooth".

Joe turned to face Ford, "Exactly".

Chapter Twenty-Eight

"Suddenly, one of the drunks swung a beer bottle..."

Felisa truly loved her "Uncle Joe". Dorotea spoke of Joe in near reverence. On more than one occasion she spoke of Joe being a savior to her and Felisa. Both women adored him as if he was their blood father and grandfather.

Dorotea's life was hard from the beginning. Her eyesight was bad from a young age. Joe heard of this and helped the family get her eyes tested and bought her eyeglasses. Just after Dorotea's sixteenth birthday her parents both contacted influenza. Dorotea was faithful to them, making sure they were fed, their clothes changed each day, and their medications given. She did the laundry, the cooking, the cleaning, and anything else needed. Uncle Joe, as well as relatives and neighbors, provided groceries, medicines, and anything else that might help.

Dorotea's father died first. Her mother appeared to rally and there was hope she would pull out of the illness. Dorotea took care of her mother without thinking of herself at a time when girls her age were only thinking of themselves. She was well passed her seventeenth birthday when her mother also passed.

Dorotea buried her mother just as she had her father. Money was always an issue but never a problem thanks to Uncle Joe and others. She found a job at a local bakery shop and was Assistant Manager in a matter of a few months.

It didn't take long before young men were taking notice of the striking young woman in the bakery. Dressed for work, her hair tied back with flour stuck to her arms and face, she was still a woman who would easily make a man stop and take notice.

Two years passed when Mr. Leo Gervasè caught her attention. He was two years older but looked two or more years younger. There was a fire in the young man's dark eyes that caught Dorotea's attention.

A respectable courtship time passed when Leo asked Uncle Joe for Dorotea's hand in marriage. Joe gave the bride away and Dorotea believed life's tragedies were behind her. Felisa was born in the second year of their marriage. A second child was hoped for but just never seemed to happen. Sadly, before five years of marriage passed, Leo was dead, a tragic victim of a bar fight. He had been sitting at a table with friends, celebrating the upcoming marriage of one of their group. Two drunken fellows were arguing at the bar, getting louder and angrier.

Suddenly, one of the drunks swung an empty beer bottle, fully missing his target as well as losing his grip on the bottle. The flying bottle hit one of Leo's friends directly in the face. Leo jumped up uttering a curse at the two drunkards. Too late, he realized the second drunk had pulled a pistol and was ready to shoot the first drunk. Leo's words had hardly died when the sound of a gunshot exploded into the bar. The drunken man took insult at Leo's words and somehow managed to shoot him in the heart.

Dorotea would have just given up at that dark point in her life if it had not been for her beautiful daughter, Felisa, and her guardian angel, Joe Moretti. Joe took care of all the funeral arrangements and made sure Dorotea's rent was paid as well as groceries supplied until she could go back to work.

Because of Joe's kindness, a new resolve filled Dorotea. Not only did she go back to work but used her skills as a seamstress to bring in additional money. It was no wonder that Felisa was such a hard-working and strong-willed woman herself.

As Ford became more acquainted with Felisa, he found she reminder him more and more of the women he greatly respected from back home. It was just as true of Dorotea. She welcomed Ford into their home, offering fellowship as well as warm and zesty Italian meals. Those meals reminded him of his Mother's cooking. In fact, it was the resemblance to his Mother's personality that made it so easy to spend time with Dorotea with or without Felisa's presence.

Dorotea asked about Ford's Mother, especially after he told her Mara grew up in New Jersey. However, she was quite surprised at how little Ford knew of his mother's past life in New Jersey.

Still, Ford loved telling the ladies stories about the large personality that was Mara Rawlings. They found equal enjoyment in the other characters that made up his past life in North Carolina. Both ladies loved the stories of the *Three Wise Men* who observed life from the porch of J.J.'s garage. They especially enjoyed the tales of Wallace and his many wives, children, and grandchildren. They were impressed with his Dad's grasp on what was important in the world and his infamous Uncle Jubal…the master of North Carolina's best *white lightning.*

Ford enjoyed getting to understand the kindness and grace which was Dorotea. Her attributes were certainly evident in her only daughter. To be a part of Dorotea and Felisa's lives meant you were also going to have the mysterious man they called Uncle Joe be a part of your life.

Being on Uncle Joe's good side was where a person wanted to stay. Staying on Joe's good side meant you would eventually be the recipient of one of his generous gifts, whether they were wanted or not.

Ford was not one to easily accept something for nothing. He knew that many times there were strings attached as well as other entanglements. There were so many times he turned away a gift solely because he didn't want to feel obligated to someone.

With Uncle Joe, it was a totally different story. Ford knew from the beginning there were no strings attached when it came to Joe Moretti. Still, it not only took a while before Ford was offered one of Joe's favors, it took even longer for him to accept it.

Joe came by to see Ford at work one day. He carried a small box of chocolate and pistachio biscotti to share with Ford. They ate, drank a cup of coffee, and talked engines as Ford continued rebuilding one of the truck motors. Just before Joe left, he shared a happy message. "Hey Ford. You been working so hard. I'm gonna set you and Felisa up with a free weekend in a nice hotel. You like Philadelphia or Atlantic City?"

Ford was surprised but rallied as he tried his best to gracefully turn him down. "Mighty kind of you Joe. I wouldn't feel right taking such a nice gift. Thank you! I really mean it…thanks!"

Every one of Fords excuses was turned away in hand by Joe. Still, Ford persisted. Of course, the infamous Uncle Joe was not to be deterred.

Soon after, another offer followed and then another. Finally, after getting a refusal for the third all-expense trip offered, Joe called for Ford to come by his office one day. Ford showed up and was led into Joe's small and cluttered office, and told to sit.

"Do you not like me, Ford? I have told you how much you mean to me. We are *paisano,* no? You surely are not trying to insult me…and if you are…well, I do not understand why."

Ford tried to rise but Joe laid a heavy hand on his shoulders. "I do not believe your saintly Italian Mother would approve of your insults. And your Father…a respectable man I'm sure. What would he say about such disrespect? No…I can't believe such a respectable young man…the son of two most respected parents would ever do such a thing."

Ford made it to his feet this time. "Now wait a minute Joe!" I've never shown you anything but the greatest respect. I don't think it one bit fair…"

Joe interrupted Ford, a shushing sound coming through his lips. "I know. I know. But you must think of our dear, sweet Felisa. Do you not think her deserving of going on a little holiday? This stubbornness of yours must hurt our beautiful Felisa. Do you not care for her?"

Ford lifted his hands to the sky, doing all he could to resist screaming. He took a step towards Joe, standing directly in front of him. "What do you think people will say if I take "our beautiful" Felisa off for a weekend alone. How's that going to make her look?"

Joe pursed his lips under his bushy mustache. Then his face lit up. "Of course, you are correct! Why did you not say this sooner? You will have chaperone's of course. I will send Dario's son, Jovanni and Felisa's cousin, Natale, along with you!" Ford tried to say something but Joe was already talking rapidly. "I will have a car pick you and the others up early next Saturday morning. It is settled. I know you will be a gentleman…no question. Everything will be paid for. The hotel manager will meet you and fill you in on everything. It will all be fine! Better than fine! You're going to have a grand time…you have "Uncle Joe's" word."

Joe walked to his desk, rubbing his chin. "Let me see…hmm, Philadelphia…maybe. No! Not Philadelphia. The hotel is being renovated still. That's it! Atlantic City! There is a beautiful hotel there. I have stayed there myself! Good rooms and good food! Oh, wait…you can go out if you'd like. I'll get in touch with the hotel manager. He will get you reservations at a nice restaurant…and a show. You must go to a show. Everything is paid for, okay?"

By now Ford was stunned. Joe laid his hand on Ford's shoulder, pulling him close. "It is important that everything is paid for. Do not try to pay for anything. Even tips…*capiche?* If you decide to do a little gambling, that too will be taken care of once you arrive. Listen to the hotel manager. Gamble in a big way. Large bets. It's all covered. Just do not use your own money…ever!"

Ford was puzzled again. "It's okay my young friend. You're encouraged to gamble, keep the patrons in the mood to lay their money down. They see you bet, they'll want to keep up with you.

Just never go back with your own money, understand?"

Ford shook his head, "no". Joe smiled, "It's simple, Ford. It is meant for people to see you placing large bets. Doesn't matter if whether you win or lose. It just puts others in a mood to gamble freely. Now, if you go back and only place small bets and someone recognizes you, they will become suspicious, hesitant to bet freely. All the people who are "comping" your stay want you to do, is play the part of a "high roller". It gives others courage to do like-wise. It's good for business. *Capiche?*"

"That doesn't sound very honest to me, Joe. We'll be *shills* for the "house". I don't think I like the idea of putting Felisa in that position."

Joe rubbed his chin. "You are a wise young man, of course. I can see where this might rub you the wrong way. You see, you will not be made to do. If you choose to participate, it will only be for an hour or two. It is one way in which the businessmen of Atlantic City use to "prop up' their investment in the City. The people going to these establishments are there to gamble. Many are drawn to the gambling for the excitement. It is entertainment to them. Your little "play acting" will only add to the excitement of the game."

Ford stared at the man, wondering how many small compromises the old man may have had to make in his life. "Okay, Joe. I can take your point. We'll see. I won't say "yes" or I won't say "no". It will be up to the others. We'll take you up on your generous offer. It will be fun, I'm sure. I'll say "thank you" and trust you that this is only a gift for Felisa. I just don't want it to become something else."

Chapter Twenty-Nine

"It was as if they'd discovered the pot of gold at the end of the rainbow"

True to his word, Uncle Joe provided the foursome with a black Cadillac limo to transport them to Atlantic City. The interior of the car was as plush as anything Ford had ever seen. A small bar was available which Joey found delightful. In fact, the whole ride was delightful as the two couples found plenty to talk and laugh about.

Their arrival at the Traymore Hotel was as impressive as the hotel itself. The hotel manager came out to greet them. Standing alongside him were two hotel staff. One opened the limo door while the other began unloading their luggage. The Manager, Mr. Sturgis, took Ford and Joey directly into his office while the ladies, along with the luggage, were taken to their suite.

Ford heard the Bellman escorting the women listing the amenities that would be available for them to enjoy during their stay. As they walked away he could see the girls were excited at the possibilities of being pampered during their stay. He couldn't help but smile a little at Felisa and Natale's excitement as they looked around the hotel lobby.

Mr. Sturgis office was as nice as anything Ford had ever seen. He offered whiskey and cigars as Joey and Ford settled into plush leather chairs across from his desk. Even Ford was impressed with the warm and generous welcome.

It didn't take long before Mr. Sturgis got down to the business end of their stay. It was similar to the basic guidelines Uncle Joe outlined initially. The only thing different was that they were requested to gamble a bit while in Atlantic City.

Joey spoke up, "I didn't think there was still gambling in Atlantic City?"

Mr. Sturgis smiled, amused at the query. "Yes, well, there's always been gambling in Atlantic City. Mind you, the local and State governments aren't always encouraging in this manner since they do not participate directly those profits. However, they reap a richness in the taxes paid by the businesses that can still provide service and entertainment to any and all visitors."

Ford looked at Joey as he wondered what was going on. "Where are we supposed to do this gambling Mr. Sturgis? And for that matter, why?"

Sturgis was lighting a cigar, not speaking until he was satisfied with the burning embers. "I realize our mutual friend, Mr. Moretti, set up this trip. He and I share some business acquaintances that we in turn support in small ways. Let me assure you that we mainly wish your stay to be completely enjoyable. However, we are a community of business enterprises that offer each other assistance from time to time. We have friends that provide a form of entertainment not formally recognized by the governments of Atlantic City and New Jersey. People like to gamble and do not always wish to travel to Nevada to do so."

Ford asked, "Okay, I get that. I'm just not sure as to how we can be helpful in promoting gambling?"

Sturgis tapped the ashes of his cigar into a crystal ashtray. He explained patiently, "It's actually very simple. There are gambling venues that are in part, associated with a group of business ventures which enjoy a mutual goal…to bring profitable business to Atlantic City."

"I am sure you are aware that our grand city has been declining over the last ten years. The Traymore Hotel and like-minded businesses are attempting to change the direction of our city with any creative means at our disposal. The Traymore has been called the *Taj* Mahal of Atlantic City. We want to maintain that image and we are doing all we can to change the direction in which our city has been following."

"You are staying at our hotel with all expenses paid. As a favor, we'd ask that you spend a few hours in one of our establishments. You'll have a good time and it won't cost you anything but your time. We will provide you with chips to bet and will also provide you with transportation. Food and drink also. Let me assure you that you will be completely safe. There shouldn't be any concern as to being arrested or running into any problems. You will play with chips given to you so that you will have the luxury of playing as the high rollers play. In doing so, others will be encouraged to follow suit. It's all part of the game so to say."

Joey spoke up, "What if we win?"

Sturgis laughed, knowing that the question would be asked. "We can only offer so much. I'm afraid any winnings will be returned to us. But, you will have a wonderful time with any food or drinks you'd like. As I say, we only ask for a few hours. The remainder of your stay is for you to decide."

Joey and Ford looked at each other, fully surprised at what they were asked to do. Finally, Ford shrugged and Joey said, "Well, why the hell not!"

Sturgis smiled again as he reached for two small leather cases. "Be wise in the size of your bets. Don't become hysterically grandiose. Consistent large bets are what you should be doing. Do not be timid but don't place foolish bets when it is obvious you will lose. Act like it is your money you are betting and act like you care."

"You are "high rollers" so I encourage you stay away from small bets. Remember, "high rollers" are daring but not foolish. You will never see a "high roller" bothering with small bets. They are playing because they wish to win large amounts of money but they never try and draw too much attention to their game. Listen, all we ask is for you to make those around you feel comfortable betting in ways that follow your lead. And by all means, have fun."

He rose from his desk and gave each man his gold embossed business card saying, "If I can be of service, please show this card to any of my staff. I wish you all a wonderful weekend. We are privileged to have you as guests. If you run out of chips, feel free to discreetly ask for more."

As they left Sturgis' office, each man was handed one of the small leather cases with the Hotel's logo embossed on the side in gold. With that, the fellows were escorted to their suite.

They stood inside the doorway, thoroughly impressed. The room was very spacious and finely furnished. A door led to a bedroom on either side. Ford guessed Uncle Joe set up the accommodations as well as the presence of another couple to give the representation of respectable co-habitation. How the two couples chose to use the bedrooms was their business and theirs alone.

Ford felt highly regarded by the old man if he provided this type of quarters with no instruction as to how they would be used. He mumbled to himself, *"I guess the old man actually does trust me."*

The question of who bunked with who was settled before there was any discussion. Joey was pouring two glasses of chilled champagne from a bottle housed in a silver ice bucket when one of the bedroom doors opened. Felisa and Natale walked out in grand fashion. Each one modeling a beautiful evening gown.

Felisa stood with her hands on her hips. "These were waiting for us. The note said to wear them as we wish and then leave them in the closet when we leave. We each have another one still in the closet! There's shoes, jewelry, and everything else. It's like Christmas"

Natale giggled, "Well, I'm not taking mine off…maybe ever!"

Two expensive looking black suits including all the accessories were laid out in the other bedroom for Joey and Ford. Joey's was double-breasted and Ford's single breasted with the faintest of pinstripe in the material. All of this had to have Uncle Joe's hand in it because the suits and dresses were all correctly sized.

Ford looked at the suit saying, "I'm not so sure I'm ready for this?"

Felisa walked in front of him, strutting her stuff. "I can tell you one thing, Mr. Ford Rawlings! If you want to escort a fine-looking lady like myself to dinner then you'd better get comfortable in that suit." She looked away in a dramatic pose. "Of course, I guess I could just find a wealthy big shot almost anywhere in this hotel who'd love to escort me."

She looked back at Ford, batting her long dark eyelashes. Joey and Natale were laughing by now as Ford gave Felisa a crooked grin. Without even thinking, he pulled Felisa to him and gave her a long, tender kiss. He then whispered, "I'll wear the suit for you but just so you know, I'll take your breath away."

Felisa was totally caught off guard. Her heart raced a bit as she smiled at Ford. "I believe you, Mr. Ford Rawlings."

Joey was immediately heard saying, "Holy Mother…!"

He wasn't responding to Ford's comment. Instead, he was looking inside the case he carried in. They all gazed at the case which was filled with one hundred dollar chips. It was as if they'd discovered the pot of gold at the end of the rainbow.

The Traymore Hotel had been a true palace in its heyday. That was when illegal whiskey flowed freely around the famous Boardwalk. By the time the 1950's arrived, the ocean-side getaway had lost some of its luster. The hotel was still a fine specimen of a grand hotel. It was not surprising that some of the shiny veneer had worn thin in the last thirty years. Still, it was a most impressive place. Each bathtub featured four faucets: hot and cold city water and hot and cold ocean water. The sink added a fifth faucet that produced ice water.

The hotel stood tall as it looked over the city and the ocean. There were plenty of places, including the Boardwalk itself that had fared worse. After all, the same types of aging and depression could be seen throughout the city. Some places just showed their age more than others.

At present, there were still plenty of visitors as far as Ford could tell. Without even knowing how everything looked before, a person could still sense the fact that the golden age had faded. The foundations of Atlantic City remained but the cracks and wrinkles were beginning to show.

The foursome's first excursion was memorable for all the right reasons. A visit to the famous *Steel Pier* to hear the *Four Lads* sing was so much fun. Felisa and Natale found themselves turning into schoolgirls again. Both Joey and Ford found it fascinating to see the girls so carefree and animated as they danced, sang along, and giggled away the night. He found himself wishing he could lose himself in a joyful moment like that.

Their weekend passed in a blur of activity. They watched the *Diving Horse,* rode the rides, and gorged themselves on crazy food from the Boardwalk. Then there were fine meals in very nice restaurants, room service for any and everything they wanted, as well as too many entertaining venues to count. Finally, there was dancing and the inevitable gambling they felt as their obligation.

Ford was still a little uncomfortable with the gambling situation. He was uncomfortable being used by the gambling house, but was will to give it a try. Ford hardly had any gambling experience outside of poker. On the other hand, Joey jumped right in as if he was a seasoned gambler.

Joey was playing "craps" and losing badly. He handed the dice to Natale who immediately began to win. As Natale continued winning, Joey's smile broadened. When she made a "hard eight" Joey shouted out, "That's my Girl! I love this woman!" Natale literally lost her grip on the dice as she overshot the table. The dice hit the floor and bounced away. She put a hand on each of Joey's cheeks and planted a hard kiss on the boy as the next shooter was handed the dice as the game continued.

Ford and Felisa were playing *Blackjack.* Neither were doing very well, mostly because they didn't understand the game that well. As Felisa placed a bet, Ford felt a presence behind him. He turned to find two heavy-set, very serious looking men standing behind him. One had a silver tray holding two flutes of bubbly wine.

The other fellow spoke in a serious tone as his partner handed a crystal flute to Felisa and Ford. "Mr. Rawlings, could I borrow you for a moment. Mr. Hash, our Manager would like a word."

The man said no more, staring intently at Ford. A few beats passed until Ford moved. The man said, "Just over this way. His office is close. My associate will stay with the Lady. She will be fine."

Mr. Hash greeted Ford with a firm handshake and the offer of a seat in yet another comfortable chair. "Mr. Rawlings, I am hopeful you and your party are enjoying your evening. We are honored to have you and your party join us tonight."

Ford nodded, wondering what in the world this man was going to say. "Thank you, Mr. Hash. Everything and everyone have been great. Is there something I can do for you?"

Hash smiled, "Of course…right to the point. I certainly don't blame you for wanting to return to your lovely lady as soon as possible."

He stood, offering Ford a cigar. Ford helped himself to two, one for Joey. Mr. Hash smiled again as he spoke. "I'll be brief. I can understand if you have not gambled in a Casino very much…strange waters so to speak. Please do not be alarmed with me speaking with you. We'd just like you and Miss Gervasè to be more magnanimous in the size of your bets. We would like you to appear to be more of a "high roller". You both appear to be a little hesitate and conservative. We will be happy to provide more chips if you run out or begin to get low."

Then he chuckled, "Of course, we hope you will enjoy the excitement of winning, but if not, there is still plenty of fun to be had. A reminder if you don't mind. Any winnings go back to the Casino before you leave. It may appear unfair, but all of your bills are being covered so it shouldn't seem an unfair trade-off."

With that, a container holding four stacks of one hundred dollar chips was handed to Ford. "Please let us know if we can provide you with any accommodation. Also, I don't think it necessary, but pass this information along to Mr. Visconti and Miss Ricci. I believe they are enjoying themselves in a grand fashion."

Before Ford could think of words to respond, he was escorted from the office. He did manage a *"Thank you!"* before exiting. He found Felisa still playing Blackjack. She had a quizzical look on her face.

Ford smiled and whispered in her ear as he set the container of chips on the table. "They want us to bet more. I guess we've been playing too cheaply."

Felisa giggled. "Well they should be happy with me just now. I won the last five hands! I don't really know what I'm doing so I just left my winnings out to play. I was getting a pretty impressive stack of chips."

Ford looked at the table to notice her stack of chips was pretty diminished. She rolled her eyes, "Lost my last two hands. Ended up busted…literally!"

Her smile warmed Ford's very heart and he found himself kissing her on the cheek. He handed her the new cache of chips saying, "Felisa, you are the most wonderful girl. I'm the luckiest man in this Casino."

She gave him a coy smile. "Why Mr. Ford Rawlings, you're the luckiest man in the whole state of New Jersey!"

And so, the weekend continued until it ended quite quickly. They rode back to Chambersburg fully spent from all their activity. Quiet conversations occurred along the way but they mostly seemed content to consider the weekend and each other's companionship.

It truly had been a perfect weekend. Unfortunately, their second trip to Atlantic City did not turn out so well.

Chapter Thirty

"You better be good to that girl. You'll never get that lucky twice in your lifetime."

The weather was beautiful, promising a warm and sunny weekend ahead. It was the second time they were invited on an Atlantic City excursion courtesy of Joe Moretti. They were booked again at the Traymore Hotel. Dean Martin was playing at the Steel Pier as well as the promise of other great music to compliment dancing and wonderful food.

Joey was acting excited, but at the same time appeared to have other emotions taking him on a roller coaster ride. He'd be quiet for a bit and then become overly animated and fidgety. Natale even asked him if he'd been drinking before the limo ride to the coast.

"No! Really, I promise. I haven't touched any alcohol in two weeks or more…and that was just to give a toast to Claudio Santoro. He had just found out his wife is pregnant! It'll be their first!"

Natale looked at him closely, then smiled. "Okay! I'm not fussing. You're just acting a little odd."

Ford chimed in, "Yeah, it's not always easy to tell with Joey. He's like a monkey shot out of a cannon sometimes!"

Laughter filled the car as even the driver could be heard chuckling. Joey raised his voice, "You guys are not my friends! I've just got a lot on my mind is all. You know I've got a lot of stuff going on that I have to take responsibility for." His serious tone surprised his three companions, Then, he added with a smug look on his face. "Besides, I don't like cannons. They're way too loud! I've got sensitive ears."

Laughter filled the car again as Natale leaned over and kissed Joey on the cheek. He beamed, "My girl! One of the sweetest women God ever created!" This was rewarded with a full kiss on the lips.

Felisa and Natale began a conversation about the new swimsuits they'd bought for the trip. They also discussed what possibilities they might find in their closet. Ford watched Joey closely as he tried to discern why the boy was so fidgety.

The greeting at the hotel was just as formal as before. The only difference being Mr. Ballentine, the Assistant Manager, met them instead of Mr. Sturgis. Ballentine went over the same aspects of their stay as Mr. Sturgis had done on their first visit. They were again presented with small cases filled with one hundred-dollar Casino chips.

As they walked to their suite, Joey whispered to Ford. "Hey buddy. You want to just take off with these chips and see if we can cash them in for the real thing?"

Ford actually became a little choked-up as he tried to answer. "Are you crazy? Don't even think about something like that! They'd have you buried under the Boardwalk before you could say, "*Cash me out*".

Joey's eyes danced at the distress he'd caused his friend. "Too late my friend. Already thought about it…would never think to actually do it mind you…but did think about it." He laughed out loud. "Now who's being fidgety?"

Ford grabbed Joey's arm, pulling him close to his side as they walked. "About that…how come you've been so fidgety and strange today?"

Joey stopped walking and looked around. He pulled something from his coat pocket. Opening the small box, he said, "I'm asking Nat to marry me tonight…at dinner! Crazy, huh!"

Ford was caught totally off guard. He looked at the sparkly ring and notice the same type of twinkle in Joey's eyes.

Joey was waiting, expecting congratulations. Ford gave him a pleasant smile as he said, "My condolences to the Bride-to-be!"

With that, Ford gave Joey a great hug. "You better be good to that girl. You'll never get that lucky twice in your lifetime!"

When they reached the door to the suite, Joey said, "Don't even think about telling Felisa. Okay? Promise?"

Ford nodded and opened the door to a pleasant surprise. Felisa and Natale were already decked out in their new swimwear and cover-ups. They looked like they were ready to participate in the *Miss America Contest.* Ford could not take his eyes off Felisa as she moved around the room saying, "You boys change. We want to get in a little sun before it gets too hot. Hurry up! Don't be standing around." She stopped, noticing Ford's lingering stare.

"What's the matter, honey? You look like you got lost somewhere. Everything okay?"

Ford grabbed his suitcase. He looked over at Joey and Natale who were in a whispered conversation. "I'm fine. Just thought of something I needed to do…when we get back, I mean."

He went into the bedroom to change. After he closed the door he sat on the bed and closed his eyes. His thoughts raced. Everything had just become so real.

Seeing Felisa so comfortable and radiant in his presence made him think of Julia. He was confused though. He and Felisa had been seeing each other for some time now. For some reason, everything seemed to become so very intimate. He felt a little awkward, out of place. Maybe it was Joey's news or maybe it was how comfortable Felisa felt in his presence as she modeled her swimsuit.

Ford knew it wasn't guilt, even though his thoughts of Julia continued. Realizing how comfortable Felisa was in his presence made Ford feel both perplexed and excited. He couldn't help but wonder where their relationship actually was headed.

Ford slipped on his trunks, then pulled his slacks on over them. Returning to the suite's common room he noticed the girls had put together a large beach bag including clothes to change into after their stay on the beach. There were decent changing accommodations just off the sand. For a small fee, their belongings would be kept safely until they were ready to change back into street clothes.

The day was warm and welcoming. The crowds weren't too bad and they all found the late morning to be very relaxing.

The sea, sand, and sun made for a wonderful day as the two couples sunned, swam, and lounged with tall, cold drinks in their hands. As the sun climbed to its apex, they began making plans for lunch. The ladies decided they wanted to quickly clean up and eat at a small café called *Geno's By the Sea.* It was right on the beach with a reputation of excellent food. A nice, formal dinner would be enjoyed at the hotel's main restaurant later that evening. As they made their way to the changing tents, Joey grabbed Ford's arm and pulled him aside.

"I can't wait till this evening! I'm going to ask her at lunch. It'll be perfect. A beautiful day beside the ocean. There's no way she could say *No*. We'll have dessert and I'll do it then."

Ford grimaced, "What are you saying? You think there's a chance she'll say *No?* Sounds risky to me Joey. You could mess up a pretty nice weekend if she doesn't agree."

Joey's blank look was priceless. Ford almost felt bad for the boy. He punched him on the arm. "I'm just kidding, you *goomba.* She's gonna grab ahold of you and never let go. You two are made for each other. In fact, I think you both will be the best thing that could happen to each other."

Joey looked surprised as he'd never heard Ford talk in this manner. He started to say something when a feminine voice called out. "If you two want to stay and watch the girls in their swimsuits we'll just go have a nice lunch and do a little shopping on our own." The tone was merry followed by both girls giggling at their wittiness. Ford and Joey faked a few steps toward the beach before turning around and chasing the girls off the sand.

True to their word, the girls readied themselves quickly so that they were sitting at the little café before an hour had passed. It seems they were serious about shopping after finishing their meal. Joey, on the other hand, had something very different in mind.

The lunch was beyond expectations. Everyone had a nice seafood salad that was unquestionably fresh. Small, fluffy garlic biscuits were served along with a tangy sauce to use with the crab bites. The light, but zesty salad dressing was very tasty and caused a degree of conversation as to what the ingredients were. A chilled bottle of Chardonnay added to the zest of the meal.

Conversation flowed as easily as the wine. Joey and Ford became excitedly engaged in an animated conversation about Ford's new automobile. The car was a 1957 Chevy Bel Air Sports Coupe. Ford pre-ordered the car with customized additions more than six months in advance.

He began adding his own touches as soon as the car was delivered. The V-8 Super "Turbo Fired" engine was already a powerful monster. It topped out at 270hp but Ford knew he could still make it do better. To him, it was a beast…a horsepower animal. He'd already changed the type of tires on the car three times. Everyone at Visconti Trucking were thoroughly amazed at both the car and Ford's expertise.

The ladies could only allow the conversation about a car to go on for so long. Natale was excited about seeing Dean Martin perform at the Steel Pier. It was an aging venue, like most of Atlantic City. Still, it pulled in many top-notch performers. As the conversations continued, they meandered from one topic to another.

Ford could see that Joey was getting nervous again. He began getting quieter, fidgeting with the last of his salad. He downed his wine glass and was refilling it when Ford announced that a surprise dessert was soon to follow. Both women looked at Ford with a bit of amused apprehension on their face. Joey didn't move, seemingly frozen in place.

"What kind of surprise dessert have you cooked up, darling", asked Felisa. She knew Ford enough to be wary of such an announcement.

Natale joined in, "I don't care as long its chocolate!"

She felt a movement at her side and turned to Joey. Surprisingly, Joey slid from his chair and was kneeling on one knee. A small velvet covered box was opened, showcasing a beautiful diamond ring.

Natale gasped as Joey gave words to his actions. "Natale Ricci, would you make me the happiest guy in this whole world. Marry me, Nat…will you marry me?"

Natale threw her arms around Joey's neck as she almost knocked him over with a passionate kiss.

Ford leaned toward Felisa. "Is that how you say yes in Italian…cause if it is, I hope Joey never asks me a question."

Felisa gave Ford a jolt with her elbow. He noticed her eyes were moist as she watched the newly betrothed couple. Seeing her so emotional made Ford feel nearly alone…caught somewhere between two worlds. He managed a smile and left his chair to give both Natale and Joey big hugs. Felisa did the same.

The two couples were oblivious to the other people in the café as their joys were consuming. It was only the wooden voice of a stranger that brought them back to reality.

"*Scusami.* I'm looking for Ford Rawlings…maybe Elvis Rawlings…I don't know, I think he goes by both names."

Ford turned to see a young, hard-looking man of obvious Italian decent staring at them. The fellow's nose looked as if it had been broken at least once in his younger days. Another fellow, approximately the same age and build was standing just to his side. He was a couple of inches shorter than the lead man. One of his brushy eyebrows was divided by a scar from an old wound.

Joey and the ladies began sizing up the two men who'd intruded on their moment. Joey used one hand to glide Natale behind him as Ford spoke to the men.

"Is there something I can do for you fellows?"

The guy in front answered Ford's question with a question. "You Ford Rawlings?" He looked past Ford to see if Joey was moving toward him as he then said, "I just wanted to see if I could talk to you about a little business proposition."

Chapter Thirty-One

"Now that there...that's my girl!"

Ford took a step toward the young, obnoxious man as he signaled the others to stand back. Both men eyed each other suspiciously. The man standing next to the speaker didn't move but his eyes began darting back and forth as if expecting something to happen.

Ford's voice was steady with a degree of firmness that merited attention. "Listen buddy…I don't know you and I'm sure I don't have any business to discuss with you. I don't know how you found me, but I'm afraid you've wasted your time."

Ford paused a beat to see how the guy reacted. Before the man could speak, Ford spoke again. "Hey, I'm sorry to be blunt but you did interrupt us. My friends just became engaged. So, if you'll be on your way, we'll continue our celebration.

A cruel smile crossed the man's face. He turned to his associate saying, "Enzio, order a bottle of their best champagne for the table. Get a nice dessert too. Let everyone continue to celebrate this special event while Mr. Rawlings and I talk."

Enzio started to spring into action as the man turned back to Ford. "Santino Caputo is my name. People call me "Cha-Cha". I've got a nice table over in the corner where we can talk privately. What're you drinking?"

Ford spoke abruptly, "Wait! Don't order anything for the table. For some reason, you're not hearing me when I say I'm not interested. I think you and your friend need to leave now. Go to your table or take a swim in the ocean…I don't care!"

Enzio stopped, first looking at his boss, then to Ford, and then back to his boss.

Cha-Cha looked mildly surprised. It was obvious he was accustomed to having his way. He raised his hand as if to offer a compromising response.

Ford spoke again as the tension around the table escalated. "Listen Mr. Caputo, thanks for thinking of me for your business. I believe I've been very clear about this thing. Again, I'm not interested in hearing your business offer. I'm sorry if this sounds rude to you, but I will not be sitting down with you. Please find someone else…I'm not interested."

Ford's face tightened as his last word came across very hard. *"Capiche?"*

Enzio was frozen, not knowing what to do. He waited for his boss to speak. Cha-Cha's brow furrowed and his face clouded.

"I don't think you really want to try a be a hard man with me. I'm no *scemo,* wasting your time. You will be wise to listen to me…and when you do…well, you're going to find yourself with a fatter wallet. You can buy your little girly some nice things."

His voice then hardened then as he said, *"Capiche?"*

The two men stood only a few feet apart now. It was obvious that this had become a difficult and inflexible stand-off. Joey whispered to Natale, "You girls move back. I recognize this guy now."

Natale gave Joey a hard look, mouthing the word, *"Who?"*

Joey pulled her closer as he whispered, "His father is Arturo "*Knuckles"* Caputo. The old man grew up on the streets. Got his start as a boxer. He was a tough fellow. Once took his gloves off so he could beat a guy to death with his bare knuckles."

Natale whispered, "That how he got his nickname?"

"Yeah, that and a few other instances. Punching a guy until his face turned to mush gets his juices flowing. Really tough old guy! After he killed that first guy he couldn't get another fight so he became a gangster. I think he did it mostly so he could keep punching people. His sons are just as crazy."

He looked closely at Ford as he continued. "Cha-Cha is the youngest. Don't know how many others he's got but I always heard Santino was the youngest. Been an arrogant troublemaker all his life."

Joey watched Ford closely to see if he was making any headway getting Cha-Cha to leave. It didn't appear either man was going to back down.

Joey continued his story. "His old man is a low-level gangster. Runs a crew around Jersey. Connected up the ladder to a New York *family,* I think. Mostly does "grunt" work for them. He runs prostitutes in a few towns as well as rackets and loan sharking. Moves some stolen goods for the Mob as well as for himself."

The last thought caused Joey to stop abruptly. A serious look crossed his face. Something clicked in his mind and it wasn't a good thing. Natale heard him mumble, *"I wonder how he found us?"*

Quietly, he said, “How about you and Felisa move over to the bar. Okay sweetie?”

Before Natale could move, Cha-Cha decided it was time to get right in Ford’s face. He moved around a chair where he found Felisa standing between him and Ford. He gave her a firm nudge to move her aside as he said, “Go powder your nose girly, the men need to talk!”

At the same time, he put his hand heavily on Ford’s shoulder saying, “I’m asking one more time…politely. Let’s not make this a “thing”. Don’t try and go all hillbilly on me, okay? Come on over to my table. I’ll set your friends up over here…whatever they want. You’ll see. It won’t take long, you’ll like what I’ve got to say.”

Ford’s stare went dead. For some reason, he felt an old familiar feeling. It was the same feeling he had the last time he was in the presence of Sheriff Royal Albert Majesty. His hands reacted before he realized he was moving.

Ford’s hand moved straight up, grabbing Cha-Cha’s wrist. He brought it downward in one swift movement, twisting it as he moved. With the other hand, he pushed hard against Cha-Cha’s shoulder causing the man to fall backwards into Enzio. Cha-Cha didn’t completely lose his balance as Enzio caught and steadied him. He shook himself loose from Enzio’s grasp as his face turned dark red.

Ford shouted, “Enough!”

The girls reacted loudly and Joey moved toward Enzio just as the wing man began to pull a pistol from a holster hidden under his jacket. He’d barely cleared his coat when Joey picked up a wine bottle, slamming it across Enzio’s wrist. There was a dual cracking sound as the bottle shattered and the bones in the gunman’s hand did the same. The gun fell to the floor as Enzio cried out in pain from the damaged wrist.

Several things happened at once. Cha-Cha let out an oath as he pulled a deadly knife from under his jacket. Ford grabbed a tray sitting on a portable stand. The tray contained dirty dishes and utensils. It made a great deal of noise as the tray and its contents crashed into Cha-Cha. The man reacted by trying to block all the debris coming his way with the knife. He tried to knock the tray away as he blocked the dishes. This was partly stymied by the fact that Ford still held onto the tray.

Ford swung the tray into the hand holding the knife. The impact of the tray on the hand caused Cha-Cha to lose his grip on the knife as he cried out in pain. Cha-Cha only had time to look up at Ford as a hard, right hand made a crunching contact on his chin. He staggered again, trying to catch himself by grabbing a table. He didn't go down but the table crashed to the floor.

At that same time, Joey followed the blow to Enzio's wrist with a left hook to the man's face. He then grabbed the guy around the neck, half running and half dragging the man through the front door. Joey got the thug through the door, then continued across the walk-way. He punched the bigger man in his esophagus causing him to grab his throat as he coughed and sputtered. Joey then grabbed the man's belt and pushed him over a handrail onto the sand below. He lay there coughing, not able to regain his feet.

Almost simultaneously, the situation inside the restaurant was becoming more volatile as Cha-Cha made a lunge toward Ford. Felisa kicked a chair into the gangster's path causing the big man to crash forward into a table and then to the floor. He lay there finding himself dazed and disoriented. He tried raising his head so he could get up. The effort was wasted as Ford landed another right to the side of Cha-Cha's head. The blow landed just behind the gangster's right ear. This resulted in an explosion of ringing in his head which left Cha-Cha ready to give up the fight.

Joey was trying to get back inside as the patrons and wait staff began pouring through the door. He caught movement to his right and then to his left. Two more thugs, who'd been stationed outside, were right on top of him. They both had drawn pistols leaving Joey helpless.

Suddenly, the front window erupted as a body came hurling through. The body turned out to be Santino Cha-Cha Caputo. Before all the broken glass settled, two gunshots exploded into the melee. The wooden boards around the feet of the two thugs erupted in splinters. They flinched, not knowing whether to duck, help their boss, or try to find a target to shoot at.

A cold female voice was heard from the doorway. "You boys best drop those pistols unless you want to be buried with them." They hesitated, then turned to find Natale standing there with a large pistol pointed at them. It was the one Enzio dropped inside the restaurant when Joey clubbed him with the wine bottle.

Since they weren't immediately responding, Natale fired again. This time the bullet tore into one of the thug's shoes. He let out a terrible yelp and hit the floor hard. He lay there holding on to his bloodied foot inside the ruined shoe as he screamed out in pain.

"What would you like to live without, buster", she said to the other thug.

He immediately dropped his pistol and began backing away. Natale wasn't happy with that as she called to him. "Hey buddy, how's about getting your belly down on the walk-way here. I think your friends will be needing some help in a little while."

Ford and Felisa stood behind the broken window, two large grins on their faces. Ford mused, "I think our friend Joey better not cross that lady."

Felisa laughed, "Her Father was in the Military. Marine Corp I believe. He was some sort of Cop in the Corp and then became a Cop in Trenton. She knows how to handle herself, so yeah, she can be a force."

They noticed Joey as he was watching Natale get the situation under control. He could be heard saying, "Now that there…that's my girl!"

The foursome thought it a good idea to make their getaway before the dust completely settled. The girls grabbed their bags as Ford picked up Cha-Cha's knife and stuck it into a support column in the restaurant. Cha-Cha's billfold, which had fallen from his coat, was skewered by the knife, held in place on the column. The Manager was behind the bar, a look of shock still on his face.

They headed toward a back door as Ford called out to the Manager, "There's a couple thousand dollars or more in that billfold. It should cover the damages as well as our food and drinks. Really sorry about the mess, but they started it."

The Manager held up his hand in a half-hearted wave. Ford called back, "We'll recommend you to all our friends. Look forward to coming back again! Better get that money before Mr. Caputo regains consciousness!" The man cringed at that last statement.

Ford turned back to the Manager with a last thought. "I'd appreciate it if you'd tell the Police it was four Cubans that did all this. Don't mention the girls…okay? *Capiche?*

Ford thought he saw the man make the sign of the cross over his chest as Joey began pushing his friend away.

Joey's excitement was absolutely exploding at that moment. "Just like the old days in Germany…right Ford?"

Natale gave Joey a stern look. Felisa just looked at Ford with amusement. Joey caught Natale's look and began defending himself.

"Now Nat…Germany was a long time ago. Ford and I don't do stuff like that now. Besides, they were bad guys!"

Natale kept her eyes of Joey, "Which ones?"

He stammered, "What do you mean which ones? I mean, they were all bad guys. Bad guys in Germany. You know, they've had some bad ones there. And these guys too! These were exceptional bad guys. They interrupted my proposal to the most beautiful woman I've ever known."

Felisa joined in, "Does that include your Mother? How about me? You used to go on and on about how pretty I was. Said you'd never look at another woman!"

Joey continued to walk and sputter. "Hey now! That's not fair. We was kids when I told you that…I hardly knew that many girls."

Both ladies gave out the same groan with Felisa saying, "Come again! That's hardly a nice thing to say. You know what, Joey? I'm very disappointed in you and so will your Mother be when I tell her what you said."

Joey was about to twist himself into the ground by now. The girl's fun was great and it did take the edge off the fact they'd had a big showdown with some sort of gangster and his men.

Joey was moaning, "Just shoot me why don't you…no, wait! Not you Natale! Hey, what'd you do with that pistol?"

Natale was having a hard time keeping a straight face by now. "I dropped the bullets and casings down a storm drain and threw the pistol in a trash can."

She hesitated a moment and gave him a big hug along with an equal sized kiss. "You're my hero Jovanni Visconti. You came to my rescue! Ford's too, for that matter. Didn't hesitate…just got in there. My man!"

She gave him another big kiss before saying, "I don't know if you heard me in all that ruckus, but I did say YES!"

Joey grabbed her and twirled her around, literally off her feet. "I never doubted it, baby. I love you, baby! I really do!"

They arrived back to the hotel without further incident. Ford sent everyone ahead to pack up their clothes. "We need to get out of

Atlantic City while we can. Throw my stuff in a bag. I need to speak with Mr. Sturgis."

Chapter Thirty-Two

"The only thing I wish you could get for me is my mind...I think I've lost it."

Ford spent over thirty minutes in the office of Traymore's Manager, Mr. Sturgis. The conversation was animated, filled with many questions by the hotel man. Sturgis punctuated their conversation by making several telephone calls as he issued orders and inquired about several things. He gently prodded Ford along in order to get each and every detail.

After the last call, he turned to Ford. "Tell me, Mr. Rawlings, do you know who this man is and what he represents?"

"Well, Mr. Sturgis, I can't say that I do. My friend, Mr. Visconti, seemed to know a little about him. All I know about the man is that he was extremely rude and aggressive with me and my friends".

"Did it ever occur to you to just speak with the gentleman which may have kept all of this hullaballoo from occurring?"

Ford ran his hand across his chin. "Yeah…well, even if I'd sat down with that clown, he still wouldn't have liked the answer I gave him. If he didn't like "No" when he was standing in front of me, he wouldn't have liked it anymore if I was sitting across from him."

Sturgis was making some notes on a pad which he handed to one of his assistants. "Yes…you are probably correct. I am sorry this has happened to you and your friends today. It is most unfortunate."

Ford leaned forward. "You know, when he tried to push Felisa out of his way and spoke to her disrespectfully…that was just too much. She didn't deserve that."

Sturgis laughed, "Yes, I would assume he realizes that now. I am sorry the lady was caught in the middle of this!" He then looked over his round eye glasses at Ford. "I actually think you did the right thing. These young punks need to be taught a lesson. There aren't many who would let a man walk away if he pulled a knife or had his men pull their guns. I must say, you are a very resourceful group indeed."

There was a knock on the office door and one of the Manager's assistants entered. He spoke in whispers to Mr. Sturgis who responded by nodding his head several times. Another person came in bringing a small silver tray of fruits and cheeses as well as a decanter of chilled wine. Sturgis wrote a couple of notes, "Please…eat, drink. It will keep your digestive system from retaining too much acid caused by the ordeal. I have also sent the same to your suite."

Sturgis stood, giving instructions to his assistant and handing him the notes. Ford didn't know what else to do so he poured himself a drink and picked up a bunch of grapes, mindlessly nibbling.

The assistant left with his instructions and Sturgis returned to his chair. He appeared to be in deep thought as he plucked a toothpick holding a small wedge of cheese from the tray.

Ford couldn't hold it in any longer. "So, what's our move? I don't want to get involved with the Police here and I'd like to go back home before another goon squad rolls in looking for us?"

Sturgis popped the cheese into his mouth and chewed slowly. "Keeping this away from the Police is something we can most certainly do. The other has more far-reaching implications. Some of which, I will not be able to offer assistance."

Ford sat his glass down. "What is the "some of which" you are talking about?

"Here's the truth, Mr. Rawlings. The Caputo's are gangsters. I don't know what they wanted with you. You were right to turn them down…probably before you even knew what they were asking. That was good instincts."

With that, he began to surmise his thoughts. "Herein lies the main problem you now have. If they somehow found you here, there was a reason. They wanted you away from the Visconti's to discuss this matter. I'm sure it has something to do with the Visconti's business…maybe something they have already discussed with the brothers and was turned down. So, one thing I would suggest is that you discuss this with the Visconti's as soon as possible."

Ford was intrigued as Sturgis continued. "Keep in mind, they found you here, they will most certainly be looking for you in Trenton. You and your friends have done damage not only to Caputo's son, but to some of his men, and just as importantly, his ego. So, I must say this, it isn't over."

Ford nodded in agreement as he thought of the implications of what was still to happen. "How did they know to look for me here?"

"A very good question, Mr. Rawlings. I would imagine they have an informant at the trucking company. It would be very beneficial to flush this person out into the open and deal with him…or her."

Sturgis stood signifying the meeting was all but over. "Mr. Rawlings, let me assure you that you and your party will be in safe keeping as we deliver you back to your homes. After that…well, please be careful. The Visconti's and Mr. Moretti will be valuable assets on the other end."

Sturgis was acting uneasy with the last statement he was about to make. "I don't think they will try anything with Miss Gervasè or Miss Ricci. However, this is not something I can guarantee. The Caputo's are like animals. They would eat their young if it benefited them. All I can say is to be very careful. Watch out for those you love. Don't let your guard down. I wish you the very best and hope to see you another time under better circumstances."

Ford was left standing outside Sturgis' office. Two young men were standing there, waiting to escort him upstairs. Instead, Ford stopped, turning to look at his reflection in a decorative wall mirror.

Ford was frozen in front of the mirror. The hairs on his neck were standing on end. He suddenly recalled Uncle Joe's comments of what was to come, *"...watch out for yourself and those you care about."*

Ford found himself rubbing the back of his neck, trying fiercely to make this foreboding feeling leave. He closed his eyes tightly and found that he discovered a ragged crack opening up in his mind. The crack was allowing something to be released into his consciousness. It wasn't a source of light coming through the crack though. It was a flood of memories…dark, ugly memories. No, there wasn't any type of light at all…it was a darkness seeping through. Suddenly, inside that darkness a face appeared! It looked as if it were crying out in pain. It looked like Julia. Not the beautiful Julia of another lifetime. No, it was the face of a tormented Julia…that is, until it changed into the face of Felisa!

Ford opened his eyes and found himself staring into his reflection in the mirror. His thoughts raced, *"This is bad! This can't happen again! Hell itself has made a pact to destroy me and anyone I care about!"*

Ford let out a cry of pained anguish as he slammed his fist into the mirror. The glass shattered, falling to the floor along with the gilded frame. The sound penetrated the walls causing Mr. Sturgis and his Assistant to come out of the office as a few guests looked on in shock.

Sturgis' eyes fell on Ford's bloodied fist. The two escorts were at a loss as to what to do. Mr. Sturgis took control immediately. He sent one of the escorts to bring the hotel Doctor to his office. His assistant took Ford by the arm and led him inside to a seat. He then poured Ford a strong drink and filled up a cloth napkin with ice from an ice bucket. Gently wrapping the ice filled napkin around Ford's fist he asked if there was anything else he could get him.

Ford looked the fellow in his eyes as he said, "Thanks! The only thing I wish you could get for me is my mind…I think I've lost it!"

The fellow, only known as Lyle, broke the intensity of the moment by laughing out loud at Ford's statement. His response pleased Ford. "I'll get right on that Mr. Rawlings. Perhaps I'll find my own as I look for yours."

Chapter Thirty-Three

"Leave them be, Joey. They've been out slaying dragons today..."

The sight of Ford's bandaged hand shocked Felisa when he walked into the suite. Before she could say anything, he held up both hands saying, "It's fine! Really! Just a stupid accident is all. Nothing to get upset about…just a cut or two. I did it to myself."

He quickly explained their situation without going into every detail. He certainly didn't want to discuss the possibility of the Caputo's bringing their vengeance down on the foursome.

"Mr. Sturgis has a limo waiting. It's at a back entrance…just to be safe. Is everyone packed?"

To answer his question, Felisa brought him his suitcase containing all of his clothes and accessories. She gave him a light kiss on the cheek…then stood back to look him in the face. Her lips quivered a bit as he could see her adrenalin rush was worn off. Instead of saying anything, he pulled her to him and gave her a lingering, intimate kiss.

Joey blurted out, "Hey you guys! We're the ones who just became engaged! You might want to slow down."

Natale gave Joey a sharp elbow to the gut. "Leave them be, Joey. They've been out slaying dragons today…let them have some fun."

The limo was parked at a supply receiving dock in a remote area of the hotel. Hotel staff made sure that no other vehicle was parked in the area to insure it stayed secure.

Mr. Ballentine saw them off, passing along Mr. Sturgis' regards. "You will have a safe trip back home. We have contacted the State Highway Patrol of your journey back to Chambersburg. A Sargent Woodard will be catching up with you shortly to insure a safe trip. You should have no worries concerning any problems along the way."

Ford was more than a little impressed with the degree of connections afforded Uncle Joe Moretti and his group of friends.

Ballentine waved them goodbye saying, "I wish you good luck in sorting this thing out. Very sorry your stay had to be interrupted, but I must say, I'm very glad no one was hurt."

Ford laughed to himself, *Well, none of us were hurt...thank goodness!"* This caused him to look over at his friends. His face clouded at the reality that any and all of them could have been badly injured or worse.

The limo pulled away from the Traymore Hotel and the foursome soon found themselves on the highway, making good time toward home. The foursome settled into their seats, quiet in their thoughts. Each pair sat very close to each other, softly exchanging words from time to time. Ford knew they understood how close they'd come to tragedy. He also knew they all believed it was far from over. He could see it on their faces.

Ford found himself wondering if he should have just sat down with the thug and listened to his proposal. Just as quickly, he dismissed the notion. His answer at the table wouldn't have changed and he knew Cha-Cha's response would have been the same. It was a certainty that the only way he walked out of the restaurant was with the same scenario. Still, he felt terrible the girls became involved. Of course, they did quite well for themselves.

This trip in the limo was very somber as if a black cloud hung inside the limo. No one spoke of the incident for fear it would become more of a reality than they'd wanted to accept.

They were soon joined by a Highway Patrol car that led them all the way into Chambersburg and then to Visconti Trucking. It actually helped the mood of the passengers seeing the big man in uniform on his bike.

The driver spoke for the first time saying he had been instructed to take them directly to the trucking company.

As they passed the *Entering Chambersburg* sign, the apprehension seemed to grow instead of diminish. They pulled through what was now a guarded gate into the company's parking lot, stopping in front of the main entrance. The welcoming scene was not what they expected.

Chapter Thirty-Four

"She says they will be "dead fish"!"

Ford exited the limo, unsure as to what was going on. He spotted an armed man on one of the roofs and noticed the two fellows manning the entrance were also armed. There were a few men scattered around the grounds, each looking as if they expected trouble. Ford didn't notice the show of any weapons on those fellows, but he was sure they were present.

Dario walked out along with Joe Moretti. Their faces were grim as they walked out to meet the foursome. Dario walked directly to Joey, putting his hand on the boy's shoulder as he spoke to both him and Natale. Within a couple of minutes, they were all hugging. Ford guessed there was both relief for their safe return and welcome news of the couple's engagement in the conversation.

Felisa and Uncle Joe met on the steps leading to the front door. He patted her on the shoulders as he said something to her. She nodded, her eyes becoming at once liquid, glistening like the grass after a spring rain. Joe gave her a great hug and looked over his shoulder to Ford. He gave Ford a knowing nod of both appreciation and understanding.

It was Dario who began encouraging people to go inside. Felisa's mother, Dorotea, and Natale's mother, Clara, were waiting for them, nervously sipping on a cup of coffee. They embraced their daughters and then exchanged hugs with the other woman. Franco Ricci, Natale's Father, was coming along as soon as he finished his shift. He was a Policeman but right now he was a Father who understood his daughter had been in danger. The fact that he would be a force in this situation was encouraging.

Ford stood watching the family reunions, understanding he was still a bit of an outsider here. It was Dorotea that first approached him, offering a hot cup of coffee and a warm hug. She inquired about his bandaged fist, accepting his explanation it was but an accident.

She hugged him again and whispered in his ear, "My thanks for protecting my daughter from those *animali*...I detest such *bestia!* She almost spat the last two words of pronouncement concerning Cha-Cha Caputo and his men.

Ford spoke softly, "Your daughter…she was very brave. She handled herself well. Stood right up to ole Cha-Cha. In fact, she was the one that first put him on the ground. I was proud of her…you'd been proud of her too."

Another voice entered the conversation as Dario's wife, Gisella, seconded the indictment towards the Caputo's. "The Caputo family are despicable, every one of them! They have made a mistake attacking this family and our friends. They will be *pesce morto* if they continue."

Ford looked at Dorotea for understanding. She smiled rather cruelly, "She says they will be "dead fish"!"

The reunions and conversations continued as more people came and went. Excited voices registered the announcement of Joey's and Natale's engagement. Felisa had fallen in with a group of ladies who were curious as to what all had happened.

Ford found himself hungry for the first time since lunch. He went looking for food and found platters of antipasto. The varieties changed from platter to platter. He was enjoying grazing through the food offerings as he was left alone in his thoughts. The sounds around the office came across as almost festive. Ford knew that this would soon end. He would soon be in a very serious conversation with the Visconti Brothers and their cohorts.

Ford was pouring himself his third cup of coffee after eating two tasty *sfogliatelle* from a platter. The shell-shaped, filled Italian pastries were among his favorites. He fondly remembered his Mother making them from the time he had memories.

Sipping the hot coffee, he caught sight of Dario motioning him to come into the Brother's large office. He joined Dario in the smoke-filled office along with several additional occupants. Dario's brother, Brizio, was there with his sons Nino and Gasparo. Joey was sitting on a leather sofa while his three brothers, Leone, Ilario, and Giapaola stood at various places along the wall.

Everyone was holding or puffing on either a cigarette or a cigar except Uncle Joe who sat on a stool, steadily puffing on a briar pipe. The man wore a grim look on his face. Sitting in one corner was a fellow by the name of Sal Marchetti. Ford was never exactly sure as to what all he did for the Company. His job seemed to entail looking into any problem the brothers ran into. He was a tough guy who never said much but communicated well all the same.

Sal would come to Ford from time to time to ask about the Company's trucks, wanting to know if any needed replacing or if parts were forthcoming from their vendors. He also spent time picking Ford's brain concerning the 1951 Cadillac Coupe Deville he was re-building. Recently, they had been discussing dropping in another engine that could exceed the standard 160 horse power engine. Sal was also considering re-doing the transmission, possibly converting to a manual floor shifter. Ford was of the opinion Sal was trying to decide whether to race the car or just make it the slickest looking and driving '51 Caddy on the road. As Ford walked into the room, Sal nodded, a very serious look on his face.

One other fellow was seated in the opposite corner. He was older and wore his salt and pepper hair in a short, military style cut. Ford was not familiar with him at all but immediately felt him to be another serious man. One look told Ford the man knew how to handle himself in any type of situation. On the man's large right hand, a heavy ring was emblazoned with some sort of Military insignia.

Brizio and Dario stood behind the desk, speaking in low, serious tones. It was Brizio who first addressed the group of men.

"First of all, you are all here because you are trusted. We must emphasis that everything you hear today must not be spoken of to anyone…ANYONE…outside of this group of men. Not only is this Company facing a dangerous time, but we, along with our families could find ourselves threatened. This also holds true for all of our drivers. I want to assure those who drive our trucks that we will begin sending an armed guard with them for the present."

Dario allowed those words to settle in as he took the lead. "About five months ago we attended a meeting with the head people of Wolf Pharmaceuticals. They are old friends and business partners. It was a productive meeting and one in which we found to be of great interest. Because of the nature of products being transported, the meeting has been kept secret. Unfortunately, we were not wholly successful in our attempts at secrecy."

Brizio spoke up again, "Trust me gentlemen…what you hear today will be the type of information that could put lives in danger. "He paused, as if needing an extra breath. "Let me be candid…I speak not only of your lives but possibly of those you love and care about. The Caputo Family are *suino! Spregenole* in every way!"

Dario spat the last few words. Joey was sitting next to Ford. He leaned over and whispered, "He called them swine…despicable. We've had run-ins with them before. Remember that idiot, Tony Fentilucci. The one who came over here to teach you a lesson about you taking a ride with his girl. He's one of their tough guys. A real *stupido*…er, idiot, numbskull… well, you could see that."

Dario was still talking. "We would step aside from this endeavor if we hadn't given our word to fulfill this task. Plus, I must add that the products being shipped will help protect many precious children. The Caputo's have caught wind of this business and wish to line their pockets with or without our help. I say to you, completing this business is both a job of honor and duty."

Brizio spoke up, "Most of you know this is not the first time the likes of the Caputo's have tried to use our business for their illegal acts. Our Father, Abramo, would not allow them to control our business and neither will we. Dario and I stand firm on this matter."

Dario spoke again. "I…we, must also tell you all that we appreciate the loyalty you've shown to the Company. You and our employees are what makes this thing we have to be successful. We don't say thank you enough."

The serious man sitting on the stool over in the corner asked a question. "Do you know how they found out about this business with the pharmaceutical company…or even how they knew where to find Jovanni and Ford."

This was followed by silence. Ford looked at Joey, wondering if there was an answer to the question along with his own question of…*who was this guy.*

Joey whispered, "That's Natale's Father, Franco…the cop."

Ford looked again at the man. "He looks as hard as a rock. You better behave yourself, ole son…that man looks as if he could tear a man's arm off and beat him to death with it."

Joey winced a little, "Well, he likes me…and his Wife, Clara, thinks I'm the "sweetest boy" …and Natale loves me." He ran his hand back through his thick black hair. "I'll tell you the truth…he does scare me a little, but he's been nice to me so far." He paused, "You know, he asked two really good questions, though."

Dario was whispering something to his brother. First one nodded and then the other. He looked at Mr. Ricci, "Franco, I appreciate your question. These are very good questions and I want to tell you as well as the others that I have an answer. You are not a part of our Company, but I will gladly share this with you also. I can only say that we do not want to bring the Police into this. I mean you no disrespect, but I'm afraid there are a few people who wear the uniform that might also have ties to the Caputo's."

Franco nodded, "No offence taken. Unfortunately, you are most likely correct. We have our share of *ratti* just like everyone else. Let me assure you that I'm only here to help any way that I can. I will be discreet."

With that, Dario continued, "The Caputo's informant was someone close to us all. He came to Brizio and myself only this afternoon when he realized what was going on. We have been able to figure many things out now that we know how information has been leaked."

There was grumbling in the room and a few questioned what was being done to the "rat". Before their question could be answered it was evident they all had their eyes on Franco Ricci to see how he reacted to the answer.

Dario rubbed the stubble on his face as if he was having a difficult time answering the question. "Here's the truth. It was Mikey."

The room suddenly became louder as several voices tried to speak at once.

Dario held up both hands to silence the group. "It's not what you think. Let me tell you the story before you start calling for Mikey's head."

The room quietened with everyone's attention now on Dario. "You all know Mikey…a sweet kid, really. He has family blood on his Father's side. He works hard and does everything he's asked to do. Because of his job with us, he picks up on many things that happen in our business. We didn't know about this, but some time ago he met a girl. He said she called herself Immacolata Leone. Through our own resources, we have found out that her real name is Luciana Caruso. She is on the payroll of the Caputo's. She does many unpleasant things for them. Some say she is more dangerous than any man on the Caputo's payroll."

Dario found a need for a drink of water from the cooler in the office. Brizio took over the telling. "This woman found Mikey and pretended to become infatuated with him…and with his work. Mikey says she is a beautiful woman which amazed him that she took so much interest in getting to know him."

Brizio paused, "We all know that Mikey has had little luck with female companionship. Anyway, they began seeing each other and before long their dates became intimate. While in their intimate moments, she began to pull information from him about the Company. She had him in her bed and then acted as if his work was very interesting to her. Mikey fell hard, giving up all sorts of information to impress her."

Dario regained the lead. "The Caputo's have been trying to find out who some of our customers are and what we transport for them for many years now. We know they follow our trucks at times. Many of our customers are obvious…but they hold little interest because of the goods we transport for them. However, there are always a few customers that provide goods of a very lucrative manner."

The dance continued as Brizio took the floor. "Old Arturo made threats to our Father many times over the years. It seems every time they need to come up with some quick money they try a hijacking scheme with some trucking company. We know they have discovered what we will be doing with Wolf Pharmaceuticals and I'm sure they believe they can turn it into a nice profit for them and their New York bosses."

There were low murmurs of conversation that ended as Brizio cleared his throat rather loudly. "You see, we too have informants. It appears the Caputo's are in some trouble with their Family in New York. They've been looking for a big score in order to pay off some debts incurred because of bad business deals they've done. In other words, they need to buy themselves back into the good graces of their bosses."

Franco Ricci spoke up, "What's going to happen to Mikey?"

The question hung in the air. Joe Moretti stood and offered an answer. "I am not a part of this business and I'm not a part of this family's blood, directly. Some of my children have entered into a Holy union of marriage with members of the Visconti family, so I can claim this family to be my own. We have been very good friends for many years. That is my claim to a right to speak on behalf of the Visconti's."

He cleared his throat, "Mikey was very forthright about everything. He realized what was happening when he heard that Jovanni and Ford were attacked by the Caputo's. Mikey is not the fool some may perceive him to be. It may be that Mikey needs to go away for a period of time. He realizes that for the time-being, he will have no access to the Visconti's business. It is more prudence than punishment. I will say this, we can thank God that Mikey caught on to what was happening. We can also be thankful that this *puttana,* Luciana, did not have opportunity to murder Mikey."

Dario's voice was full of emotion as he interrupted. "We talked it over with Mikey and came up with a plan where he would just play along and see if we could take advantage of this situation. He tried to contact her today but she no longer lives in the apartment she used. We believe that Luciana was either finished with Mikey or may have become fearful she was exposed. She has disappeared it seems. This does concern us because we know from our sources that she is also used as an assassin by the Caputo's. It is another reason that we…and I mean our families also, must be of constant vigilance in safeguarding each other."

Brizio added, "We have used all of our resources to figure this out over the last six hours of so. I'm sure the Caputo's are trying to be very careful so as to not tip their hand. As for now, our resources have dried up for the most part, but we did find out many valuable things today.

These troubles will be reconciled and we will not allow the Caputo's to persevere. They've overstepped when they chose to do violence against Jovanni and Ford. Santino Caputo has the temperament of his father with little sense of restraint. We will meet their violence with violence if necessary. My brother, along with counsel from Joe Moretti are working out a plan. It has, by necessity, been put together quickly so I'm sure we will need to adapt it as time goes forward. It is a plan that will require many parts working together. Gentlemen, you are the parts that will make this plan work."

Chapter Thirty-Five

"...He hasn't called me "son" yet...but he will."

The plan was set, more or less. Five of the Visconti's largest trucks were designated to pick up the merchandise at Wolf Pharmaceuticals early the next Wednesday. The merchandise in question was vaccine used to prevent the awful disease of polio. They would travel in caravan style from the trucking company to the pharmaceutical company. From there, t caravan would carry the vaccine to a New York dock and loaded on a ship. Normally, this would be a simple job for any trucking company. This time, there would be nothing simple about this job.

Louis Salk developed the vaccine that was first distributed in 1955. There was already a noticeable drop in children contacting the terrible disease in the United States. This shipment of the latest version of the polio vaccine would be going across the Atlantic. The shipment was going to an organization that would begin distributing the vaccine into poor and hard-pressed areas. It was just the type of products that could bring a good price on the "black market". The whole matter only underlined the fact that a criminal's avarice outweighed even the basic needs of poor children.

The Visconti's and Wolf Pharmaceuticals had been business partners for over two decades. They had worked together through good times and bad. Dario and Brizio understood loyalty and they understood the position of stewardship they accepted as a trusted business partner. Another thing they understood was the value of children. If they lost money on this contract they were still determined to keep the polio vaccine from falling into Arturo Caputo's hands.

The fact that the Visconti's knew of the Caputo's treachery and plans to hijack the shipment was of great help. Franco Ricci was helpful as he discreetly gathered information about the gang, the number of thugs that might be available to the Caputo's, and any rumblings from the many informants available to the Police Department.

It was indeed sad that the Visconti's did not fully trust the Police to deal with this matter. The combination of a lack of hard proof and the possibility of leaks through the Department made it seem more prudent to work this out on their own. They could have hired a private army of armed guards to protect each truck, but that wouldn't have worked forever, plus the cost would be much too expensive. It seemed best they go about their business while luring the Caputo's into a scenario that might put an end to this for good. It wasn't what they wanted but neither did they want to continue running their business while looking over their shoulder each and every day.

It was hoped that the Caputo's had an urgent need to create revenue for their bosses. That, and greed, should cause them to try and hit this first load of vaccine. All that was certain was that it would not be long before they found out how badly the Caputo's needed the shipment and how much they actually knew.

Routes were checked and re-checked. The best probable spots for an ambush were noted. As best they could, everyone tried to look as if they were just going about business as usual with no hint of what the Caputo's were planning. If the Caputo's still held to the belief they would have the element of surprise on their side, it could all end quickly. Even though the Caruso woman was not to be found, they hoped her information would still be perceived infallible.

Mikey was now secreted away in a safe location. They were afraid the assassin would come looking for him since he could recognize her at some future date. They could only hope Mikey was the only leak. There was concern and uncertainty as to why the Caruso woman dropped from sight. If they were lucky, she felt her job finished and wished to be through with Mikey. As for Mikey's long-term safety, that would need to be addressed later.

The remainder of the preparations were coming together as quickly as possible. Only the very top people at Wolf Pharmaceuticals had any idea of what was about to happen. They lobbied to call in Law Enforcement from either a State or Federal Government Agencies. The Visconti's prevailed however, setting their own plan into action.

Ford Rawlings stood outside the garage, a smoldering cigarette dangling from his mouth. He rarely smoked but found a little quiet solace in the burning tobacco. His thoughts were connecting the string of events that had brought him from his home to this exact spot. Visions of North Carolina, of Julia, and of his Parents flooded his mind.

One very unpleasant thought that kept popping up was the image of Sheriff Royal Majesty. Ford thought, *"One of these days I'm coming for you Royal. If I survive all of this, it's going to be sooner than later. I'm going to find out all of your deepest secrets and then I'm going to burn you down with them. I'm going to find out what you know about Julia's death and then you are going to pay for every hair on her head you are responsible for harming."*

"Hey buddy, that's the sourest look I've seen on anyone's face since the beginning of time. You okay?"

It was Joey of course. Who else could be so light-hearted at a time like this? "Don't overthink this thing, man. We've been driving these routes for a long time now. You'll know what to do anywhere along the line. Besides, the Caputo's may decide to forget the whole thing. They've got to be wondering if we know anything."

Joey brightened as he said, "Besides, who in the world is going to catch the famous moonshine runner, "Hot Rod" Rawlings"?

Ford smiled at this. It'd been a long time since anyone had called him "Hot Rod."

It was true, Ford was well acquainted with the highways and bi-ways from Virginia to New England. Ford had been following a dual role for the company for many months now. He still kept the garage working efficiently but was also driving some for the company. It had been good to get out of the garage and feel the open road blow by again. He'd driven to the port in New York on a few occasions and was well aware of the routes that were safest as well as alternate routes if trouble occurred.

They knew the Caputo gang had people watching the firm. Their men were posted discretely around the property to watch the watchers. Precautions were being made to make sure family members were safe from abduction or could be compromised in any way.

All of this was being done with as little show as possible. A few new men were seen patrolling the Company's property. They tried to maintain a low profile while adding extra eyes to the scene. All of them were cleared by either the Visconti's or Joe Moretti.

Ford's mind was pre-occupied with what was going to happen and what could happen. Joey kept talking away but was being ignored.

"Listen Ford, I was thinking about something we need to do as soon as we get past this thing."

Joey finally had Ford's attention. "What?" Before Joey could answer, Ford finished his thought. "Listen, I didn't mean what were you saying…I mean what are you thinking about instead of what you should be thinking about?"

It sounded harsh and Joey looked at his friend wondering what was going on in his head. "Hey, look…I just wanted to talk about something besides this big showdown. It's going to all work out. It's a good plan!"

Ford felt bad that he'd sounded short with his friend but he had so many things on his mind at the moment. "Joey, it's okay. Sorry about sounding so short. I shouldn't keep so many things on my mind. Now what are you saying?"

Joey smiled, knowing his old friend was conflicted on so many levels. He could tell Ford's mind was back in North Carolina more than it had been for a long time. He didn't want to be someone who wasn't sensitive to his friend's turmoil. At the same time, he wanted Ford to think of the other side of this run-in with the Caputo's. He wanted him to see possibilities.

"I don't know about you, old buddy, but I was thinking we'd try another trip. I don't like having that fiasco with Cha-Cha as my most recent memory of a vacation. I'm sort of soured on the Atlantic City scene, anyways. I was thinking the four of us could go to Philly or maybe get a little extra time and do the sightseeing thing in Washington, D.C. I'm always up for New York, too."

Ford frowned a little at this idea but Joey plugged on. "We'll all go on our own dime…leave Papa Joe out of it. Our own little vacation with no strings attached. I think the girls would love it! What do you think? I bet Felisa has never seen D.C."

Ford still not reply…at least at first. He flipped the cigarette stub away as he looked into the sky and then back to Joey. "Yeah, that might be okay. You know…if this turns out without too many problems."

Joey's smile grew but quickly diminished as Ford said, "Look…I know you've found the love of your life in Natale. I think you two are great together and I wish you all the best of happiness." He paused, searching for words. "I'm just a little worried about me and Felisa. She is everything any man should want and more than any man deserves…including me."

Joey started to protest when Ford cut him off. "I'm just saying I'm grateful. To Felisa and to her Mom…and you and Natale. It just worries me…I don't have too good a record with my love life. I'd never do anything to hurt her or let her down. I just don't want to take her down a path that might hurt her in some way. She's much too fine a person to be disappointed in her life again. I'd drive off a cliff before I'd do that."

Joey put a hand on Ford's shoulder. "Don't worry Ford. If you hurt that little lady, her Uncle Joe will personally take you to that cliff and give you a push."

Ford smiled, "You better take your own advice old son. I have a feeling that if you mess this up with Natale, Mr. Franco Ricci will cut your nuts off and Natale will fry them up in a hot skillet."

Joey smiled at first and then the visual struck him. He defended himself, "Hey now! Natale loves me and so does her Mother. And just to be clear, me and Franco are becoming real *buoni amici*...er, good friends. I think he was impressed that I handled that goon of Cha-Cha's when he tried to pull that gun."

He grinned broadly, "He hasn't called me "son" yet...but he will."

Ford looked at Joey for a long minute. Joey felt a little uneasy so he asked, "What? Why're looking at me like that? You're acting a little strange my friend."

Ford chuckled, "Nothing...really. I was just picturing you talking in a much higher pitch when Franco and Natale get through with you." He laughed again, "Trust me, it's not a pretty sight. If I were you, I'd wouldn't do anything to poke that old dog...or his pup either."

Chapter Thirty-Six

"That's the most hellacious looking truck I've ever seen."

Tuesday came quickly and so did Tuesday evening. The planning was finished and all the trucks were ready to go. Ford and Joey were just finishing up some final modifications to a Company truck. It was a 1949 Dodge B1B ½ ton pickup. Ford had previously modified the engine to exceed the standard 95hp it normally topped out. The flathead, straight-six engine could be counted on to haul all the extra weight that had been added to the chassis.

There were remnants of the original dark green paint still to see but other than that aspect, it looked little like the 1949 Dodge. The rear window was missing and the actual opening was made larger. There was a heavy rectangular piece of heavy metal welded to the back of the truck where the tailgate once sat. It rose about four and a half feet from the truck bed. Heavier tires and larger side mirrors were added to the vehicle giving it a unique look. Underneath was a heavier suspension. There were several crates set along the sides of the bed that held surprises.

The oddest look of the modified vehicle were two round metal posts that now protruded forward through the front fender wells, ending ahead of the steel bumper.

Joey was heard to say, "That's the most hellacious looking truck I've ever seen. Those Caputo boys will take a look at this thing and run right off the road."

Ford stretched out of his coveralls. "That'd be great, but I don't imagine it'd be that easy. Wish we had about a half dozen more of these. I guess one will do plenty of damage, though."

He lit a cigarette and blew the smoke into the darkening sky. "Your cousins have the flatbed truck ready to pick this up tonight? The cover for it is in one of those crates on the bed. They need to get it there by sun-up tomorrow."

Joey was out of his coveralls and combing his jet-black hair. "They'll pick it up in about an hour. Lucio and Isaia are going in separate cars but they'll meet up with the truck along the way. I don't think there'll be any problems along the way but they can make sure of that. Both will have a guy in their truck with a shotgun just in case. I really don't know why anyone would follow a single flat-bed truck anyway. It's gonna be fine."

Ford dropped the cigarette after only three deep drags, crushing it with his foot. "Jovanni Visconti, always the optimist! That must be a good feeling Joey…always seeing the best side of everything. Does disappointment ever bring you down?"

Joey looked away, out of the shop. A hardening of his features was noticed by Ford. "Look Joey, I was just messing with you. Nothing intended…really!"

Joey turned, that old haunted look of his crossed his face. "It's okay Ford. I didn't take it wrong. It's just this is the first time in a good long time that I started doubting myself again. I'll be fine, really."

Ford felt bad he'd said anything about his friend, even in a mildly kidding way. "Look man, I'm sorry. Yeah, it's going to be fine. The Caputo's may not even show up…you know, catch a whiff in the wind that something just doesn't smell right."

Joey half grinned, "Aw, it's not that." He paused as if he was deciding on some major decision. "You know all those long rides I used to get you to take me on. I mean, I really didn't need to see that much of Germany. Heck, I've even had you running across the highways since we came back. I appreciated you never had to have an explanation."

Ford nodded, "Yeah, that' been a puzzler. I knew there was something there, just figured you'd tell me if you ever wanted to. You always seemed more relaxed when we hit the road and more like yourself when we got back."

Joey sat on a nearby stool. "I can't tell you the number of times I almost told you to just keep on driving…just drive to the end of the world and take a left or something. It's been hard for me, Ford. I never expected so much and didn't think I even wanted it. Hell, I never thought I'd be the one doing it and certainly didn't believe I could live up to it. I guess I still think that way at times."

Ford was a little confused, "I don't think I know exactly what you mean. What kind of "it" made you so antsy?"

"This Company, Ford. Running this Company. I never thought I'd be the one who'd be doing it one day. I mean, I've got brothers and cousins. My Pop and Uncle Brizio could have picked any one of them…or maybe one from each family. Hell, they could have done almost anything. Instead, they decided I'd be the one to take their place someday."

Ford pulled up another stool. "What do you mean they picked you?"

"It's like this. I'm the youngest. I never thought they'd look to me to take over running this Company. It's this way, I'm out of High School and I begin taking a few business classes at a nearby college. Made good grades without even trying that hard. It just all clicked. I mean, I never had any problems in High School with any subject. College didn't seem to be much different. I went three years and everything was fine. I was studying and making good, solid grades. Dating some fine college ladies. You know, having a great time."

Joey reached for a pack of cigarettes lying on a work bench and lit one. This was very rare for Joey, Ford thought. He liked his cigars but he'd never seen him touch a cigarette.

"In my senior year of college my Pop and Uncle take me out to dinner one night. It was a great meal. Best steaks…a few drinks and really good cigars. I felt on top of the world. I mean, here's two men who I would try and walk on water for and they take me out and treat me like I'm the greatest guy on earth. Then they tell me."

Joey took a long draw from the cigarette and slowly released the smoke.

Ford felt like he'd missed something. "So, what did they tell you? Was it that you were going to have to work the rest of your life?"

Joey smiled, "No, it wasn't that. That, I already knew. No, they told me it had been decided I'd be the one to take over running the Company one day. It was all going to be put on my shoulders. Everyone would be working for me and everyone would be relying on me to continue the family legacy. I thought I'd lose the best steak I'd ever eaten right there on that restaurant floor."

He crushed the cigarette. "It just floored me, man. I never expected it or saw it coming. They said I had the abilities and the smarts to take the Company into the future. I was smart but it was more than that. I also understood both the American ways as well as the old Italian traditions. They told me it would stand with my brothers and my cousins. They would support me and be loyal to me. I mean, it was decided. I had no choice…I had no way out. I felt trapped…and badly ill-equipped."

Ford pulled a cigarette now. "So, you joined the Army. Not much of an escape if you ask me."

Joey laughed. "I figured it would put off the inevitable long enough for them to change their mind. Either that, or it would give me time to wrap my head around the whole thing better. But, that just wasn't happening. I'd get these feelings that I was going to fail…just mess it up for everyone. Everything my Grandfather built would come crashing down. I'd just let my whole family down and then what?"

Ford walked over to an old vending machine and bought two Root Beers. "Best I can do for now. Nurse this for a while."

Joey took the bottle and downed half of it in one long gulp. A loud belch followed. "I can't tell you how much I appreciate those long rides. I'd just about be ready to explode, then I'd get you to take me on a long ride. That was the only thing that would calm me down. Man, I think you saved me more times than you could ever know. I'd never made it without those rides. I just don't know how I can ever thank you enough?"

Ford looked down at the floor as silence filled the garage. Finally, he took a sip of his drink as he looked around the room. "This here is plenty thanks enough my friend. I don't know where I'd have gone…if you hadn't brought me here. The closest thing to having a plan was to get an old car and drive off to Alaska or somewhere and just eventually die. If not that, I would have gone back to North Carolina half-cocked and tried to kill the Sheriff or something else mostly stupid. Either way, I was going to die alone and probably not in the best of situations."

Ford leaned over and tapped Joey's bottle. "So, here's to you my friend. Maybe we saved each other. I'm still going back to North Carolina but not for revenge…maybe a little vengeance. If that happens, I'll know exactly why."

Joey looked up smiling. "Here's to you, Ford. Best damn moonshine runner I've ever known. I only hope you can find peace one day."

Ford smiled back, "I can see you running this place one day. I think you'll make a hell of a Company President. Heck, if I was you, I'd make Natale your Vice-President. That girl will keep you straight while you're running this place. You two will have trucks running from here to California."

Joey's expression softened at the mention of Natale's name. "She's great…I can't imagine doing anything or being anybody without her." He paused and swallowed a little. Looking over at Ford he simply said, "Felisa?"

Ford sighed, a forlorn look on his face. "Just can't say partner. I've got to go back to North Carolina and I just couldn't take her with me…not now…maybe ever. I've got a lot of ghosts that will not leave me alone till I settle this. And when I do finish it, well, it may have just finished me. Surviving it won't mean I've completely won. My life will have changed but I'm not sure I'll be better for it. Guess I've just got to see what happens."

Finishing his drink, he held the bottle by its neck. "The only thing I know for sure is that Felisa has had a lot of troubles in her life and all I might be able to offer her is a lot more…at least right now."

Ford's voice became hollow, as if adding any emotion to it would cause him harm. "Felisa and Julia are similar…in a way. Both of them…completely generous, warm and honest. Both have made me laugh as well as touched my most tender feelings. I'm a better person because of them. And…they both have made me feel scared to death. Julia died because of me and I can't help but wonder if knowing me will cause Felisa to become another victim."

With that being said, Ford threw the empty bottle into a wall of the garage. He did nothing but stare out into what could only be the emptiness before him.

Joey rose, startled at the sudden change in Ford's demeanor. "You can't look at your life that way, Ford. It's not fair. Not to you and certainly not to Felisa. Hell, man, I don't think it's even fair to the memory of Julia. You've just got too many things on your mind right now. Stop thinking of what's behind you and don't worry about what's further down the road. Take care of what is right now, man."

Ford stood there, not moving or responding. Joey spoke again in a more even tone, "You know, Ford. Felisa might like to have a say in your decision. She's a very capable person. I think she's already invested a lot in you and she could become your best asset. Don't make your choices just based on how you feel about your past. That's not fair to you or Felisa."

Ford mulled the words over in his mind. He could see a life with Felisa as easily as he could see the sun rise in the morning. Knowing her was the closest thing he had experienced since his days with Julia. At that moment, another thought flashed across his mind. The thought was like a bolt of lightning across a black sky. He saw himself standing by Julia's grave and he saw the smug look of Sheriff Royal Majesty staring at him from the crowd of people offering their last respects. He looked up at Joey, only saying, "We'll see!"

Chapter Thirty-Seven

"I love you Ford...I always will."

Joey used the shower at the garage, then left to see Natale. He was accompanied by one of Brizio's men and one of the tough-looking men Papa Joe sent over. The security made Joey feel ridiculous even though he understood the necessity.

Natale was so concerned for her fiancé that she offered to join him on Wednesday. Joey, of course, would not let her go. He didn't doubt her sincerity, bravery, or ability to hold her own in a fight. He just couldn't let her be aware of the crazy part he would have in a possible running battle with the Caputo gang.

Natale wasn't the only one not going. Joey's brothers and first cousins were told they would not be a part of the caravan. They were all married and had children. Therefore, their positions would be more auxiliary and backup.

Joey and Natale's evening together was brief. Franco, Natale's father, pulled Joey aside and spoke briefly about the next day. Natale was ever amazed at how well Joey could win people over, even a hardened man like her Dad.

Franco left to take care of some details, not really telling his family where he was going. Natale's mother was a woman of strong faith, always active in her church. Joey figured part of that came from being married to a man whose life had always been in a dangerous profession.

But in truth, Clara's story was much more than that. Yes, she was always concerned for her husband as well as her children. She did pray a lot and she did read her Bible a lot. Joey began to notice that the prayers, which she often said out loud, were much more than selfish requests or memorized sentences. They were sincere, repentant, and filled with joy. He also noticed that many of the Bible verses she memorized were often a part of her prayers.

So, when Clara Ricci sat down and asked Joey and Natale to join her in prayers for the coming day, they felt no other option but to join her. The prayer time lasted barely five minutes. It was a prayer of faith instead of some rote sentences strung together or a blanket request for safety for all, especially those she loved. No, Joey was left with the feeling he had been in the presence of the Almighty God. It was a good feeling and one that left him truly optimistic. Not that God was on their side and not the Caputo's. Joey just knew that the important vaccine they were transporting would reach the children in need and that those involved with this transfer were doing a righteous service.

Joey left the Ricci's house in an upbeat mood. Even the presence of his two bodyguards didn't bring him down. He was beginning to look forward to the day in which he would be the one leading this company into the future. Natale and him. It would not be an easy task for either of them but he finally felt he could be the person responsible to do what was required. He just had to live through tomorrow.

Ford planned on swinging by Felisa's house before heading home. He knew he wouldn't stay long and he was sure he would not require any bodyguards. Ford headed to his car only to find Sal Marchetti leaning against the fender, a burning cigarette hanging from his mouth. A trail of lazy smoke lifted from the half burned-up sleeve of tobacco. He was so still it appeared he'd drifted off to sleep while smoking.

"Hello Sal. Don't suppose you're just resting here a few minutes before you head home?"

Sal removed the cigarette and looked at it like he'd just discovered it was there. He dropped it on the ground and slowly ground it out as he spoke. "Yeah, I'm going home. Just so you know, I'll be following you to yours first. So, I'd appreciate it if you don't stay too long at Felisa's. Listen, I understand. You got to go see your girl. But you see, it's a long, hard day tomorrow and the sun will be up before you know it."

Ford protested. "Just go on home Sal! I'll be fine. I've got no need of a babysitter."

Sal spat out a loose piece of tobacco he'd just discovered. "Right. You ain't no baby and I'll not be sitting for you. But I will follow you to Felisa's and then I will follow you home. And if anybody comes to mess with you they'll be having a conversation with Mr. Smith and Wesson here." He patted the holstered weapon hanging just under his jacket.

"It's not your choice and it's not mine. Joe Moretti and the Visconti's all say it's their choice. Last time I checked, two of them signed our paychecks, so I guess it's the way it's going to be. That sound okay, Chief?"

Ford just didn't have the stamina or the patience to argue the matter just now, so he nodded his head and climbed into his car. Almost twenty minutes later he was standing at Felisa's door. He'd have to admit that the two familiar faces he noticed outside the building gave him a comfortable feeling of peace concerning Felisa's and Dorotea's safety.

Ford was barely inside when Dorotea began fixing him food as Felisa set him a place at the table. He felt a little awkward at the fuss but had to admit he was hungry. The meatball sandwich at lunch was barely a memory by now.

After eating the fine meal, he wanted to curl up and go straight to sleep. Dorotea began clearing the table and encouraging Felisa and Ford to the living room. As they were talking, Dorotea came into the room to say good-night. She kissed Felisa on the cheeks and did the same to Ford. "Ford, we'll be praying for your safety tomorrow. You are doing a Godly work for the children. Be safe. You must come back tomorrow night for a proper meal. I'm sorry I didn't have you something better tonight."

Ford stood, giving Dorotea a hug and a kiss on each cheek. "That was a great meal. Reminded me of my mother's cooking. I can't give you any better compliment. I'll see you tomorrow!"

With that, Dorotea left the room and a heavy silence followed. Ford moved from his chair to the sofa where Felisa sat. She put her hand in his as they sat a little longer in silence. It didn't feel awkward at all. It only felt that once either one spoke, the world would begin changing, perhaps forever.

After a few moments, Ford started to say something. Felisa shushed him. She did it again when he started to speak a second time. After another minute or two she spoke.

"It's going to be fine. I'm positive. I'll not be worried. I'll be concerned, but I won't be worried. You can handle yourself and I won't be worried. I'm not sure the Caputo's will be brave enough to even show up tomorrow. If they do, they're fools. They're fools anyway…they aren't brave. Just cowardly fools."

It looked as if she was going to keep right on with this nervous line of thought, so Ford pulled her close and gave her a long, deep kiss.

"You sure have a way of making a girl stop talking, Mr. Ford Rawlings. I can see why all those Southern girls must have been so terribly sad when you left."

The horror of the words she'd just spoken made Felisa gasp. Before the last syllable left her mouth, she realized how cruel her jesting must have sounded to Ford. She stared at him as her eyes glistened with almost ripe tears. She was one of the very few people

Ford had shared his tragedy.

"Oh, Ford honey! I didn't mean…I was just being silly. I was thinking…I wasn't thinking at all. That was so wrong. I'm…I'm so ashamed of myself."

Ford took his hand and brushed a lock of her silky hair away from her face as small breaths were about to become sobs. "Felisa. You may not realize that I know something about you, so let me tell you. You are one of only about six of the kindest women I have ever known in my life. If it wasn't for shoe leather there'd be days I wouldn't have any taste at all in my big mouth…you know, from sticking my foot in my mouth. Anyway, I know this and I would never believe anything else. You are a sincerely kind person. You couldn't change if you wanted to. Couldn't happen."

Ford took her hands just as a solitary tear began riding down her cheek. "Felisa, I never believed I'd ever feel this close to someone again. It wasn't that you're incredibly beautiful or that you are so very smart, and brave, and funny, and just…lovely. I could only feel this close to you because you have the biggest heart of anyone around you."

She pulled Ford to her and squeezed him as hard as she could. More than a few tears ran down her cheek at that moment but she didn't care. The moment overwhelmed her and she too felt as close to anyone as she had ever felt. They relaxed their embrace and she was surprised at the look on Ford's face.

"Felisa. I wish I could say that I love you. I don't want you to think that I don't or would ever have trouble saying it…but I can't say it…just now. I can't now because it would be selfish. I've got a road to travel and it's going to be long and it's going to be ugly at times. I don't know what will be found at the end of this…this dark road. I hope when I find its end I'll still be around…but, I can't make that promise. Even if I am, I don't know how much of me will be left. It's just a hard road and there's no way to know how it's going to end."

Felisa bit her lower lip as she squeezed his hands tighter and tighter. "Ford, honey. I'll go with you…I want to go with you!"

Now Ford held both her hands together with his. "I know you would and I know just as well I'd be selfish to let you. Maybe you think I sound cruel or selfish by saying "no", but I wouldn't allow any of my own stinking hell to ever touch you."

Felisa sobbed, wanting to speak but afraid it would unleash a flood of tears.

"Listen Felisa. I hope I'll be able to come back. I want to be able to come back. I really do. If I can, I will…I mean, if I'm still me. But you have to see this for what it is. Almost every real possibility has a very bad ending. It will probably take a long time. I'm not going to North Carolina to solve this whole situation in a week or two. But listen, I promise you this. I'll do it the right way. That's the only way I'll do it. I'll try to get me through this whole thing and not become something I'm not right now. I'll do it right, even if it k…" Ford stopped just short of finishing the last two words.

Felisa forced a smile. "So, this is the part where you taste some shoe leather I'm guessing." Her words lightened the moment immediately.

She continued, "Ford, I won't go on about this. I'm pretty sure I understand how you feel…at least a part of it. I won't say I love you, even though I'm sure I do. And one other thing, I won't let you see me cry when you have to go…but I'll probably cry after you do. It's okay. It's all okay. We are merely human. Any human who gets the chance to care for someone who's very special and feels the same way about them is very lucky indeed. We're lucky Ford. Remember, it's what my name means. You've made me feel lucky…you've made me feel loved."

With that, they remained seated on the sofa…holding on to each other and wondering how they both could be so lucky together and what it would mean if they weren't.

When Ford re-entered the dark street, he felt as if he'd shed a large bag of burdens. At the same time, he felt like the biggest fool to ever walk the earth. How could anyone not love Felisa? How could he even think about leaving her? It had to be the right thing. If it wasn't he knew he'd be turning around, rushing back upstairs and taking her on one of Joey's long trips to the end of forever before they took their first left turn. Maybe that day would still come. Hope was a good thing and he was truly filled with hope. All he had to do was live through the times it took to realize hope's reward.

Felisa looked down, past the curtained window. Her emotions were as conflicted as they'd ever been. She saw Ford nod to Sal Marchetti as they both got in their cars. Ford also tipped his cap toward the darkened streets. She knew it to be a subtle gesture toward the men guarding her and Dorotea's apartment. Suddenly, a visual reality of the dangers that lay ahead for Ford Rawlings became extremely vivid to her. She shuddered as he drove off into the still night. Saying a silent prayer for him brought shivers to her body. She put her hand on the window and breathed, "I love you Ford…I always will."

Chapter Thirty-Eight

"Everything looked as it should be and nothing was what it really was."

It was a rainy Wednesday morning as Visconti Trucking came to life. Ford could not remember a time when there was so much tension around the Company. Joey, who was usually the most hyped up individual was found to be the calmest today.

In little time, the five trucks were lined up at the gate. The engines emitted a low rumble as if they were awaiting a great battle. Ford was in the lead truck and Joey drove the last one. The trucks lumbered onto a wet and dreary street as those inside the compound watched them out of sight.

As the last of the trucks rumbled into the dim morning, a man sitting in a window across the street took notice. He set his binoculars down by a cup of stale coffee and picked up the telephone. The call lasted only two minutes as the man provided every detail of the caravan and the direction they traveled.

At the other end of the line another man took down the information, then made two calls himself. One call went to Arturo Caputo and another one to a man set up to watch the progress of the caravan. The game was on and both sides were fully committed.

Ford drove the roads with one eye ahead and the other seeking anything out of the ordinary. He saw no reason for anything to happen yet. The time for the Caputo's to act was not on the way into the pharmaceutical company. Ford was almost certain that any attack would take place several miles away from Wolf Pharmaceuticals. There was a stretch of isolated road that ran up to the State Highway leading to New York. It was the area that made the most sense. It was also the area that the Caputo's would avoid.

The gangsters needed an area that would allow them time to change the crates into their own trucks. An area that the Visconti trucks could be abandoned and not found for a while. A place where bodies might be hidden away.

Ford knew an ideal place that met all their needs. The Visconti trucks could be identified so the hijackers would not want the vehicles left along the roadside. About thirty-eight miles from the factory was a small, cut-out road angling off the highway. It was originally used as a logging road but in recent years was more an access for sportsman traveling into areas for hunting and fishing. A small lake, known as Chaseburn Lake, offered a good area for recreation as well as making bodies disappear.

The lake area was developed decades before in the rolling woodlands by a young tycoon who felt he could create a resort area. He could see there were multiple streams running into a depressed area so he had a dam built and the small lake came to be. The area never developed so he began to pull resources from the land. After several years, he walked away from the land entirely when the sources of his finances finally dissolved in the Great Depression.

The Caputo's choice of this stretch of highway served two purposes. First, the logging road wasn't on current maps. It was a rough and narrow rod used only on occasion by sportsmen. Secondly, the logging road wound through the low forested land until it finally came out on a State highway several miles away. It would make for a perfect back-up escape route if it became necessary. Hiding the hijacked trucks and dead bodies would be easily done in the forest.

Ford and Joey walked down the row of trucks making sure everyone understood their roles in this dangerous race to the port in New York. Each truck held a driver and a passenger plus another surprise. Joe Moretti and the Visconti brothers had called in a few favors that would certainly be a surprise to the hijackers. One of the main rules was to stay together so they wouldn't become a solo target.

There would be a lead car and another trailing the five trucks. They symbolized the security detail to give the hijackers a reason to believe the Visconti's had taken summary precautions. Everything looked as it should be and nothing was what it really was.

Again, a pair of eyes stared after the convoy as it left the pharmaceutical company, noting every detail. After two quick telephone calls, the man left the small roadside café in his black Buick, following along behind the five trucks and two pickups. The owner of the little restaurant stood watching the man drive out of sight. Three twenty dollar bills were left in his hand for the service rendered. He was also left with the threat of harm if he ever spoke of this to anyone.

Franco Ricci provided five World War II vintage two-way radios for communications within the convoy. Ford had one in the Dodge truck as did the lead and following cars. The other two were given to the first and last trucks in the caravan. Natale's Dad also managed to get hold of a surprise piece of ordinance that could be a difference maker.

Ford drove for several miles with little conversation. He used the two-way radio a few times to remind the other drivers that the hijackers would be coming in "hot" when they hit them.

Joey was not his usual talkative self. Instead he kept singing softly the same words to the Tennessee Ernie Ford ballad, *Sixteen Tons.*

After the fifth round of singing most of the verses, Ford interrupted. "What's with that song, partner. How do you even know who Tennessee Ernie Ford is?"

"Why? Is he a relative of yours?"

"A relative? How is that supposed to be possible?"

Joey laughed, "Well, you both have pretty decent voices. Then there's the fact that you both share the same name…kinda. I mean you may look and sound like Elvis, but I can see the resemblance to ole Ernie…plus I don't know how cousins share their names in the South!"

"You *cantonata!* Yeah, I can speak a little Italian too. I learned it in North Carolina where my Italian Mother spoke it fluently. And you are a goof…you *cantonata!"*

The small amount of dialogue left both men smiling. The truth was that their minds were both on that "long drive" to anywhere else before they took a left turn.

Several miles passed and before long they were approaching the area Ford believed the attack would take place. The radio crackled as the lead car reported. Got a couple of vehicles on the right. Appear to be broken down. It's a small truck and an old Packard. Looks like they're changing a tire on the passenger side."

Ford radioed back. "Tighten your belts boys! I think it's about to begin."

The hijacker's orders were to take out the lead car and in the process, block the line of trucks. At the same time, the last car would be taken out in such a way as to block the road from behind. Armed men would rush the trucks from the woods along the road. They would directly attack the men in the cabs as soon as the caravan slowed or stopped. Violence was not addressed as they all knew it was expected.

Cha-Cha Caputo's last words to the gang of thugs was, "Whatever it takes boys…just don't make it unnecessarily bloody to begin with. We'll need some help loading the merchandise in our trucks." Then he added, "If you can get hold of that guy they call "Elvis" or that Visconti runt, Jovanni, bring 'um to me. I need to settle up with them myself. *Capiche?"*

Ford's eyes held fast to the road. Joey asked, "I think it's time, don't you?"

Ford nodded and Joey climbed through the enlarged area of the cab where the rear window used to be. As soon as he reached the bed of the pickup, he pulled on the awkward "flack-vest" his father handed him before they left that morning. "It'll give you some protection if they aren't too close. Be careful my son!"

Ford and Joey were following behind the convoy in the modified Dodge ½ ton pickup. Ford began to speed up as he anticipated the attack in only a matter of moments. Joey readied himself in the bed of the pickup as he geared up for the fight.

Ford and Joey came up on the spot where the truck and car feigned the act of fixing a flat tire. The truck suddenly lurched across the road to block their progress. Two men stood at either end of the pickup while the driver was still in the cab. The two men began waving for them to stop with one hand while the other hand held a shotgun.

Ford dropped the truck into another gear and punched the accelerator. Too late, the three hijackers realized Ford's truck was not stopping. Ford drove fiercely toward the truck blocking the road. The two men leveled their shotguns at the rapidly approaching truck. Just then, Joey popped up over the top of the cab and strafed the pickup with machine gun fire.

The thugs dove for cover rather than face the spray of bullets. Joey didn't know where his future Father-in-Law had come up with the Thompson machine gun but he knew he enjoyed the firepower. Almost instantly, Ford plowed into the parked truck, hitting it just behind the cab. The two battering ram posts made a mighty crunching sound as they contacted the sitting pickup at maximum impact.

The driver in the truck only had time to scream and duck to the other side of the cab. The explosive sound of the impact was followed by the pickup being spun around and then flipping sideways completely off the road. It ended up on its top, only a pile of worthless metal. Joey, who had ducked behind the cab, looked back to see the two thugs trying to pull the driver out of the pickup.

Ford kept his speed up as he rushed toward the convoy which he knew was now in jeopardy. Joey turned to look back when he heard a loud thud from down the road where they'd plowed through the pickup. He caught sight of black smoke billowing from what must have been the pickup. He wondered if they all had survived. When he turned back to look forward he could see the convoy coming up quickly.

Ford shouted at him through the hole in the back of the cab. "Behind you!"

Joey turned back to see two cars coming up behind them. They must have been just off the side of the road, hidden from view. Ford was traveling fast but they were catching up. The sound of gunfire was followed by the sound of bullets striking the heavy metal plate welded to the back of the truck. Several shots passed over the plate not far from Joey's head.

Joey duck-walked toward the plate as he checked the action of his Thompson. He raised enough to set the barrel of the gun into the notched area that had been cut away at the top of the plate. Raising up, he leveled the gun toward the road and began firing back, rotating from one side to the other.

The immediate effect was the luckiest of shots as it took out the whole windshield of one of the cars. He knew the driver was hit but he didn't know how badly. The car veered from the road and crashed between two trees, wedging the doors closed.

To Joey's surprise, there were still two cars following instead of one. A black Buick had joined the chase. He ducked down and grabbed one of the small crates, removing the top while shouting at Ford to speed up. As he felt the truck surge he tossed the wooden crate over the plate onto the road. The box exploded scattering a mass of sharp roofing nails onto the roadway.

One of the cars immediately lost its front two tires causing it to swerve off the road, ending up on its side in the ditch. The other car, the heavy Buick, avoided the nails by quickly moving to the shoulder. The powerful engine brought the vehicle steadily to the rear fender of the truck. The Buick hit the rear fender of the Dodge pickup causing Joey to be thrown hard onto the bed of the truck. His machine gun went flying as Joey's head made contact with one of the crates, stunning him momentarily.

Ford held the steering wheel tight in one hand and managed to call out on the radio, "Alonzo! Pull your car to your left of the truck! Georgio! Pull the truck to your right! Hard, then brake!" At the same time, Ford cut his wheels to the left allowing the speeding Buick to go past Ford's Dodge. Too late, the driver of the Buick saw the rear transport truck slowing down. The Buick driver tried to stop but his momentum carried him right into the higher bumper of the

White Motors truck.

The truck was jolted forward a bit as the heavy Buick's front end was destroyed. The driver was now a part of his steering wheel and his passenger was lying in a bloody mass half way through the windshield. One of the rear doors managed to open as a man tried to crawl out of the back seat. He managed to only fall out on the pavement, not to move any further.

Just then the radio squawked loudly. "Ford! If you're all right, I need you to get up here…NOW!"

Ford pulled to the shoulder of the road, coming to a rolling stop. The convoy was now stopping as they found an old road grader pulled into the middle of the road with two pickups on either side. The convoy's lead car was stopped in the road, smoke coming from under the hood. Both front tires were flattened and the windshield destroyed.

The men hiding in the woods began to rush the trucks. Ford shouted into the radio. Fire 'um up boys…don't let those men get to you!" Immediately, the side windows of the transport trucks lowered and the barrels of shotguns, rifles, and pistols began firing into the rushing line of men who were also firing. Smoke canisters were tossed out of the windows of the trucks, obstructing the eyesight of the on-rushing gangsters. The men in the trucks laid down a line of fire in the direction of the on-rushing men.

Ford shouted to Joey, "Stay low Joey! I'm running the gauntlet!"

The shout to Joey was fruitless because the young man was still lying on the bed of the truck, only half conscious.

Ford ducked down as far as he could and started up the left side of the convoy, half on the road and half on the shoulder. The truck was immediately a target. The windshield was destroyed and the body of the truck was pounded by slugs. Ford was living lucky as bullets tore into the cab but missed him. The reinforced door helped protect him.

Ford was able to clip a couple of the hijackers running to the trucks as he plowed forward. The firepower coming from the cabs was having an effect on the on-rushing gangsters. Those still rushing forward suddenly realized that they were also getting fired upon by another source. Small slots had opened up in the sides of the trailers. Shotgun and rifle fire added to the deadly barrage of bullets. The attackers began losing their nerve. They continued to fire, but did so as they retreated.

Meanwhile, Ford made it to the front of the convoy. He was met with more gunfire as he plowed forward. The Dodge pickup drove straight into the front of one the trucks by the road grader. The men firing their guns dove for cover as the two trucks exploded together. The stationary truck was knocked heavily backwards, its front end crushed. The impact left dust flying as well as truck shrapnel.

The jarring impact roused Joey from his semi-conscious stupor. He found himself lying up against the back of the truck cab. He began rubbing his head while realizing he was lying on something hard. Reaching down, he happily felt the frame of the Thompson machine gun.

Joey grabbed the gun and stood up to survey the carnage around him. As his eyes focused he realized Ford was having trouble getting to his weapon that had bounced into the floorboard. A man was creeping up to the driver-side window ready to fire on Ford. Joey leveled the Thompson and cut loose a short burst that tore into the man's shoulders and upper torso.

A second later two gunshots were heard from the back, driver-side of the Dodge. Joey felt the impact as it knocked him forward into the back of the cab. The pain seared into his back and side but he didn't go down. He tried to bring the Thompson around and fire at the man as he jumped up into the bed of the truck. Joey pulled the trigger of the Thompson as the pain shot through his body fouling his aim. The man ducked and was surprised to see he wasn't hit. Joey pulled the gun back up to fire again only to find he was out of ammunition. The man pointed a .38 caliber revolver toward Joey's head as he envisioned the ultimate kill shot.

The two gunshots came from within the cab instead. Ford's shots hit the gangster fully in his chest, destroying his heart instantly. Joey fell to his knees as the gangster fell hard against the hard metal plate welded to the truck bed. He glanced inside to thank Ford but instead shouted, "DUCK!"

Ford lunged toward the seat as a shotgun blast came through the front window. The sound inside cab was deafening. The man with the shotgun jumped on the trucks damaged hood and made ready to fire again. He started to stick the barrel through the shattered windshield just as three gunshots exploded as one.

Joey was firing the pistol of the fallen thug who'd jumped into the truck bed. His shots caught the shotgun man in the right leg and lower abdomen. The third shot came straight upward from the seat of the truck. Ford had rolled over and shot straight up, catching the gangster under the chin, blowing out the top of his head.

By now the gunfire had all but subsided. The remaining gangsters either had fled into the woods or were lying on the ground on their stomachs. They were being guarded by the Visconti's men who were hidden inside the cargo trailers. They had them grouped between two of the trucks. One of thugs looked up at the now opened trailer doors. He noticed the backs of the trucks were not filed with cases of inventory.

One of the Visconti's men noticed the man's gaze and asked. "What you looking at gangster?"

The man raised up to look further inside. Where's the vaccine? Looks empty from here. They change their minds?"

The Visconti's man laughed. "Those crates of vaccine are well on their way to the docks by now. You boys went to a lot of trouble for nothing. You got played, you pack of hyenas!" He pushed a shotgun barrel into the back of the man's head. "We ought to do to you what you were going to do to us!"

The wounded were being cared for and all the damages accessed. The Visconti men had four fatalities and several wounded. All in all, a small total for the amount of lead that had flown through the air. Every truck was shot up but could be driven away.

The hijackers had not fared well. They had rushed head on, feeling they had superior firepower against only mild resistance. Among the dead gangster's, was one of the Caputo brothers. However, it wasn't Cha-Cha. A few gangsters escaped into the woods. There was no need to chase them.

Ford sent a couple of men on further down the road to see if there were any surprises ahead of them. The car came rushing back as several weapons turned to face the oncoming vehicle.

The truck skidded to a halt and the passenger side door opened. A man known as "Fleck" jumped out and ran toward Ford. "There were two cars up ahead that took off when they saw us coming. I think Cha-Cha Caputo was in one of them. They made a run for it and turned off that old logging road that takes you by the little lake. Didn't know what was ahead for them so we turned around for help. We left Sammy hidden beside the road in case they decided to turn around and come back before we could get reinforcements."

Ford turned to find Joey seated on the running board of a truck. He'd shed the flack vest as well as his shirt. Underneath the tight undershirt was already found some colorful bruising around his ribs and under his shoulder. He stood, grimacing in pain.

Ford asked, "You going to be okay partner?"

Joey painfully put his shirt on. "I guess that damn vest saved me but it still hurts like hell!"

Ford was not sympathetic. "Just be happy he wasn't any closer. That jacket won't stop a gunshot if it was fired any closer." He hopped into the damaged Dodge saying, "Come on Joey! We've got one more run today. I'm going after the Cha-Cha and end this thing."

Joey moved to the passenger door, crying out in pain as he climbed inside. "I think my ribs broke…not that you care!"

Ford let the clutch out and punched the accelerator. "Don't whine…you've got plenty of ribs!"

Chapter Thirty-Nine

"It's saying things like that, that can get a fellow shot out here in the woods."

About an hour after the Visconti caravan left Wolf Pharmaceuticals, a steady stream of delivery and service trucks left the facility. They headed toward New York via an alternate route than the one taken by the convoy. There were trucks with words on the sides that noted Electrical Companies, Plumbers, Industrial Supplies, and food services. It appeared normal, howbeit, a very busy stream of such vehicles coming and then going from Wolf Pharmaceuticals.

The real truth was that almost each of the trucks leaving the facility were loaded with crates of vaccine headed to the docks in New York. It took a lot of vehicles to carry all of the crates to be delivered. Inside each truck was a driver and a hand selected and trusted off-duty Policeman called into service by Franco Ricci. Joey's future father-in-law was himself in one of the trucks as was Sal Marchetti. This was indeed going to be a very expensive day for the Visconti Trucking to deliver on their promises.

Meanwhile, Ford and Joey were on their way toward Chaseburn Lake. They picked up Sammy from his hiding place. He was now riding in the bed of the pickup while holding on to the fully loaded Thompson machine gun.

Ford looked over at Joey, staring at him intently. Joey noticed, "Hey! Don't be looking at me! I'm not singing now!"

Ford smiled grimly. "That's the nastiest looking knot on your head I've ever seen. Looks like your head is about ready to explode. Is that splinters sticking out? I always knew you were a knot-head, but this is definite proof."

Joey unconsciously rubbed his head, then cried out in pain. "Now look what you made me do! This hurts worse than my ribs! You think it's funny don't you!"

Ford was amused. "I think you're getting some good loving and sympathy when you get back to see your Natale. She may even pull those splitters out for you. Plus, ole Franco can't deny how much of a man his daughter is marrying."

Joey sat back in the seat, a pleased smile on his face.

The moment ended as Sammy shouted from the back of the truck. "Lakes ahead. I think I see a parked car…no, I see two."

A small wooden framed house sat about seventy yards from the lake's edge. The condition of the house was pretty bad. An equally badly aged shed was off to the side of the house and an outdoor crapper sat just toward the back of the house. Someone was here but it was obvious that the property had not been used for living for a long time.

Ford slowed to a stop, his eyes darting back and forth. Something was not as it should be. One of the car doors stood open, a bloody smear down the side glass. They noticed the car was spotted with bullet holes and the rear glass was punctured with holes radiating veins of cracks.

Ford could see the front door of the old house stood partially opened. Another smear of blood was seen on the door's frame. His foot was antsy on the clutch pedal and the other foot was hovering over the accelerator.

Sammy started to hop off the truck but Ford whispered loudly, "Wait!"

Joey's eyes widened as he too felt there was something not exactly as it looked. He was alert and tense. Speaking in a quiet voice, he said, "I'm not so sure about this. It's like they're leading us toward the house."

Ford looked beyond the shed as he noticed an old tree stump just beside the failing structure. A large spot of shiny, dark substance was on the top and side of the stump drawing a goodly number of flies.

Ford turned slightly toward Sammy. "Get ready Sammy. I'm going to start slowly toward the house. Just everyone keep your eyes on the front door. When I say "Now", I want you to turn that Thompson on the shed and light it up. I'm going to plow right into it so get ready to duck right before I hit it."

He looked at Joey. "As soon as Sammy starts to fire I want you to bail out the door and use that decoy car for cover. Shoot anybody that comes out of the house. We'll have the shed covered."

Ford slowly rolled forward. As he pulled up to the decoy car he took a quick look at the interior. It was definitely empty. He hesitated just a beat and shouted, "NOW!"

In one fluid motion, Joey bailed out the door and Sammy opened up on the building. Ford popped the clutch and punched the accelerator. The battering posts had taken a lot of punishment but were still functional. Ford headed right for the center of the shed. He wasn't worried about the decaying wall as much as what might be on the other side.

Suddenly gun fire erupted from the shed but Sammy's strafing fire kept the shooters low and fouled their aim. Just before impact, he ducked down behind the cab.

The impact was filled with a great crashing sound as pieces of old wood flew in all directions. Ford kept plowing forward as it was discovered the building was mostly empty. The already weakened roof came down quickly as it fell on the two shooters inside. As soon as the truck cleared the shed Sammy stood up and began firing on one of the downed men to the left of the truck. He went down without having the opportunity to fire another shot. Ford jumped out of the truck and quickly found the other shooter. He was not moving due to a rafter's impact on his skull.

Shots were heard from the opposite direction but not from the house. Ford and Sammy ran toward the gunfire as they noticed a butchered wild animal on the other side of the tree stump.

Two bullets kicked up dirt and wood chips on the tree stump. Sammy began firing toward the tree where the shooter was hiding. Ford fired on the other side of the tree and the man threw his gun down. He held his hands straight into the air as he moved out from cover. Sammy ran toward him but suddenly was hit with a shot coming from the side of the house. One more shooter had been hiding just off the small porch. He took one step out to take a shot at Ford only to be cut down by Joey.

Ford ducked by reflex and then rushed toward Sammy. He reached the young man who was holding on to his leg. A bullet wound was found in his upper thigh. Blood was spreading but it didn't appear to be an arterial hit. Ford pulled off Sammy's belt and made a temporary tourniquet to stop some of the bleeding.

Joey ran past him as he picked up the Thompson. "There's one more running toward the lake." Ford heard him say, "I think it's Cha-Cha! He better be ready to take a long swim!"

Ford raced after Joey, angling off to one side. The running man carried a shotgun in one hand and a pistol in the other. Realizing he had been discovered he changed directions and ran back toward the woods. The only problem was that Ford had him cut off. Ford fired a warning shot just in front of him. The bullet hit a tree in front of Cha-Cha's head causing wood splinters to fly in his face, and encouraged him to halt his momentum.

He stopped abruptly, falling to one knee. He turned the shotgun toward Ford shouting, "Eat this Elvis!"

Ford leaped to the ground just behind a tree as the shotgun blast ripped into the tree. He cried out as a few buckshot caught in his calf.

Cha-Cha chambered another shell only to hear Joey's voice behind him. "I can either blow your head off or shoot your heart out. Your choice."

Cha-Cha stopped abruptly, "Okay…you win. Little Jovanni got the best of me. I guess you'll live another few days…just don't get used to it."

He threw the shotgun back toward Joey. The gun landed just beside Joey, distracting him for just a split second. In that instant, Cha-Cha rose to face Joey, a .45 pistol in his hand. As he lifted the pistol his finger tightened on the trigger but he never fired the weapon.

Ford instantly fired a bullet into the center of Cha-Cha's back as Joey unloaded a burst from the Thompson into Cha-Cha's chest. The two simultaneous blasts actually stood the man upright for a second. His finger twitched then, firing the gun toward oblivion. His mouth opened as he fell to the ground but no sound was heard. He lay in a pile, blood seeping from multiple wounds.

Joey stood over the fallen criminal. "So, if you shoot a gangster in the woods, we now know he falls without making a sound."

Ford rolled his eyes at the failed joke by his friend. He muttered, "It's saying things like that, that can get a fellow shot out here in the woods."

They walked back toward Sammy who was holding a gun on the thug that had surrendered. Checking the bodies, Joey discovered one of the men in the shed was the other Caputo brother. It was the fellow whose head was crushed by the fallen beam.

Joey said to no one in particular. "That only leaves old Arturo. He going to be one mad SOB!"

Chapter Forty

"Joey walked up smiling, Remember Ford, no whining."

"Fleck" Marini was busy getting the mess along the highway cleaned up. Some of his fellows were monitoring traffic and getting citizens moved along the highway. The bodies were quickly moved to one truck and the wounded and captured were placed in another. Guards were placed in the truck with those men. Those that needed it were bound and sat in the back of the truck. There weren't any real medical personnel available so it was imperative for trucks to get the human cargo delivered to a place that they could get their wounds cared for.

The truck with the wounded Visconti men was just pulling out as Ford, Joey, and Sammy pulled up. Joey and Sammy were in the bed along with the captured hijacker. Joey waved the truck down to add Sammy to the Visconti group of wounded. Two men helped a very pale Sammy into the truck. Joey called out as the door was shutting. "Sammy! You did a grand job out there. I'll be sure and tell the Brothers! They'll take care of you, my man!" The truck pulled away, heading toward the nearest hospital. A couple of the guys had serious wounds that needed attention immediately.

"Fleck" walked over to Ford. "You need a little attention don't you Ford? Got a few bloody holes in your pants."

Ford gave "Fleck" a "what are you talking about" look. "Just a little bird shot caught my leg. I'd be concerned if it had been my head."

"Fleck" laughed and slapped Ford on the back. "You should be more concerned about the leg. That shot would have bounced off that thick head of yours."

Joey was talking to a group of men about what to do with the two trucks filled with living and deceased hijackers. "Just take the whole group of them over to the State Patrol's headquarters. It's about twenty-five miles or so from here. Just be careful and don't let any of them try and jump you or cause problems. I'll call when I get to a phone and let them know what happened and what to expect. One of the brothers will be calling them also. Keep your story simple. You were hijacked and survived. Answer any questions, just don't offer too much detail. "Fleck" will do most of the talking. Okay? Oh, and don't be flashing any guns around the Patrol Headquarters when you get there. Tends to make those boys a little jumpy."

He walked back to Ford who was gently placing a dressing inside his pants leg over the wound. He then tied a belt around the wounded area to keep the dressing in place.

Joey walked up smiling. "Remember Ford, no whining!"

Ford walked stiffly by him. "How about you driving us back, hero. I'm sure your girl will want to hear of your heroics and begin nursing you back to health."

As the two friends pulled away from the remaining carnage, a trio walked down the street in Chambersburg. Joseph Moretti was walking Dorotea and Felisa back from their vigil at Saint Andrew's Catholic Church which was just down the street from the ladies' home. Joe walked behind the two women as they were locked arm and arm, whispering back and forth as they walked.

An old lady was on the sidewalk re-packing the groceries that had spilled from her overturned two-wheeled cart. Several things lay on the sidewalk. The ladies spoke to her, asking if they could help. The woman waved the women on as they heard her mumbling about what a chore it was to get her groceries home after shopping. Dorotea took a long look at the old woman, finally shrugging as they went on.

Joe stopped to pick up two cans that had rolled away from the cart. The old woman didn't look up as he handed them to her but was heard to say, *"Grazie! Lei è molto gentile!"*

Joe smiled saying, *"La benedizione di Dio, Signora."*

He walked on, noticing the two women were now separated as Dorotea was fishing in her purse for her apartment keys. Joe stopped walking, something was picking at his mind that didn't exactly feel correct. He began to turn back toward the old woman just as she stood straight up, tossing away the faded shawl that had been draped around her shoulders.

Joe reached under his coat and began pulling his pistol from the holster underneath. He just cleared the coat when a gunshot exploded into the late afternoon air. Because he was moving, the slug caught him in his shoulder instead of his chest. The impact knocked him around and his pistol flew toward the women.

A second shot was immediately fired but missed Joe by a couple of inches, hitting the sidewalk and kicking up concrete chips. Felisa shoved her mother toward the pavement, falling forward herself. Dorotea's body twisted and her knee caught as it twisted in an agonizing angle. She pitched forward and her head slammed into the concrete steps of the stoop. Felisa screamed as she saw her Mother's body seem to exhale its very life from its possession.

The woman, Luciana Caruso, now walked toward Joe, watching him carefully. He rose from the ground to one knee. She stopped short and aimed the gun at his head. He looked her straight in the face and said, "Don't you want to know why?"

She stopped, a puzzled look on her face. "What do you mean, why?"

"I mean why do you think I turned around?"

"Sure! Enlighten me old man."

Joe grinned, "First of all, you bought two cans of kosher fish for your ruse, only mildly curious. Then…I noticed your shoes. They're an awfully expensive pair of shoes for a poor old woman to be wearing. Not very professional, Luciana!"

Luciana laughed out loud. "What a smart old man you are…or was. Yeah, I know…the shoes. Forgot my old frumpy shoes in my apartment. You know, old man. It's the little things that can get you killed. By the way, this is from Arturo Caputo if you were wondering."

Before she could fire she caught movement from the corner of her eye. Felisa dove for Joe's pistol grabbing it on the first attempt. Joe shouted out and lunged toward Luciana, giving her a shove as he landed. She staggered back, pulling the trigger of her pistol just as Felisa fired. Two shots sounded simultaneously. Felisa's bullet crashed through Lucian's left eye. She fell backwards, her mouth open, a shocked look on her face.

Joe landed hard on the pavement, hitting his face straight on. He was dazed, finding his vision was instantly blurred. He could see well enough to tell that Luciana was not going to be getting off the pavement on her own. Blood streamed from her fatal wound, her right eye wide open, staring directly at him, but not seeing anything.

He pushed himself off the pavement, suddenly realizing he'd heard nothing from Felisa or Dorotea. He turned quickly toward them but was still finding it hard to focus as blood from his scraped forehead was running into his eyes.

Joe realized Felisa was lying on her back. He stumbled toward her and gasped at what his eyes finally saw. Felisa lay there, heaving hard breaths. Her face had changed. It wasn't the beautiful, flawless face he knew from the time she was born.

Felisa's eyes were wide open. She wanted to speak but found she was choking on her own blood. Her face was filled with both pain and numbness. She reached to feel her face and pulled a bloody hand away. Her eyes rolled back in her head and she passed out just as Joe grabbed her and pulled him toward him. Luciana's bullet had struck Felisa's face just as the young woman's bullet penetrated the assassin's head.

Felisa had been struck in her lower jaw. It had passed through her cheek damaging teeth and cartilage as it went. Joe held her crying out, "Please! God! Don't take her." He then looked over at Dorotea and realized she still had not moved. Then, all he could do was sit there, holding on to Felisa and heaving great loud sobs for help.

Chapter Forty-One

"Hello children, now we can speak freely. But first I must talk."

Ford limped down the hospital hallway towards his friend. Joey sat alone, sporting a fresh dressing wrapped around his head. In addition to a mild concussion, the young Visconti had to have splinters removed from his head. The impact with the wooden crate left a serious abrasion and took away a patch of hair to treat. He held a cold compress to his head and looked like a man with a tremendous hangover.

A heavy bandage could be seen under his shirt wrapping his upper torso. Ford watched Joey grimaced in pain with even small movements. The flack vest had just stopped the bullets from penetrating Joey's body but he was going to be very sore for a long time. He probably should have been in a hospital bed, but refused out of stubbornness.

Joey saw Ford and got to his feet only to have to sit right back down again. Natale and her mother, Clara, came walking up the hallway just then. They were carrying a cardboard tray holding paper cups filled with coffee. Natale handed the coffee off to her Mother and hurried over to the two men. Clara followed close behind with the same worried look on her face.

Natale sat by Joey, taking his hand while her gaze remained on Ford. Clara walked over and hugged Ford after sitting the coffee down. "How are you feeling, Ford. Are you in much pain? You should sit down. Here…have a coffee."

Ford forced a small smile and declined the coffee. "I'm okay Mrs. Ricci. Just a few random shotgun pellets caught my leg. They removed them, gave me some anti-biotics, and dressed the wounds. All superficial…so, I'm fine."

He looked down at Joey, wanting to hear some positive news. Joey looked up but grimaced as his eyes caught the bright hallway lights. "Ouch…dammit, that hurts worse than hitting the crate."

He looked over at Mrs. Ricci saying, "Sorry, Mrs. Ricci. Sometimes my mouth can be a problem."

She walked over and gently kissed Joey on the exposed side of his head. "You've been through so much today. I understand. I'm so thankful that you're not hurt any worse! It must have been terrible out there! You both have lived in God's grace today."

Joey smiled at her kindness. "Sal called the Company Office and spoke with my Father. All the vaccine was delivered. I think there was some confusion since so many vehicles made the deliveries. But they sorted it out and it's on a ship heading East."

He looked up at Ford who was staring at him without blinking. "I'm sorry Ford. My brain is not working very well at the moment. He then stood up with Natale's help. "Look, Felisa is still in surgery…last I heard. I was in a trauma room for a while, getting my body and head checked…not examined…just checked and treated." Ford did not smile at the humor.

"She's going to be in there for a while yet…then recovery. She's stable, but we just don't know the extent of the damage. She saved herself as well as her Mother and Papa Joe's life. Look, you just have to believe she'll be okay. She was remarkable today. She's going to be all right…I really hope she will be."

Ford stole a look down the hall, hoping the door would open and someone would be bringing Felisa out with a smile on her face. He then wondered if he'd ever see her be able to smile again. He turned back to Joey, "Dorotea?"

Joey's voice was a bit haunted. "They don't know what damage there is, yet. She's still unconscious. Her head smacked the edge of the concrete step. They stitched it up after cleaning the wound. She's stable, but it may be a while before she regains consciousness. They'll know more when that happens." Her knee is swollen where she turned it when she fell. It should be fine by the time she gets to use it."

Then he added, "My little head bruise looks like a scratch compared to her head, I guess." Again, no one smiled and Natale gave him a slightly jarring punch which settled him down as he yelped lowly with pain.

Ford could only shake his head. Dark memories of Julia's death seemed to be crushing his very soul. He felt disgusted…with himself. *"How can every woman I really care about be punished because of me?"* At that moment, Ford felt like the best thing he could do was go out to the car, pick up his gun, and blow his own brains out. He thought, *"If I do that, then no other woman will have to be punished for my sins."*

At that moment, Mara's face came to Ford's mind. She was smiling and waving for her son to come to her. Her face was suddenly filled with horror as she stood over a bloodied body. The body still had part of a face. It was Ford's own face. He knew then he could never take his own life and be responsible for destroying even another woman's life.

He snapped back to the conversation when something was said about Joe Moretti. "What's the news on Joe? What's happening with him?"

Joey pointed over to a desk situated in the Nurses office. Joe sat in a wheel chair with a telephone pressed to his ear. His left arm was in a sling as a heavy dressing covered the shoulder. He was shouting into the receiver causing a Nurse and a Doctor standing nearby to cringe. This went on for several minutes before Joe finally began to calm down. He hung up and ordered the Nurse to roll him out of the office. He pointed to the group of friends and had the distressed lady roll him in front of Ford and company. He dismissed her as she started to protest his stopping to talk to the group.

"Please, please, Mrs. Treadway! I'll go back to my room in just a few minutes. Then you can do anything you want to me…except give me an enema. Please, go have a cup of coffee and settle your nerves a bit. I'll call for you as soon as I speak with my friends. Thank you!"

The exasperated Nurse walked back to the Nurses Station and stared holes into Joe Moretti. He turned to the group of sad looking faces. "Hello children…now we can speak freely. But first I must talk."

They gathered around him as he began. "We lost a few good men today as well as several wounded protecting the Visconti's business. The thieves were stopped and paid a heavy price. Only Arturo Caputo remains of that evil family. He sacrificed his very children in his greediness. The local and State Law Enforcement agencies are now involved. They've arrested those captured and wounded. Two more of the gangsters died at the hospital. They paid for their evil deed with the forfeit of both their body and soul."

He stopped, a burst of shoulder pain from his wound taking his breath. The Nurse started over but he held up his hand. "Please…just a few more minutes, Mrs. Treadway." She stopped but kept a steady eye on Joe.

He started again. "Just so you know, the Police are not very happy with any of us. Do not be surprised if you are asked to answer some questions. Just tell the truth. It's really all we have to offer them. Franco will be helping with that as time goes by. He is a very capable and resourceful man. He even has taken to our own Jovanni here. Who could have imagined?"

There were smiles on everyone's faces as even Joey's face gained a touch of color under his pallid skin.

Joe stopped, his shoulder obviously causing him a lot of pain. The Nurse started toward him again, but he held her back by holding up his hand and mouthing the word, *"Please"*. Clara handed him a cup of the unclaimed coffee and waited for him to take a few sips.

He handed the cup back with a thank you and a smile. "I was most fortunate today. I should have been wary of that old fool, Arturo. He will never stop as long as he lives, I'm afraid. With all three of his son's now deceased, he will blame us when in fact it was his own doing."

Clara bent beside the old man and held onto his hand. He continued. "I have been told that Dorotea may be unconscious for some time. They won't know how badly she was damaged until she awakens. For now, she breathes life's breaths and her heart beats steady. It is truly sad. I think the Caruso woman meant to kill us all. She didn't anticipate the grit of our Felisa."

Ford felt woozy at the mention of Felisa's name. Clara notice and rose to make him sit beside Joey.

Joe looked sadly at Ford. "This is terrible for you Ford. I wanted to protect them. It is I who failed, not you. The Doctor told me they do not believe her life to be in danger. They have to be very careful because of infection. That would be very bad."

His eyes glistened with a painful sadness. "She will have a great deal of recovery time and her beautiful face will be forever altered. Just remember, her spirit is still sound. She will always be the beautiful person inside as she has always been. She will be loved and that is what is most important. The Visconti's and myself will make sure her and her Mother will be taken care of, forever on."

At that, Joseph Moretti began to sob as his body shook in uncontrollable heaves.

The Nurse rushed over and whisked him away to his room. The Doctor walked over now and spoke to the group. "I just received the latest on the surgery involving Miss Gervasè. The initial surgery is over. The patient is stable and we perceive nothing life threatening to occur. She was very fortunate the bullet hit her a more glancing blow. It has destroyed some areas of cartilage and a few teeth were affected. The bullet actually bounced a bit and exited through the cheek without doing further harm except for some tissue damage."

"Some forms of what is known as plastic surgery will need to be performed in the future. This can be done at a more prestigious hospital than this one. Right now, we must guard against infection as well as any bleeding and seepage from the wounds. Do you have questions?"

Ford spoke before the question even settled. "When can I see her? Is her Mother, Dorotea Gervasè doing any better."

Doctor Harmon looked through another chart before he spoke. "Mrs. Gervasè is still unconscious. As best we can tell all her vitals are functioning fine. We will know more as she returns to consciousness."

Ford interrupted, "And when do you think that will be?"

"Yes…Mr. Rawlings, is it? I'm sorry but I don't have a specific answer to your question. Her head trauma is severe. She could awaken in the early morning or it could be weeks from now. There is cranial swelling which should go down over the course of time and that will help a lot. She may come out of this with only a very sore head or she could come out of it with severe limitations"

This brought a groan from all who were listening. "What kind of limitations?" Natale looked at the Doctor as if she scared herself asking the question.

"This could bring about reoccurring headaches, loss of some or all of her speech, problems with the cognizant thought processes can develop, and sundry other possibilities as time goes by. As I said, we need to get more information once she regains consciousness."

Ford spoke up again, "And what about Felisa…uh, Doctor Harmon?

The Doctor went back to his other clip board and then spoke. "As to your earlier question, Mr. Rawlings You may see her tomorrow providing she has gained consciousness after the surgery. It must be a short visit with as little emotional stresses tossed into the conversation as possible. She will be asking about her Mother of course. Try and be delicate in this matter initially. In a day or two she should be able to communicate with you, howbeit in the form of writing on a notepad."

He looked around the group. "Her jaw will be wired shut so that the mending will begin. That will be temporary. We must keep her under observation for infection or other internal stress. You should realize she will experience a great deal of emotional distress. She will be on several strong medications for some time. Some of those for pain will cause her to drift in and out of consciousness. An injury of violence brings about lingering emotional changes as the patient tries to understand exactly what happened and why. It is difficult for some patients to move forward with their lives."

He paused to see if anyone had a question. Continuing, he said, "She will be concerned about her mother as well as Mr. Moretti. Everyone should expect wide swings of emotions. Since it is her face that is affected you should be aware she will wonder how she will be forever affected and how her looks will change. It is a great deal more than vanity. This type of injury is a very sensitive area both in body and mind. Please, just check with the Nurse's station tomorrow Mr. Rawlings. They will tell you when you can see her."

He looked up and over his clip pad, "Remember, a short visit…no more than ten minutes at a time." He looked over at Ford's leg, "I believe you should be getting some rest yourself. Please pay attention to those wounds. There was a great deal of tissue affected but the wounds should heal quickly if you care for it. Don't let any infection get started! Legs can still be lost as well as your permanent health itself."

Just then the Doctor was called upon by a Nurse to upgrade some medications for a patient. He excused himself and left the still stunned group staring at each other. No one seemed to have an idea as to what to do or say next.

Clara stood first. "Come with me children. I have food prepared at home. We all need some nourishment. It will be good for all of us. Franco will be home soon and we can all talk about what we need to do. It is bleak but God will care for us all. Put your hope in Him in all things. He is our Heavenly Father after all."

Ford spoke up, "Thank you for the invite, but I'll just stay here. I don't want any of them left alone tonight."

Joey stood now, adjusting the dressing on his head and tossing the cold compress aside. "I don't think they'll be alone tonight. The Brothers had Franco set up two off-duty Cops to guard the rooms as well as sending two of our own guys to watch over them. They'll be safe and we'll get a call if anything changes. Come on over, Ford. But first, it would be great if you got a bath and a fresh change of clothes. You're overpowering even with all this great anti-septic smell around here."

Ford gave in, following Joey and the ladies out of the hospital. He offered to drive home first to clean up. They made him promise not to change his mind and reminded him they would be setting a place at the table for him. He stopped at his apartment, quickly cleaning up and changing clothes as he continued to debate what he was going to do.

By the time Ford arrived at the Ricci home, Franco was already sitting at the table nursing a cup of coffee. The food followed directly. Conversation was shared by all as soon as the food was served.

Franco shared the latest news. They were disappointed but not surprised that Arturo Caputo had gone into hiding. It was likely that the New York *family* was not happy with the botched robbery. Local and State law enforcement agencies were looking for him. Both agencies had voiced unhappiness with Visconti Brothers but Franco felt that would die down eventually. Joey ventured a hope the Police would not arrest any of them for the results of the day. Franco looked at him with the slightest hint of a smile.

Everyone at the table waited to hear Franco respond. Instead of speaking, his smile increased a bit and he continued eating. Franco took a sip of wine, then spoke. "I think the Police are actually glad a great number of gangsters have been taken off the streets in one fashion or another. I believe a slap on the hand will be the most any will see." He held up his glass. "Salute!"

Ford politely picked at the food but his heart wasn't in it. After a short time, he excused himself saying he needed to go home and rest a bit. Hugs, kisses, and handshakes followed as Ford finally found himself inside his car. He realized his head was pounding and his heart was racing. There was an on-going stinging pain in his leg. He started the car, driving directly back to the hospital.

Chapter Forty-Two

"A million words filled his head but all he could say was, "No! I'd hate myself."

Two days passed as a lifetime for Ford Rawlings. He only left the hospital to go home and change clothes. The visits to Julia were always short. Sometimes he would get into the room only to have to leave immediately. Nurses and Doctors came and went at a steady clip. Dressings had to be changed as well as other, more personal matters attended to. There were many times she would fall asleep from the drugs before he could even speak to her.

Meanwhile, his life was being lived on bitter coffee and stale food from vending machines. Several people came by to visit Felisa, Dorotea, or Joe only to end up spending most of their time with Ford. The best part of the visitors stopping by was that it kept Ford's mind somewhat occupied.

Several ladies, some he only barely recognized, began bringing him homemade food to keep his strength up as well as his spirits. Ford was gracious for the food that was left for him. Truth be told, the majority of it found a welcome recipient with the guards posted by the Visconti Brothers.

Ford began spending a lot of his time sitting with Joe Moretti, speaking of what had happened, what was happening, and the many possibilities of what could happen. They spoke of Felisa and Dorotea in long volumes. Joe shared more stories of both woman from years past. Ford even opened up about his life in North Carolina and the tragedy he left behind. Both men carried burdens few knew about. Joe sadly included his own family's background and how he lost his brothers. In the end, it became cathartic for both men.

The visits with Felisa were kept short. Sometimes she was only just aware of his being there because of the pain medications she was taking. She couldn't really smile when Ford came in to see her but her eyes danced with delight as she held on to his hand tightly until she drifted off to sleep again.

By late afternoon on the third day, Dorotea began to stir. It took several hours for her vision to clear. By that time, she began speaking in concise, but weak, sentences. It was readily noticed that she was having some memory difficulties as well as trouble moving her limbs in a stable, fluid motion. The doctor stressed that these things could take time to reconcile themselves. He warned that the recovery might not be 100%.

She soon began asking about her daughter and her friend, Uncle Joe. Tears ran in streams down her face as their injuries were explained. She desperately wanted to go see Felisa but neither woman could leave their rooms or the medication lines running into their bodies yet.

By the fourth day, Ford was more encouraged by Felisa's improvement than Dorotea's. Dorotea was awake but not always alert. As for Felisa, it would be a long time before she could speak again or be through with medical care. She quickly took to writing on a pad to converse with Ford and others. Some of what happened was a blank to her which was understandable. The Doctor told him that the human brain sometimes repressed traumatic events so that the body has a better chance to heal.

Each time she saw Ford she asked about her Mother and her Uncle Joe. Her eyes always glistened as he gave her a small amount of information concerning her Mother. Ford would not share everything he knew about Dorotea and neither would the medical staff, friends, or family. Still, she always asked with each visit and each visitor. Before each visit ended, she would write boldly on her pad, *How Are You!!!*

She would not allow Ford to get away with a simple answer such as, *"I'm fine."* Ford would be forced into details or she would keep showing him the pad with her question, shaking it toward his face.

One time, when she was persistent in knowing how he was healing, he threatened to drop his pants to show her his wounds were fine. He regretted it immediately. Felisa almost broke out in laughter except she couldn't laugh. A spasm of pain ran through her jaw which Ford felt himself in his very heart. He realized at that moment how deeply her wounds, wounded him.

Joe Moretti was undoubtedly getting better because his demeanor became a little worse each day. A man whose life was in constant movement did not take well to the sedimentary hospital life. He had even thrown a dish of gelatin across the room at lunch. Then, with the help of his wife's chastisement, he profusely apologized every time one of the medical staff or housekeeping came through the door.

Ford was summoned one late afternoon by the old man. In a very serious voice, he asked Ford to pull a chair close to his bed. Ford didn't know exactly what to expect.

Joe put his hand on Ford's and began. "First of all, we all appreciate the compassion you are showing through this terrible time. You are a man of great character."

Ford nodded his head, not having words to respond to the sentiment.

Joe continued, "Arturo Caputo is still in hiding. We have heard he is deeply grieved for the loss of his sons. He is raving about revenge and vengeance on all involved. He is being hunted by both the Police and certain members of a Mob family he answers to. He is limited on what he can do…at least for now. But, that old skunk…well, he has means and he has money. So be on your best guard. He is a conniving old reprobate and will need to be dealt with as soon as he can be found."

Now, Joe hesitated. "This mob family I mention…they know of you through the Caputo's. We have heard they may reach out to you because they would like to use your skills in their employee. They will use the excuse that you cost them profit from this botched hijacking and the deaths of their money-makers, the Caputo's. It is all a ruse. You owe them nothing. Once you do one favor for them they will believe they own you. Be very careful my friend! It will probably be something that will blow over in time. It would be of your best interest if you could disappear…at least for a matter of time."

Ford looked at Joe with utter confusion. He started to stand up but the old man held on to his wrist with surprising strength as he pulled Ford toward him.

"These men…these *animali sporco*, they are despicable. You will find they will not be brushed off. They run their business as *uomini duri*...uh, hard men. Do not confront them if you can help it. You really need to disappear…give them time to put you out of their mind." He squeezed Fords hand tightly. "Believe me on this, son. It is for your own good and everyone else's!"

Fords eyes widened. "But Felisa…and Dorotea. I want to help them. I need to help them. It's my fault. They should never have been involved!"

Joe lunged at the boy, grabbing him behind the head with his good hand. "NO! It is my fault! I am the one they came after. It would have happened even if you'd never met Felisa! Arturo Caputo is an evil man. He destroys not just who he hates but everyone around him if it suits him…and it always seems to suit him."

Joe released Ford's head and fell back on the bed, deeply heaving in strained breaths. "Ford…I know you would stay with Felisa and Dorotea…standing by their side in every way. But once you try to do this you will actually put them in danger as they will become targets for a new enemy. You must leave Ford…everyone knows and understands this. Even Felisa will know this to be true!"

Ford stared at Joe in total disbelief. A million words filled his head but all he could say was, "No! I can't leave her, Joe. I'd hate myself."

Joe shook his head as he reached for his water glass. He fidgeted with the straw as it kept avoiding his mouth. As he started to throw the glass across the room, Ford reached out and steadied his hand. Joe took a long pull on the straw, holding Ford's stare.

"It won't matter if you stay, Ford. We are sending both women away to another facility. It will be a very private location and only myself and the Visconti brothers will know about it. They will be taken care of in the very best manner. Felisa will need more surgeries and Dorotea is facing some extensive rehabilitation. You cannot go with them because you won't be able to be around them at this place. They will use different names and backgrounds. It will not be possible…it will take a very long time. It is the way it is…I owe them my life and I will do all I can to give them their lives back."

The finality of the matter made Ford feel deadly cold. He sat back in his chair, staring into the nothingness his life had suddenly become. He whispered, "I could stay here…you know, do what I can do."

He already knew the answer as Joe said, "You would become a lability to both yourself and those around you. No, you must leave. I can't tell you where you should go but I'd like to make a suggestion…"

The next twenty-four hours passed in a flurry. There were many quick goodbyes spoken, tears shed, and promises made…few, if any, that might ever be fulfilled.

Felisa had written Ford a letter but decided instead to give him a sheet with only these words. *"Ford, go find your next lifetime. I will do my best finding mine. You will always be a part of my heart. I have no regrets. That is only because I have lived, as you say, a wonderful lifetime with you. With all my love, Felisa."*

Ford was in a shocked void. He either felt deadened to his emotions or was so overwhelmed with them he'd lost discernment.

Without thought, Ford loaded his basic belongings into the trunk of his new Chevy. Joey and Natale saw him off. Natale was in tears and Joey was close to crying himself. Their lives together had been so wonderful that they could not imagine losing so much so quickly.

Ford had a destination but no idea of what he would find there. If he guessed correctly it would be much as it had always been with the exceptions that Julia would not be there and the mystery of her death would be. With little thought, Ford found himself driving away from his lifetime in New Jersey and toward his next lifetime…back home…toward the Brown Mountain Lights in North Carolina.

PART FOUR

Another Lifetime / A Familiar Place

Chapter Forty-Three

"Don't Italians make a toast at times like these?"

Ford finished his story and waited. He didn't know what to expect, but silence was not anticipated. The coffee was all gone as was a pitcher of Uncle Jubal's wine. Everyone appeared to want to hold a glass or a cup rather than speak first. Ford noticed a small amount of cold coffee in his cup so he downed it in one swallow.

"Well sir, I guess that was a lot more than you expected. I couldn't tell you just a part of the story...it wouldn't have made much sense, I guess. It's sort of funny, I didn't see any violent action the whole time I was in the Army, but I've seen a lot more than I wanted to ever since. I didn't want it, I didn't look for it. I guess the Army prepared me for it. Now, I'm not so sure I'm done with it yet. I just know one thing..."

He looked around the table. "I don't want anyone else hurt because of me...especially anyone around this table."

Looking around the table, he noticed Holly staring intently at the woven detail in the tablecloth. J.J. had both hands clasped on the table in front of him. His lips were pursed and his brow was a bit wrinkled as he thought over all that Ford had just said.

Ford looked at Mara, holding his eyes on her, feeling she would be the one most likely to respond first. She held his gaze, not blinking or fidgeting. Her eyes glistened and he could tell her mind was whirling and calculating about all he'd just said.

Mara finally moved as she released the empty wine glass that could give her no comfort. Her eyes did not release Ford's. In fact, they seemed to draw him closer even though they sat at opposite ends of the table. To his surprise, a slight smile appeared to accompany her now sparkling eyes.

"You never have disappointed with a story, son. From the moment you were conceived, you have lived a bit of an extraordinary life. I…well, shoot Ford...I had no idea what a life you've been living. I'm not disappointed and I hope you aren't."

Ford was astounded at Mara's first words. There were several things he expected to hear from his Mother. Nothing she said was anything he expected.

"Mother, I just..."

She held up a hand, interrupting his words. "Listen Ford. I mean it. I think your life...your other lifetimes have been extraordinary. Really. Knowing all of this means so much. It'll help us help you. I'm just glad you've gone through challenges of this life and made it back to us in one piece. You've been blessed by God's grace, my son! Now you're home. There's no other place you could get any better support."

Ford's thoughts hit him like a hammer as Mara spoke. First Carla, Natale's mother, spoke of God giving Ford grace and now Mara was saying almost the same thing. Ford tried to see past the tragedy and loss that surrounded his life. If there was "grace" to be found, he was having a difficult time seeing it.

Ford slapped both hands on the table, a little harder than he meant to. "Mother! You aren't going to help me. That's not why I told you this. I'm not putting you in danger. I can take care..."

This time J.J. interrupted him. "Ford! We are all sure you can take care of yourself. You've done just that or you wouldn't be among us right now. Just remember, you should know any threat or a burden to one of us is the same for all of us. It sounds as if you've been helping folks ever since you left. Well, you're getting help now!"

"I expected you to come back and try to solve Julia's murder…find out what really happened back then. I knew you'd do that one of these days...we all did. We just didn't expect you'd go through so much to get back here."

Ford thought of Holly as J.J. spoke of Julia's murder. He noticed she was staring in Mara's direction, her jaw set. He wanted to say something that would ease the pain she was probably feeling.

Before Ford could speak, his mother spoke up. "We know you didn't come back here because of these people following you. It just happened they decided to follow you when you came back. It was a mistake. Not your mistake…theirs. They'll find out they should have stayed in New Jersey or New York...wherever!"

Her voice dropped an octave as she said, "They'll find out they made a huge mistake. They'll find it out when they see themselves bleeding out. They didn't come to North Carolina to die...but they're going to be surprised."

Ford was astonished to hear Mara speak in such a way. J.J. looked over at Mara but spoke to Ford. "These fellows really don't know what they've got themselves into, son. Maybe they'll leave while they can. Once they see what they're up against, I mean.

They'll leave if they got any sense."

Mara laughed lowly, shaking her head. "You don't really know these *fellows* J.J. They ain't normal. They ain't right." They have *palle* instead of *cervelli.* Their *arroganza* makes them *stupido.* They are *animali, beastia.* They have no *anima*...no soul. They believe themselves invincible.*"*

Her eyes fell back on Ford. He didn't know if he'd ever heard her speak so animated...so filled with fury. The Italian words she used only enhanced her angry tone. Mara was always known to fill her sentences with Italian words when very agitated or angry. There was a certain bite in each word of Italian expression.

Mara's eyes turned soulful and her words quietened. "Ford...darling. I'm afraid I know these people. Not these exact people but ones mostly the same. I know what they're capable of doing. I know them as well as you. I'm not glad that I do. I left New Jersey because I met your Father, the most wonderful man I've ever known. He's truly, the very opposite of everything these men are."

She set her jaw as she said, "But, I want you to listen. If I hadn't left New Jersey when I did...I don't think I'd still be alive today. You don't know this story and your Father only knows a little...but he knew enough. From the very beginning...he knew. It's men just like this that would have killed me if I'd stayed. So, yeah...I know something about these people. If they have come this far they don't plan on being turned away. I'm glad you are home…you did the right thing by coming back."

She reached over and took J.J.'s hand, giving it a squeeze. "Look, Ford. If you told these men "no", then good for you. Just remember, these men are filled with unhealthy *oroglio.* Their pride drives them. They are *stupido.* Everything is about *rispetto* to them but they know little of respect...all they know is how to put *paura* in people's hearts. Anyone who stands up to them puts fear in their own hearts though. They are *vigliacchi...*they are the cowards...but they are still dangerous cowards."

The table was silent as Mara's words filled their thoughts. They all knew that what she said was true. Ford looked toward the ceiling, "Yeah, I don't know what to say. I did come back for Julia. I expected a war, but it was going to be here...not starting in New Jersey. I was ready to go to war to settle this once and for all. I couldn't have expected this war."

Holly's voice surprised everyone at the table. "I'm ready to go to war, Ford."

He gave her a quick look, surprised to see such a determined expression on her face.

She was composed, but forceful. "Look, I get it. You'll always see me as a girl. Julia's little sister. I get that. I'm just a lot more than that...now. You don't know it...but I've been to war already. My own war. You'd be surprised how dirty and dangerous it became. Just so you know, Ford…I never backed down because of it. I'll promise you this...I'll not back down now."

Ford reached over to lay his hand on her arm. She pulled it away and looked at him with fiery eyes. "No! You want to tell me I don't understand these people. You need to tell me how dangerous they are and how I just can't get involved with them. Remember when I told you I needed you to be my "big brother". I hope you didn't think I'd be anything less than a sister to you! You won't stop me from helping you. If you're afraid I'll see bad things…those things that I shouldn't ever think about."

She paused and took a deep breath. "Let me tell you something...I've already seen too much!"

Holly's voice had a hard edge now. It was like she turned into someone else entirely. It was almost as if she became a creature...one that was ready to even die to protect her own.

"Ford...like it or not, I'm family. You don't have a say-so in the matter. Mara is your Mother and J.J. is your Father. They will not allow you to be harmed. There are plenty of people in this community that will not let you be harmed. I, will not allow you to be harmed. Those damned *stupido* Yankees can go back to New Jersey or they can go to hell. They will not come here and mess with my family!"

Holly's face was crimson and her breaths were hard, but she continued, "You just listen to me. It doesn't stop when those gangsters are sent home. We're going to run those Yankee's off and then I'm going to help you find out what happened to Julia." She looked over to Mara, "This ain't the Civil War...we've got advantages this time. We're not going to let this stand. Like it or not...you've got me on your side."

She paused and picked up her empty glass. Looking at the bottom of the glass she grumbled, "Hell, I'm even better than a sister. You never, ever had to share any of your toys with me!" She looked up grinning, "Not yet anyway." Then she turned to Mara, "Don't

Italians make a toast at times like these? What have you got to put in these glasses, Mara?”

Chapter Forty-Four

"Ford matched the fire in her eyes with his own hard look."

J.J. left to go out by the barn and feed the hogs. Ford figured his Dad needed to clear his head and process his son's story. It was obvious J.J. planned on going into town with Ford...something Ford really didn't want to happen. The initial conversation with Vincent DiPoli was going to be short but that didn't mean it was going to end nicely.

Mara and Holly headed toward the kitchen to clean up the dishes. They were doing their best to ignore Ford who stood beside the dining room table holding on to a chair.

Ford started shaking his head as the two women spoke in hushed tones as they rattled the dinner dishes. Finally, he walked to the kitchen door. "Look...I've got to go! Before I go, I've got to tell you something! I don't know what you two were trying to say, but you did a lousy job saying it. I don't appreciate these veiled, secretive sentences. I thought when I got home I'd be done with people talking all around the truth without ever saying anything. I guess I was wrong!"

Ford started to leave but turned back. "What exactly is this, "the mob would have killed me", or "I've already gone to war"? What on God's green earth are you both talking about? Could you not just tell me the simple truth of what you are saying. I'd like to be focused when I see DiPoli instead of wondering if you're both in some type of trouble."

Both women stared at each other and then back at Ford. Mara began putting leftovers in a small bowl, "We've said too much. I'm sorry...you don't need this right now! Just drop it. J.J. will go with you into town."

She started to walk away when Ford grabbed her by the arm. She tried to pull away but his grip was a bit more than firm.

She whirled around and heatedly said, "Let go of me! I'm your Mother. A little respect please...mind your manners!"

Ford matched the fire in her eyes with his own hard look. He let go and she pulled away, rubbing her arm.

His eyes still smoldered as he walked away, heading to the front door. "Fine! Keep your secrets. I spilled my guts and what do I get in return? This is not a game...at least not with me! To hell with all of you! Bye! Maybe I'll see you in another lifetime...if I live through this one."

The door slammed behind him. Holly tried to push past Mara to chase after him. Mara caught her by the arm. "No! Just stay here...maybe he's right. I'll tell him. Wait in here, please." She looked into Holly's eyes. "It's just I'm so damned scared! Please...stay in here, for now."

Mara walked outside and hurried off the porch directly into the path of Ford's car. He was just about to let the clutch out when he saw her plant herself in front of him. She put both hands on the hood shouting over the sound of the engine. "Please! Come back to the porch. I'll explain...I'm sorry. Really, it's just not an easy thing. I didn't want you distracted by what we did."

Ford turned off the engine only to hear Mara quietly say, "Because...it's still not over."

She led him to the front porch and sat beside him in the hanging porch swing. Reaching over, she grabbed on to his hand and squeezed before she started.

As she started, a haunted look crossed her face. "It was your Uncle Jubal that first put me on the scent. He and Billie came by one Sunday wanting to visit and talk to J.J. about a new carburetor or some such thing."

"We all ended up on the porch, drinking lemonade and eating a piece of freshly baked pound cake. You know the one where I fix that special orange sauce and dribble over it while it's still hot. Well, Billie was just going on and on about how tasty it was and asked about my recipe. That's when I overheard Jubal mention something about Harris DePaul getting some moonshine from him. Said Harris was planning on selling the 'shine so he could get money to leave North Carolina."

"Now, you know your Uncle Jubal as well as I do. He's never been one to give credit...especially to the likes of some sad sack like Harris DePaul. I excused myself to get Billie a copy of my pound cake recipe. I stopped inside the door and listened to Jubal go on about how Harris had come to him in dire need of money. Said he needed to leave town and move away from here. He joked with J.J., saying he wished he'd known all it would have taken to get rid of Harris DePaul was a load of moonshine. Said he'd paid that price a long time ago to get him out of Burke County."

"I pressed my ear against the screen door because Jubal was talking lower by then. You know how your uncle likes to drink a little of his product on Sundays. It always makes him a little mellow and forlorn, unless he has too much...then he becomes a hellcat."

Ford was getting antsy by now, wondering what the point of the story was going to be. "Mother! You maybe should move this story along some, given the nature of things. Does this have anything at all to do with why Harris ended up shot in his car down that swampy hole?"

Mara acted a little offended at Ford's intrusion into her story. "My lord! I let you tell the world's longest story without interrupting or offering commentary." Ford held up his hand indicating he'd be quiet.

"Let's see now, where was I? Jubal...yeah, your uncle said Harris was acting real fidgety. Well, that weasel never did act right as far as I was concerned. One time he..." Mara stopped as she realized she was about to get herself sidetracked.

"Anyways! Jubal was saying that Harris was begging him to buy a load of moonshine so he could sell it and make enough money to leave North Carolina. They haggled over the price of a load and finally Harris said he'd need two loads so he'd have enough money to get set up."

"Jubal knew there was more to the story than Harris was telling but he decided to let him have it anyway. Only thing, he made him promise not to tell where he got it. In fact, he told him he'd pound his head flat with his biggest skillet if he let it be known where it came from."

"Jubal then went on about how Harris paid him for the first load and half of the cost of the second load. Seems he was good to his word and came back from his first delivery without a hitch."

"That's when things went sideways. Instead of giving Jubal the remainder of the money for the second load, he begged off paying the balance. Harris said the money he made off the first load was used to get him set up out where he was going. Harris then went on about how the money from the second load would be enough to pay Jubal and get him away from Burke County."

"He went on to say he had a Friday night delivery over near Brown Mountain. Some guy from Marion was meeting him there to buy the whole load. He told Jubal he'd give him an extra hundred if he'd trust him till Saturday morning when he'd bring the money. He promised to pay him and be gone for good."

"Jubal laughed, saying he wouldn't be losing much money at all if he didn't come back since he made out well on the first load. He said Harris promising to leave helped sway him into risking the money from the second load. The thought of him leaving the area for good was most appealing. I think Harris had a little fling with two of Billie's nieces. It didn't end well because he was seeing them both at the same time. They were sisters who not only ended up mad at Harris but with each other."

Realizing she was off track again, she corrected her storytelling. She went on. "Harris didn't get to make his delivery that Friday night. He did end up "gone for good" though. We saw to that."

Ford became more confused about the story the longer his mother spoke. "Mother, what in the world are you talking about? You're not making sense. What in the world does this have to do with Julia?"

That's when Holly walked out on the porch, speaking directly to Ford. From the look on her face and the tone in her voice, Ford knew then, it had everything to do with Julia.

"Ford, this will be hard to hear. If you want to know the truth...at least what there is to know, you've got to hear it. Just listen, okay?"

"Your mother got to thinking about what in the world would make Harris DePaul so anxious to get out of Burke County. Leave for good. Then she remembered something. It was something that happened at Julia's funeral. Do you remember Harris being there?" Ford shook his head as he tried to search through the fog of that day.

"The preacher finished his words and we were singing *Amazing Grace*. That's when Mara noticed Harris standing by the grave. I didn't know why he was standing there, so obviously upset. He looked awful and we thought him to be drunk. He kept looking around like he was expecting something might be said to him. He actually looked scared."

Holly had to take a deep breath to continue. "Sheriff Majesty and his wife walked up to the family to offer condolences. He looked over at the Sheriff, turning even paler as he backed away into the crowd. I saw him reappear after the Majesty's left. Mara said he was sweating even though it was a cool, pleasant day. She thought he might be sick since he looked as if he might vomit at any minute."

"That's when he came over to the family. I remember him standing there. It was like he wanted to say something but just couldn't find the words. My father took his hand and shook it, thanking him for coming. Harris was shaking a little when he finally spoke. He said something about what a beautiful young lady Julia was and that it was a tragedy her life was taken. Then, he just stood there like he couldn't move. One of the Funeral staff came over and led him away."

"Mara noticed he stopped a few yards away from the gravesite. He just stood there, just looking at the grave for the longest time. In fact, he didn't leave until he noticed Deputy Shell walking in his direction. The Deputy was on his way to his squad car but it appeared to spook Harris. I looked away and when I looked back, he was just gone." She looked over at Mara. "There were just so many ridiculous emotions going on that day that we forgot about Harris even being there. I mean, you don't remember any of it, do you?"

Ford searched his memory again but was unable to find one thought that included Harris. He looked at Mara, "What happened? What does all this mean?"

Mara took over the story now. "You were long gone by the time I heard Jubal's story. Something stuck in my mind and wouldn't let go. We were all so upset about losing Julia. I just could not understand why Harris had been so distraught? It kept me awake all that night. So, the next day I went down to the garage for a while. Told your Father I was going to go through paperwork and do some filing."

"I dug through his paperwork until I got to the work-orders that fell right after Julia's death. Finally, I found a work-order for Harris DePaul. Seems he had J.J. do some tie-rod and front-end work on his car. J.J. noted on his work sheet that the bumper had been removed by the customer and the car had a new headlight, not installed correctly because of a fresh dent in the housing. J.J. noticed the headlight because it looked to be pointing way high so he corrected it's positioning."

"Another note on the work-order said the customer had hit a deer and was planning on picking up a used bumper from a junk yard over in Avery County." She paused then, "You know your father. Always very thorough in his notes on work-orders. Says it saves him a lot of time and argument when a customer isn't satisfied or has questions."

"This was all a bit curious but it didn't really cause any bells and whistles to go off until I saw a note on the back of the work-order. The note read: Found under front seat – one blue, lady's embroidered purse, slightly damaged and a left, lady's navy leather shoe, size 7. I asked J.J. about this. He said he was looking under the seat for a screw driver he dropped when he found the items. He noted them on the back of the sheet in case it was said he damaged the purse or there was question about the other shoe. Unfortunately, he didn't open the purse...just laid both items on the seat."

Holly spoke up, "Julia carried a blue, embroidered purse. It was a gift from Aunt Eleanor. She also wore a size 7 shoe and she was only wearing her right shoe when her body was found. The left shoe was never found."

Ford found himself breathing rapidly, a cool sheen of sweat forming on his forehead. His heart pounded in his chest. "Does this mean that Harris..."

Holly interrupted. "That Harris killed Julia. That's what we decided. I should say that's the conclusion we came to when Mara told me all about this. We didn't have any actual proof and we weren't in the mood to waste a lot of time trying to find it. If Harris was the murderer, then we decided we'd just ask him!"

Ford closed his eyes. There were demons screeching in his head. In the midst of the whirlwind in his head, he had one clear thought. He knew the story was not going to end well and he was just as certain that the end of the story was not going to be the end of it.

It was Mara now. "I thought about confronting Harris at Uncle Jubal's place when he picked up the rest of his moonshine. Then I decided I'd leave Jubal out of it all together. Better for him, better for me. I figured Holly and me could get to him before he had a chance to make his delivery. So, I told J.J. that I had to go to Asheville for a couple of days. Holly and I got together and began planning. We drove out to Brown Mountain to pick a spot along the road where we could ambush him after he left Jubal's place. I knew it would be risky but we wanted so badly to nail that son of a bitch."

"I was in my Ford, running without lights as I followed Harris. It was tricky but I stayed back and took my time. Holly was up ahead, already on the roadside. She was faking a breakdown just on the shoulder of the road. Didn't figure there'd be any cars on the road that late at night. We were lucky in that.

Holly took over. "Sure enough, Harris pulled over as soon as he saw me. I knew he didn't recognize me. He hadn't seen me since the funeral. I'd changed a lot by then."

"I was standing by the road holding my dress up a bit too high to keep it from getting soiled. He saw a flash of thigh and stopped immediately. I knew he was always chasing women so I figured I'd go with my gifts." She blushed a bit at this.

"I thanked him for stopping. He acted all interested so I had him looking under the hood right away. I didn't give him my name and I knew he couldn't see my face too well in the dark. Of course, he wasn't looking at my face that much. He started telling me that he'd give me a ride home as soon as he did a little piece of business. I thought his heart nearly stopped when he looked up to find a gun in his face. He grinned at first and then saw I was serious."

"Before he could say anything to me, Mara pulled up. We had him up against the car in a second, both of us asking him questions. Mara emptied his pockets and the questions continued. He was beginning to act really nervous, literally shaking in his shoes."

"That was when Mara suddenly fired her .45 into the air. Only thing was, she was holding it right behind his head. I think he may have peed himself a little and nearly passed out. He had the smell of whiskey on his breath which didn't help him any. Mara took the pistol and pushed it right behind his ear. She started telling him about the purse and the shoe. Told him they were Julia's so it was clear he killed her. Then she asked him why he did it. To make her point, she pushed that pistol right into his ear."

"Finally, he began crying, his whole body shaking. That's when he began talking. He admitted abducting Julia at gunpoint as she put her groceries in the trunk of her car. He said he was supposed to take her up on Brown Mountain and threaten her before leaving her there. He swore he was only supposed to rough her up a little and scare her."

Ford stopped her, "Why? Why was he doing all that? What did he want?"

Mara spoke up, "He wanted to get to you. He wanted to use Julia to send a message to Jubal that he couldn't continue being stubborn about sharing his business anymore. It may have been a message but it was a very ugly message. Harris said that if Jubal didn't change his mind, things were going to get ugly for him, for you and for your loved ones as well."

Ford was in shock. It was a terrible nightmare!

Holly spoke, "He wouldn't tell us who had him do it. He said the man threatened him in terrible ways and he was scared to death of him. He was too afraid not do what he was told to do."

"He went on to say he wanted to run away but knew the man would track him down. I guess he was too scared not to follow his orders, so he grabbed Julia and tried to make it quick...not scare her too badly."

Holly hesitated. "This is kind of a hard part. He said he was driving down the highway toward Brown Mountain when she stabbed him with the sharp pin on the broach she was wearing on her jacket. She lunged for his face but he got his arm up and the sharp metal pin dug right through his jacket and stuck in his arm. He said he knocked her backward with his forearm and her head hit the passenger side glass. She seemed stunned so he pulled off the road. She was still conscious though, and quicker than he expected. She opened the door and jumped out running into the field by the road."

"It made him so angry he started chasing after her in the car. He said he was bouncing along hoping she'd get tired and stop. Suddenly he realized the clasp was still stuck in his arm. He stopped watching Julia just for a second to pull the broach from his arm. That's when he felt a hard bump and heard a scream that ended suddenly. He didn't see Julia anymore so he stopped. He found her and realized he'd hit her, run right over her. He thinks she stumbled just as the car came up on her. He thought he'd turned the wheel accidentally when he dislodged to broach. Harris swore she died instantly. He said he was so scared he got back in his car and fled."

Ford was beyond sick. He felt ready to die himself. Finally, he said, "What else happened? I know there's more."

Mara's voice had a hard edge to it. "By that time, we were both so upset we wanted to throw up. I turned him around to face us. Holly had her gun on him and I thought she might pull the trigger any moment. I actually felt the same way but I needed to know for sure who started this tragedy. I asked him one more time, telling him I wouldn't ask again. I put the pistol right in his face and he heard Holly cock her revolver."

"His mouth was open and he was about to speak when we heard heavy footfalls come around the car. I heard an angry growl and realized a big, black animal had come into our little party. Wisps of breathy frost came from its nostrils and the mouth was covered in nasty looking mucus-like stuff. Its breaths were coming in heavy, staggered snorts. It scared the bejeezus out of both of us."

"The growling became more menacing. We knew it was probably mad and ready to attack. The moon came out from behind a thin cloud so that I could see it better. It was really big, some sort of wild dog and it was surely rabid."

"In one flurry of action it all fell apart. I turned to face the dog. Harris thought he had an opportunity, suddenly grabbing for Holly's gun. She fought him off as the gun fired wildly. He jumped at the sound of the shot and Holly hit him across the nose with her pistol."

"I turned and immediately fired, hitting him square in the forehead. Blood, bone, and I don't know what else seemed to blow over both of us."

"Holly took a step back, noticing the dog had hesitated at the gunshot. Then, just as suddenly, the dog started to attack. She fired and I followed. We shot that animal until we'd both emptied our guns. It ended up dead at Holly's feet…right beside Harris."

"Looking around at the carnage, we helped each other over to a rock not far from that stinking sewer of a pond. We both felt violently ill but we didn't lose it. I'm not sure how long we sat there. We sat there wiping the scatterings of Harris' head off us as best we could. I remembered discussing how we wished we had more ammunition. We wanted to reload our guns and empty them into the sorry carcass of Harris DePaul. Then we both cried a few minutes before sorting it all out."

"We shoved Harris in the back seat first. Neither one of us wanted to touch the big, mangy dog. Surprisingly, after handling that scum of a man, the dog didn't seem that bad at all."

"It took both of us to get the dog into the front floorboard. Just didn't know what else to do with him. We were afraid he'd float in the pond and besides, the car was closer. Holly managed to get the car out of gear. It was tricky, but we got it moving and headed it to the pond. We hoped it would be deep enough. The ground was softer there so it was difficult to get the last few feet. Fortunately, there was enough of a slope that the pond just seemed to suck the car right on down. By the time the car settled below the surface, we were spent. It was all we could do to climb into our cars and drive to Asheville. I'd already checked into a motel just outside the town. Used another name and wore a droopy hat to hide my face. Put down the wrong numbers on my license plate and hoped they wouldn't notice."

"The rest of the night was hard. We cleaned up but couldn't feel really clean. We cried some...for Julia, for ourselves, and mostly for the fact we didn't get the name of who put Harris DePaul up to this atrocity. Holly was so brave. She never wavered through the whole mess."

Holly spoke up. "Your mother is a warrior, Ford. She did not let this go. We were so close to a name. That damn dog messed us up."

At that point, Mara said something that surprised even Holly. "I've got to say this. Don't get upset with me, but I have to tell you something. I saw the lights again. That night, I saw them. Holly, you had your head down, sobbing on my shoulder about Julia. It was just a moment."

Mara took a deep breath, knowing both Ford and Holly were looking at her like she was crazy. "I saw them behind you. You wiped your eyes and stood up. The lights were already gone, that quick. We were both already so emotional, I didn't say anything. They were really there, Holly. I saw them just above us, coming down from the mountain."

"I don't think they were there to save us, though. I think they were there to give us strength to do what we had to do. They did give us strength to do what we had to do. How else could we have gotten that car pushed down in that water? How else did we manage any of it? You don't have to believe me...but it was the angels. They came by to help us get through the rest of it. You don't have to believe me…but I know it was them. The angels came to help us."

Ford and Holly looked at Mara incredulously. Mara smiled, saying "Don't think of me as crazy. I did see them...I've seen them before. They always come to me when I really need them. Some say they're just lights but I know exactly who they are."

Chapter Forty-Five

"She's a spitfire...but one of the best spitfire's you'll ever know."

Mara rose from the swing, then leaned over giving Ford a hug and a kiss. "We'll speak more of this…later. It's too much to process at one time." She squeezed his shoulder, "Now I'm going to have to tell your Father. Thanks a lot, pal!"

Ford started to ask his mother what she meant about men wanting to kill her when she lived in New Jersey. She was already at the front door, though. Besides, he didn't know if he had enough energy or stamina to deal with another story. The truth about Julia's death had him drained physically and emotionally.

Mara quickly disappeared into the house as Ford sat staring into the diminishing light of the early evening. He felt dazed as Mara's story washed over him. In fact, he jumped when a quiet voice asked, "Are you okay?"

He had forgotten that Holly still remained on the porch, standing behind a large wicker chair. For some reason, she looked like the younger sister of Julia again as the chair hid many of her features. He'd been away so very long that he'd really forgotten the innocent beauty that had always been Holly. *"My lord...she's changed since I've been gone but she's still that wonderful girl I remember!"*

Ford stood, trying to find exactly the best words to say. "I'm sorry, Holly. This whole thing…this last month…well, it's been far and away more than I could have ever imagined. I'm not so sure where my head is right now. It's like I have almost all of my lifetimes crashing together."

She started to come around the chair toward him when he held up his hand and pointed a shaky finger in her direction. "You and Mara…you really did kill Harris DePaul…ambushed him and killed him…just like you said?"

Holly's eyes grew misty but she held a determined look on her face. "Yes. That's exactly what we did. He killed my sister and he deserved to die. It was justice being served. You'd have done the same thing if you'd found out."

Her green eyes flashed as she said, "It may not have been his idea to involve her, but he was responsible! I never thought I'd be part of such a thing, but I was…and I'm glad I did it."

Her face showed more determination than ever now…almost defiant. She raised her chin, "Tell me Ford…what would you have done differently? You left, joined the Army. You said you loved her and was intending on marrying her. Bur you left…you left us all! The people who loved you the most…you left us to try and put our lives back together. Her voice rose now as she let loose. "Then you wouldn't even come home when you got out of the Army. Found a new family. Found a new woman to love! How can someone do that to his family? How could you just forget about everyone? How could you forget Julia…and even me!"

Holly finally broke. Ford realized this was what she had held on to all these years. She buried her sister and she mourned her…but she never really was able to grieve for her in a healing way. Part…maybe all of it, was his fault. He saw it now. His life had become so connected to Julia's that he didn't recognize how he was also connected to Holly's. *"One more woman I've brought pain to. One more time I couldn't see past myself."*

Ford reached out for Holly and pulled her toward him. He held her firmly in his arms and absorbed the staggered heaves of her emotions. He felt even more at a loss than standing at Julia's grave-side or sitting beside Felisa's hospital bed. He knew then that it was time to stop running…it was time to confront the devil himself if that was what it took.

A full minute passed as Holly began calming down. Suddenly, she pushed away from him and the defiant stare returned. Then she softened, "I never thought I could ever talk to you that way. Maybe I should say I'm sorry…but I probably wouldn't mean it."

They stood only a foot apart but Ford sensed an even greater distance had developed. "Holly, I have no excuses. If there were a thousand reason that I've acted the way I have, then there's probably two thousand reasons I shouldn't have. All I can say…all I can promise you is that I'm here to see this to the end. I'm not going to let anything stop me…including myself." He took a deep breath, "And I'll be damned if I let some sorry New York gangsters try and stop me either!"

Holly wiped her running nose on her three-quarter length sleeve. She smiled at Ford, it was a weak smile, but still a smile. As she turned her head a little to the side she mused, "I don't think those Yankee boys have a chance in hell with you, Ford Rawlings…or should I say, us?"

It was just then that J.J. was heard to clear his throat and walk around the porch. How long he'd been standing there was anyone's guess. There were lightning bugs flying now and the other night-time insects were beginning to sing their rickety-sounding songs. J.J. walked up on the porch, his eyes never leaving Ford. Holly took this moment to excuse herself going inside to see if she could help Mara.

Ford looked toward his car saying, "Guess I better head into town. It's a little later than I meant to get started. I'll see DiPoli at the hotel and tell him to go home."

J.J. continued to stand on top of the porch step. For the first time today, he actually took in the man his son had become since the day he rode the bus to Fort Sanders. "You know son, I understood why you needed to leave Treemont when you did. I really do believe if you'd stayed around much longer, you would have killed Royal Majesty…or he'd killed you. I don't know what part he played in Julia's death but I've always believed him to be dirty. I guess tonight I found out at least a part of it. I believe you and I both know who was making Harris DePaul try to scare Julia."

Ford didn't say anything. Instead, he nodded toward his Father, wanting to hear what he would say next.

"Here's the thing, Ford. If I was half as smart as I consider myself to be, I'd have figured this out before my very smart wife did. And now I know she did more than figure it out. Even little Holly knew more than me."

He walked over and leaned against the porch railing. "I just don't know. Maybe I was hoping someone else would figure it out one day and I…we, could just be glad they did. You know son, you may have left town but I stayed here and still did too little trying to solve this thing. Tell you the truth…it still makes me damn angry every time I think about her. That young woman did not do anything to be abused that way!"

Ford was feeling an anger in his gut. The rise of bile was inevitable. He could almost taste the distaste he felt for his life. He looked hard at J.J. saying, "I gotta go."

J.J. stood off the railing and reached out to lightly grab Ford's arm. "Do me a favor, Ford. Wait till the morning. It's too late to see this fellow tonight. Trust me in this. It'll go a lot better over at the Diner than in his room. He won't be as likely to get riled up in a public place. Plus, you can spend the night planning just how you want to handle it. You've been told a lot of disturbing information this evening. You need to think about it and you need to rest. Tonight…tomorrow morning, it won't make a difference."

Ford realized he was actually exhausted. The day had begun with such ease. The last dozen hours or so had taken a tremendous toll on Ford's body and mind. He heard J.J. continue, "Look, I'll go with you in the morning…or I won't. Whatever you need. Think about the logistics in this. See him in the morning just before he gets to drink his second sip of coffee. Tell him this is your home or whatever the hell you need to tell him. You're not going to be alone in this. There's not anybody in these parts that will let some Yankee gangster come in here and tell anybody what to do."

Ford could see the logic in it. He knew his Father was not trying to get him to leave it alone or even ordering him to comply. He knew it would be wiser to wait till early morning. Maybe he'd get lucky and they'd just eat their breakfast and leave. Ford found himself smiling, *"And yeah, maybe the Brown Mountain Lights were really angels resting up from their earthly chores before they ascended back to heaven."*

"Sure thing, Dad. I guess that would be the smartest thing to do. I'll be out of here by first light. Maybe he'll even listen to some reason. Ole Cha-Cha didn't want to be told *no*, but maybe this is a different type of gangster…smarter, maybe."

J.J. smiled. "Your room is ready for you. You might want to escort Miss Holly back to her house before you turn in. She's a helluva a girl, Ford. That's the only kind of girl that family raises. She's a spitfire…but one of the best spitfire's you'll ever know. Trust me on that, son. I know, because I married one myself."

Ford started to walk back inside when his Father spoke one more time. "I don't know what kind of racket you may hear when you get back from Holly's, so don't be surprised. It appears my lovely wife and I have some serious catching up to do concerning the demise of the late Harris DePaul. Seems I've been left out of the loop for some time now.

So, if you hear some loud conversation, name calling, or just down-right gnashing of teeth…don't be surprised!

Chapter Forty-Six

"Don't worry boys…I've got your backs…me and the angels."

Ford slept little. When he did, it benefited him even less. He drifted in and out of shadows, never finding a peaceful landing place. Finally, he completely awoke with a start, a sheen of light sweat covering his body. He got out of bed and attended the standing salute in the small bathroom. He washed off in the sink basin and finished by toweling his face and torso until his skin slightly glowed in a pinkish hue.

Returning to his room he added a fresh shirt and pulled on his jeans hanging from the bedpost. Carrying his boots into the kitchen he saw his dad had already been stirring about. A plate with a bacon and egg sandwich was sitting by a large mug of steaming coffee.

With his boots on, he picked up the sandwich and coffee and proceeded to look for J.J. The was a light on in his old man's workshop just to the back of the house. It also housed a garage on one side of the structure and Mara's potting shed attached to the other side. There was an orderliness in the workshop not always found in J.J.'s office at the garage.

Ford eased inside the door to find J.J. talking on the extension phone he'd strung out to the shop from the house. "That'll be fine. I'll have to swing by the garage first. Don't imagine they'll be out and about at very first light. Just stay cool and let it all play out. Thanks, man. Appreciate you."

As J.J. hung up he must have sensed Ford's presence. Without turning, he offered, "How's the sandwich? Didn't figure you'd have time to eat at the Diner."

He turned to see Ford push the last bite of sandwich into his mouth. Ford swallowed, then spoke to his Dad. "Early doings around here it seems."

J.J. picked up his own coffee cup and tossed some old dregs through the door. Unscrewing a thermos, he poured another cup of black, steaming and bitter coffee. "You know I got used to strong coffee in the Army and just never went back to it any other way…at least when I fix it. Your Mother tolerates it but says it's not civilized."

Ford laughed lowly, "Yeah, the Army will definitely change or destroy your taste buds. I'm about the same way. Strong, black, and full of bite. Never fails you in front of a full day."

J.J. turned off the small radio that had just finished it's morning news show. "I need to run to the shop first thing. Parts Man is making an early morning stop on the way up to Boone. I promised Mrs. Richards I'd have her old Chevy pickup ready by the end of the day. I've been waiting on the parts for two days now."

Ford drained his coffee, turning down a refill from the thermos. "Is that all? Don't suspect you've turned into Mara, have you? You know, little surprises and all."

J.J. flicked off his light as they walked out the door. His two dogs came bounding around the building after a chase through the woods. Ford cried out, "Ike! Patton! Where have you guys been? I didn't know if you'd run off or what?"

J.J. pulled a bag of dry dog food out from just inside the door and poured the dogs a heaping helping into two large bowls. "Don't know if these two are any good as watch dogs. They're too busy running around and chasing every rabbit and squirrel they see instead of keeping an eye on the place. They're good company though…when they stay home."

The shop door was closed. and locked as Ford realized that to be something J.J. rarely used to do. His Father reached for his thermos and used it to emphasize his point. "Your Mother is a woman who doesn't let her mind settle on useless things. Her "little surprises" always have to do with trying to do a good thing. Right or wrong…still, trying to do a good thing. If you never understood that, then I'd advise you to re-visit her story from last night."

Ford grinned slightly, "How'd your conversation go last night?"

The look on J.J.s face was a cross between being amused and ticked-off. "Well son, it may come as a little surprise to you…but that's just none of your damn business."

With that, the two men walked to their vehicles and went their different ways. Meanwhile, Mara sat by the dining room window, watching the two people she loved the most drive off in search of their forthcoming destiny." In a low voice, she said to herself, *"Don't worry boys…I've got your backs…me and the angels."*

Chapter Forty-Seven

"Life ain't lived in a Diner, Ford!"

The road into town was a mist of fading darkness as the sun began streaking soft red lights across the blue-gray mountain ridges. Even at this early hour there was plenty of traffic on the mountain roads. This was a community filled with hard-working souls that relied on their own effort and ingenuity for their livelihood. Each work day started early and didn't end until everything was accomplished that could be.

Ford was beginning to get anxious. He wanted to get this over with, regardless of how Vincent DiPoli reacted. He knew if DiPoli was like others of his kind it wouldn't be finished today. The fact that he chased him down so quickly was disturbing. He couldn't understand how DiPoli knew he'd left Jersey or how he knew where to find him. It appeared there was another rat in the Visconti operation. He made a mental note to call Joey or Dario and mention this to them.

Ford knew from his conversations with Dario and Joe Moretti that these men had some sort of scheme involving him. Considering the crime element represented, the plan could easily involve ending Ford's life.

Ford drove through town before turning back toward the Diner. He parked across the street from Mary's Diner and observed two black Buick's parked in front of the hotel. Two heavy-set, serious looking men leaned on the shiny fender. A half-smoked cigarette dripped from both their lips and crushed paper coffee cups lay at their feet. Ford thought to himself, *"Typical goons! Think they can leave their trash anywhere they want."*

Ford was on edge. When he was in this state of mind he was primed to act without thinking. He willed himself to walk to the Diner and not confront the two thugs over their littering.

Mary's Diner was very busy this morning…but then, Ford remembered it usually had a booming breakfast and lunch business. The thoughts of Miss Mary's biscuits and red-eye gravy made his stomach rumble. Of course, the rumbling could just as easily be a result of J.J.'s potent morning coffee. Even Mara found it difficult drink his harsh concoction. She'd say it was laced with starch and cinnamon sticks because it could stand straight up on its own.

Ford walked in, immediately greeted by many of the patrons as he made his way to the back of the Diner. He walked to the big round table in the back of the room. Vincent DiPoli and Dino Bellini sat with their faces behind Mary's large menus. A bodyguard stood on either side of the table. They looked at Ford as if they suspected him ready to pull a gun and begin firing. *"Maybe that wouldn't be too bad an idea!"* mused Ford.

The goon on Ford's left reached forward, touching him on his arm and indicating he should just stand right there. Ford shook off his hand as he heard the guy say, "Mr. DiPoli, that Elvis fellow is here to see you." As quick as a struck lightning bolt, Ford swung a hard right into the man's face. The thug hit the floor hard, completely dazed. The other guy grabbed for Ford but stopped abruptly as Vincent shouted, "NO!"

The entire Diner went suddenly silent, everyone's attention turned toward the back of the room. Ford stared down the seated Vincent DiPoli as Dino jumped to his feet, his hand reaching inside his suit jacket. He stared angrily at Ford as Vincent appeared unconcerned. DiPoli shrugged as to say, be calm.

"Well, good morning Mr. Rawlings. Sorry if my associate offended you. You go by, Ford? Correct?"

Ford's adrenalin rush waned. He hadn't planned on hitting the guy but it certainly demonstrated that he was a serious man. The fact he didn't get shot straight away gave him hope in this meeting.

Vincent's smile was uneven as he offered, "Let me buy you breakfast, Ford. 'Mother Mary' here will put the meat on your bones." His voice was smooth and steady with no signs of malice.

He continued as Ford remained standing. "I'd like to apologize again for the misunderstanding. To be honest, we've heard your name referenced in several ways." He stared up at Ford with that same uneven smile. "I really can see why some would call you Elvis, but I've got to say…you've got a lot more manliness going on than that singer. Please, no offense intended, just an observation."

Ford looked around for the first time. He was ignoring Dino entirely. "Well sir, I've just got to say it gets a little tiring hearing people call me Elvis. Sometimes the timing can be wrong…plus, you never can anticipate what affects my Dad's morning coffee will have on you."

Vincent stared seriously at Ford and then burst out laughing! "Please, Ford. Eat breakfast with me. Best meal of the day!"

Ford found himself sitting across from DiPoli. The thug that was still standing helped his companion to a chair. The man was still looking dazed. A waitress approached cautiously and Vincent ordered a table of food. Dino took a seat and the whole Diner found its center again as low conversations began to whirl.

Coffee was served around the table and Vincent began pouring sugar and cream in his cup. Dino's look never left Ford, even as he turned up his coffee cup. Vincent leaned forward, "Thanks for coming over to meet with me. I understand you've had some troubles. The Caputo's have always caused more trouble than they're worth. They overstepped this time. You see, they've made a lot of bad choices in the last year. My Associates in New York have not been happy with them for a long while. They were trying to find a way to repay us for losses they caused."

He sat back now, "Let's just say…they won't be missed."

Ford's voice was steady and hard. "What about the old man, Arturo. I hear he's swearing vengeance on everybody involved. I mean, he sent an assassin to kill an old man and two women. That's a pretty angry thing to do. I'm guessing that's another reason he won't be missed."

Ford let the statement stand, not offering any additional thoughts on Arturo. Then a thought crossed his mind.

Vincent was smiling until Ford added, "I also hear the Police would like to find Arturo and sweat some information out of him. What do you think it'd take to make him talk…say about his 'business'…or maybe, his associates?"

Vincent had been nursing his coffee cup but pushed it aside and spoke directly with no hint of the smooth tongue he'd been using. "Let me be clear about this and any other part of our business. We will take care of Arturo Caputo and we will take care of any and all things that pertain to our business. Do not let my accommodating demeanor fool you."

For the first time, Dino chimed in on the conversation. "I'd be careful with your words Mr. Rawlings. This is a serious conversation and you should treat it as so. You may have killed off a few Caputo's but we are much more."

Ford looked at Dino and smiled. "Yeah, Cha-Cha and his brothers met a bad end. I'm kinda glad I was able to participate in that fact. By any chance, would you have been one of the guys that turned tail and ran away when the bullets started coming back at you."

Dino was half way out of his seat when DiPoli grabbed his arm and pulled him back to his seat.

Ford shook his head saying, "Tell me something. I don't want to sound rude, but is it too early for me to tell you, *No*? I don't know what you planned to ask me, but my answer is *No*. I told Cha-Cha Caputo, *No.* He had a difficult time understanding what I meant. Maybe a language barrier of sorts. Now, you fellows certainly have a good understanding of the English language. So, when I say, *No*, I can assume you will understand what I'm saying. I mean, *no* is still *no,* in Italian…correct?"

This got a rise from Dino and Vincent shifted uncomfortably in his chair.

"All I really have to say is the same thing I told Cha-Cha. I was serious then and I'm even more serious now. I left all of that *Mafioso* stuff behind in New Jersey. Didn't want any part of it then and damn sure I don't want it now."

"All of that may seem to be a short time ago to you, but to me, it was a former lifetime. I've moved on to another lifetime now. You fellows just aren't going to be a part of what I plan on doing. I hope you can understand this and go back home. I'm sure you have plenty of business to keep you busy in New York."

Vincent didn't say anything right away but Dino was very agitated by now. "Listen, you stubborn hillbilly. We had a good sum of money coming our way with that vaccine deal. We still feel it needs to be accounted for. We've got an offer for you and you'd be wise to accept it. Because you screwed up that deal means you owe us…whether you like it or not."

Ford just pushed his coffee cup away as he said, "Nope! I guess I was wrong. You don't understand what *No* means."

The tension immediately replaced the small amount of tranquility that had settled around the table. Both guards were on alert.

Dino spoke with a firmness in his voice as if he were lecturing Ford. "Don't be a stupid, dumb hillbilly! You need to shut your smart mouth and listen to what we're saying. It's really simple. You're going to get some good cash out of this deal and we'll get some pay back on our end. You'll be fine! Listen, you'll be able to buy any little girlie around here enough baubles to make her fall madly in love with you. Hell, you can even add indoor plumbing to your house!" He smirked at his last remark as both of the bodyguards broke out into odd smiles.

Vincent again put his hand on Dino's arm, saying, "Enough!" His look turned hard and it didn't appear all of the anger was directed at Ford. "Listen, Ford…my friend. Please let me speak with you without all of this drama. Dino gets a little too passionate for his own good. I apologize for his rudeness. We're only here to discuss a matter. It's purely business and we truly are just trying to be cordial and informative. This is not meant to be personal or disrespectful." This time, Vincent's voice was not soothing at all.

Ford had not taken his eyes off Dino as Vincent spoke. He slowly stood up just as a waiter was bringing a large tray of breakfast foods. Dino also stood, facing Ford as the waiter hesitated putting down the first plate.

Ford glanced over at the older man who'd been a part of Mary's Staff for years. "Hello, James! Nice to see again…Why don't you just sit that tray down on the other table there? I think we're about done here!"

James carefully sat the tray down and motioned for a waitress named Claire to hold off on the other tray. He quietly walked back to the kitchen, turning his head to glance back ever few steps.

The two bodyguards stood just behind Ford as Dino stood staring him down. For the first time, Vincent stood to look Ford directly in the eye. "Look Ford…it's this way. I meant for this to be more amenable. It is not in my best interest to have my associates thinking ill of me or the work I ask them to do. I'm only here to work out a reasonable solution to this situation."

About this time, the smile came back and his soothing voice attempted to return. "I've heard what a good driver you are…resourceful, brave, and smart in what you do. I only want you to do a few jobs for us, make some good money for both of us, and then go our separate ways if you so choose. It's simple as that. We came down to find you in North Carolina with little difficulty, but it does take time to get here. I wanted this to work out so that we don't need to come back."

The threat was not even attempted to be veiled. Ford reached over to the tray on the table and picked up a warm biscuit. He carefully pulled it apart, then laid a round patty of pork sausage between the layers. He looked at Vincent and grinned at the mobster."

"You boys are about the dumbest, most thick-headed fellows I've ever run into."

Everyone around the table began to tense up as Ford spoke.

"Telling you fellows, *No,* is like trying to talk an old mule into coming along when he don't want to. Now, I'd like to say this just one more time. Please listen and I'll talk slowly." He munched on the biscuit until he was satisfied he had all their attention. The Diner fell into a church funeral silence.

"First of all, Dino. You've called me a hillbilly twice now. I know you don't mean it as a compliment but that's what you Yankee's think it is…an insult. I am a hillbilly and proud of it. But just so you know, the next time you call me a hillbilly to insult me, let's just say you'll be eating breakfast through a straw."

Ford was grinning as Dino seethed. "Hey now, if you don't believe me ask the last chuckle-head that did it. You know him. Cha-Cha Caputo…just ask him. No, wait. Sorry, you can't ask him. He's dead because I killed him. Of course, first of all I busted up his face some and then threw him through a window."

Dino started to make a move on Ford but Vincent grabbed his arm harder this time.

Ford turned to Vincent. "Listen Vincent. I appreciate that you want to give me a fine job in your criminal organization. I want you to try and understand that there is no way in hell that I'll ever do that. You can't promise me anything that is going to change my mind…you can't intimidate me…and you sure as hell can't threaten me into working for you. I know how it works…I know how it always works out for fellows like me. I'll not be your pawn and I'll not do your dirty work."

Ford took a last bite of the biscuit, then said, "You may think of me as a stupid hillbilly but I think the likes of you are worse than a *ratto di fogna.*"

At this, the bodyguards began to reach inside their coats and the large vein on Dino's forehead looked as if it would burst.

"What? You boys don't like being called 'sewer rats'? Well quit living like one and maybe it won't come up again."

Vincent started to say something but Ford cut him off. "No…it's not something we are going to discuss. In a very few minutes we are going to come to a point of no return. I'm going say some things that are going to sound worse to you than anything I've yet said. Then you are going to lean on me, threaten me further…threaten my family and then just get downright ugly. Let me save us all a lot of time and hurt. Okay?"

The men around the table seemed to calm just a bit until Ford added, "I left a bunch of dead gangsters scattered around the country in New Jersey only a few weeks ago. Didn't hardly know any of them…didn't have a chance to know them or think too ill of them. So, I want you to believe me in this moment when I say this to you."

Ford picked up a napkin and wiped his mouth for effect. "See, I've met you fellows now and I've come to know you. Just so I'm clear, now that I know you, I'll be damned if I see any way I could ever like any of you. You fellows better just go find someone else to run your dirty little jobs because if you don't leave here today, there'll be a lot of dead gangsters left to rot away in these old mountains…maybe more than in New Jersey!"

Dino could hold it in no more. He forgot where he was and paid no attention to Vincent's hail to stop. His hand was inside his jacket and the other two goons were following his lead.

The next few seconds all happened in a blur. Ford had moved easily over to a cart holding a full pot of hot coffee. Ford's hand had already found the handle of the glass coffee carafe that was resting on a side cart. He swung the hot liquid container directly into Dino's face before the thug could pull his gun. The glass shattered and hot coffee soaked the man's face and chest.

The two goons were pulling their guns out and even Vincent was reaching inside his jacket. It all came to a dramatic stop when a terribly loud gunshot blasted a hole in the ceiling of Mary's Diner. Phil Sizemore stood just to the kitchen side of the table, a smoking .45 Colt in his hand.

The bodyguards tried to bend into smaller, more defensive postures, their eyes wide with amazement. As they looked across the room, they realized they were looking into the barrels of at least eight weapons being held by some serious folks.

It appeared that a fair portion of this morning's breakfast crowd was there for more than the biscuits and gravy.

Dino grabbed a waiter's towel from under the large tray of uneaten food. He was wiping hot coffee and blood from his face, hands, and shirt. The two thugs stood awkwardly, not really knowing what to do next. The two guys outside the hotel were still standing by the cars, apparently unaware of what was transpiring inside.

Vincent straightened himself. He walked in front of Ford as he eyed the menacing crowd. Carefully, he wiped splatters of coffee and pieces of broken glass from his suit coat. He spoke carefully and coldly as he turned to walk by, "Life ain't lived in a Diner, Ford!"

The two bodyguards fell in behind them, both still wide-eyed from the amount of firepower suddenly pulled on them. Dino walked out last. He threw the towel at Ford's feet. In a voice filled with contempt, he snarled, "This is fun Ford. You ain't gonna believe the kind of fun you're in for!"

The crowd began settling down, returning to their breakfasts. Laughter was heard spilling into the conversations and Ford's hand was shaken several more times. A few of the men watched the gangster's return to their car and then file into the hotel just down the street. The two bodyguards around the car kept looking up and down the street as if they expected to be ambushed on Main Street.

Ford walked over to Mary who stood behind the counter. He held a fist of twenty dollar bills in his hand. She was partially laughing but started shaking her head as he laid the money down. "You don't need to pay for those holes in my ceiling. I just hope that lead didn't find my soaking tub I have up there. Now that would be real shame! Besides, it was worth the show to see them boys run out of here."

Ford smiled at Mary and reached over, giving her a hug. "Missed seeing you Miss Mary. Your biscuits are as tasty as ever. Hope I didn't cause anybody to lose their appetites this morning. I just wanted to get this over with." He pushed the money forward. "Here, put it on the food. Anything left over give it to James and the other waitress…Claire, I think it was. Next time, I'll try and do my business elsewhere. Don't want you getting any bad publicity. This ain't the old wild West."

At that, Mary laughed out loud. She grabbed onto his forearm saying, "It's good to have you back, honey. Do be careful! Looks like there's trouble coming for you from outsiders as well as the trouble that's already here. You just remember something, okay honey? There's plenty of folks around here that'll help you with either problem." She pulled him over to give him a hard kiss on the cheek and then said, "Love you, darlin'."

Phil Sizemore walked up about that time. His .45 still in his hand. "Believe you've made a few enemies there, Ford. Think I should have shot one of them instead the ceiling?"

Mary motioned for Phil to put his gun away. "Phil Sizemore, all I can say is that if you spend your powder plugging Yankees then I wouldn't be having to fix a leaky roof. Probably cost less too!"

Ford laughed as he pulled out another twenty. "I'm buying Phil's breakfast. Put the rest toward patching the ceiling. Again, I'm really sorry for the damages." He looked at Phil. "Thanks for keeping me covered, my friend. You sure startled those old boys. I thought they might shoot each other!"

Phil laughed, "Appreciate the breakfast. I'll take care of your ceiling, Mary. Won't be a big deal. Ford, you need to be careful with these boys. I don't think they'd mind if you turned up dead."

It was true and Ford knew it. Even if he did a few jobs for them, they'd eventually kill him. It was in their nature."

Ford walked out onto the street after shaking a few more hands. A voice drawled out as Ford adjusted his eyes to the sunlight. "Had a morning meeting I see. Looks like it didn't go to well."

Ford looked over to see Deputy Sheriff Lon Shell leaning against the wall of the Diner. He was sporting his dark sunglasses and held a cigarette in one hand. Ford stretched in the early morning sunlight as he said, "Just trying to do your job for you, Lon. I know how busy the High Sheriff keeps you."

"Well, what kind of job are you doing for me, Ford?"

Ford looked over at his sometimes friend and smiled. Why, running rats out of town, Lon. Yankee sewer rats. They're the worst you know. Right up there with those Louisiana swamp rats."

Ford started to walk away when Lon called out. "You may have missed one of those rats, Ford."

Ford's look was question enough. "There's one of them over at J.J.'s this morning. Had a low tire that may hold a nail and some kind of oil leak. I told him he'd get good treatment over at your Dad's garage. Maybe he'll fare a bit better than those other boys."

Ford could only bite his tongue as he stared at Lon. His mind considered the possibilities. *"This was probably not the best of things to happen today."*

Chapter Forty-Eight

"Just like my old man used to make."

Beppe Carbone sat on a wooden crate, drinking a Nehi Grape Soda. The wooden crate creaked in complaint from the sheer weight of the big man. Just down from him sat two elderly Negro men, each parked in a weathered chair. Both had spoken to him as they arrived at the J.J.'s Motor Pool, wishing him a good morning and noting the man was already sweating in the early warmth of the day. Sitting there in a snug fitting suit, he was a bit of a contrast compared to the old fellows sitting on the porch. Along with their third partner, they were fondly known as the *Three Wisemen.*

J.J. had the Buick Roadmaster up on the rack checking for an oil leak. He had already fixed a small hole in one of the tires.

Wallace, the third member of the *Wisemen* trio, walked into the garage before finding his chair. He handed J.J. a greasy brown paper sack. "Here's three pork sausage biscuits from Matilda. She put a little jar of sorghum in the bag for you, too. She's says her old LaSalle's running just fine and she appreciates you finding her those used parts.

J.J. took the bag and grinned at Wallace. "That's one fine old car. Tell me again, how was it she came by that old masterpiece?"

"Well sir, I think it belonged to her second husband who got it off the old man he worked for…uh, just prior to his death. Think the old man took a liking to her second husband or maybe didn't like his family that much…I don't remember. Anyways, Matilda puts a lot of stock in that old car…her old husband too, if the truth be known! Sometimes, I think she still likes him too much…maybe more than me. 'Course…he did give her three young'uns…and then, the LaSalle."

J.J. was already eating on a biscuit and smiling at Wallace. "Man, I tell you something, Wallace. Matilda makes about as good a biscuit as anybody I know…and that includes my wife." J.J. held his index finger to his mouth as if to say, *"Don't tell Mara!"*

Wallace grinned, "I think it's her well water she uses. Comes straight out of the mountains. Don't run through any of those old pipes in the ground. I believes the water picks up…uh, impurities in them pipes. At least that's what I'm thinking."

J.J. finished off the first biscuit, smacking his lips and licking his fingers. He pulled out the second biscuit and poured a little sorghum across the top. Taking a glorious bite, he exhaled as he said, "Tell me, Wallace, how is that you so often end up at Matilda's doorstep on so many early mornings? Doesn't Missy get a little jealous?"

Wallace smiled mischievously. "Aw now J.J., what's a fellow gonna do. There's a lot of women that have many needs. I'm just the sort of fellow that likes to be helpful."

The old fellow tipped his hat back on his head and nodded toward the door. "Getting you a little better class of customer looks like." He peeked around the door. "Looks hungry!"

J.J. swallowed the last bite of his second biscuit. "Looks can be deceiving, Wallace. Well, maybe not the hungry part. He's traveling with some sordid types of fellows." J.J. looked longingly in the bag at the one last biscuit, then tossed it back to Wallace. "Here! Feed that pitiful looking Yankee before he eats one of the *Wisemen.* It ain't my fault he shows up here without eating breakfast."

Beppe looked as if he was about to fall asleep in the early morning sun. He almost dropped his grape soda bottle when startled by the shadow of Wallace's body crossing his face. "Boss man in there said for you to have a bite to eat, 'fore you pass out. He's coming along on your car."

Wallace watched Beppe stare inside the bag. "I'm Wallace, pleased to meet you! Eat that last biscuit there. One of my fine ladies, Miss Matilda McNabb made it fresh this morning. Roll some of that fine sorghum across the top of that golden-brown biscuit and taste the sweetness of life."

He shuffled off to his two companions and took his chair as they all chuckled to themselves. Beppe looked at the biscuit with a little amazement. He looked from the bag toward the *Wisemen* and back to the bag. Shrugging, he pulled the last biscuit out of the bag. The *Wisemen* encouraged the young Italian fellow to pour the sorghum across the top of the biscuit. He smelled the sorghum jar and reluctantly poured the golden-brown mixture across the top of his biscuit. The expression on Beppe's face as he bit into the biscuit set the fellows to hearty laughter.

"I knew it! Just look at that fine fellow. I knew he could eat if he couldn't do anything else", said Wallace. Harv cackled, "Can you imagine living to be that stage of life and just now having your first taste of a fine Southern biscuit or sorghum molasses. Lordy,

lordy…and they say we're backwards in the South." This brought a roar of laughter from all three men.

Meanwhile, Beppe was already swallowing the last bite of biscuit. He pulled a handkerchief to wipe his mouth as he waved a *'thank you'* to his three new friends. Just then, J.J. walked out with a crusty looking mug of coffee. He handed the mug to Beppe who took it with obvious appreciation.

"Got you fixed up there my friend. There was a small nail in the tire…patched it for you. Folks been getting them a lot lately with that new Bank being built on Main Street. Now, your oil leak needs a little more attention. You've got a seal leaking is all. I can fix it but you'd need to leave it with me for a day…day and a half. I put some *"magic oil"* in the engine that'll slow the leak down till you get home if that's what you'd prefer."

Beppe found himself thanking J.J. who handed the big man a bill for the service. Beppe was a little surprised as to how small the charges were. He looked at the bill while taking a hearty slug of coffee. In the moment it took the hot liquid to reach his stomach, the man began coughing and sputtering. J.J.'s morning coffee had cut another man down to size in one swallow.

J.J. slapped the man on the back as Beppe got his throat back under control. He had to give the Italian fellow credit because when the coughing stopped, he took another hard swallow. "Friend, that's some mighty serious coffee. Tastes like what my old man used to make. I like coffee with a bite! It just surprised me at first."

The *Wisemen* were being thoroughly entertained this morning.

J.J. watched the man finish his coffee in two more hardy gulps. Three twenty dollar bills appeared in his hand as he pushed them into J.J.'s hand.

"That's too much, friend. I'll make some change."

"Keep it all. Tell you truth, it's a small price to pay for a break from the fellows I'm traveling with. Besides, that was the tastiest thing I've had to eat since I've been here the last couple days. I tell you something else about that coffee my friend. It was worth the whole sixty!"

Beppe's voice trailed off, "Just like my old man used to make."

J.J. tossed a car key to Beppe. "Travel safe, Mr. Carbone. Your car is sitting around the side there. J.J. hesitated as Beppe added the key back to a key chain. "You fellows about to get your business finished here. I'm sure it's a different place than home, huh."

Beppe gave the mechanic a curious look. "Guess that's not up to me. Tell you the truth…I'm ready to go home. I mean, this is a beauteous place you live in here…but I got family at home. Like to see my girls and lay down beside my wife. It ain't been that long…but I miss 'em."

J.J. continued to size up the man. He wasn't exactly what he'd expected…but he was still here with some people who did not have the best interest of his son in mind.

Beppe reached out and shook J.J.'s hand. Tanks for the hospitality. Appreciate youse helping me out this morning!" Beppe looked down at the bill again and noticed J.J.'s last name scribbled at the bottom. "Your last name, Rawlings? I spoke to a real nice lady yesterday on the phone…a Mrs. Rawlings. Guess you'd know her?"

J.J. looked the man up and down. "Yeah…that'd be my wife. I like laying down beside her at night too!"

Beppe hesitated before he asked, "You know a fellow goes by the name of Ford Rawlings?"

J.J. gave the man a hard look. "That'd be my son. And just so you all understand, I'm right partial to both of them."

Chapter Forty-Nine

"They are a different breed, Deputy."

By the time Beppe Carbone re-joined his associates they had the two Buicks packed up and ready to go. Vincent was in a bad mood and Dino was in an even worse one. Dino's face looked as if a drunk hedgehog had been dancing across it. The cuts looked bad and the flaming redness looked even worse. Beppe also noticed a wild red mark on the chin of Aldo Santoro, one Vincent's personal bodyguards.

Beppe informed Dino the car had been taken care of and was good to go. Cutting him off, Dino said, "What do want…a medal! We got your stuff in the other car so let's get out of this stinking hole!"

Beppe climbed back behind the wheel of the Buick and started the powerful engine. Vincent and Dino climbed in the back, with the older man saying, "Get us to Asheville, Beppe. I've got a few calls to make. Keep an eye out for a decent place to stay when we get over there."

Beppe sighed to himself, *"Don't appear we're going home yet! These guys gonna get us all dead before we leave these mountains."*

As the three cars left Treemont, the telephone lines were already reporting their departure. One call connected directly with the High Sheriff of Burke County, one Royal Albert Majesty.

"Yes, I did hear of the confrontation at the Diner this morning. Very fortunate no one was injured, I'm sure. Those fellows represent a rough element. We're all glad to see them go. Thanks for the information."

Royal hung up and addressed his young second-in-command, Lon Shell. "It appears Mr. Vincent DiPoli is in the process of leaving our County. Now the questions remain, *"What brought them here exactly"* and *"when will they be back?"*

Lon was polishing the lens of his sunglasses. "You think they'll be back? Seems to me they'd be more interested in their business back home."

Royal lit a cigarette and blew a thick, blue-gray cloud of smoke. "They are a different breed, Deputy. Men with too much pride, the constant greed for power, and the hopes of easy money. They've got a whiff of something they want and they'll not believe they can be denied. Men like that are too hard-headed for their own good."

Lon nodded, out of habit. "I've got a couple of my fellow's following them so we'll know for sure what they're up to, and how far they actually go." He grinned, "I heard Ford knocked one of the tough guys on his butt in one punch. Some things never change!"

"Listen Lon, I need you to stay on top of this thing. Don't worry so much about the Harris DePaul murder at the moment."

"I've received information through contacts in the New Jersey area. It appears there was a bloody event involving our friend Ford Rawlings and his recent employer. An attempted hijacking of medical supplies by some hired guns of one of the New York *families.* Name of Caputo is what I've heard. It is apparent *New York* feels Ford to be greatly responsible for the fiasco's failure. I believe they came down here to prove a point that he couldn't just walk away from fouling their hijacking…that they need restitution. In other words, they have a score to settle."

Lon took all of this in without making even a gesture that any of it mattered. "Sounds like something Ford could find himself in the middle of…knowing him. I doubt they're coming down here would intimidate him in any way. He's got his own brand of stubbornness."

Royal smiled, "Yes he does…gets it from his Mother if I were to guess. Not that his Father isn't formable…but that Mara Rawlings, she's a pistol indeed."

He added, "Here's the thing, Lon. I'm having a premonition that this Vincent DiPoli and his friends think they have a smell for some easy money to be made right here in our little County. I hope they reconsider…but those fellows rarely choose to do something like that."

Royal put his cigarette out and moved to the window, "Keep all of your many eyes open Deputy Sheriff Shell. I think they'll be coming back and possibly with a larger force to make their point. There's something here they think they want. The only thing is, what they think they want is already mine!"

Chapter Fifty

"Going into the logging business, Vinny?"

Vincent DiPoli sat at a table in his room at the stately *Grove Park Inn,* overlooking the city of Asheville. He'd been on and off the telephone ever since he'd checked in.

Vincent said he was tired of staying in some "little dump", so he booked rooms at the *Grove Park.* According to the brochure Beppe picked up at a gas station, the hotel was the product of a successful pharmaceutical business man, Edwin Wiley Grove, and his Son-in-law, Fred Seeley. It was built as a compliment to the historic George Vanderbilt home, Biltmore, in the growing city known as Asheville. The hotel was over forty years old now and had a fine reputation across the Southland. Vincent felt it was a fine place for a fellow like him to rest up and make plans.

He thought to himself, *"Who knows, maybe I'll have my own 'little' place like this one day. Yeah, that'd could be possible if I was to get a hold on this area. Maybe I could just forget about New York and New Jersey...run my own empire from one of these pretty mountains. That'd be one to run by the bosses. Be interesting what they'd think of that. Of course, money is still money...no matter where it comes from."*

Vincent knew the first thing he needed to do was deal with this punk, Ford Rawlings. He needed to get that matter wiped off the books as soon as possible. Doing that would make him look much better in the eyes of the *bosses*. He knew now that they'd just need to kill him and get it over with. He wouldn't come to work for them. Besides, they would have killed him anyway at some time. *"Smart mouthed punk!"* He thought.

If that was the first thing to do then perhaps the second thing would be to leave Dino Bellini buried in one of these cracks between the mountains. The only trouble was that he might need Dino in making his third thing happen. Vincent didn't expect Sheriff Majesty to be a push-over, but he didn't have time for the man to be too stubborn.

Dino was busy in a bathroom, applying creams to his reddened face. There were several small, ragged cuts caused by the glass coffee carafe that Ford used to smash into his face. As he stared at the image in the mirror he could not imagine all of the harm that he planned on doing to that "hillbilly"! This was the second time he'd made him look bad. *There won't be a third time!"*, Dino promised himself.

A knock sounded on the door causing Dino to leave his image behind and angrily answer the door. On the other side stood Beppe Carbone and the fellow called Aldo. They came in with a cart of food ordered from the kitchen.

Dino shook his head, "Like they won't deliver Room Service from the kitchen! This operation is like a clown show!"

Beppe and Aldo walked inside and covered the room table with all manner of food. "Boss told us to go get it and make sure it's right. He didn't want to have to send it back and waste more time. Plus, he wanted to keep his business to himself."

Dino went back to the bathroom, shaking his head and mumbling into a face towel. Another knock was heard. Beppe spoke to the room, "That's the drink cart. They were sending it up right away."

It was indeed the drink cart, filled with coffee, tea, and a couple of bottles of hard liquor and two bottles of red wines. The cart included cups, crystal glasses, napkins, and an under-tray, filled with assorted pastries, cheeses, and fruit. Beppe tipped the server at the door and rolled the cart inside. Vincent appeared to be satisfied with the food and drink. He gave a nod to Beppe as he hung up the telephone.

"That worked out better than I expected. Drago Rinaldi is going to bring some guys and meet us back in Treemont. That should give us plenty of manpower to get this thing in motion."

Dino's head popped out of the bathroom. "You're bringing that *boombots* down here?"

Vincent shot him a look. "Hey, "Blinks", I wouldn't let Drago hear you calling him an idiot. He's not a very forgiving kind of guy."

Dino stared back into the mirror where he noticed his nervous blinking "tick" was going crazy. It often happened when he was excited or frustrated. The twitching added a rather comically demented dimension to his already messed-up face. "He don't worry me any. He just needs to know to keep his place. I got no problem with the guy…really. He's got his talents…just gets a little too bossy at times for my liking."

Aldo poured Vincent coffee while Dino opened a bottle of whiskey, filling his glass liberally. Vincent spoke to no one in particular, "Eat up boys…looks like some good food. This ain't no

'Mother Mary's Diner'."

The five fellows, including Beppe filled plates to almost overflowing. They were all starved by now. The men took their positions inside and outside the room as they chewed heartily.

Dino sat down at the table and began nibbling from the various plates of food. Vincent was busy making notes, drinking his coffee and pulling various pieces of paper from every pocket in his clothing.

The truth was that Vincent was facing the biggest moment in his life. He knew the little *sanguisuga* sitting across for him was not only positioning himself to take over his own spot, but was planning on moving way past him…possibly leaving him in a shallow grave along the way.

Looking at Dino, Vincent lit a cigarette and observed his cohort. "You know, Blinks…we came here for the wrong reasons. This Ford Rawlings was someone I thought we could use…push him around and make him work for us before we put him in the ground. Thought we could get some payback for the Caputo slime. Here's the thing I've discovered. There's money in these backwoods."

Dino re-filled his glass. "How you gonna pull money out of all these pine trees. Going into the logging business, Vinny?"

"Let me tell you something. I've been checking around while we've been waiting for the Rawlings kid to show up. Now it ain't the glorious days of Prohibition, but there's a lot of folks around here that make a cheap but profitable form of some pretty good liquor. They call it moonshine. I've tasted some of it and I tell you, it's not too bad for a lot of people's taste. I think we could bring in some of our guys and set up a good organization in a hurry."

Dino looked at him in amusement. "I can see you think this a joke, Dino. I think with a little commitment I can get most of these rubes to work with us. It's the same old, same old. The cops don't look to be too sharp in these parts. We pay off those fellows using some money we skim from the moonshine."

"This stuff can be sold as fast as it can be produced. We can get these people to up their production of this stuff. Those that won't work with us at first will come around…one way or another. If they don't come around, we'll use the ones that will work for us to kill off those who don't. But hey, they're human…they'll come along."

Dino was shaking his head, "Vinny, this ain't Prohibition. People can buy alcohol. Good stuff…not that nasty stuff. It'll peel the hair off your arm."

"I'm not speaking of fine drinking whiskey that men in tuxedos drink. I'm talking about tax-free whiskey. I'm talking about enough whiskey pouring out of these mountains to fill up every drinking joint in the whole south. We can get the cops on board and we can transport and bottle this stuff cheap. Trust me, there's an army's worth of producers up in these mountains. Then, once we get started…there's the other stuff."

This got Dino's attention. "What other stuff?"

Vincent tossed a sheet of paper across the table with a long list of items. "There'll be more than that once we get going. I mean look, there's fresh resources here. We could be pulling farm-fresh girls out of here for the brothels. There's mining around here that we can use to skim from, use the transportation they got…hell, bury bodies!"

Dino had enough. He stood up shaking his head. "I think you lost it Vincent. You're talking about a lot of work and head-knocking and it still might not pay off. These hillbillies are hard-headed…just look at the Rawlings kid. Why are you so interested in these mountain people all of a sudden?"

"Investment my friend. I can see new horizons here, Blinks. We can run hijacked goods into these mountains and then move the stuff up the coast, down the coast, or send it out West. This place is like a hub. It's gonna grow. There's land we can get on the cheap and set up scams for developments."

"What in the hell do you know about developing anything? You're just like me…a street kid who made a life for himself in the City. You ain't gonna push these folks around. I say we just snuff this Rawlings kid, cut our losses, and get back home."

Vincent waited a long minute before answering. "No…I think not. I'm looking into all of this and more…there's "gold" in these hills!"

Dino didn't know what had happened to Vincent. Maybe it was time to push this old man off, sooner than later. He'd lost his mind…that was for certain. He went back to the mirror to check his face. He mumbled, "I'm not wasting a lot of time trying to bring these *cousins* into line."

Vincent was quiet, looking over another sheet of paper filled with his own scribbling. "I want you to help me with this Dino. I just want to see what might be done. You help me and I'll see to it you get a nice slice of the pie. What you got to lose 'Blinks'? Let's just look into it some more…you know, find the angles.

"So, what you want done, Vinny? I'll give it a few days for you. Just so we're clear though…I'm mostly here to take that kid down. He messed us up in New Jersey and now he's messed up my face. I'm ready to put the punk in the ground. I'm not sure there's much more worth doing in hillbilly land."

The telephone rang as Vincent said, "Get that, Beppe…I've got to start making arrangements to meet up with the High Sheriff of Burke County…one, uh…Royal Albert Majesty."

Chapter Fifty-one

"Here it is...no secrets around here."

J.J. found Ford staring down at him when he rolled his 'crawler' out from under Joe Fosse's 1946 Chevy pickup. Looking at his son, he reached for a hand up as he said, "Have a good breakfast meeting?"

"About as good as could be expected. Knocked a guy on his butt…so that went well."

Shaking his head, "Lordy son, you know you don't always have to hit somebody to make a point!"

"Yeah, well, he called me Elvis and it was much too early for that non-sense. Plus, he said he didn't like your coffee."

J.J. squinted a smile, "Tell me, how did he know anything about my coffee?"

"Right…it was probably more like he didn't care for the way your coffee affected me as I punched him in his face. It worked out okay though. They didn't shoot me and it didn't hurt the fellows looks at all."

Ford went on to tell his Father about the meeting with Vincent DiPoli in detail. "Don't suppose you had anything to do with all my chaperone's down at the Diner this morning?"

"Now son, people are just neighborly around here…you know, like to be helpful. Besides, I think you made a call or two yourself yesterday afternoon."

Ford smirked, "Just left a message for Phil Sizemore in a couple of places. He never did call me back. Busy man, I guess. Showed up at the Diner this morning, though. Shot a hole in Miss Mary's ceiling."

This brought a chuckle not only from Phil but snickers were heard from behind them as the *Three Wisemen* were found to be ease dropping.

Ford eased over to the drink cooler, pulling a cold RC Cola from the offerings. "Heard you had some company too?"

Harv was heard to say, "Here it is…no secrets around this place."

J.J. wiped his hands and began telling Ford the story of his time with Beppe Carbone. He commandeered Ford's drink, motioning him to get himself another one.

"I hate to admit it, but that old boy didn't seem half bad.

Think he's homesick and don't have much reason to like the company he's traveling with. Hard to say where he'd fall out in a fight. Probably on the wrong side I'm afraid."

J.J. smiled then, "Said he liked my coffee. Reminded him of how his Dad used to fix it."

Ford smiled warmly, "Well that's scary! Hopefully they're done and won't be coming back?"

"You believe that, Ford?"

Ford stared a few seconds, "I believe they'll be back…I believe there'll be trouble…and I believe it's going to get bloody." He turned grim, "I'm not sure what I'll do the first time they hurt someone around here while trying to get at me. I'd have to go after them hard." He looked sad. "If I was to do that, I'm not sure I could stay or even come back again, Dad?"

J.J. looked at his son, realizing the pain and anguish he was going through. Words failed him at that exact moment.

Ford spoke lowly, "Given the circumstances, I'm afraid I ought to just leave anyway. Maybe this time just disappear and not come back. I can't have anybody else hurt because of me."

J.J. noticed the trio of elderly gentlemen nudge each other and quietly shuffle out of the garage. "To tell you the truth son, I think those old boys are coming back here for trouble, whether you're around or not.

Chapter Fifty-Two

"So, they will be back on our doorstep sooner than later it seems."

Deputy Sheriff Lon Shell was no stranger to any of Sheriff Majesty's quirks. His most irritating habit was expecting Lon to complete minor tasks that the Sheriff never bothered to mentioned. There seemed to be several wheels in motion at the moment. Lon was sure he'd already missed something that the Sheriff would bring up to him.

He could see that this new development with DiPoli and his gang was going to problematic, especially for him. He knew down deep that no matter what these thugs brought to the County, the Sheriff would most likely want Lon to hold the fort down while he dealt with it himself. Royal had a core of Deputies that formed his personal task force. They followed Lon's orders but they answered to the Sheriff. He knew there were many things done for the Sheriff that he was never privy to. He hated living and working in a job that was filled with so many secrets.

Lon wanted the Sheriff to call in outside help, but Royal would never do that. He was emphatic that Burke County problems were always handled internally.

No, he wouldn't see fit to contact surrounding Counties or State and Federal Agencies. No sir, he would "lone wolf" it like he did so many times. Lon's opinion was that one day the Sheriff's stubbornness was going to end up biting him in the rear.

Lon sometimes wondered why even stayed with the Department. He might be Royal's Chief Deputy, but he knew Royal kept him blind to his various enterprises that had to do with the Majesty's personal wealth. Lon's responsibilities consisted of keeping the Department run efficiently, putting a good face on for the public, and making sure the Sheriff was re-elected every four years.

~

Deputy Jonas Starling and Deputy Ron Greer followed DiPoli and his men into Asheville where they had taken up residence at none other than the swanky *Grove Park Inn.* The two plainclothes Deputies were to watch the gangsters and report their every movement. They found the trio of Buicks in the parking area. They used a couple of tricks to monitor the vehicles whereabouts. A chalk mark left just inside the passenger-side front tire illustrated if the car had been moved and a little money to the attendant made sure nothing was missed.

They noted the men had so far stayed close to their rooms, even shunning the dining room at most meals. It had only been two days, but it was agreed that this place of habitation would soon have to end. Something was being planned. Like the Sheriff, they too thought it to be something that would bring them back to Burke County.

Lon's most reliable Deputy, Jonas Starling, had been most resourceful. Using his badge, some soft, sweet words, candied treats from the gift shop, and his dark, good looks, he was able to sweet-talk some of the ladies on the switchboard. They had been kind enough to share with Jonas the general areas being called by DiPoli and his guests. They even provided a few numbers as well as the origination of several of the in-coming calls.

Lon had the accumulated information and was already inside Royal's office when the Sheriff returned from a lunch with his wife, Angelica Grace.

Royal hung his hat on a hook and flopped into his leather-covered chair. "What you got for me, Lon?" He was still picking at his teeth with an ivory toothpick.

"So far, DiPoli has been on the phone ever since they arrived. Both placing and receiving calls. Don't know the particulars since we don't have any kind of warrant to allow us to listen into the conversations. The calls all center around either Trenton, New Jersey or New York City is all we know for sure."

He paused to see if the Sheriff had any comment. He didn't, yet. "Jonas caught the second in command, Dino Bellini, asking at the desk about a place to stay in Burke County for a crew he had coming in for some survey work. Wanted enough room for about twenty guys and wanted it as private as possible. The Clerk recommended a small hunting lodge a friend's family owned just outside of Treemont. Jonas listened to the desk guy call from a hotel phone and set up the lodgings. Turns out he was calling Jim Seeley."

Royal acted pleased as he threw the toothpick to the desk. "That's good work, Lon. Give Jonas my compliments.

He leaned back in his chair as if creating a grand plan. Pulling a bottle of bourbon from a desk drawer, he poured himself a healthy slug without offering any to Lon. Rising from the chair, he began pacing. "So, they will be back on our doorstep sooner than later it seems. Now what would they be up to, I wonder?"

Lon waited. He'd played this waiting game with the Sheriff on many occasions. "First and foremost, I still think they want Ford Rawlings. I'm sure of that. I hope you have been keeping close watch on the boy so we will know his whereabouts if we need him. I think those fellows are still interested in getting him either working for them or dead as Aunt Nellies petunias."

Royal chuckled either at his old joke, or maybe, the thought of Ford…dead. But with Royal, it could just as well have been something else.

Royal walked over to the telephone to make a call. He talked low and upon hanging up, made another call which turned into a lengthier conversation.

Upon hanging up, he turned to Lon. "This is all helpful. I've learned a bit about Mr. Vincent DiPoli and the crime family he works for over the last several days. I have several reliable sources that keep me informed on such hotspots as New York, New Jersey, New Orleans…all places that give me interest."

He continued, "Let us say that Mr. DiPoli could use a boost in his standing with his employers at the moment. It is thought that his companion, Mr. Dino "Blinks" Bellini does not have DiPoli's best interest in mind when it comes to loyalty."

"The New York family in question does not care for the fiasco that the Caputo's put on the front pages of several papers in the New Jersey area. Plus, they did not like losing both the profits from the hijacking and the loss of manpower used up in the messy results. All in all, Mr. DiPoli, who gave the go-ahead to the Caputo's, must do a lot of damage control or he is most certainly to be an ex-member of the family. Not sure about Bellini's standing with the *Family*. He appears to just be another jackal in a long line of jackal's."

Royal directed a few words toward Lon, meaning both to sting and inform. "You see Deputy Shell, Mr. DiPoli has been spending some of his time doing a little research on our fine community as well as nearby Counties. He seems to have grown a peaked interest in not only the availability and production of moonshine in these parts but also a few other resources our fair

County possesses. I do believe these aren't a mild curiosity to gain stories to tell the fine folks back in New York during a cold winter's day. Tell me Deputy, are you aware of any such goings-on?"

Royal poured more brandy into the tumbler and swirled it around. Lon was getting both irritated and a little bored by now. "Since you already have been informed by those reporting to you, I'm sure you've already come up with your own thoughts concerning the curiosity of Mr. DiPoli. Would you like to share your thoughts on what they're up to Sheriff? They're not bringing all those fellows down here just to kill ole Ford."

The telephone rang again so that the Sheriff ended up involved in another conversation. Again, he spoke in hushed tones. Hanging up, he looked at Lon with amusement on his face. "Well now, Lon. To answer your question, I think we may just need to wait a little while longer as the answers appear to coming to our own doorstep indeed."

Lon shook his head at the Sheriff's words. "That was Jonas. You have picked a good man there, Lon."

Royal sat on the desk, facing Lon. "According to our intrepid sleuth, Deputy Starling, they have been following the three black Buicks as they left Asheville a few hours or so ago. Two of the cars turned onto Old Sawmill Road after entering Burke County. That, of course, is the road where Jim Seeley has his hunting lodge. The same place where the DiPoli crew will be launching their enterprises."

Lon finally tired of sitting and waiting. "Tell me then Sheriff, what are these 'enterprises' they will be launching?"

Royal smiled, "Patience, Deputy. We will both find out very shortly. You see, our Deputy Starling believes Mr. DiPoli and a couple of his associates will be walking into my office very shortly and enlighten us on that matter."

Chapter Fifty-Three

"Find Ford! I need to meet with him..."

An odd atmosphere hung over the Sheriff's Office. Aldo remained with the car which was parked across the street from the Sheriff's Office. Beppe was stationed outside the office door, standing stoically, like an Italian version of the old American Indian figure that stood outside stores that sold cigars and other tobacco products. The people coming and going around the office could not help but notice the very large man in the dark suit.

Inside the office, Vincent DiPoli sat facing Sheriff Majesty from across his desk. The visitor's hat was parked on his right knee causing him to look a bit like some sort of salesman making a business call. Dino was not with DiPoli. He was sent with the others to the small hunting lodge for the purpose of welcoming Drago Rinaldi and his men. Vincent found it amusing as he thought of the look on Dino's face when he issued him his duty.

The truth was, Vincent just needed a break from Dino. Plus, the sight of his confederate's face was a little off-putting. He felt good sitting in the Sheriff's Office by himself, making a deal without prying eyes and ears. He watched Royal light a fancy monogrammed cigarette pulled from the initialed, polished oak box on his desk. A Deputy stood to the side of the Sheriff, keeping his eyes stoically on Vincent. He smiled at the Deputy wondering if the man had ever seen such a "serious" man like himself before.

"Sheriff, you have a very unusual name. Your Father surly had great expectations for you. A very interesting family I imagine."

"Mr. DiPoli", Royal said with a flourish as he expelled a cloud of smoke from the freshly lit cigarette. "You have no idea how interesting my family is. However, I'm sure you didn't come by to hear about my family. In fact, it seems we should say, welcome back to Burke County! It seems your stay away from us did not last long. I assume you have found business that brings you back so soon. How may we assist you?"

Vincent's amusement now fell on Sheriff Majesty as he found the man's attempt at Southern charm to be anything but cleaver. He laid his hat on the Sheriff's desk as he leaned forward, noticing the Sheriff's eyes dart to the placement of the hat.

"Thank you for seeing me Sheriff Majesty...without an appointment, I will admit. I am very appreciative." He could play this type of game as well as any. He wasn't sure about this Deputy but figured he'd do whatever the Sheriff said. Anyway, if they were going to do business together, the people in his department would also be involved.

"I must say, Sheriff…these mountains are a beautiful land. There appear to be a plentiful amount of resources available to make a man a more than decent living. I must say, I came here originally to see about giving one of your local fellows an opportunity of employment, but my eyes have been opened by the additional opportunities here."

Lon spoke for the first time, "How did that go with you and Mr. Rawlings…I mean in your offer of employment?"

Royal smiled at the question but gave Lon a quick glance that may have meant for him to back off. However, Royal said nothing as he waited for the man's response.

As Vincent slightly shook his head, he said lightly, "Let's just say we are still in the process of negotiating. Mr. Rawlings has strong opinions and a great resolve in the way he regards his position. I believe we will be addressing the topic with further conversation in the near future. Then, we'll see."

Royal's eyes had not left DiPoli since he sat down. "So, I must assume that you have business to discuss with me other than employment issues with a Mr. Ford Rawlings."

DiPoli leaned back in his chair, sizing up the Sheriff. "That would be correct, Sheriff. I can see many ways in which an investment of time and money could be turned into a great deal of money for all who wouldn't mind some hard work and commitment. I can foresee a core of businesses centered here in Burke County that would grow throughout much of this region…even into your larger 'sisters'. Of course, I speak of Asheville and Charlotte."

"In fact, I can very well see enterprise that would flourish not in North Carolina, but into the surrounding States. Given time, of course."

Royal continued to study the New York gangster. He was intrigued by the man but was already tiring of this cat and mouse game. He was a patient man as long as he was the one leading the game. When it came to waiting for others to lay their cards on the table, he bored easily.

Looking at Lon, he felt he could get DiPoli to say what he was here to say if they were alone. He also considered that Lon might not need to hear all that might be said in this meeting.

"Deputy Shell, I believe I can continue the conversation with Mr. DiPoli without your assistance. Would you please look into the matter we discussed earlier? I'm speaking in regards to the man we may need to bring in for questioning. I'd like to get that matter settled as soon as possible."

Lon was surprised at Royal's request. The 'matter' was actually a mystery to Lon, that is, until Royal handed him a freshly written note. He folded it into the Deputy's hand and Lon left the office. He curiously took a look at DiPoli's massive man at the door. He'd been called something that sounded like *Beh-pee.* An unusual name for sure. The man stood straight as he nodded at Lon when he left the office, then continued to gaze across the room. Lon thought, *"This surely wasn't the guy Ford cold-cocked in one blow. It'd take a two by four timber to put him to the ground in one blow."*

Lon walked away as he unfolded the single crease of paper. The note simply said, *"Find Ford! I need to meet with him...at his Father's garage if possible? As soon as possible!"*

Lon wasn't sure what the Sheriff had in mind but he didn't believe it would be anything that would bode well for Ford.

Chapter Fifty-Four

"His hand landed on something with sharp-feeling, saw-toothed edges...something man-made."

Lon Shell was not the only person looking for Ford. Phil Sizemore was also searching, going first to the Rawlings' house, then to J.J.'s garage. Mara told him Ford had left early without telling her anything. J.J. was unaware of Ford's plans for the day.

A third person seeking Ford was Holly. She dropped by and spoke with Mara which led to coffee and a long conversation. Both women knew Ford was still 'chewing on' the surprising news concerning the death of Harris DePaul. Neither woman was sure as to how Ford was dealing with the revelation. They both decided they needed to be ready for every action or reaction that Ford might take.

In the heat of the moment, it appeared to be the correct thing to tell him. However, now that they'd had a chance to reflect, they just weren't sure as to how he was affected.

Ford had been restless all the night. Finally, he gave up and dressed for the day. Leaving early, he did manage to get some of J.J.'s coffee in his belly. It wasn't food but it certainly added octane to his system.

First, he retraced all he knew of Julia's route on the fateful day of her death. He picked up a couple of ham biscuits at Hiller's Gas and Market along with more strong coffee. After a little munching and some conversation with Mr. Hiller, which included some subtle questions about that day, he headed up towards Brown Mountain on Rucksack Road.

Ford pulled off the road by the swampy sink hole that had been Harris DePaul's grave. It was odd to think that something so random as a young boy's fatal car accident ended up uncovering such a bizarre and startling event. He wondered what the man who forced Harris into committing such a crime thought of the discovery in this old sink hole. Ford laughed to himself, *"Who was it that said "dead men told no tales"?*

Ford squinted, trying to stare into that past night when Harris' life ended. His mind's eye watched the drama play out between Harris DePaul, Mara, and Holly. As he came to the fateful shooting he found himself thinking of the same words Holly said, *"That damn dog!"* He found himself clinching his fists, *"If it hadn't showed up I'd already have my hands around the neck of the person who started this whole thing. That is, if Mara hadn't already killed him."*

There was really nothing here to see. Time had replaced the events of that night with mundane layers of life. There were still signs on the ground where Phil Sizemore pulled Harris' car from the murky water. Ford stepped out of his Chevy and began walking around the area where the car was first examined.

Ford's frustrations were just as palpable now as they were all those years before. Sitting on a large rock…possibly the same one where Mara and Holly sat after their final encounter with Harris, his thoughts drifted again. He thought back of Julia and of happier times. Those thoughts jumped suddenly to the graveside as Julia's coffin was lowered into a deep, earthy hole. Ford felt he'd been falling into a similar hole…ever since the day it happened.

His mind quickly changed to thoughts of Felisa. Her beautiful, innocent face a cluster of bandages as she tried to communicate with Ford. He could still see the daze of drugs and pain in those beautiful eyes that once twinkled with liveliness.

It hurt Ford to the bone to think of the pain and horror she faced. Who could know how long her suffering would continue as she went through more surgeries and rehab? Ford knew people were hurt just as much by emotional scars as they were by physical scars. He also knew which ones hurt the longest. The pain that was now her life was brought about because of her connection with him. Joe said he was the one to blame. Ford's mind argued that point.

Just like Julia, Felisa's pain came from nothing she did to deserve it. In fact, her only weakness was letting someone like Ford into her life. Ford wondered about Felisa's mother, Dorotea and her "Uncle" Joe. Ford had walked away, leaving all of them with injuries that would not quickly heal. He could tell himself he was sent away or forced to leave, but that did not change the truth that he left. And yet, trouble was still at his doorstep.

"*Julia! Felisa!* Ford's mind screamed out into the dim swampy area, *"There can't be another one!"* He jumped to his feet and screamed, it was primordial, the sound a gravely wounded animal would make. For some reason, he picked up a heavy rock lying close to the edge of the stinking pond. With great effort and another terrible scream, he pushed the rock over his head and slammed it into the edge of the brackish water and mud.

The sludge erupted as the rock impacted the water's edge. Due to the consistency of the water and muck, there wasn't that great a ripple in the surface of the pond. The angry emotional release made Ford feel light-headed.

Ford's breaths were heaving in hard shudders, a combination of emotion and exertion. Tears filled his eyes and he fell to his knees to compose himself. It took him a minute to feel he was able to get up and leave. His hand went down to the muddy sand to push himself upright. He quickly pulled his hand back as it was stuck by something with sharp-feeling, saw-toothed edges…something man-made.

It was about three inches long, made of a dull brassy metal. He picked it up, wiping and blowing the dirt from its surface. Ford spit on the surface and wiped it on his shirttail. It was a key! He looked around the site, realizing this was probably the point where the car had been pushed into the muddy waters. It could also be the location where Harris' car was pulled out of its muddy grave. From what Phil Sizemore told him, the car was opened up, drained, and the contents examined on the spot he first pulled it from the muck. It was most likely the same spot where Mara and Holly questioned Harris. He remembered her saying she emptied his pockets.

It was dark when Mara emptied Harris's pockets. It was muddy when the Deputies opened the water and mud filled car to examine it. Either time, a single key could have fallen to the ground to be buried by a single or multiple footsteps.

Ford looked at the key, turning it in his hands several times. He realized it might not have belonged to Harris DePaul…but then, something seemed right about it being a part of this mystery.

There were familiar looking markings on the surface of the key. It was not a common looking key, but still, it was a key with a familiar look. A smile crept across Ford's face as he realized what he was looking at. Ford flipped the key up in the air and caught it. He knew exactly what type of key it was and was also confident that he could find the door it would open. The answers he was looking for might not be behind that door, but it most certainly offered him an interesting possibility.

Chapter Fifty-Five

"I haven't shot a real SOB in a long time. I believe it would feel...excellent!"

The two men had been wary of each other at once. Both felt they knew more about the other than was realized. There was a truth that they actually did have a lot in common, both in personality and desired goals. Unfortunately, this very truth was that which would cause their personalities to ultimately clash.

Royal left the conversation open for whatever Vincent needed to discuss. Vincent appeared a little more at ease since Lon was sent on his way. The Sheriff waited for Vincent to lay his cards on the table. He felt him a curious man, not really powerful enough to assure great success in any grand plan, but still having enough clout to make a messy start of anything he felt necessary.

A thought crept into Royals head…or maybe it was only a whimsy. *"I should just pull out my Colt Python and put a quick bullet in your face. I've got a pistol in the desk that I could throw down to make it look as if it was pulled on me."* Then the thought occurred, *"Probably wouldn't need it though, I'm sure he's already carrying a weapon."*

Royal rested his hand under his coat, lightly patting the Python. *"I haven't shot a real SOB in a long time. I believe it would feel...excellent!"*

DiPoli was choosing his words carefully. These types of meetings usually required a certain finesse…even amongst these Southern rubes.

He had been talking almost twenty minutes about the many ideas he felt would bring profits. Now he was ready to move to the heart of the matter.

"I think you can see that I'm very appreciative of the many resources this area offers. The things I've touched on can become great sources of revenue…expanded and grown. The thing most needed is an initial income source creating a very liquid flow of revenue. A catalyst, so to speak. We need a product that can produce the consistent amount of cash that will serve as the foundation of a great enterprise. This cash stream will not only pay for the expansion but will also begin making those invested in the enterprise a tidy sum of money from almost the first day."

Vincent acted pleased with himself in his carefully chosen flow of words. If he was so pleased with himself, then this back-county Sheriff should be very impressed. He eyed Royal closely, trying to read his reaction. The Sheriff finally added to the conversation.

"That sounds extremely interesting, Mr. DiPoli. I'm surprised you have chosen me, the High Sheriff, to discuss the economy of our area instead of the elected officials who oversee such things. I suppose I should be flattered."

Royal crushed a cigarette butt into his ash tray. "I guess then that I am to assume you have already found this great source of ready and fluid cash. I must say, I will be surprised to hear of this mysterious source of overlooked revenue. Perhaps our County leaders need to seek your personal financial counsel?"

The tone of Royal's words left Vincent with the taste of angry bile rising from his stomach. This man was smug and pompous. He obviously had been the top dog around here for too long. If anything, it might be worth it to just plunge ahead without him. A thought occurred, as his hand twitched just outside his coat pocket where a thirty-eight, snub-nosed pistol was carried, *"Maybe I should just remove you from Office, Sheriff. Perhaps, shooting this arrogant fellow would be the very thing to do so I could go on about my business."*

Royal pulled another monogrammed cigarette from the polished box. As he lit the cigarette, he encouraged DiPoli to continue enlightening him with his presentation. But before Vincent could begin again, Royal surprised him by reaching into his desk for a bottle of bourbon and two glasses. He poured a double shot in each tumbler and pushed one over to Vincent.

Vincent eyed the liquid, hesitating to take a sip as he appreciated the gesture. Royal nodded his glass toward DiPoli and took a pleasing sip. As the glass left his lips, he softly said, "This is mighty smooth Kentucky Bourbon, Mr. DiPoli. It is a far different product than the industrious lads of our County make in these mountains. I believe you have found your 'liquid stream' of income, as you call it, in your inquiries about one of our local industries. That would be the production and distribution of a product known as moonshine. I am curious as to how you plan on making this product your own personal river of cash to fund all of the enterprises you suggest?"

Vincent was both surprised and impressed with Royal's perception. He waved the glass in 'salute' and threw the bourbon down his gullet. Smiling, he held Royal's gaze, saying, "I see I am speaking with an intelligent and perceptive man today. Tell you the truth, Sheriff…I'm relieved. I think I am in the presence of a man who knows how to turn a buck."

Leaning forward, he felt confident as he began his offer to the Sheriff. "I see you also do your homework, Sheriff Majesty. Yes, it is true, I've been speaking to a number of people concerning moonshiners and the moonshining business. I must admit, these people around here are friendly but not very forthcoming about the business of making "corn licker" as they call it."

"However, I've come to believe that with your assistance we could really get this business to pay off in a volume you couldn't imagine. I believe you are the very man who could persuade these local fellows to join together in a unified enterprise. You sir, could help motivate all the moonshiners to fall in line with us in expanding the production of the product. Of course, I could be of great help on the distribution and transportation end of the business."

Vincent now had the sound of a smug man. "I'm sure you can have your Department look the other way as the production and transportation grows. I realize you would have to make an occasional show of an arrest here and there. There are many ways in which your Department and your leadership could contribute to this enterprise. I'm sure your creativity knows no bounds."

He then went for what he considered the 'kill' shot. "You shouldn't have to ever be worried again about money. Seriously, you or your family should never have to be without anything…ever again. After two or three years of getting the moonshine business where it needs to be, we can then begin turning to the other enterprises I've addressed. Wholly legitimate enterprises I might add. I mean, I'm speaking of a truck load of money with each passing day. We could own this whole region...my goodness, the State."

Royal made a bit of a show as he returned the bourbon to his desk drawer. *"This cocky little man is sitting in my own office and acting like the High Sheriff of Burke County was no more than a 'pimp'…with nothing more to do than work for a bunch of gangsters."*

"Mr. DiPoli, I think you have actually struck on the most blatantly obvious of answers when you speak of moonshine. It isn't taxed, overhead is reasonably low as is labor. There is a constant demand and some people actually prefer it to some of the more refined spirits. Congratulations!"

Vincent was about to come out of his chair as the sarcasm rolled from Royal's tongue. Still, the Sheriff continued. "I think this is a good time to remind you of a few truths you may find…uncomfortable."

Royal waited a beat to see if Vincent was willing to listen to what he had to say. "Very good. First of all, the making of moonshine has been going on around here for well over two hundred years. It has always been a very highly independent enterprise. It still fits the temperament of these people to remain independent. This is not your confined city area made up of pliable shopkeepers and craftsmen. These people do what they do because they remain autonomous, free will and all of that."

DiPoli acted unimpressed as Majesty continued. "Vincent, the very idea of you trying to unite these people under your domain would only cause them to unite…and run you and your organization to ground. They would die before they became servile to an organization such as yours."

This time, Vincent opened his mouth but was cut off. "You see, sir, your business plan would have a near impossible path to success…regardless of the number of cutthroats you'd bring into play. You could make it a bloody affair but you'd still lose. I think you should understand a bit of this simply from your encounter with the local populace at Mary's Diner just the other morning. That all came about from just a couple of telephone calls. The really nasty folks around here weren't even contacted."

"These mountains have seen many a bloody feud over the past two hundred years or so. The ancestors of these folks stood against the people originally native to this land and carved out their own home. When the Civil War raged, our men went to fight in horrible battles. Our people represented both sides of the picket line. We have men who have fought both the Germans and the Japanese. These are not timid men and women in these mountains. You are not the first to believe you could tame them. Others have made that mistake and many have been bloodied because of their folly."

"Mr. DiPoli, you may take these words as a history lesson but I hope you will take them as wisdom from a source that knows. I hope I can make myself clear in one more thing. And trust me, this is just as important a point as any. This is my land. I am the one who profits from the resources of this county. My family has been doing this longer than you have breathed breaths. I admire your desire to prosper, but let's be clear. Do it somewhere else!"

Vincent shuffled in his seat. He reached for his hat and began to stand. "No, please stay with me another moment, Mr. DiPoli. You see, we should address the other element in play." Vincent's attention was at once alerted and he stared into the Sheriff's fierce, gray eyes that held his gaze. An amused smile was on his face.

"We have not addressed the original purpose of your visit, Mr. Ford Rawlings. I hope I have explained thoroughly that I am heir to a legacy handed down from my Father and Grandfather. However, I think you should take care of your original business before you return to the Northern climes where I hope you will find success."

DiPoli stood, taking his time to place his hat on his head. "So, am I to understand that my 'original business', is just that, my business. My affair with Mr. Rawlings is solely my affair?

Royal's voice indicated he was tired and bored with this conversation. "It is my opinion that this affair started in New Jersey and should have remained in New Jersey. This type of vengeance, or revenge, should not have left the State of its origins. We do not need or require other people's problems brought into our community. I prefer to maintain my own status quo in Burke County. So, allow me to say this…and please do pay attention. I am not a gracious person to those who would disrupt the natural order of things around here that has been so carefully devised. I am not immune to anger and I would not hesitate to put you and yours in a very strong jail cell."

Royal leaned back in his chair. "As far as Mr. Rawlings, do what you need to, reconcile this matter quickly. It is not any of my business or concern unless it spills into the affairs of Burke County. So, please do what you will, then leave! I'll give you three days."

Royal rose but did not offer a handshake. "Let us say we have an understanding. I see no reason for us to meet again. Please resolve your business with the Rawlings boy and find your way back to New Jersey…or New York. I really do not care where you go Mr. DiPoli…I just want you to leave Burke County and stay the hell away. As I say, I can become less than a gracious person if irritated."

Royal pushed a button under his desk that set off a silent alarm at a desk just outside the office. An Officer immediately walked past Beppe before the man realized the door of the office had been opened. The slender Officer stood beside Beppe, dwarfed by the bodyguard's size. Vincent looked to the door and then back to Royal, slightly impressed and thoroughly irritated at the man.

Royal added in a subtle voice, "Let me say again, you will be through with your business in my County over the next three days…one way or another. A pleasure to meet you Mr. DiPoli…don't come back."

Chapter Fifty-Six

"I've had a little trouble headed my way for most of my life it seems."

Two surprising things happened to Ford on his drive back from Brown Mountain. The first thing was that a Deputy by the name of Arvil Smeltzer pulled up behind him, red lights flashing as he frantically waved at Ford to pull over. The other surprising thing was that Ford did just that. He grinned as he thought, *"This is probably the first time I've ever pulled over for a lawman."*

The Deputy was talking on the two-way radio. He finished and walked briskly to the driver side window. Ford was debating on whether or not to get out of the car. He watched the Deputy from his rearview mirror, uncertain of his intentions.

Arvil appeared at Fords door, acting antsy as he stated, "Sorry to bother you, Ford, I've got a message for you." Ford remembered Arvil from years ago when he and others tried to stop his moonshine runs.

Ford waved his hand to dismiss any apologies and asked, "How you doing, Arvil. Been a while, huh. Looks like they've got you stuck in that same old Plymouth you were driving when I went into the Service. What's up…what can I do for you today?"

"Just wanted to tell you that Deputy Shell is looking for you. I caught him on the radio a while ago. I tried to get back to him just now but these mountains knock the radio signal down to nothing in places."

Ford waited to hear the message as Arvil paused and released a large stream of chewing tobacco. Ford remembered the Deputy was always chewing, dipping, or smoking. "I got a message that the Sheriff wants to see you. Lon said you needed to meet up with him at your Dad's garage early this afternoon? Sheriff Majesty looking to have a word. So, can you do that? Meet up, I mean? I'll radio in when I get to where I can catch someone to pass it to Dispatch."

Ford could tell that he wasn't going to get any more information from Arvil. "Arvil, just tell Deputy Shell I'm heading over to the garage now. If the Sheriff wants to see me there, he better come on. I don't know how long I'll be there."

Arvil gave Ford a look that registered plainly that he didn't approve of his tone. "All right Ford. I'll pass that along. Be seeing you. Stay out of trouble."

Ford didn't find it odd that Royal was calling for a meeting. In fact, Ford expected it before now. The fact he didn't want him to come into his office was curious. *"Well, at least he'll have a hard time arresting me at the garage. Shoot, he might not like it but I'll take my leave anytime I want."*

There was plenty to think about as he drove to the garage. A brass key from a murder site…and yes, it was a murder site even though the victim deserved to die. The sorry life that was Harris DePaul was worth hardly a consideration. The harsh fact that his own Mother and the sister of his late fiancé were the murderers of Harris DePaul was a hard nut."

A boy growing up would never think his mother would become a murderer. It was hard to wrap his head around the fact that two of the women closest to his heart had murdered someone. Ford's mind almost twitched as he thought, *"They killed the man who was responsible for Julia's death. The very thing he had sworn to do. I should be glad they did what they did even though I'd rather been the one pulling the trigger! Oh well, I left…they didn't."*

His thoughts became settled until he began thinking of that unspoken name who put the whole tragedy into motion. Ford found himself gritting his teeth as he thought, *"I think I may just want to see you too, 'your Royal Majesty'. I believe I'd like to poke the bear a little. I think your time of corruption is about to come to an end."*

As Ford pulled into his Father's garage he noticed Phil Sizemore having an animated conversation with the *Three Wisemen.* They were all seated except for Phil. It was obvious they were not in total agreement. Ford smiled, knowing disagreements often happened when trying to discuss something with Wallace, Harv, and Trace.

Ford wanted to speak with his Father alone. He wanted to show him the key and get his thoughts. It seemed half the County was determined to show up here today which might become a problem.

Pulling his Chevy over to the side of the building, he got out and gave Tom, Roy, and Gene a hamburger cooked rare. He'd picked the sandwiches up at Dulcey's Bean Pot. On the drive back, he began to realize he'd barely eaten all day. The dogs were excited to received such a treat in the idle of the day. "Should have got you boys an order of fries. You act like you're starved to death."

Walking toward the front of the building he felt the stare of Phil and the three residents of the front porch. Phil spoke up, "Boy howdy, you're not easy to locate some days, Ford. I've been trying to figure you out all morning."

Wallace spoke up, "Leave that boy be. A man's business needs some privacy."

Harv spoke up, "Wallace, you sure don't want people looking into your business. Might find you been visiting somebody's wife on the way to see one of your girlfriends while your own wife is home fixing your supper."

Trace laughed, "I do believe that's happened to old Wallace on an occasion or two. Which wife of yours was it that threatened to sew a squirrel in your pants if you didn't leave Miz Inna Mae Wilkes alone?"

Wallace grinned, "Why Trace, I think that would be hard to answer…cause I think just about every one of them told me that at some time or another."

This brought rolls of laughter at Wallace's expense. He walked over to the cold drink machine muttering. "You are all a bunch of old fools. How am I supposed to help it if I'm loved and desired by so many women? You're just a bunch of jealous and pitiful old fools." Everyone noticed the broad smile on his face as he walked by.

Phil took hold of Ford's arm and pulled him over to the side. Ford was still grinning at the fellows poking fun at Wallace. "Listen Ford, you may have yourself a little trouble headed your way."

Ford was still grinning. "A little trouble? I've had a little trouble headed my way for most of my life it seems. Is this new or old trouble, Phil?"

Phil looked over at the *Wisemen*, not wanting to be overheard. "I'd say both. That Yankee fellow and his men are back…you know the ones from the Diner the other morning. I don't think they're back to finish their breakfast, either. There's something else though, which makes it even worse."

Ford's look turned serious as he knew Phil rarely became excited over nothing. "I ran into Jim Seeley's man, Earl Edwards, this afternoon at lunch. He had been up to Seeley's hunting lodge earlier. Said he was getting the lodge ready for some of those Yankee gangsters to move in. He heard some of them talking like there was a bunch more of those fellows coming in. Maybe twenty or more men."

"I asked him if they were coming to hunt, but Earl said he thought they were supposed to be doing some survey work. Said he they were definitely coming in from up North somewhere. A man by the name of DiPoli was the head guy. He figured with a name like DiPoli, the guy had to be from north of the Mason Dixon."

Phil took a deep breath, "So, I'm here to tell you, Ford. That man's name is either the biggest coincidence in the world or I'd say that was the same fellow who came down here to settle scores with you."

Ford's mind was sobered now. He wondered what exactly Vincent DiPoli was planning. If he was bringing more men into this, then surely there was more to it than a vendetta. But what?

J.J. came out of the garage, wiping grease from his hands. Ford looked over to see him nod toward the highway. Turning around, he saw Mara's Ford convertible pulling in. That was awkward enough, but she had Holly in the passenger seat as well. *"Well, isn't this just getting more and more interesting!"*

The *Three Wisemen,* as always, perked up when Mara came around. They never knew what to expect when Mara stepped on the property but it was usually amusing. All three gentlemen were on their feet as Mara walked over to greet them. She shook each pair of hands, asking about their well-being. She handed Trace a tin filled with homemade ginger snaps which brought great smiles to their faces. Mara could certainly command any stage.

Wallace held on to her hand a moment. "Tell me Miz Mara, how is that Elvis doing? I always enjoy seeing him down here at the business."

Harv punched him on the shoulder, "Aw Wallace, you just

miss seeing all those young women coming by to talk to him when he's around."

Trace guffawed, walking back to his chair with the cookies saying, "Lordy…lordy!" He was quickly followed by the other two hungry *Wisemen*. Mara offered, "Elvis is doing fine. Not to worry Wallace, I'll bring him by soon to spend the day."

Holly was already speaking to Ford as Mara walked over. Phil stood by Ford, not ready to give up on his conversation with the young man. Mara winked at Phil, "How you doing, Phil? Slow day or are you here on business?"

Phil muttered, "Little of both. I'm fine…hope you're well Mara." He looked at Ford, realizing he'd lost his place in line. "I'll be inside Ford…getting me a drink." He looked a bit frustrated.

J.J. joined the little family gathering, figuring there was something said that in some way involved him.

Mara was saying, "Ford, honey. We've been looking for you today. Guess you've been busy. What have you up to, today? I hope you are being careful!"

Ford was not in the mood for games so he glibly said, "Let's see now. Drove by Hiller's and ate a biscuit. Went by the field where Julia died. Stopped by the cemetery and left flowers I got over at Margaret's Floral Shop. Let's see, then went up on the mountain where you and Holly killed Harris DePaul."

Holly let out a small gasp at Ford's direct statement. Mara pursed her lips and gave Ford a displeased look.

He went on, "Stayed around that ole stink hole for a while, contemplating life and death. Seemed an appropriate place, you know. While I was there, I found something most interesting laying in the mud over by the pond." He held up the key so that everyone could see it plainly. "Found it right where they pulled Harris' car out of the muck. Probably close to the spot where you frisked him. It could've fallen out of the car when the Sheriff's boys cleaned it out or maybe it came out of Harris's pocket at one time or another. Either way, I may have found an interesting piece to the puzzle. Depends on what's behind the door it opens."

Ford expected Mara to grab the key from him. Instead, J.J. reached over. His Father began turning the key in his hand as Mara and Holly watched as if the piece of stamped and cut brass would reveal some magic answer.

While they looked at the key, Ford added, “Oh! I also just found out from Phil that the Mob guy…Vincent DiPoli, is back in Burke County…and he’s sent for reinforcements. Looks as if they’re staying up at Jim Seeley’s hunting lodge until they get around to whatever they plan on getting around too.”

Ford ran his hands back through his hair as he said, “I think that’s about it. How are you ladies doing today? Anything exciting happening in your lives?”

Before Mara or Holly could respond a noise was heard from the highway. Deputy Sheriff Lon Shell’s patrol car pulled in, followed by Sheriff Majesty’s black Cadillac. Ford looked at his Mother. “Oh yeah! The Sheriff needs to have a word with me. Busy day, huh, Mother?”

Chapter Fifty-Seven

"Oh honey, if you like that, I'll tell you some words that will peel the meat right off the bone."

Lon stepped out of his car, surveying the parking area and making note of those who were there. The Sheriff's driver, Ferrell, also got out and walked to the passenger side rear door. He waited there in stillness even though his eyes continued moving. Lon positioned himself about ten yards from the car as he wiped the lens of his sunglasses.

Ford sighed, "May as well get this over. I'll be back shortly, so don't go away. It'll be interesting to see what the High Sheriff needs of me. If he tries pulling off with me inside, just shoot his tires out." Ford was the only one laughing at this.

Climbing into the Cadillac, he immediately noticed how well appointed the car was. The engine was still running and Ford was immediately hit with coolness from the air conditioning unit. He plopped down beside the Sheriff. "Nice car, Sheriff. Guess the Office is paying well these days."

Royal offered a smile and his hand to shake. "I see you still have the same personality and rapier wit about you, Mr. Rawlings. I would assume your stubbornness hasn't improved much either."

Ford shook his hand. "Some folks say that's the thing they like best about me."

"Well, as you know, I am not one of those 'folks'. Regardless, I'm not here to trade subtle barbs with you. I have something of importance to tell you and something of prudence I wish to ask you."

Ford stretched back in the seat as he continued to look around the car's interior. "Sure…take your time. I'm just enjoying sitting in this fine automobile of yours."

Royal pushed back the urge to smack him but continued instead. "A Mr. Vincent DiPoli, of New York City, came to visit me earlier today. I believe you are acquainted with the gentleman."

Ford turned to face Royal. "No, I'm not acquainted with the 'gentleman', but I have run into that pompous gangster recently. I would think you'd know all about that. In fact, I'm not sure why you two fellows didn't get along. Wasn't there enough air in the room for both of you?"

Royal smiled, "I see you still enjoy pushing your luck around people who could either help or harm you. But, for the sake of argument, let's just say that would be an accurate description of Mr. DiPoli."

Royal pulled out his monogrammed cigarette case and held it as a lecturer does a pointer. "Upon our agreement that DiPoli is no more than a gangster, I think it obvious that I do not like the idea of a gangster and his thugs finding a reason to visit our peaceful little community. Furthermore, I do not like the idea of a pompous gangster making threats and setting edicts as to what he is going to do within Burke County."

Ford pulled a toothpick from his pocket saying, "Are you saying you want me to do something about it, Sheriff?"

Royal pulled an envelope from his jacket and laid it on the seat between the two men. "I have come to understand there was some nasty business in New Jersey just before you decided to come home. I also understand your time with the Army was spent well in Germany. In fact, you made a good friend in Jovanni Visconti whose family owns the trucking company you worked for over the last few years."

Ford gave Royal a knowing nod. "Look Ford, you see, I appreciated the fact you joined the Army after going through the ordeal you were dealing with at that time. I was even more pleased that you'd made a life for yourself elsewhere…putting the past behind and all."

Royal took time to light a cigarette as he continued. "But now you are back here…in Burke County. Maybe a visit, maybe planning on staying…I wouldn't venture a guess. The problem is not in that you are here. The problem is that you have brought your own particular set of problems back with you. Gangsters and thugs coming into our community is not a thing I can allow. Since they appear to be here because of you and your recent history…I am not pleased. I do not think I should put the citizens of my County or those that serve to uphold the peace in a position where they might be injured or worse."

Ford appeared to take the Sheriff's words seriously. "Sheriff, I didn't invite those boys to follow me here and I've already told them once and for all that my answer was, *No*! I even told them to leave and not come back. Might have mentioned that their health would not improve by staying around these mountains."

Ford added, a little frustration in his voice. "It seems every time some old boys get 'mobbed' up, they get stupid. Doesn't appear they have enough sense to get in out of the rain. They don't understand the simplest of language. For some reason, they think a straight *No,* means *Yes,* if they keep asking."

Royal laughed, "You are correct about the mind of a hoodlum, Ford. In their world, a *No* is almost always turned into a *Yes* as they push their agenda forward. If they can't change a fellow's mind then they change his status from living to dead."

Royal paused for effect and to draw on his cigarette before continuing his lecture. "You see, Ford, those who do the asking have a limited time frame to get the answer they desire. Their bosses will not hesitate to replace those doing the asking if results aren't forthcoming. Their business does not thrive on people telling them *No*. Those that are the *handlers* in their organization make sure their employees understand that they will send others to turn the *No's* into *Yes's* if they cannot be successful. So, you see, those doing the asking only get so many opportunities to get results. Staying alive is a great incentive for most."

"Helluva way to run a business, huh Sheriff"

"It certainly has its merits as well as its downside, Mr. Rawlings. It's just that it can play hell on the personnel list available at any given time. Of course, most businesses, legal or not, thrive on people saying *Yes* instead of *No.*"

Royal shifted in his seat as he blew smoke out the window. He returned the glass to a closed position. "Here is the crux of the matter, Ford. I'm not sure as to what those men want you to do for them. It's obvious you wish no dealings with them. They are persistent by nature and will become more forceful the longer they stay. In fact, I think your presence here endangers many people in our community. People you still love and care about."

It was becoming clear as to the reason Royal wanted this meeting. Ford knew what was going to be next on the Sheriff's agenda. He decided to beat him to it.

"So, you think I should run…leave Burke County and have the bad men try and follow me. That could end up becoming a long time of running…maybe the rest of my life."

Royal turned his hand upward as if to say, *"If that's what it takes."*

"Look Ford, I understand you've been away a long time. Your Father and Mother are both here and this is the place you'd want to return to. The fact that this criminal element has followed you here is most unfortunate. I'm sure it isn't your fault, nevertheless, it's what has happened. I think you need to consider the safety of your family and friends. I think leaving would be the mature decision…a way of keeping the innocent safe. Perhaps you might return one day under different circumstances."

The look on Ford's face turned dark. It was apparent he wasn't happy with what the Sheriff had to say.

Royal tossed the envelope to Ford. "Take this Ford. It'll help get you a fresh start somewhere…wherever you'd like to go. You're not employed, I understand that. Maybe you don't want to go back to New Jersey…and I understand that. There's two thousand dollars in there…enough to get you set up wherever you want. You can get a job anywhere with what you know about engines. Take the money and get you a good life started somewhere. Let's make sure you keep the folks around here safe from these Yankee gangsters."

Ford shook his head, letting out a low laugh. It was too obvious he found the Sheriff's offer amusing. "Well, I tell you Sheriff, I thought keeping the innocent safe was the whole purpose of your Department. I mean, you fellows are still in the business of protecting the innocent from the evils of society…is that not correct? From what I'm hearing, you don't feel your people are up for the task."

He tossed the envelope back to Royal. "As far as this *hush* money or *running away* money, I think you can stick it right back up that black hole you pulled it from. I'd thank you for your generosity but I think it sounds more like you're pretty desperate to get me away from here. I'm not sure what is going on but it seems people keep thinking they can buy me off. I'm just not for sale, Sheriff."

The envelope ended up falling to the floorboard but Royal made no effort to retrieve it. "You really haven't changed in the time you've been gone. Maybe I should just threaten to arrest you. That might convince you to leave town again. It worked before."

Ford's dark eyes sparkled now. "You need to understand the difference in the man I am and the one I was when I left this town. Let me make it perfectly clear to you, Sheriff. I left to keep myself from fulfilling my great desire to kill you. I still hold you responsible for the events leading up to Julia's death. And you've sure made little effort to try and find her killer."

The breaths of each man were becoming heavier now. "Royal, if I hadn't changed any from the boy that left here, then we'd be having a different conversation. I would have come back and done the job I wanted to do a long time ago."

Royal's face began to flush and Ford noticed Ferrell move closer to the door.

"I want you to listen to me, Sheriff. Let's make sure I'm being clear. I'm a more dangerous man than you ever knew me to be. I'm dangerous because I'm here to bring you down. I'm here to identify everyone responsible for Julia's death. I'm not running away again!"

Royal was seething. "I could arrest you! You've gone way too far. You're still upset about Julia…but now you go and threaten an elected County official, an Officer of the Law. I should arrest you right on the spot and lock you up till hell freezes over."

Ford spat out, "So if you can't buy your way out of a problem, you'll arrest me but won't lift a finger against the real gangsters. Listen, you can threaten me all you want. The truth is, I doubt you could find a dozen people in this whole County that would stand up and protect you under any circumstance. Shoot, I could find almost a dozen who'd stand up for me in this parking lot…and they wouldn't be paid to do so."

Royal tried to calm himself as Ford continued. "You're not going to arrest me, are you Sheriff? You've got a few of carloads of gangsters planning to take care of your problem with Ford Rawlings. Hells bells, they've already sent for reinforcements to get their business done. That sure tells me something. It tells me they may have more than little ole me in their sites."

Ford laughed as he looked out the window, giving Lon a wave. "A couple grand would stand to be a pretty small price to have one of your problems go away. I guess the question should be, would it make all of your problems go away?"

Crimson red began crawling up Royal's neck. The impudence of this…mechanic…to speak to him in such a way. He had to calm down since there were witnesses around…but he really didn't want to. He wanted to choke the very life out of this cocky little SOB.

Royal couldn't calm himself so he exploded! "You little worm! I made you a fair and generous offer to take your troubles elsewhere, but you've think you've become some hero since you've been gone. I guess you won't mind your Mother and Father seeing you get gunned down. Maybe they like going to funerals. I just hope there'll only be one grave dug in your Family's plot. Get out of my car you stupid SOB. It'll be a sad day around this County when your arrogance ends up getting innocent folks killed."

Royal's voice steadied a bit. "I mean it, get ready for more funerals, Ford. You'll think a lot different if you survive only to find yourself looking down at your Mother's or Father's coffin. Who knows, even little Holly might be joining the family plot before this is over!"

Just as Ford started to launch himself into Royal, the car door swung open and he was grabbed in mid-leap. It took both Ferrell and Lon to drag the angry man from the car. By the time they had Ford on his feet, they were joined by J.J., Mara, Holly, and Phil.

Ford calmed and smoothed his shirt before saying, "I think we understand each other Royal. You know what makes my blood boil and I know the same about you. To be completely honest, I've already found out some of your secrets and look forward to knowing more. In fact, I found the key to one of your secrets up on Rucksack Road today. You know the place…where Harris DePaul met his end. Looks like Harris didn't take all his secrets to the grave after all."

Royal calmly responded, "Don't think your imaginary evidence will amount to anything or even cause me to be concerned. You've had your chance to leave. The consequences are on your head."

With that, Ferrell closed the door. He walked to the driver's side, never taking his eyes off Ford. The Cadillac threw gravel for some distance as it drove away.

Ford looked at Lon and shrugged his shoulders. "Well, that was fun. Anything else we need to discuss today. My office door is open, it seems."

Lon threw up a hand and walked toward his car. "Be careful, Ford. You're in untested territory. Royal won't be trifled with."

Everyone watched Lon drive out of sight. Then as one, they turned their eyes on Ford. J.J. spoke first, "What the hell was that all about? From the look in his eyes I thought he was going to pull that Python and shoot you in the face."

Phil chimed in. "My goodness, Son. That's what I call *poking the bear* in grand style. I don't know what you said to the fellow, but he sure as hell didn't like it." Phil hesitated before leaning in close to Ford. "So, what did you say to that fellow?

Ford looked at this group of loyal family and friends. He knew he had to tell them because like it or not, they were a part of this *dance*.

So, Ford told them. He told them about the thugs from New York and he told them of Royal's not so veiled threats to his family and friends. It didn't take long for him to tell the story fully, at least what they most needed to hear. When he finished, he said something that surprised everyone. "If you want, I'll leave. I can't put any of you in danger because of any of this. I'll go and figure out another way to bring the High Sheriff down.

"No, no, no…you're not leaving again. We can handle this. That *maiale disgustoso* is not going to run you out of town. I'll fight him myself if he thinks he's going to run over this family." Mara's words had a deadly edge.

Holly eased up to Mara, saying lowly, "What does *maiale disgusoso* mean?"

Mara leaned over to Holly, "It means disgusting pig."

Holly tried it out over her own lips, then said, "I like that!"

Mara smiled, "Oh honey, if you like that, I'll tell you some words that'll peel the meat right off the bone."

J.J. was not waiting any longer. "What are we going to do with this key? If it's what I think it is, we can't just march in and use it." He wiped on the key some more and held it out to further exam it. "Harris has been dead a while now. The box may have been cleaned out by now."

Ford took the key. "I don't think so. Especially if he paid ahead on the box. Since he was just identified as being deceased they might not have heard or even realized he had a box. That being said, I think we need to act on this real soon. The longer we wait, the more likely it will be emptied out…maybe even given to the Sheriff."

Holly asked, "What is the 'blamed' thing to, anyway? How do you even know what it fits or if there's anything there that will help us?"

Ford held out the key to Holly. Unless I'm badly mistaken, this is a key to a lock box inside the Burke County Savings and Loan. Harris wasn't the type of fellow who'd put anything in safekeeping unless it was of great importance. He'd have to have a good reason. I think there's something in that box that connects Harris DePaul to the man who put him up to kidnapping Julia."

He looked around the little circle. "I think there's evidence in that lockbox that will connect him to Mr. Royal Majesty himself. It could be enough to bring that pompous ass down and put him away for the rest of his life."

"Don't you know it would be fitting to have Royal locked away with a bunch of men he may have put in prison himself. Don't think he'd live long enough to make parole…but that'd be okay." Everyone looked at J.J. as his words settled.

Mara added, "Okay boys and girls. Put your thinking caps on, we've got a lockbox to get to and no authority to do it."

Chapter Fifty-Eight

"...he doubted they'd ever run up against anything like the Haddish clan."

Royal fumed in the back seat. He was more disturbed about Ford's tone than the actual words he spoke. There was something there that wasn't bravado or arrogance. There was a serious sound in his words that made Royal wonder what exactly Ford might know. The obvious question that needed answering would be…who else has he told?

The boy just was not going to let this thing about the murdered girl go away. Royal thought the whole issue was nearly over when he found out Ford had settled in New Jersey. He had been biding his time as he waited for the right opportunity to deal with Mara Rawlings and even the Harmon's other daughter. Like his Mother, Ford was just as stubborn, which was going to cause problems.

It wasn't like before, when it was just Ford and the Harmon family sticking their noses into the investigation. Ford was a kid then and didn't have any idea as to what to do. Royal used people inside the Detective Agencies hired by the Harmon's to find no trace of the killer. The issue was easily controlled then but this time around would be different.

Royal re-considered just arresting Ford to see if he could get him convicted of…well, anything. Once he had him under his control, he could put him somewhere he'd find less than healthy. In a place like that, Ford would never survive. Royal considered his missed opportunity, *"Oh well, water under the bridge."*

Ford was a problem but Royal knew he had bigger fish to deal with. The idea of gangsters moving into the community could be a severe problem. Maybe DiPoli was just doing a little 'fishing' of his own by meeting with Royal. It was hard to tell how serious these fellows were when they spoke of new *business opportunities* in his County. Royal frowned, *"It doesn't matter what they think they want, they've had their chance to leave."* Royal was not going to take any chances. They could kill Ford for all he cared. He really preferred it that way. Heck, he didn't care if they took out Ford's whole family. But that was all. He was not about to let them get a foothold in his County.

Whatever DiPoli had in mind would be dealt with. After all, he had his own contingency plan to deal with the thugs. They would never see these fellows coming.

Royal mused, *"I don't know what kind of fellows these Yankee gangsters have to deal with in their world, but he doubted they'd ever run up against anything like the Haddish clan.* He despised using them, but those he used them against, hated them even worse!"

"Ferrell, radio the Office and have Mildred find my brother. Tell her to either confirm he is at his home or that he will be there shortly. Tell her to tell him we are on our way."

Royal laughed to himself, *"I'll let my brother deal with the Haddish clan. He needs some bloody work to do on occasion."*

Chapter Fifty-Nine

"From what I hear, 'Elvis' won't die easy."

If Vincent DiPoli was dissatisfied with his meeting with Sheriff Majesty, then his arrival at the Seeley Hunting Lodge didn't put him in any better mood. He expected to see a long line of cars in front of the lodge. Instead, there were only the two black Buicks that Dino and the fellows drove and four dust-covered Packard sedans. There was no small army arriving in only four cars.

Three of Vincent's men were on the front porch along with six new men. They were all munching on some type of sandwiches. Every man stood as Vincent walked directly inside.

Dino stood by the fireplace in the great room. Drago Rinaldi and another fellow were sitting at a table eating some kind of beans along with a meaty sandwich that hung off the bun. Vincent walked straight over to the table, stopping just to the right of Drago. He leaned forward and spoke in a menacing tone. "I hope there's more men coming than this, Drago. I asked for three or four times as many. You want to tell me what's going on?"

Drago looked at Vincent as if he hardly cared to answer. "Mr. Silvestri has other business going on at the moment. He didn't appear your little trip down South was very important. You got lucky we were on our way up from Florida. We happened to be close so we made a detour for you. You should know, we got issues on the docks that need attention." He wiped his mouth with a handkerchief and stood. "You should count yourself pretty lucky to get anybody at all. Mr. Silvestri seems to think you already had plenty of men to take care of that 'Elvis' guy."

Both men stood staring at each other. Drago was calm but Vincent was steaming. Suddenly, Vincent slammed his hands on the table. DiPoli couldn't see it, but this reaction brought a smile to Dino's face. The other fellow at the table picked up the remainder of his sandwich and left for the porch. The two men stood, staring at each other for several long beats before Vincent walked away, running both hands through his hair wile Drago returned to his sandwich.

Dino spoke up, "Vinny, it wasn't personal. The Family's got lots of stuff going on. Manpower is a little on the slim side, especially since the Caputo's burned up so many guys.

Vincent shot Dino a hard look. "How come you're so educated all of a sudden?" DiPoli certainly didn't care for Dino inserting himself between him and the higher-ups in the Family. He was getting more power hungry and it seemed he didn't care to hide it.

Drago pushed away the remainder of his sandwich and walked over to face Vincent. "Mr. Silvestri told me to let you know you've got four days. He wants everybody back in the City in five…sooner is even better."

Before Vincent could respond, Drago asked, "So, where do we find this Elvis character? Let's snuff him and get back to the world of civilized food." He looked down at the sandwich remains. "I must say though, that was a tasty pork sandwich. Believe I like that spicy sauce on it. I could eat that again, especially with a bowl of *gnocchi.*"

Vincent now had a total of fifteen guys and himself. It would be over-kill just to knock off one guy. Of course, Vincent had much bigger plans beyond Ford Rawlings. At present, he didn't have enough manpower or time to really lean hard on the Sheriff of Burke County.

However, a plan had developed in his mind. A plan that could change his life and just as importantly his position in the Family. He knew that if he had the time and some local cooperation he could begin pulling some decent money out of these mountains. It wouldn't take much time before he could make amends for the losses due to the Caputo's failure. The money would come. It would take a little time and manpower, but it would come. He felt he could find local Politicians to lean on but the first obstacle would the Sheriff.

The sooner he could get his plan started the quicker New York would see him as an important person to be recognized. His whole vision was beyond anything his bosses had ever considered.

Vincent knew that as it looked now, he was going to come out of this looking weak. Maybe he could at least get rid of Dino in this mess as well as blaming any suspicions on him. That could certainly work to his advantage. Dino would make a good scapegoat if any part of this went sideways.

Vincent made a show of pacing, stopping at the fireplace. He picked up a long fireplace poker to emphasis his control. "There's no reason we can't get this done two nights from now. Let's find out where this Rawlings kid is weakest, where he lives, what he does. We can get that done tomorrow. We'll find him and hit him the next day or night."

Drago sat down, deciding to finish his sandwich. "We don't leave any witnesses, right?"

Vincent nodded, "No witnesses. Collateral damage happens if it's the right place and time. Don't make it any bloodier than it has to be. We don't leave any bodies lying around to be found…at least easily. Simple enough, right?"

Drago sarcastically laughed, "Ain't nothin' ever simple about killing somebody. From what I hear, 'Elvis' won't die easy

Chapter Sixty

"What kind of hullaballoo is that?"

Mara's plan sounded ridiculous. In fact, it was ridiculous. The biggest problem was that it was the only plan anyone offered. J.J. and Ford tried talking the women out of it as they traveled into town. Ford and Holly were in his Chevy while J.J. and Mara traveled in her Ford. As they arrived in town, Phil Sizemore pulled up in front of the Bank with his wrecker.

Phil double-parked and waited for the women to go inside the Bank. The two ladies walked purposefully inside. They were dressed in their 'going to town best', including high heels. Holly walked directly to the desk of Sue Marion, an old friend and employee of the bank for some ten years now.

The two women hugged as Holly answered the usual forthcoming question. "Why yes, Sue…you certainly can help me, I think I'd like to look into getting a security box. Where to you keep those by the way? I'd really like to see one."

Sue looked at her friend closely. Holly seemed to be acting a bit hyper. "Have a seat Holly. We have three sizes available unless you need one of our Commercial boxes. If that's the case, I need to tell you we don't have any available at present."

Before Sue could go on, Holly blurted out, "I need the smallest one. Just show me the smallest ones."

Now, Sue was a little perplexed. "Okay then. This is the form you would need to fill out. As you can see…"

Before Sue could finish, Holly jumped in. "Could I see the small boxes. I just might need the medium size. Let's just have a quick look, Sue.

Just then, another voice entered the conversation. Mara walked up behind Holly. "How you doing, honey. I think J.J. is already getting antsy. We need to move this along before he leaves us here."

Sue was feeling a little perplexed by now. Holly stood and looked at Sue expectantly. Sue seemed to have no other choice but to stand with the ladies. "Okay then. Let's go over to the vault and I'll show you the different boxes."

Mara noticed Sue had a key in her hand. "Is that a key to a box? Looks unusual."

"It's a master key, Mrs. Rawlings. The customer has a key to the box and the Bank has a key. It takes both keys to open a box."

Holly and Mara gave each other a quick look and then a negative shake of the head. They stopped in front of the security box area where Sue opened an empty box using the master key and the key that was already in the box. Suddenly a great commotion was heard from outside the vault. There were sounds of two men shouting at each other. The resulting clamor of commotion was heard throughout the bank.

Sue went to the vault door to get a look while Mara moved in behind her, saying, "What kind of hullaballoo is that?" She nudged Sue a little outside the vault as the Bank employee tried to understand what was going on.

Phil Sizemore was inside the Bank now. He was loudly asking who called for a wrecker. Ford walked in behind him, shouting at him for leaving his wrecker double parked and blocking the street. The Bank Manager and another Bank employee were trying to calm things down which added to the commotion.

Meanwhile, J.J. slipped up to Sue and began asking her a question about what type of rates the Bank had on savings deposits. It was all getting very confusing to Sue. She leaned closer to J.J. to try to understand what he was asking.

By this time, Holly had grabbed the Bank master key which Sue had inadvertently left in the box when the commotion began. She frantically scanned the numbers on all the boxes, paying the most attention to the smaller boxes.

Sue broke loose from J.J. and started to re-enter the vault. Mara stepped up, pointing to the Bank lobby. "Oh, my goodness! Look, it's Ford. You remember my son, don't you? I think he's become even more handsome since he's been gone, don't you?" Mara produced several old photos of Ford from her dress pocket and began showing them to Sue.

Holly was not doing well at all. The number on the key was not matching any of the numbers of the boxes. In fact, as she looked at the master key, it didn't exactly match the one Ford found.

Mara couldn't hold Sue any longer and Phil and Ford were made to take their argument out to the street. Sue came into the vault as Mara looked over her shoulder. Holly shook her head slightly indicating she could not find the box. She did have time to slip the master key back into the box Sue had started to show Holly.

As Sue picked up the box, Holly place a hand on her wrist. "I'm so sorry, Sue. I'm going to have to come back. I'm feeling sick to my stomach all of a sudden. I think the egg salad sandwich I ate earlier wasn't so good. I'll come back another time. It looks like you're pretty busy right now anyway. Thank you for your time! By the way, Sue, that's just the cutest dress!"

Mara grabbed Holly's arm and began leading her outside when the girl turned back to Sue. "One question, Sue." She pulled the old key out of a pocket in her dress. "I found this old key in some of Julia's things a while back. Do you recognize what kind of key it is? We have no idea what it might fit. I was going to throw it away but thought I'd ask around about it first. It may have meant something to her."

Sue took the key and looked it over carefully. Studying it closely, she mumbled, "Well, it isn't a safety deposit box key…at least not ours. It only has a two-digit number on it. Ours have a letter and then three digits."

Just then, a Mr. Townsend walked into the vault. He was one of the Department Managers and a long-time employee. Sue spoke up, "Mr. Townsend. Do you have any idea what type of key this is or what it goes to?"

Mara and Holly held their breath as another person was added to the conversation

The man pulled out his reading glasses and eyeballed the key closely. He began to smile and then answered. "I've seen a key like this before. It was probably used at the old *Mountain Laurel Inn*. They had a group of security boxes for their customers. Of course, all of that was hauled away after the fire so that the new Bank could be built." He then added in a disgusted voice, "Like this small town needs two Banking establishments. It's ridiculous if you ask me."

He started to walk off when Mara asked, "Who was

responsible for tearing the building down? They may still have the boxes."

Townsend stopped, stroking his chin. "Oh yeah, that had to be Earnest Horton. Ernie's got stuff piled all around his house. His fields are littered with junk he's hauled away. Don't know if he ever gets rid of anything. I guess everyone finds their happiness in their own way."

With that, Holly and Mara headed to the door. They picked up J.J. standing just outside, but wouldn't tell him anything. The women jumped in the two cars before telling the men, including Phil Sizemore, they should meet back at the garage.

As they pulled away from the Bank, Holly burst out in laughter. It came from a relief that the drama was over and how ridiculous the whole thing played out. Mara was in the car with J.J. looking very pensive as she considered their next step. Suddenly she burst out in loud laughter. "I believe poor Sue was totally baffled at that whole stupid circus we put on."

Inside the bank, Sue Marion watched them leave through the window. She didn't understand what had happened over the last thirty minutes, but she knew something strange just took place.

Chapter Sixty-One

"You sellin' somethin' or passin' out religious tracts?"

Ford and J.J. were talking about chasing down Ellis Banks, one of the few remaining people who ever had regular dealings with Harris DePaul. J.J. knew Ellis was having hard times. He was sick and he had no money. He thought just maybe they could get some information from him using one of his predicaments as leverage.

Mara and Holly argued they needed to head over to the Horton place to see if Earnest might still have some of the old lock boxes.

J.J. offered, "That's a terrible long-shot if you're thinking of finding those boxes. Even if you found the right box and even if it hadn't been opened, what do you expect the chances are that whatever was inside is still intact? I mean, it was in a fire, for goodness sakes. And, it's been sitting in a pile out on the Horton property for a long time now. It's just a real long shot."

Mara countered, "I don't care if Ellis Banks was on his deathbed and could get a reprieve from the Lord Almighty for all his misdeeds, he still couldn't be counted on as a reliable witness. That man forgot what the truth was a long time ago. Besides, if he knew anything at all I doubt he'd tell you just out of spite. He's always been a pain in somebody's rear end. He just enjoys seeing how angry he can make someone. You'd be a heck of a negotiator if you can find the truth in him. Besides, he might not know one single thing that matters."

Finally, the four compromised. J.J. and Ford would try and locate Ellis while Mara and Holly headed to the Earnest Horton place. Phil offered to snoop around to see if he could find out any more information on the New York gangsters. Ford called out to Holly as they headed to their cars. "Bet you a homemade dinner on who gets the best information."

Holly responded, "Yeah, well, who's going to cook for you. I expect something nice when I win a bet."

"Now Holly, you should understand I've become almost as good a cook as my very talented Mother. You'd be lucky to get a taste of my *Veal Milanese.* Melts in your mouth. Taught to me by an old Italian gentleman by the name of Joseph Moretti."

Mara called back over the top of the Ford, "Fix plenty, cause I'm coming too!"

With that, the two cars pulled out…each on a mission. What was not noticed was the car pulling out to follow Ford and J.J. Immediately, another car pulled out to follow Mara and Holly. Then another odd thing happened. From another location, a car pulled out to follow the car following Ford. It was becoming obvious that none of this was going to end well.

The women headed directly over to Earnest Hortons place. He had about twenty-five acres filled with scrub pine, hilly stretches, and an enormous amount of materials salvaged from all over the County and beyond. His property also included five ramshackle barns, a few cattle, and a little land left for growing vegetables, corn, and sugar cane to make molasses.

The yard around the house was uneven and ill-kept. Just walking up to the house in high-heels was challenging. Dogs barked loudly in the background. It was hard to say if they were penned or loose. Mara pounded on the door three times before it was answered by two boys, both under twelve.

"Hello boys. My name is Mara Rawlings. My friend is Miss Holly. Is your Father home…or maybe your Mother?

They stood there several seconds before the older one asked, "You selling somethin' or passin' out religious tracts?"

"Oh my…no! Neither one, just looking for your father so we could see if he has something we might buy. Is he home?"

The older boy simply said, "Nope" and shut the door. The women were left staring at the door. Looking a little closer, they noticed the younger boy standing there, looking at them through the glass part of the door. Holly held up a dollar bill as she called out to the boy, "If your Mother's home, fetch her and this is yours."

The boy took off into the house. A couple minutes later loud voices began coming from inside the house. Eventually a smallish woman came to the door, wiping sweat with one hand and holding a canning jar filled with sweet tea in the other.

"Well, hey-oh, hello Mrs. Rawlings. I didn't know you ladies were here. I was in the back, hanging laundry to dry under this hot sun. Excuse my presence, there's just too much work around here to afford a woman to clean up much." It was just then that she noticed who Holly was. "Glory be, I want you to look right here. Miss Holly Harmon. You're so grown-up and pretty. It's been so long since I've been close enough to talk to you. I've seen you in your Daddy's store a few times. Just working like a bee so I never bothered you. You were always so pretty, but you've truly blossomed since last I saw you at..."

Mrs. Horton's voice trailed off as she started to say, *'your sister's funeral'*. "Oh, Mrs. Horton...you're just fine. I remember you and the family at Julia's funeral. You brought by a mixed berry pie, some homemade bread, and a wonderful casserole to the house. They were just delicious and we really appreciated them."

Mrs. Horton beamed. It was obvious she did not receive many compliments. "You're so sweet...just like your Mother. You get your good looks from her. I just love your Momma." She stepped outside, saying, "What can I do for you ladies today?"

Since Holly had her attention, she led off. "We were told your husband was the one that cleaned off the old Mountain Laurel Inn after it burned. We heard he collected some salvage from what was left...maybe some lock boxes?"

Mrs. Horton took another drink of her tea and sat on a weather-beaten chair. "Yeah, that's right. He cleaned that place right off of Main Street. It was a mess. Had a few things he kept for re-sale. You know what, there were some metal boxes in that mess."

Mara jumped at this. "Does he still have them? Are they here?"

Mrs. Horton walked to the edge of the porch and surveyed the property. She pointed toward a certain hilly area. "Pretty sure they're sitting right over that hill unless he's sold them. See that white post. Just go about fifty yards to the left of that post. You can drive to the post if you don't mind getting your car muddy but you'll have to walk from there."

All three women found themselves staring at Mara and Holly's high heel shoes. Mara spotted a few pair of old, muddy boots near the door. She walked over to pull off her heels and slide her foot in one of the boots to check its size.

Mrs. Horton called out, “I’d shake those boots before I put my foot in them. Critters crawl in sometimes.”

Mara jerked her foot out of the boot, realizing she was blushing a bit. “We’d like to rent a pair each of these boots if we could. Say, five dollars a pair.”

The business woman in Mrs. Horton surfaced as she countered. “Let’s say five dollars for each boot?”

Mara caught a glance at the two boys. “That’d be fine. I appreciate it.” She proceeded to pull a twenty-dollar bill from her purse while Holly shook some boots and checked her foot against the sizes available. She then handed the younger boy the dollar bill which left a scowl on his brother’s face.

They laughed at each other in their fine dresses and nasty looking boots as they walked back to the car. “How does your footwear feel? I’m still not sure my toes are alone in my right boot.”

Holly laughed, “I think there’s a hole in my left boot. I just hope they don’t fall apart on me.” She turned to Mara, “You were generous with Mrs. Horton.”

Mara shook her head. “Aw, that woman and those boys could probably use a little *found* money.”

They stopped at the white post, looking down the rugged row. It was a wild tangle of old wooden beams, rusted metal of various sorts and shapes, and a good harvest of wild and thick weeds.

Both women were a bit overwhelmed. Mara offered a thought. “If there’s critters crawling into boots, then I wonder what sort of critters are in that mess?”

Holly offered, “Wish there had been some hip waiters on the porch.”

Mara laughed, “Now that’d be a pretty sight in your girly dress.”

With that little levity, they began climbing and pushing their way through the wild piles stashed alongside the path.

Holly heard her dress rip as it caught on a ragged piece of metal. She untangled it as another jagged piece caught the other side of her dress. “These old boots may be all I’ve got on by the time I get out of here.”

Mara cackled a laugh just as her dress caught in several places on a large barbed weed. "Dammit! I mean darn it. I really liked this dress, too. Damn thing already has as many holes in it as sieve."

She heard Holy gasp, and then yelp out in pain. "Holly! Are you okay? Where are you?"

"I'm fine Mara. I think I found the boxes but I also found some kind of thorny bush. My thumb is going to be sore as the devil!"

Mara was immediately by Holly's side. Holly was trying to get the remains of the thorn from her finger. Mara grabbed Holly's thumb and bit down hard. Holly screamed out in pain from the bite as Mara squeezed the thumb between two fingers. She had the briar out of the finger while Holly was holding her breath and turning bright red.

Flipping the thorn away, Mara said, "I'd dip that thumb in alcohol when you get home. An ice cube will draw the swelling down."

Holly released her breath as she exploded. "What in the hell was that? You almost bit my thumb off. Son of a b…I mean, gun…son of a gun, that hurt. I almost hit you when you bit down on my thumb!"

Mara grinned at Holly, "Don't doubt it a bit…but if you knock me out you better not leave me out here in the weeds…even if you killed me. I wouldn't be caught dead in these ugly ole boots."

Mara moved toward the pile of metal boxes. "I think Mrs. Horton forgot to tell us that her husband or somebody busted up some of these boxes. Probably trying to find something of valuable. That doesn't bode well for us."

They continued working in the heat, weeds, and grime until Holly burst out, "It's here! It's here and it's still locked. Number Eleven, just like on the key!"

They began to open the box or at least test the key when they heard a motor coming toward them. Holly put the key away and Mara grabbed up two more of the small boxes. Walking out onto the open row they saw Earnest Horton coming their way on an old Harvester Tractor. They moved into his path as he slowed and stopped.

"Good afternoon ladies! Surprised to see you all climbing around in this ole briar patch, especially on a hot day like today. Looks as if you've been hard at work. Hope you weren't too partial to those dresses. Not much of a place for fine dress clothes."

Both women had forgotten about the rips and tears in their dresses and did feel a bit embarrassed as they wondered if they were exposed in any area. Mara dropped the two boxes and Holly threw hers down. They then began to explain they were searching through the lock boxes because Holly had found a key in some of Julia's belongings that might go to such a box.

Earnest looked a little puzzled. "Well, did it? Fit one of the boxes, I mean. I see you've got three boxes pulled out."

Mara answered, "No, it didn't Mr. Horton. I've been looking at these boxes though and I've decided they'd make a nice decorative addition to a cabinet J.J. is building me. I think I can clean them up a bit and make something nice. How much for the three?"

Earnest had the look on his face like he was doing some serious calculating. "Fifteen each…forty-five dollars. They're solid pieces."

Mara countered, "Would you consider twelve dollars each? That would be thirty-six dollars on top of the boot rental we paid."

He studied a minute before saying, "Sure. That's okay. You're going to need some money left so you can replace those nice dresses. Just leave the money with Abigail when you take the boots back." He re-started the tractor and began to pull out as he said, "Thanks ladies! Come on back anytime. Hope you didn't run into any snakes in that pile. Oldest son said he saw five out sunning themselves over there just yesterday. Hate them myself but they keep the rodent population down."

Mara looked at Holly who was staring back at the weeds and piles of junk. "Guess that's something else Abigail forgot to tell us about."

Holly picked up the boxes, her eyes still wide with fear. "Take me somewhere…anywhere away from this place. I don't know which scares me more…snakes or rats!"

As they climbed into the car, Mara mentioned. "I think we're about to find out who the real snakes and rats are. Trust me, the two-legged ones are worse than anything in that rubbish pile."

They drove straight back to Mara's. Both women felt utterly filthy which prompted them to take a quick bath and find a change of clothes before trying the boxes.

Holly found Mara in the kitchen after she cleaned up. She was wearing some fresh clothes Mara found for her. She also sported a bandaged thumb.

The radio was playing. A news story was ending about President Eisenhower signing the first civil rights bill since Reconstruction. The newscaster was pointing out that Senator Strom Thurmond along with some others in the Congress and the Senate were still protesting the new bill. A couple of commercials followed, then the voice of Ferlin Husky was heard singing, *Gone.*

Turning the radio off, Mara came into the dining room carrying a tall glass of sweet iced tea. "Just sip on that tea Holly. I added a little of Uncle Jubal's best. Thought we might need a bracer before opening that box."

Holly asked, "How come you pulled out two more boxes? I wasn't sure as to why."

"Oh, just thought Mr. Horton might see it more of business transaction. If we only bought the one after saying the key didn't fit then he might have been suspicious or a little less likely to let it go. I figured he would let three go without much thought of overpricing them. He needed to feel like he made the deal. The twenty-dollar boot rental probably helped. He's not a greedy man but he needs to feel as if he made a profit. That may be all the money he makes all week. Plus, I do kinda like the idea of using them in some way. A bit of local history, you know."

Mara brought an old towel to spread across the table. Holly carried the lock box and gently sat it down. Fortunately, the boxes had not been exposed to extreme heat or direct flame in the fire. Gently, Holly inserted the key and turned it. Her attempt brought no results. She turned harder, jiggling the key as she turned. Mara appeared with a hammer. With Holly putting firm pressure on the lock by trying to turn the key, Mara gave the box a hard whack on top.

There was a click and the lid opened! Holly opened the box as if a snake or rat might jump out. Looking inside, both women let out a small gasp!

Chapter Sixty-Two

"I have usurpers and trespassers in the mountains."

Ezra Majesty was madder than a hornet caught in a glass jar. Royal was irritating at the best of times. Ezra could deal with that version of Royal. There were the other times though, when he just went too far. This was one of those times he wished could do some type of harm to his brother…permanent harm.

"He should be responsible for his own sordid affairs. Problems with some Mob types should be handled by the Sheriff! What good was his Office if he couldn't use it to get rid of these thugs?"

The whole thing with the DiPoli fellow was bad enough in Ezra's eyes, but now there was the Haddish clan being called into play. And to make matters worse again, he was the one Royal sent to deal with them. He detested every last one of Haddish clan. The elders claimed they were decedents of some lost tribe of Israel which gave them special dispensation in regards to the ways in which they acted.

The Elders consisted of three brothers, Hezekiah, Ezekiel, and Solomon. They ruled the decisions of the clan in all things. Hidden away in a long mountain hollow, the family mostly kept to themselves. When they did venture into the outside world, they acted as if they were mingling with people below their status. They made a habit of looking upon others as if they were servile in regards to the needs of the Haddish.

They were indeed a rough bunch, staying in packs to further intimidate others. Still, there was always one thing that caught their interest from the outside world. They would always listen to any opportunity concerning making money. They rarely cared about the legality of any proposition as they believed themselves above the law. The opportunities just needed to fit their code…whatever that was at the moment. The laws that governed those below the mountain were made by heathen minds, so they felt they held little authority concerning them.

As he anticipated the meeting he found himself rubbing his hand on the ivory grip of the pistol in his leather holster. He believed he would have more regret shooting a stray dog than he would shooting all three of the Haddish brothers.

Ezra needed to calm down before speaking to the brothers. Making them angry was the last thing he needed. Not that he was afraid. He carried the .45 caliber Colt in a holster on his waistband while an ankle holster held a Smith and Wesson .38 Special as back up. His cane could become a deadly weapon with the twist of his wrist. Also, inside the car was two Mossberg pump shotguns primed to go. Then, there were the two Bob's.

Ezra had two bodyguards that watched over his well-being. It just so happened that both men were named 'Bob'. He called them Bob 1 and Bob 2. Neither man had a choice in the matter. Both were built for action and were always heavily armed. His use of a bodyguard was first brought up by his wife, Raven Agata.

Raven Agata Majesty was at best mysterious and at worst a demoness. Ezra, like his ancestors, brought her to the mountains from deep in Louisiana. Unlike the other wives brought to the mountains by one of the Majesty's, Raven Agata LeClaire Majesty came with a sister. Serafine Estelle LeClaire. She was made an employee to justify her quarters in the Majesty household. Supposedly, she was the housekeeper, part-time cook, as well as confidant to her sister.

One sister was creepy, but the two together made a person's skin crawl. At least that was how most people who had contact with the women felt. This, of course, was not the case with Ezra. Rumors were spoken in hushed tones attributing Ezra of bedding both women and taking part in wicked voodoo rituals. All in all, there were plenty of reasons for people to have as few dealings with Ezra and the sister's as possible.

Ezra's car had been met at the lower end of the hollow. He was escorted to the main enclave by four men on horses. They rode just ahead and behind the car, two to a side. Carrying heavy caliber rifles the men wore grim faces and wild long hair covered their head and face. Neither of the riders offered any word as they took them to the group of buildings serving as the quarters of the Haddish clan.

Ezra climbed out of his black, 1955 Cadillac Fleetwood, surveying the encampment. This was the second time he'd been here to facilitate the unique services they offered. The compound had not changed very much. Smoke hung heavy from the different fires around the compound as well as from several chimneys. It was like stepping back in time as he looked at the old buildings and the people making up the populace of the compound. Most stared back at him and the two Bob's in a disinterested or disgusted way.

The two Bob's stood on either side of Ezra as the three brothers approached. They exchanged a greeting which consisted of Ezra acknowledging each brother's name. Two brothers merely nodded to Ezra as Solomon spoke, "Ezra Majesty, welcome to our home".

"My thanks to the Brothers and to your Clan for this meeting. I have work for a few men if you are so inclined. I need twelve, strong and full of heart. I have usurpers and trespassers in the mountains. Foreigners and troublemakers from New York who have come to lay claim on what is not theirs. They bring a demonic set of laws to enslave all the peoples of the mountains. They plan on getting a foothold by making those who live independently in the mountains do their bidding. We want to stop them below the mountains!"

He paused his speech for effect. "We wish to show them retribution and drive them back to the North…to their heathen brotherhood where their laws corrupt and enslave. If they do not choose to leave we would gladly give them a new home deep within the earth where the worms will have their feast. Ten men would be appreciated, twelve would be even better. No more than a week will be required."

The brothers were stoic, not offering any emotion of response. They turned and discussed the matter. Several minutes passed. Turning back to Ezra, Solomon spoke.

"Ten men can be provided. They are all strong, with great heart. Two hundred dollars per man to fight these usurpers. It is a fair price."

Ezra stared into the blank face of Solomon. "Let's say, fifteen hundred dollars total and I'll provide food."

Solomon cocked his head to the side. "One hundred fifty for each man…including food, lodging, and ammunition."

Ezra could see Solomon was taken with his black cane. He held it in front of Solomon, the silver snake head with ruby eyes staring directly into Solomon's eyes. "Done! I'll even sweeten the pot, Solomon Haddish, I'll give you my cane! Furthermore, if the task is done satisfactorily, I'll provide a similar fine cane for Hezekiah and Ezekiel."

Ezra tossed the cane to Solomon. "I'll need these men immediately. They will need to bring weapons and transportation. Meet us at our old mine at five o'clock. It is the one known as "the *Spivey"*. Instructions will be given there.

Ezra returned to the car with the two Bob's cautiously following. Both Bobs were glad to be leaving the compound. They were confident men, but the Haddish clan scared the crap out of them.

One Bob drove. Ezra spoke to the other Bob. "Get on the radio to the Sheriff's Office. Tell my brother the Haddish will meet him at the *Spivey* mine at the prescribed time."

Ezra then mumbled to himself, *"If you dance with the devil himself my brother, you may too soon see the fires of hell firsthand."*

Chapter Sixty-Three

"I said, He is a dead man, I promise."

The box's contents were carefully removed. It was obvious the contents had been exposed to the heat from the fire. Still, everything was intact, including the letter inside. The paper itself was brittle, discolored a bit. The writing was faint in places but still legible enough to read.

Holly pulled out a decorative broach, looking at it as if it was Queen Elizabeth's royal jewelry. The metal pin was slightly bent. "This was Julia's. It's the one she was wearing the day she died…the one Harris said she used to stick him. I wondered if he'd just thrown it away."

Holly continued staring at the piece of jewelry. She felt it odd she wasn't crying, overwhelmed with emotion. Instead, all she could feel was a numbness, something akin to the chill of death. In her mind, all she could see was Harris DePaul's face. He was trying to speak, but couldn't, due to the fresh bullet-hole in his head. His mouth gaped as if he was a fish out of water, gasping for its next breath.

Mara put the paper under a lamp to get the best look at the writing. She read out loud so that Holly could hear.

To anyone who discovers the contents of this box: Please give this letter to the State Police only! Do not give it to anyone in the Burke County Sheriff's Dept. This is a confession! It is not written to make excuses myself. This letter is written to bear witness against the evil man who conjured up this tragedy and pulled me into his evil plans.

Mara looked over to Holly. She was staring at the letter, her breath barely noticeable.

Mara continued but kept a wary eye on Holly.

I did not set out to cause the death of that young woman. That is a fact. The only reason I was coerced into abducting her was due to a great mistake I made. You see, I picked up a young woman at a place called Froggy's. It's a place featuring music, dim lighting, alcohol, and other indulgences. She approached me and appeared to enjoy my company. We danced and drank moonshine liquor for some time. The alcohol took its toll on my senses and my judgement. The young woman and I soon moved outside and into the backseat of my car. We were immediately involved in a most amorous situation. She quickly removed her clothing and was working on mine when a Sheriff's Deputy interrupted.

I never saw the girl again as I was taken directly to the Sheriff's Department. They told me the girl was identified as only being fifteen and I was in all sorts of trouble for providing illegal alcohol to a minor as well as rape, and several other things.

That is when the 'Big Man' himself came in to tell me I would be sent to "Old" Craggy Correctional after a quick trial. He could easily see the sentence to be at least twenty-years hard time. He kept telling me the things done to child molesters in prison. I admit, I was terrified.

The Sheriff's threats piled up until he finally sat down close to me and offered me the hope of having all the charges go away. He said he could make it all go away if I'd do something for him. I asked about the girl but he said not to worry about her. For all I knew, it was just a pure "set-up" so he would have leverage to coerce me into helping him.

"He promised to pay me five hundred dollars and wipe away any trace of my arrest in exchange for putting a good scare into a woman by the name of Julia Harmon. He wanted to send a message to Ford Rawlings and Jubal Rawlings. He said he needed them to 'see reason'. I accepted out of fear, never realizing the consequences or tragic ending. I admit I messed up the whole scheme. I didn't want to do everything I was told to do to the girl. I confess I was feeling so badly for the girl even before I grabbed her. I was so scared I almost backed out several times.

I finally followed the instructions I was given and waited for her to come out of the market. I wore a mask and grabbed her outside Hillers Gas and Market as she put her groceries in the trunk. I came up behind her quickly and got a sack over her head. It was a heavy material so no one heard her scream. I stuck a knife to her throat to get her to calm down and forced her in my car. My car was already running so I took off with her, threatening her with my knife.

That girl turned out to be a fighter, though. I pulled over in a dark spot by the road and tied her hands in front of her. At least I thought I had them tied. Along the way, she slipped the ropes and stabbed me using the metal pin in her broach. (The broach is included in the box.) I was able to block her aim with my arm but the pin stuck deep into my muscle, all the way to the bone. I reacted by hitting her in the face with my elbow to get her off me."

Her head hit the side window and she appeared to be unconscious. I pulled over but before I could reach for her, she screamed and jumped out of the car. It was really dark by then so I couldn't see her too well as she ran away, crossing a field. I was so angry and in pain. I should have just driven away but I was terrified by then. She'd seen my face I figured and I had to at least speak to her. I began chasing her in my car thinking she would become winded and stop. I bounced through the field, sometimes losing her for a second in the darkness.

My arm began throbbing and I realized the broach was still sticking in my arm. I glanced over at my bleeding arm just a second as I painfully pulled it out. I remember screaming just as the car hit a large bump. It caused me to lose control of the steering wheel for just a second. I jerked the steering wheel just as I felt another bump. She must have fallen. All I knew was I didn't see her any more. I knew I'd run over her. I got out and walked back only to see her crushed body. I was sick and at the same time, scared to death. I left her there and drove away. It was truly the most cowardly act I've ever committed. Please know, I am truly sorry!

In this box is a page from a notepad telling me where to watch for the girl and when the best time would be to abduct her. That is all that is on the pad except for the Sheriff Department's letterhead. However, on the back is a handwritten note. It is from a Sheriff's Deputy, Arvil Smeltzer, which reads: 'To Sh. R.A.M.: The girl in question stops at Hiller's Gas and Market on Tuesdays and Fridays. Usually parks to the side of the building. If no one around, a good opportunity. Dpty Smeltzer'.

I am gathering additional proof that will be helpful in putting that evil man where he belongs. My friend, Ellis Banks agreed to hang on to it for me. Tell him this, 'Roosevelt sent me'. He will respond, 'Which one?' Answer then, 'Both of them'.

That is all I have. I'm sure I am dead if this is being read. I think Sheriff Majesty planned on killing me as soon as I completed his job. Since it didn't go as planned, he has kept a close watch on me. I have been threatened and re-threatened about telling anyone. He said he had another job for me to do. I have not heard the all of it but I know some. As soon as I get the rest of the proof I will give it to Ellis Banks for safekeeping. I'm am sure he has plans for me to do murder and I can have no more part of that type of thing.

(Also, you will find one of the Sheriff's special monogrammed cigarettes that I stole from the box on his desk and an envelope he threw in the wastebasket. It is dated to show further proof I was in his Office and approximately when. It's probably all weak evidence except for my word and my detailed accounting. I hope to God it will be enough.)

I wish good luck to whoever has the chance to bring this man to justice. If I am most fortunate, I will be secretly re-located when someone reads this letter. I am planning on sending the key and a letter of explanation to someone who will act upon the contents. If the Sheriff gets hold of this or decides he is through with me, my body will not be found.

Harris DePaul

Mara's blood was boiling. She was ready to spit any number of vile words when she looked at Holly who was still holding her sister's broach. Holly's face was a porcelain white, unmoving as she stared at the broach. Mara leaned over, putting her arm around the young woman's shoulders.

Holly's trance was broken. She looked hard at Mara. "I'm glad we killed that coward. I wish we could kill him again! We need to get Majesty…he has to pay! Tell me we are going to get that filthy bastard, Mara. I need to hear it. I need someone to tell that to me!"

Mara hugged her tightly. Her voice was cold as she said, *È un umo morto, lo prometto!"*

Holly looked up at her, obviously not understanding.

Mara's voice softened, "I said, He is a dead man, I promise."

Chapter Sixty-Four

"Just finish your story, old man."

Ellis Banks lived about a mile off the paved road, five miles from the Treemont town limits. The cabin had been nice in its day. After several years of neglect, lack of interest, and lack of funds to keep it up, it sat as an ugly shadow of its former self.

As a younger man, Ellis made a lot of money through various enterprises. He made money in mining, timber, land speculation, and on several businesses unreported. Now, he puttered around the ramshackle cabin, coughing up phlegm and blood, and living on a diet of oatmeal, peanut butter, and alcohol. Ellis was never known as a pleasant man and now was as bitter as bitter could be.

Ford and J.J. pulled onto the property ignoring all the signs warning trespassers. At one time Ellis kept two mean German Shepard's as watchdogs. Both dogs were dead now and Ellis never found the time or energy to replace them. At least, that's what the two men hoped to be true as they walked to the front porch.

J.J. called out, "Ellis! Ellis Banks! Are you decent? It's J.J. Rawlings and Ford. Can we come in? Hello!"

There was silence. Then J.J. called out again, this time louder. Finally, J.J. shouted, "If you don't let us in, I'm going to break the door down to check on you. You don't want a broken door now do you?"

A shuffling of steps was heard along with low mumbling. After a couple of minutes, the door was opened just enough for Ellis to stick his head out. "What in the Sam-hill do you want, J.J.? I don't owe you no money. I'm a dad-burn sick man…don't feel like jumping up and answering the door!"

Ford tried not laugh at the old at the old cuss. J.J. tried to soothe his ruffled feathers. "Now Ellis, I realize you are a very sick man and I'm sorry to hear of your problems. We were hoping you might be able to answer a few questions that have come up. We won't stay long and I brought something to leave with you for your time."

J.J. sat a large jar of Jubal's moonshine on the table beside the chair Ellis had collapsed into. Ford held a similar jar in one hand causing Ellis to look over expectantly. J.J. got his attention by saying, "We'll see about that jar, Ellis. I've also got a fifty-dollar bill for you. Depends on whether you're civil or not and if you try to help us.

Ellis started cussing under his breath and J.J. picked up the jar he'd sat on the table. "Now don't be that way, J.J. I'm a sick old man, you've got to give me a little slack.

Ford was immediately fed up with Ellis' games. "Listen, old man! You've been an ornery sort of fellow all your life. I remember you kicking my dog once because you said he was ugly. If I'd been more than just a little boy I would have pounded you then. I ain't no little boy now and we don't have the time or patience for your nonsense. We bring you something nice because it's the respectful thing to do and you immediately start your act. You haven't even heard what we came here to ask you."

Ellis curled up his lip just before he started a coughing fit. Picking up an old coffee can that was half-filled with cigarette ashes, he spat a terrible load of phlegm and thick-looking blood into the can. He finished and began wiping his mouth on his sleeve before he spat back.

"Who do you think you are coming into my house and talking to me that way. I don't take bribes and I don't put up with sons-of-bitches like you!" He suddenly pulled a pistol from beside the seats cushion.

Ford was at his side in a flash. He grabbed the revolver and in one smooth move had the gun cocked and under the man's chin. "Listen to me you fool! The last time somebody cussed me and pulled a gun on me, I shot them through the heart. And, by the way, he didn't insult my Mother by referring to her as a female dog!"

"Now, if you think I won't pull this trigger because I know you, well, let me tell you something. The first time I met that fellow, I threw him out the front window of a restaurant. The second time I met him I blew a hole in his heart. Now, with that being said, even though I killed that man, I still liked him more than I like you right now. So, it would be really best for your health if you choose your next words very carefully."

Ford screwed the nozzle of the revolver into the underside of Ellis' chin and held it there. A long five seconds of silence passed as small sweat beads began forming on Ellis' forehead. Ford broke the silence. He looked at his father as he said, "This pile of old bones is about finished anyway. Why don't I put him out of his misery? I can make it look like a suicide. He won't be any more missed than his old buddy, Harris DePaul."

If it was possible, Ellis' eyes widened even further. His mouth opened but he suddenly couldn't find words to speak. Ford un-cocked the revolver and pulled it back. He unloaded the bullets from the revolver's cylinder and kept them in his hand as he tossed the weapon to Ellis. "Don't make me take this away from you again, old man."

J.J. opened the moonshine jar and poured Ellis a double shot in a dirty glass sitting on the table. The old fellow breathed deeply after swallowing the moonshine in one long swallow. A fit of coughing ensued but nothing was hacked up this time. He held the glass for another drink but J.J. closed the jar. "Drink every drop of it till it kills you, Ellis, but not until you try and satisfy our questions."

Ellis started to protest but slumped back into the chair as he eyed Ford. He almost whispered, "Go ahead. What is it you need?"

J.J. started, "You used to have dealings with Harris DePaul. We believe he had something to do with Julia Harmon's death, but he wasn't alone. We want to know what you know about Harris…right before Julia's death and right after. What can you tell us, Ellis? Her family deserves to know so they can close out that terrible event in their lives. An innocent girl abducted and then run down in an old field…left for the varmints and birds to have their way with her body."

The words hung in the air. Ellis looked a J.J., a hollowness in his eyes. He glanced at Ford but would not try to hold his stare. The sweat beads came back and a slight tremor began in his hands. "I don't know a thing about that poor girl's murder…I certainly wasn't there and I had nothing to do with it."

Ford slammed the jar of moonshine onto another table causing Ellis to jump. "He didn't ask you if you had anything to do with it. He asked you about Harris DePaul. Do I need to put the bullets back in your gun?"

"Look fellows, he was a shady man for sure. He could have

been mixed up with any number of people. He didn't travel in very righteous circles, you know."

Ford pulled a ladder-back chair over by Ellis, straddling the seat and leaning on the back. He stared hard at the man, almost daring him to continue this line of denial. Carefully, he mouthed, "For the last time…what do you know about Harris just before and after Julia's death? Last time I'm going to ask, Ellis.

Ellis turned his head away from Ford. "J.J., why do you treat me like this. I've never done anything to you or your family. I'm sorry for the girl…I really am!"

Ford leaped to his feet. He picked up the chair and slammed it into the floor. The chair shattered and splintered. All that was left was the top of the ladder-back in both of Ford's hands. He drew it back and was ready to slam it into Ellis' face when the man cried out, "Nooo! Don't! I'll tell you what I know!"

J.J. poured another drink for Ellis, saying, "Last one."

Ellis downed the drink and began to talk.

"Harris told me he got into some bad trouble with the Law a few weeks before the girl's death. He never told me exactly what it was but he was in deep. We were drinking one night when he told me something about an underage girl playing him. He swore he thought she was older than a mere fifteen. He just couldn't decide if she was playing him to rob him or just wanted sex. Then he said that the Sheriff may have put her up to it to hold over his head and make him do something. He passed out about then and I never mentioned it to him later."

A coughing fit started, causing the old man to almost pass out. After a while he composed himself and lit a cigarette, inhaling deeply. "That's about all I can tell you as far as anything peculiar happening before the girl's death. About a month afterwards, he shows up here wanting to know how he can come by some money. Said he needed to leave and go somewhere and disappear. I didn't have anything for him, so he left. He was scared though. Looked like he hadn't slept in a week. Just looked terrible."

Ellis then slowly got up out of his chair. "I got to take a piss."

Ford grabbed his arm. "Just finish your story, old man."

Ellis wanted to lash out at Ford but was too afraid of him.

"Look, I didn't see him again until about a week…maybe week and a half before he disappeared. Still needed money. I gave him a note to give your brother, Jubal. Told him he might let him buy some moonshine if he thought he could resell it and make a profit. I know he worked something out with Jubal. Figured he got enough money from the moonshine and left town. I mean, we weren't close. We had a few business dealings every so often and would get drunk on rare occasions. So, he didn't have a lot of reasons to tell me much. That's all, I'd swear it."

A squeak sounded from the screen door to the front porch opening. The front door had been left open when J.J. and Ford walked inside. All three men looked up to see Mara and Holly walk inside.

Mara spoke directly to Ellis. "Except that's not really all you know, is it Ellis?"

Ellis turned a little paler if that was possible. He looked as if some apparition had come through his door.

Mara spoke three words, "Roosevelt sent me."

Ellis' mouth opened as his chin twitched. "Which one?"

Mara spoke one other word, "Both."

Chapter Sixty-Five

"Be forewarned, there will be an accounting."

Deputy Billy Horne was anxious to get his latest news to the Sheriff. The Sheriff needed to know of this development immediately but he was afraid to put it over the two-way radio. He felt it was so important, he needed to pull himself off of his detail. He did leave Oz Tanner to monitor the situation and keep surveillance active.

There had to be an important reason why Ford and J.J. Rawlings showed up at Ellis Bank's house. To make it something really interesting was when Mara Rawlings and Holly Harmon ended up at the same place not much later. Ellis was too much a disagreeable fellow to warrant that much company.

The Sheriff was headed to a meeting at the old Spivey mine which was not that far. He would hurry there and come back before much could happen.

Stepping out of the black Cadillac, Royal Majesty had the look of a man who lived up to his name. He surveyed the old mining office as if it was a part of his kingdom. The old 'Spivey Mine' had been shut down for five years now. The land was still owned by the Majesty brothers. The Majesty's still found a use for the office and the land ever so often.

Majesty greeted his Deputy, "Good afternoon Deputy Horne. I understand you have some important news for me. Why don't we sit in my car as you enlighten me?" With that, Royal allowed Ferrell to open the back door and he climbed in, tossing his cigarette.

Deputy Horne followed, happy in the opportunity he was bringing something valuable to his boss. He waited for the Sheriff to give him the opportunity to speak. "Deputy, you have been following the Rawlings woman, is that correct?"

"Yes sir, that was my assignment. I've only pulled away to tell you just what has developed. Those Rawlings' have something going on. First of all, the whole bunch of them, along with Phil Sizemore, met at the Brown Mountain Savings and Loan in Treemont this morning. After a few minutes inside, there was a commotion started just after Phil Sizemore and Ford Rawlings went inside. I started inside, but hesitated as I didn't want to give my presence away. It wasn't long until they all hurried outside, stopping just a minute to discuss something before all of them drove away. They met at J.J.'s Motor Pool and talked a while more before driving off in different directions."

Deputy Horne hesitated to see if the Sheriff had questions. Royal told him to continue.

"Mrs. Rawlings and the Harmon girl drove to the Earnest Horton property and began digging through some of the junk he's dumped there. After a while, they came out of that junk pile with three old metal boxes. They weren't very big boxes and appeared be some sort of lock box. Those women were a mess after digging around in that rubbish. They paid Horton for the boxes and headed back to the Rawlings home where they cleaned up and changed clothes before driving over to the Banks' property. When I arrived, Ford and J.J. were already there. Deputy Tanner had followed the men there and told me they'd been inside for over a half hour."

Deputy Horne looked at the Sheriff who remained quiet, thinking about the information. "That's all Sheriff, it just all peculiar to me. I don't know what Ellis Banks has to do with it but they've zeroed in on whatever he's got or what he knows. It's hard to say what that old coot would have that is so important."

"Yes, it is, Deputy. Please see if you can raise Deputy Tanner on the radio. Tell him to keep an eye on the house and let us know when everyone leaves. Tell him to let us know if Ellis gets on the move. Then tell him we will join him soon, after I see to some business."

"Oh, by the way, Deputy…I don't suppose you were able to get hold of those boxes after the women left?"

Deputy Horne looked shocked. "No, Sheriff. I mean, I was following the Rawlings woman and couldn't stay at the house and go after the boxes. I'm sorry…I just didn't want to lose her!"

Majesty seemed lost in thought. He lit a cigarette as he thought. "That's fine, Deputy. Difficult to do two things at once I suppose. Best you contact Tanner and get back to the Banks house. I'll see you shortly."

The Deputy left for his own car to radio to Tanner. Majesty spoke to his driver. "Ferrell, please radio Mildred on my private frequency and ask her to call my brother. Ask if my meeting is still on at five o'clock. Tell Ezra I expect him to join the meeting."

He leaned back into the deep seat and let out a sigh. "I wonder what was in those boxes, Ferrell. I guess we can look into that later. Perhaps Mr. Banks will enlighten us."

Royal looked at his driver as his mind continued to spin. "Oh, and Ferrell. Please make sure you have adequate firepower at ready in case the meeting with the Haddish does not go well."

Royal then went inside the old mining office for a while. The mine was 'played out' but Royal and Ezra still used the office at times to work on *Majesty LTD* planning, especially when they wanted complete privacy. Both had offices but the mine offered a different degree of security. Sometimes it was a great place to ask someone some hard questions when extreme privacy was needed.

After a bit, Ezra showed up with Bob 1 and Bob 2 in tow. The two men nodded at Ferrell, but that was all. There was a definite feeling of each wanting to be the *alpha dog*.

After a while, they emerged from the office, climbing into the Sheriff's car. Another twenty minutes passed before four old pickups pulled into the parking area. The Haddish's arrival was met with cold stares by the Majesty brothers. Everyone met in the middle of the parking area. There was Solomon Haddish and seven of his men. Facing them was Royal, Ezra, the two Bob's, and Ferrell. Tension was already in the air.

Ezra brought his back-up cane. He pointed it at Solomon as he spoke. "You appear a little light on man-power Solomon. I needed all of them here today. Where are the other four men?"

Solomon spoke to the Majesty's in almost disgust. "Where indeed? Where is the whole truth when you speak? Why do you try to deceive the Haddish? We thought you a man of some honor, but your words are hollow now because of your deception."

Ezra spat out, "What deception? We hired your men out at a fairly bargained price. I gave you my own expensive cane and promised one for your brothers if the job was completed successfully. What deception?"

Solomon twisted and pulled the silver snakes' head from the cane, revealing a long, deadly-looking blade. He pointed it at Ezra which heightened the tension around the circle of men.

"This cane has the same sort of deception as its owner. You did not tell us the usurpers and trespassers were gangsters…mobsters from the North. You led us to believe they were something else…like a plague coming out of Egypt. You gave us not the opportunity to know who we were facing in battle. It is not the righteous war you made it sound to be. Deception! No matter what your arguments!"

"Why would that matter? I didn't think it necessary. Your men are reliable and hardy fighters. What does it matter who they are up against?"

Solomon stepped forward bringing the blade only inches from Ezra's throat. "It matters! You are a deceiver!"

The two Bobs' were about to pull their weapons when Royal signaled them to hold back. He stepped forward. "All right. My brother neglected to give you all of the information. It was a mistake and we both apologize. Now, what do we need to do to move forward? You have promised to do a job for us at a fair price. We have erred, but we have apologized. So now, what else do we need to do?"

Solomon lowered the blade but continued to eye Ezra in a disgustful way. "We will only provide you with six men…good men and three vehicles. They will be yours for four days…no more! You will pay us five hundred dollars for each man…three thousand dollars, no haggling. It is the penalty for your decep…no, your error. Half of the money today…no haggling!"

Solomon looked at both parts of the cane, then threw them at Ezra's feet. "There is no honor in this piece of deception!"

Ezra realized Solomon's words were more directed at him rather than the cane. His anger began to boil but he felt like spitting fire when he heard his brother speak.

"Allow me to make you this offer. Five hundred for each man and five hundred for you and your two brothers. That would be forty-five hundred dollars, but we may need them for a full seven days. The money and the days are both righteous numbers."

Solomon stared at Royal for what seemed a long time before saying, "It is done, then. And, by saying it is done, I mean we are done with deceptions…or it will be finished!"

Royal and Solomon shook hands. Ferrell produced a small case, holding it open. He pulled out stacks of currency in the correct amount and handed it to Solomon. "If your boys are everything they should be, you will have the balance of the cash very soon. If they aren't…we will bury them or bring the bodies to you."

The man to Solomon's right took the cash. Solomon nodded and turned to leave. He stopped at the pickup. "Casualties are sometimes a part of business, but if they are all casualties, it will be very bad for business. Be forewarned, there will be an accounting."

With that, Solomon left leaving six of his clan and three pickups to add to Royal's force. Royal ordered, "You two men…Bob's! There's food in the office there. Take care of these men!"

The two Bob's looked at Ezra who was putting his cane back together. He was seething. He motioned for them to go ahead. "Why did you give them all of that money? That's not how you deal with these people?"

Royal turned to his brother. "I don't have time to squabble. This is how I deal with a situation. I don't leave out details that will upset potential partners! Learn from your experience, Ezra. Besides, the extra expenses will come out of your pocket!"

Chapter Sixty-Six

"Have you ever killed anyone, Ellis? Are you a murderer too?"

"What's going on? I thought you two were over at Earnest Hortons' place."

Mara walked up to Ellis. "He knows. Tell them Ellis. For once in your life, just tell the whole truth."

Instead, Ellis walked over to the fireplace. Reaching down to the side of the hearth, he pulled a small stone loose, reaching under the next stone until a click was heard. Two pieces of board to the side of the fireplace eased away from the wall revealing the face of a built-in safe. Ellis slowly bent down and dialed in the combination. The door opened revealing a sizable, but nearly empty box. Ellis handed a small canvas bundle to Mara. He then returned to his seat and collapsed, breathing heavily as he began coughing.

Inside were a .38 caliber pistol and two sheets of paper. One had the creases and wrinkles of having been wadded up at some time. Mara started to read it out loud, but J.J. reached over, taking it from her. "Let's do this somewhere else." He nodded toward Ellis.

Ford asked, "Is that all there is, old man?"

Ellis' face looked like a death mask. "All I can tell you is that Harris was scared to death of Sheriff Majesty. He never said exactly why. All he would say was if I knew anything it would put me in great danger. He said once I knew I would be ashamed to know him. All I knew for sure was that it had to be dangerous information about someone. I've always hoped no one would ever come asking for it."

He reached over and picked up a jar of the moonshine. He took a long drink. "I heard they pulled his body out of that swampy area out near Brown Mountain. Guess the Sheriff or somebody got to him before he had a chance to leave. It's a shame, I kinda liked Harris. He could keep life a little lively. He'd even bring a couple girls by from time to time for a little socializing. I guess whatever he did probably wasn't any worse than anything I've ever done."

Holly reacted, "Have you ever killed anyone, Ellis? Are you a murderer, too?"

Mara grabbed Holly's arm forcefully. "Don't Holly! It won't help. We need to be careful!"

Ellis looked up at the girl as a certain realization occurred to him. Then something strange happened. Something he hadn't done in almost a lifetime. Something no one living had ever seen Ellis Banks do. Tears rolled down his cheeks.

Chapter Sixty-Seven

"You've come a long way just to kill a couple of hillbillies, Vincent."

Vincent spent the morning and into the afternoon pacing the room, fidgeting on the porch, and snapping at anyone if they asked him a question. He went over County maps several times, making notes and lists of how he wanted the men divided. He would have Dino lead one group. They would attack the Rawlings home and bring in anyone they found there. He would also be responsible to look for any of the Rawlings family out on the roads. Again, they would chase them down and bring them back to the lodge.

Part of his group, led by Drago, would find Ezra Majesty and bring him to the lodge. With hostages in place, he would get word to the Sheriff and Ford Rawlings to come to the lodge for a set-down. The fact that there was no telephone at the lodge irritated him to no end. He did seem to find some solace in the lack of a phone when Dino reminded him, "At least nobody can bother you with questions…like from New York, for example."

It was late afternoon when Vincent's 'scouts' returned. They began to fill him in on the movements of Ford Rawlings and Sheriff Majesty. Both men appeared to be having an interesting day. Ford was chasing around the County and the Sheriff ended up at an old mine where a group of scraggly looking men joined up with him. Most of the men stayed. Vincent figured he'd called in reinforcements.

Vincent thought, *"It won't matter Sheriff. A few more hillbillies to kill won't make a bit of difference!"*

Dino, Drago, and Vincent sat at the lodge table discussing how to go about everything. Vincent was speaking. "I think the best thing to do is to hit, and hit quickly. If we can, we need to take out the Rawlings kid…get him out of the way. He's a wild card anyway and he won't change his mind. Tomorrow, we find him or get him to come to the lodge. Either way, we put him in a ditch. He drives that fancy Chevy so he shouldn't be hard to find."

He looked both men in the eye. "Don't worry about anybody that's with him. Just bad luck on their part. Make it messy if you want. The Sheriff could care less about him. They've got this 'thing' between them. We'll be doing this Sheriff a favor. But, that's okay, he may not be living long his self."

Drago gave DiPoli a curious look. Vincent noticed. "Drago, I know what you're thinking. I want to finish dealing with this Sheriff now so that when I come back there'll be someone here that will be willing to listen to my deal. It's just business. It'll look like one of the Rawlings killed him."

Drago laughed lowly. "Sure Vincent. You're the one that will be explaining it to the bosses. Just remember, you'll have to survive it all to do that."

There was merriment in Dino's eyes at Drago's words. Vincent's eyes appeared to darken as he looked at both the men.

He waited, taking a breath as if contemplating his next words. "We've got plenty of men. Dino, you take a crew and go to the Rawlings home. If the kid is there, go ahead and kill him. My gift to you. Drago, you take another crew and find that Sheriff's brother. He's likely to be at his house. Bring him to me. He might be willing to do business his brother won't."

"As far as Royal Majesty, I'll give him one more chance. It won't be as sweet a deal as before but that's the price you pay for being a smart-mouthed hillbilly. If we need to, we'll put him in the ground so maybe we'll get a better reception when we come back. Just make sure of one thing, we can't have any witnesses left. Anybody happens to be in the wrong place, I say kill them. I don't want somebody snitching to the State Police causing them to be coming after us."

"If we have to, we'll go on up to the Sheriff's house and drag him out. Blinks, you should be back by the time we know whether the Sheriff is coming to see us or we have to go for him. If we have to go, I'll come with you Drago. I wouldn't mind seeing that arrogant hillbilly shot full of holes in his nice, tan suit."

He looked for any argument, but finding none, he went on. "Remember! No witnesses. Dead bodies won't bother me…squealers bother me a lot!"

"It'll be better if we do this after dark. Maybe all these rubes go to bed with the chickens!" He laughed at his humor. No one else saw the joke.

"We know where they live and we know where they work. Just make it clean and we'll be out of this wilderness and back to

New York before they even realize what all happened. This kind of 'wet' work is nothin' new to you guys. Just remember, don't leave any witnesses! *Capesh*?"

Drago ventured, "You've come a long way just to kill a couple of hillbillies, Vincent. I hope it's worth it. I have to tell you, there's some questions inside the *Family.*"

Vincent stared blankly at Drago, his thoughts grinding inside his head. *"One of these days you're not going to have all the blessings of the Family. Maybe, before you know it, I'm going to put a bullet in your head, Drago."* He smiled at Drago as he thought. *"Maybe I'll get lucky and somebody will do me a favor tomorrow."* Vincent stood up to walk away. "Talk to your guys and get organized for tomorrow. Get rested. We've got a long drive tomorrow night."

Chapter Sixty-Eight

"You don't realize how much of an education you've given me, Mara."

Ford and Mara were almost racing as they drove from Ellis Banks' house to the Rawlings home. Their arrival was a dead heat as both tore up dust and gravel as they raced side by side up the driveway into the front yard.

Mara jumped out of the car, obviously pleased with herself. "Thought they used to call you "Hot Rod" Rawlings around here!"

Ford laughed. "That was because I used to run people off the road that got in my way. I played nice today since you had Holly with you."

At that, Holly laughed out loud. Ford thought, *"She's got that same spontaneous laugh that Julia had."* He looked at his forearms as he noticed chill bumps covering his skin.

Holly brought him out of his thoughts by saying, "Guess you owe us a dinner, Mr. Ford Rawlings."

"What…hey, no, I think you owe me one. Banks was holding the prize!"

"Yeah, well we got the box from Earnest Horton and it held the critical information. Plus…we got Ellis to give up what he had. You fellows were just spinning your wheels!"

J.J. put an end to the banter. "Let's just see what all we've got and you two can figure out your dinner plans later. I didn't spend a whole day chasing around Burke County just so you two can bicker about who did what. Get in the house and let's see if this makes sense."

As J.J. walked through the door, he declared, "You two have done made me hungry with all this food talk! Mara! Put a pot of coffee on and let's pull some leftovers out of the fridge. I'm starving!"

The thought of food made everyone realize they hadn't eaten all day. It was decided to have a working meal as they examined what Harris DePaul had left behind. The lock box and the canvas bundle were set on one end of the table while the food filled the other end.

Mara produced a plate of ham, a bowl of potato salad, a jar of homemade sweet pickles, a couple of freshly sliced tomatoes from her garden, and a loaf of homemade bread. The foursome filled their plates.

Everyone was just chomping down on their first bite when a vehicle was heard roaring into the yard. Ford and J.J. were on their feet immediately. Footsteps pounded onto the front porch. Whoever was coming, was coming hard.

A pounding at the door was heard as a voice called out, "Hey, Rawlings family. I need to see you!" Ford, who'd made his way to the door first, swung it open to see Phil Sizemore standing on the other side.

Phil blew past Ford into the room. "Boy, howdy…you folks are hard to run down! I've been looking for you half the day."

Phil stopped suddenly as he noticed everyone staring at him. He became embarrassed as he realized how he had burst into the room. Glancing at the dining room table he noticed the plates of food and fixings. "Guess I could slow down and let you finish your meal."

Phil continued to look longingly toward the table. Mara offered, "Sounds like you've had a full day, Phil. Ours has been plenty busy, too. Why don't you join us? We'll eat and you can tell us your news.

Phil blushed a little but headed directly to the table. It only took a minute for him to find a seat in front of a plate of food. He began eating right away. When he looked up, he found everyone watching him as a they waited on his news.

The wrecker driver swallowed a large mouthful of food, almost getting choked. Again, he blushed. "Oh yeah. My goodness, if I had a brain I'd be dangerous! I've got news. You shouldn't be watching me chewing my food. Here it is."

Phil wiped his mouth and tried to decide the appropriate place to lay his napkin down. Finally, the napkin found his lap and he found his tongue.

"I ran into Jim Seeley's man, Earl Edwards, again this afternoon. He'd been back up to Jim's hunting lodge. Those gangsters we ran off are getting settled in up there. He said it was the same crew, but now they got more men coming in. Earl said they all looked to be thugs…rough-looking fellows. He said, so far, eight more men arrived in four cars. He thinks that makes a total of sixteen of those fellows."

Phil started to take a gulp of coffee. He looked at Mara. "This ain't J.J.'s coffee, is it?" His smile disappeared when he looked over at J.J.

He continued, "Anyways, Earl said when he got there, three of them were looking over a County map and looked to be planning something. They were marking the map and writing notations on sheets of paper. Before they covered the table with a blanket, he noticed 'Ford Rawlings' written at the top of one sheet and 'Sheriff Majesty' written on another. Earl was up to the cabin to check a problem with the water pump. Earl said the one guy they called Dino hurried him into the kitchen and watched him closely. As soon as Earl got through, the Dino fellow almost pushed him out the door. Earl didn't know what it all meant, but he said it couldn't be a good thing."

Ford looked at his father, "Guess they've come back for me. I told you they didn't have sense enough to take "no" for an answer."

J.J. added, "Seems they may also be interested in Royal. Can't imagine that DiPoli fellow and Royal hitting it off too well."

Phil laughed at the sarcasm. "I heard the DiPoli fellow had a meeting with Majesty at the Sheriff's office. It must not have ended well, though. Deputy Whitehead told me a little about it."

Phil leaned forward. "And, let me tell you what else Mel Whitehead said! He told me he heard part of a conversation between Deputy Horne and Deputy Timms about the Sheriff going to a meeting with the Haddish clan. Now, that can't be good either. You think he's getting ready to do battle with those New York thugs. Now that'd be something."

Ford and J.J. looked at each other as Phil's words sank in. It was Mara who spoke though. "That sounds to me like they're both planning some bloodshed. I can tell you all this one thing. I don't trust any of those *feccia.* They may be after each other but I think both of them have every one of us in their gunsights. I think there's a war about to start. We best be getting ourselves prepared!"

As Mara's words faded, so did everyone's appetite. It was Holly who brought everyone back into the moment. "Then I'd say we better get all of this stuff from Harris DePaul sorted through right now. If we don't do it now we're not going to have much of a chance later."

J.J. walked to the other end of the table. He opened the lockbox, emptying the contents. Next to it, he unwrapped the canvas bundle from Ellis Banks' house. As he did this, Mara told Phil most of what had happened since they parted ways earlier. After finishing, they looked across the table as Holly picked up the hand-written letter that was in the bundle. She began reading.

October 8, 1953

To the finder of this legacy: I hope you will use it wisely. You have most likely been led to this letter by opening the lockbox at the Mountain Laurel Inn. I hope you were led to the lockbox by the fact I sent you a key with instructions to begin an investigation. If you have found the lockbox otherwise, then I am sure I will have been murdered. Please remember, my friend, possibly my only friend, has put his life at risk by hiding this bundle for me.

Included with this letter, you will find two additional pieces of evidence that I believe are damning to Sheriff Royal Majesty. This letter offers detailed information concerning Sheriff Majesty's blackmailing me to commit murder for him.

Sheriff Majesty picked me up in his Cadillac on the evening of October 3, 1953. I had been ordered to wait for him where Rucksack Road intersects with the County Road. His car pulled up and I was told to get inside. Ferrell, his driver, then drove away into Brown Mountain. To be truthful, I felt I was going to be killed and left to rot on the mountain.

This was especially true when the Sheriff pulled a pistol and pointed it toward me. He checked me for a weapon as he held the gun on me. Then he told me he had another job for me to do. He said when I did this job he would pay me three-thousand dollars. I was to do the job and leave North Carolina forever or risk a sure death.

I knew then, that the Sheriff was planning on having me killed as soon as I did this job for him. As I sat there in shock, Sheriff

Majesty handed me the pistol. I remember taking the pistol by the trigger guard.

The Sheriff pulled out a small box and laid it on the seat. He let me know what he expected of me. He said, "The gun is empty...bullets in the box here. Didn't want an accidental shooting in my car." He laughed at his own words in a malicious way.

He continued, "I've been monitoring a certain person of interest over the last few months. It seems she is hell-bent on finding out what happened to the Harmon girl. I think she could be a problem for you and possibly myself. So, what I need you to do for me is to kill Mara Rawlings...as soon as possible. If it means killing her husband, or even the other Harmon girl, I need you to finish this thing. You're in too deep to let this get blown up. You do this for us, Harris, and you can go somewhere and make a new life for yourself with a good bank-roll."

The Sheriff then took hold of my hand, squeezing it with great force. He said, "I need this done as soon as possible. I need it done this month. Will you do it for us, Harris?"

I knew I was trapped. If I didn't agree to what he asked, I knew I'd never leave Brown Mountain alive. So, I agreed.

The Sheriff then squeezed my hand even harder saying, "Then get it done...get it finished and go live a life on your own." Then he added, "I'm feeling generous today, Harris. You do it in the next ten days and I'll bump your pay-off up to five-thousand dollars. Okay? Good man!"

I'd set the pistol on the seat along-side the box of ammunition. Just then Ferrell swerved the car sharply. The Sheriff hollered out at Ferrell. The driver was saying he saw a deer run in front of him. But what caught the attention of both men was a bright light shining right in front of the car, about fifty, maybe a hundred feet above the car. It had to have been one of those ghost lights people see on Brown Mountain.

I ducked down to retrieve the box of ammunition that had slid off the seat. My hand felt a wadded-up piece of paper. Picking it up, along with box, I shoved them into my jacket pocket. I then picked the pistol up by the trigger-guard again, slipping it into my jacket as the Sheriff turned to me saying, "Wasn't that a sight! Never seen one of those lights this close. Amazing!"

Sheriff Majesty told Ferrell to take me back to my car. He didn't say much as we drove back. Ferrell pulled up to my car and I opened the car door. Before I could get away, the Sheriff called out, reminding me not to disappoint him. He then handed me a type-written paper with a list of when and where I might best locate "my target". There were no names on the paper, only times and places.

He left and I immediately grabbed a flashlight from the glovebox in order to read the paper I'd picked up. It was a report on the surveillance of 'M. Rawlings' by a Deputy Smeltzer. The report gave places frequented and the roads traveled. There were times listed for each of her trips. There were also notations of when M. Rawlings was usually alone and the hours J. Rawlings normally worked. There were a few other notations. Then, on the back of the sheet I noticed something scribbled, 'Give Martin's pistol to Harris'.

I first thought 'Martin' to be a first name, but then I remembered that a fellow by the name of Jeff Martin, a moonshine runner, had been found shot to death just a few days before. The next evening, I spoke with a guy at the County morgue as we shared a jar of moonshine. I got him to tell me that the bullets pulled from Martin's body were .38 caliber. I believe the gun now in your possession is the gun that was used to murder Jeff Martin. In addition to matching the bullets, you should find the fingerprints of Sheriff Royal Majesty on the pistol grip and possibly other areas. I only handled the trigger guard.

Any of these things alone may not be absolutely conclusive evidence. I think that together with the contents of the lockbox a compelling case can be made. I believe Sheriff Majesty was planning on murdering me after I'd killed Mara Rawlings. Then, he would place the blame of her death as well as Jeff Martin's murder on me, using the gun as evidence.

This is a poor legacy for a man to leave, but I hope at least it will bring an evil man to justice. I leave you this evidence as a sorrowful and repentant man. May God grant me mercy. I'm sure I don't deserve it.

Harris DePaul

Holly handed the paper to J.J. to read again as she picked up the wrinkled paper. "I somehow doubt he was that much of a repentant man. Didn't take him a second to stop on the road that night to try and pick me up." Suddenly realizing what she'd just said, she glanced at Phil who looked at her a little puzzled.

Mara diverted Phil's attention from Holly by taking the page from J.J. saying, "I'd be surprised if the good Lord had anything to offer that *pezzo di sporcizia* except a quick trip to eternal hell!"

Holly shuddered, "That's all he was…filth."

When everyone looked at her, she spoke up. "What? I hear words…I remember things. You don't realize how much of an education you've given me, Mara!"

~~~

As Ford, his family, and his two friends discussed the implications of Harris DePaul's letter, two figures walked away from Ellis Banks' house. A shiny black car was already pulling away from the cabin as flames began flickering at the windows of the old structure. Inside, the badly beaten body of Ellis Banks had already released its consciousness and soul into eternity.
~~~

Chapter Sixty-Nine

"...kill them all and go get a beer."

It was a long night for most of the participants awaiting the coming battle. What amounted to three warring groups were all trying to figure out which of their opponents would strike first or which group they needed to attack first. It was a bizarre and equally ridicules scenario.

Sleep became restless for some and impossible for others. The plans being formulated were being changed and re-changed in the planner's minds.

Confidence was running high in both Royal Majesty's and Vincent DiPoli's minds. Both knew it was about to get bloody and that was the one thing that did not bother either one of them. They just both had different ideas as to whose blood would be shed. Well, they both did agree in thought that it would be Ford Rawlings and his family that would shed the most.

One of those finding sleep most evasive was Beppe Carbone. He wasn't worried as much as his mind was filled with conflicts. He'd never planned on living a gangster's life, but here he was, getting ready to do bloody battle for the sake of a prideful and delusional leader.

Tonight, his thoughts were on everything that had brought him to this place. He remembered a boyhood filled with too many beatings by a drunken Father. The 'old man' fought his many demons by taking out his frustrations on Beppe or his brother. When not in a drunken rage he would become a loving father, willing to sacrifice anything for his sons.

The day Beppe found him dead from one of his alcoholic over-indulges was an empty day for the teenager. He and his brother lost their place to live after their father's death. His mother had been lost soon after his younger brother was born. They'd lived their young lives with little adult supervision or assistance. There were no relatives to take the boys and the few acquaintances the family had could not take on a couple of half-grown boys. The boys were suddenly thrust into an even harder life, now completely on their own.

Georgio, Beppe's brother, was soon picked up by authorities and sent to a facility for orphaned children. Beppe remembered seeing his brother hauled away, a terrified look on his face. Hiding behind a fence, he witnessed the whole thing as he stood on a barrel, peeking over the rough wooden planks. It was the last time he ever saw his brother.

Beppe's life on the street required every survival instinct he could muster. Because of his size and his daring skills, he soon became a part of a street gang known as *the Devil's Hand.* The gang was made up of young men with little or no family. In Beppe's case, he was given a family of comrades and felt like he was going somewhere for the first time in his life.

Then, to make life even better, he was sought out by someone who offered him a permanent job. In only a short time, he found himself working for the Silvestri *Family* as a bodyguard and occasional enforcer.

It was Benny "Bones" Sala that saved Beppe from running with a street gang. Benny found Beppe to be as loyal and trustworthy as he was tough and determined. He also found him to be very grateful for giving him a way to make a decent living. It was this new-found life that afforded him to marry a sweet woman who bore two daughters. Beppe had more than he ever expected out of life.

Beppe's mind was in turmoil now. Benny had recommended Beppe for the responsibility of keeping an eye on Vincent DiPoli. The bosses were taking a hard look at DiPoli since he was responsible for several questionable undertakings over the last year. His last fiasco was the Caputo hijacking attempt. They were not happy with the bloodshed or the outcome. Mostly they were unhappy with all the publicity it brought.

Beppe had been tasked to keep an eye on Vincent and his lieutenant, Dino Bellini. New York wanted reports on what was going on with the two of them. This usually ended badly for someone.

Dino was known to be a manipulative, cold-blooded hood. His willingness to do anything made him valuable at times. His hot temper and thirst for power made him just as much a liability as an asset.

Vincent on the other hand, had served the Silvestri Family for years. He supervised, planned, and made sure the Family was served well in many enterprises. But the last few years Vincent was found to be slipping in his abilities. His plans were often flawed, falling apart in execution. Because of his failures, he had become dangerously paranoid at times and appeared to lack focus. Some felt he was more interested in how he could benefit from any circumstance instead of putting the *Family* before everything. Beppe personally felt Vincent was falling into a deep pit of delusion and insanity.

Beppe knew this whole enterprise was about to go badly. The biggest problem was that there was little he could do to change the circumstances. His ability to report regularly was hampered by the lack of telephone service at the lodge as well as his inability finding privacy and a telephone.

The addition of Drago Rinaldi made everything worse. The bosses may have intended for him to end this fiasco but Drago loved the expectation of a bloody outcome. It was said Drago's motto was *"kill them all and go have a beer"*. That wasn't too far from the truth

Beppe was frustrated that he was unable to perform what he'd been tasked to do. Just as importantly, he missed his wife and daughters. And, he missed his wife's cooking. Beppe suddenly had a great urge for a plate of his wife's noodles, sausages, and gravy. He wondered if he would ever see his wife and daughters again.

He was thankful that one way or another this trip to North Carolina was almost over. Truthfully, he was beginning to wonder if any of them would survive the next few days.

He didn't want to take part in Vincent's war with the Sheriff and he certainly didn't want to take part in the cold-blooded murder of Ford Rawlings and possibly his family.

Beppe rose from his bed about three in the morning. His body was covered with a heavy sweat despite the coolness of the evening. He walked to the front porch of the lodge, nodding to the two men Vincent placed as a lookout. The coolness of the night air had Beppe's bare skin crawling with goosebumps. He found the night air calmed him as well providing a bit of clarity he desperately needed. There was only one path he could follow. It was risky but it might go a long way in saving his life and maybe his immortal soul. He just hoped the *Family* would find his actions appropriate.

Beppe sat on a rustic porch chair covering his bare shoulders with the blanket he picked up on the way outside. He breathed in the cool, refreshing air and listened to the night sounds of the mountain woods. *"This place ain't all bad."* Beppe closed his eyes, allowing the night air to continue to soothe his conflicted mind.

Chapter Seventy

"You've made this personal and that's usually a mistake."

The first attack took place at five o'clock in the morning. There was a heavy mist across the land giving plenty of cover to the two assassins approaching the Rawlings house.

Drago had sent them ahead to do the *job.* Dino had plans to come later, but Drago found it hard to trust the guy. He was a hot head and was known to go nuts when he got the smell of blood. Drago figured if his men could finish off the Rawlings they wouldn't have to divide their forces and he could better keep his eyes on Dino. Besides, if they were successful, at least half of the job would be finished.

The men were moving to the house without hearing or seeing any signs of life. There weren't even dogs barking which seemed unusual for a country farmhouse. It appeared to be easy…maybe, a little too easy.

They climbed the steps as they heard dogs barking off in some nearby fields. Communicating by hand signals, they decided who would take which direction as soon as they were inside. The lock was simple and allowed easy entrance for someone who did such things for a living.

Each eased their way in separate directions as they looked around the first floor. One of them bumped into some sort of empty cage attached to a floor stand. The noise put both men into a defensive stance as they listened for any sounds that could mean the people here had been alerted.

They waited almost a minute before deciding they had not been detected. Assured that the first floor was clear, they began creeping up the staircase. A squeak sounded out on almost every step. They continued steadily, trying to ignore the complaints of the staircase boards that seemed to echo through the quiet house.

At the top of the steps they identified bedrooms and crept up to the doors to listen for any sounds of movement. The quietness was as overwhelming as the creaking noises they made on the steps. They looked at each other, counting down from three with their fingers. As soon as the 'number one' motion was made they threw back the doors and immediately began firing their pump shotguns towards the beds.

The shotgun blasts tore into the beds. More shots followed as they made sure no one was hiding in the dark corners of the room. Both emptied their shotguns and immediately pulled heavy caliber pistols as they waited for the cloud of smoke and goose down feathers to settle. There was no movement or sound made in either room. Both men stepped back into the hallway, checking to see if the other was okay. They scanned the remainder of the upper floor which consisted of two storage closets and a tiny bathroom.

Stepping back into the bedrooms, one of them turned on a light as he scanned the room. The second room's light followed. Both men looked under the bed and into the closet. No bodies were to be found. The thug in J.J. and Mara's room was heard to say, "Smart-asses!"

At the same time, the other thug walked over and removed a sheet of paper pinned to the wall above the bed Ford used. It read, *"I'm coming for YOU! Better go back to New York while you still can!"*

He crushed the paper in his hand and returned to the hallway. The other thug walked out holding a paper of his own. They showed the papers to each other. The second paper was written in red, *"You'll Pay For This!"*

Both men wadded their papers, amused by the childish stunt. One thought to himself, *"Still, the people who was supposed to be here weren't...they knew someone was coming for them."*

The other thug laughed as they carefully walked down the steps. "Bunch of stupid hillbillies think they can leave us a note and scare us off. Maybe they think we won't kill someone that stupid! They'll be surprised at how much I enjoy killing somebody stupid."

They reached the first floor only to realized they might have been set up. Tensing, they lowered their reloaded shotguns as they scanned the dark room. They eased over to the front door, carefully opening it as they peered out into the dark morning. Feeling safe, they walked onto the porch. Both of them stopped short as they noticed for the first time a piece of a cardboard box was nailed to the porch post. In red paint, there was another message. *"Tell Vincent*

DiPoli he is going to die in North Carolina if he doesn't leave NOW!!!"

They returned quickly to their car hidden by the highway. The rays of morning sunlight were beginning to crease the darkness and the sound of barking dogs was getting louder. They hurried away from the small house and headed back to the lodge. Neither one was looking forward to telling Drago what happened.

The two men were met on the steps by the guards stationed there. Walking directly past them, they only took notice of the sleeping giant wrapped in a blanket as he lounged in a large porch chair.

The great room was empty with only a small table light shining. "Hell, they're all still sleeping. I thought they'd be awake by now. Who do you think we should wake up first?"

The second thug did not get to answer as a voice carried from the kitchen. Drago walked out with a coffee cup in one hand and a cigarette in the other. "Did you kill him? Anybody else there?"

One of the thugs threw the sign from the front porch on the table as he said, "Nobody was there, but they left this. Bastards knew we were coming!"

Drago smiled as he picked up the sign board. "I hate funny guys! Funny guys think they're smart guys. Hell, I've killed all the smart guys who've ever gotten in my way."

Another voice entered the room as Vincent DiPoli strolled in wearing a long robe. "Who is it you've been killing, Drago. I don't recall giving you the go-ahead for murder this morning."

"Well now, good morning, Vincent. I was just trying to get an early start. Thought you'd like at least half the day's work done before breakfast."

Vincent walked over and took the sign from Drago. He looked it over as he shook his head. "Well Drago…it looks to me that breakfast may be late this morning." He threw the sign into the fireplace. "Doesn't appear your early morning vendetta went according to plan."

Drago's lip curled up as it always did when he was angered. DiPoli was one of the few people who could get under Drago's skin. He swallowed, then took a step towards Vincent. Drago caught movement to his left. He looked over to see Dino was standing at a doorway, cigarette smoke rising from a freshly lit cigarette.

Dino was wearing pants held up by suspenders, but no shirt. Instead, he wore a double leather holster holding two Colt .45 M1911 pistols. He winked at Drago, then dropped his cigarette on the floor, crushing it out. The two men stood staring at each other. There was a long, hard look between the two. Both knew that they'd have to wait a while longer to settle who was real the alpha dog.

Vincent walked back to his room. "I'm going to finish dressing. Get your boys in here and tell Armo and Gianni to fix some breakfast. I've got some things to go over with everyone after breakfast. I suppose you and your men will be ready to listen…that is right, isn't it, Drago?"

Instead of answering, he said, "They knew we'd be coming. How'd they know that, Vincent. Maybe you need to be talking to your own men. Somebody's not walking the straight and narrow. It ain't none of mine…I can tell you that!"

Vincent stopped as Dino straightened up in the door way. A few seconds passed before DiPoli walked away. He called over his shoulder, "We'll talk about it after breakfast, Drago. I need you on top of this. I want to be on the road to New York tonight. This mountain air can make a fellow a bit crazy. Let's just say we need to work together on this. I've got a plan…let's just follow the plan, Drago."

Vincent walked away but Dino stood his ground. Drago walked up to Dino, stopping only inches away. "I'll be ready to do what's needed today…just don't get in my way, Blinks. I think you've got that Rawlings kid in your head. You've made this personal and that's usually a mistake. I mean, just because 'Elvis' roughed you up the other day and ran you off from that hijacking fiasco don't mean you should get yourself killed because of it." He then winked at Dino, a smug look on his face.

Dino's hand went for his gun but Drago was quicker. Drago grabbed Dino's hand and pushed him against the wall with a great thud. With Dino pinned to the wall, Drago whipped a knife from his belt and held it under the young man's chin. Drago smiled cruelly at Dino until he felt the pressure of the barrel of a .45 against his ribs.

Now it was Dino's time to smile at Drago as he pushed his other pistol a little harder to make his point.

The two men in the room had their hands on their guns as they waited to see what was going to happen. One of the men on the porch came through the front door followed by Beppe Carbone.

Drago moved the knife away from Dino's throat. "You're pretty good when you're not too angry or heated, Dino. Keep your damn cool and we'll find out how those hillbillies knew we were coming for them."

With that, Drago walked outside followed by his two men. Dino glared toward the door, then at Beppe. "You're a lot of help!"

Beppe walked back toward his room. "He ain't wrong, Dino."

Chapter Seventy-One

"Think I may need to call 'Lightning Charlie' in on this."

It was not unusual for Jubal Rawlings to have visitors. Due to their various enterprises, people came to Jubal and Billie's home on a regular basis. They sold honey, molasses, homemade jams, apples in the Fall, and whatever else that allowed them to make a dollar. If Jubal or Billie had a few extra minutes, their customers were also treated with a good story or two to go along with their purchase.

However, the enterprise that made them the most money came from one of the finest versions of moonshine in all of Western North Carolina.

Jubal and Billie lived in a remote area of the mountains near Treemont. Their home was not where their moonshine was sold…for obvious reasons. The production of their main enterprise was not made near their home either. No, that was in a secret location…or several secret locations.

Law enforcement agencies were always on the prowl, so Jubal kept them guessing and searching. Jubal stayed in business because he was careful, always watchful, and did not push his luck. The couple's sons, daughters, their spouses, and even their older grandchildren looked after the many business enterprises with a fervor.

It was and always had been a family business. Ford was Jubal's nephew who made hauling moonshine runs look like a day at the races. Before he was old enough to drive, Ford spent countless hours under a car hood, becoming a top-notch mechanic. He was usually found either at his father's garage or up in the mountains at Jubal's, learning how to build the best moonshine running vehicles around.

Ford was already a legend as a builder and driver of fast cars when he suddenly left for the Army. Jubal knew and understood the reason. He had surely missed the boy when he departed the mountains. It wasn't that he missed the boy as a driver as much as he missed the boy he was so fond of and admired. Now, Ford was back, but it appeared troubles were still following the young man.

Yes, Jubal and Billie had plenty of visitors. What they rarely had were guests. That all changed on this night when two vehicles pulled slowly up the narrow, tree-lined dirt road that led to Jubal's rural compound. By the time Ford's Chevy and J.J.'s pickup parked in front of the main house, there were at least eight rifles or shotguns trained on the party.

J.J. knew his brother well. He knew coming here in the middle of the night was a little risky. The truth was that it was the safest place he could go right now. Holding a flashlight on his face he called out to Jubal and identified himself. A sigh of relief from each of the refugees could almost be heard as Jubal called out, "You're travelin' mighty late Brother! Come on up to the house!"

J.J., Mara, Ford, and Holly were joined by a few members of Jubal's family as they were made welcome with a fresh pot of coffee and some recently made fried apple pies. The foursome helped themselves to refreshments.

While the group settled in to the refreshment, Mara went back to the pickup to bring in a bird cage. Inside the cage was her pet, the very agitated, Elvis. He was squawking as he walked back and forth on his perch. Mara attempted to calm him by offering morsels of nuts.

"Elvis shook up!" "Awk, all shook up!" "Hey baby! Elvis wants a treat!" The agitated bird danced back and forth on his perch. He noticed J.J. which caused more excited dialogue from the bird. *"J.J.'s here! Hey baby, check your oil. J.J.'s here. Want to go for a ride, boys!"*

Finally, Elvis turned his attention to the nuts Mara fed him. She closed the cage door to see that everyone had become Elvis' audience. Billie was smiling and Jubal was chuckling to himself. The younger of the Rawlings clan were gleeful. J.J. shook his head as Holly and Ford whispered to each other as they shared some inside joke.

Finally, they began telling their story, well, at least most of it. The implications were obvious. Their stories skirted around the fact that Mara and Holly had ambushed Harris DePaul and eventually killed him. Mara and Holly had a strategy of what to say if that information ever leaked. It was simple "self-defense". Holly's car broke down. Harris stopped and tried to attack her just as Mara pulled up. A gun was pulled but it was Harris who caught the bullet. They wouldn't mention the dog unless pressed to do so. They'd gone over their story so often they'd begun to believe it themselves.

Jubal and Billie listened intently, only asking an occasional question. It was quiet for a moment after the story was told. Billie broke the silence as she stood, saying, "It's gotten mighty late folks. I'm goin' fix you all a place to sleep on these revelations. Breakfast is at six-thirty, sharp! Don't be late or you'll go hungry."

She looked at Holly as she said, "J.J. and Mara will be in the extra bedroom. Somebody can have the couch and the other can have the chair or the floor. Sorry we don't have more beds."

Holly and Ford began to speak at the same time. Ford spoke over the young woman saying she should have the couch. He followed by saying, "I can sleep anywhere. The Army taught me that much. Give me a blanket Aunt Billie and I'll sleep on the porch if you don't want us sleeping in the same room."

Billie spoke back, almost too sharply. "Wasn't thinking of you, Nephew. Just thought Miss Holly might want some additional privacy. Sleep wherever you want, Nephew. Just not my kitchen…I'll have work to do in there soon." Her features then softened. "Ford, honey, just make yourself comfortable. There's pillows and blankets in the closet upstairs. Love you honey, bless your heart."

Holly looked over at Ford as she shrugged. "It won't bother me, Ford. Don't go outside in the damp. You'll be all stiff and sore in the morning if you do. Let's just all get some sleep, I'm beat!"

Billie hurried upstairs to help get pillows and blankets. Jubal downed the last dregs in his coffee cup. He had a most serious look on his face as he said, "You all get rest. War room meeting after breakfast in the morning. Think I may need to call 'Lightning Charlie' in on this. The old coot owes me…time for him to pay up. Good night all."

Holly whispered to Ford, "Who is Lightning Charlie?"

Ford grinned, then began to whisper. "Jubal and Charlie go way back. He has what you might call, talents, I guess. Haven't any idea of why he's needed but I guarantee it'll be interesting."

As J.J. and Mara snuggled into the extra upstairs bedroom they felt a tenseness in each-others bodies. Mara whispered, "Do you think they came to the house tonight? What do you think they did when they found us missing?"

J.J. said lowly, "Which ones, Mara? We've got two different groups that want our heads. I hope they both show up tonight and kill each other." There was silence for a minute when he added, "I can say this…whatever they did will be paid back ten-fold."

Mara shuddered. She rose up in the bed before pulling J.J.'s face close to hers as she leaned down. "All I know is Royal Majesty is going to pay for his sins! I'm going to *uccidere quell parssita* if I get the chance. He has to die! I'm going to put Royal Majesty down just like I'd kill a rat. He's going down just like he deserves…he's going to die badly just like our sweet Julia did."

J.J. pulled his wife close to him saying, "Just breathe, darling girl. We're all going to finish this whole mess. Julia will be avenged and then we'll find a way to go on with our lives…even Ford, God willing."

Downstairs, Ford was propped up in Jubal's big chair. He did not feel much like sleep. His eyes went from the door to the shape of Holly lying on the couch. The room was dark, but Ford's eyesight had always been good in the dark.

His mind floated from Julia to Felisa and then to Holly. He couldn't help but feel himself being pulled toward the young woman with the waterfall curls. It seemed so wrong, though. She was Julia's sister which made him feel like his thoughts of her were almost incestuous.

He turned his thoughts to Felisa, a woman any man would be fortunate to have in their live. He remembered the hospital and looking at her beautiful face wrapped in horrible bandages. He didn't even know where she was now. Was she was healing or suffering in some unspeakable way. Maybe he should have stayed…insisting to go with her to wherever she went for medical care. He should have stayed with her until she was healed. Maybe stayed forever if she wanted him. Joe Moretti insisted he go. Her "Uncle Joe" was an insistent man who was determined to have his way. Joe was a hard man, but he had his soft spots. Felisa and Dorotea were two of them. Ford would never know if he made the right choice in leaving. He felt he would never have the opportunity to even see Felisa again. In fact, he doubted he'd ever know the answers to any of his questions concerning that lifetime.

Guilt overwhelmed him. He had strong shoulders and could endure a lot. However, the weight of Julia's death and Felisa's terrible injury were almost more than he could bear.

Ford remembered Clara Ricci and even Mara saying he was blessed with God's grace. Was living with the rawness of those you care about being harmed so terribly the *grace* God gave? He shook his head. *"I can't believe this is what God's grace leaves you. I must be missing something."*

Looking back to Holly, he felt even more pressure crushing him. Would she be victim number three? The same could be said for his Mother. They were both in hiding because of him. Their lives were at risk…all because of him. He couldn't allow himself to act on any feelings toward Holly. He couldn't risk another woman getting close to him only to be rewarded with suffering and grief. He had to save Holly by distancing himself from her. That was what he had to do. However, he knew it might be something he could not control.

Keeping Holly safe was a top priority. J.J. made an arrangement for a few fellows to keep an eye on her parents. He shuddered to think of them being pulled into this.

His eyes lingered over the sleeping girl. He whispered lowly, *"I'll protect you Holly. I'll keep you safe even if it kills me. You'll have plenty of time to join your sister… just not now. After you've fully lived all of your lifetimes. Then…you'll see Julia...maybe, me too.*

Chapter Seventy-Two

"The only certainty about war is that some will die, some will be hurt, and some will be left to pick up the pieces."

So, it began…one of the most frightful, confusing, violent, and, redeeming days in the annals of Western North Carolina. Some of what happened would become legend. Other parts would be argued to the extent no one could tell the difference between myth and fact. In the end, what mattered most would be the ones still standing. The legacy of this day would be determined by who remained.

Each group of participants devised their own plan. Some felt their plan assured them victory while some had more than a few doubts. As it has been said, "The only certainty about war is that some will die, some will be hurt, and some will be left to pick up the pieces."

It would become a day consisting of good versus evil, past versus present, hope versus hopelessness, virtue versus vice, honor versus deception, as well as revelations and repressions. It was a day that would change so many lives…both in the present and the future.

~At the Majesty Brother's Old Spivey Mine~

The High Sheriff of Burke County had his plan. He would use the six men from the Haddish clan to neutralize the Rawlings family. He knew DiPoli was the immediate danger. The only thing was the Rawlings family could do him just as much damage if they did indeed have evidence of what happened to the Harmon girl.

One of his men, Deputy Goins, who was used for the more unlawful side of his business would go along with the Haddish men, but stay in the background. He figured this way there would be plausible denial if something went sideways. Deputy Goins would only present himself if it appeared the Haddish's couldn't handle the situation or if he needed to clean up the scene. He would also be around to finish-off any survivors that could create a problem.

Royal knew that if the Rawlings' situation didn't get reconciled today he'd still have to deal with them later. They weren't going anywhere…of that he was sure.

It was DiPoli and his gang of thugs that offered the most immediate danger. One way or another, they needed to be dealt with today. He was sure they were ready to take action of their own. If it was only against Ford Rawlings, well, that was fine. Let them kill off the whole family if they wanted. Royal just couldn't depend on a gang of thugs making that happen. He'd blame the gangsters even if his own men killed the Rawlings'. Who would be around to say different?

Royal decided to go back to his home and make ready for DiPoli. He could fortify it most easily. Deputy Goins was to bring the Haddish back there as soon as they tried the Rawlings place. He'd need every man he had. The thought of setting up at the Sheriff's office in Morganton was easily dismissed. It was much too public and attention was not what Royal needed. If the night went along peacefully, he could gather his combined forces and attack the lodge where DiPoli was staying. He just needs both his men and the Haddishes for an assault.

He knew if DiPoli got to the Rawlings' family first it would not keep them for coming for him. He understood their type and the mind-set that drove them. He'd turned DiPoli down with insults and threats. These men went crazy if they felt disrespected. Pure ego caused these men to react in most violent ways. They could not be perceived as weak. In their world, the weak would be devoured. Perceived weakness was always a fatal flaw.

Royal knew running this type of scum out of the County would do no good. After all, they'd left once only to come back. He told them *No,* as did Ford Rawlings. Still, they remained…ready to do battle, for what? He wasn't entirely sure of all their reasons. They thought they could make country folks bend to their will as they did in the city. It was all pure stupidity but that wouldn't stop them. He knew his words to DiPoli made him the first obstacle they would have to overcome. Royal's thoughts were all hard, *"Come ahead DiPoli. Walk right into my trap. I'm going to chew you up and spit you out. I may even send your heads to the bosses in New York. Let them see what happens to those who would try to take anything from the Majesty's!"*

Royal had six Deputies he could count on to do anything that was required, legal or not. If needed, he could also call in Deputy Sheriff Lon Shell and the four remaining Deputies on the Force. They were held back in many situations that was not straight-forward law enforcement situations. The Sheriff kept his chief Deputy in the dark about his nefarious enterprises. His relationship with Lon was important and worth keeping him from becoming involved in many of the things that added to the Majesty family wealth and enterprise. Besides, he had plans for Lonny Shell.

Lon was made Chief Deputy Sheriff for reasons beyond the norm. The young man was steadfast in his work, a smart and industrious Deputy. He'd learned what was needed to keep the Office in accordance to the highest of standards. Even at his young age, he'd gained respect from the other Deputies and Staff. Even the six Deputies who helped Royal with the darker side of the Majesty business gave Lon due respect.

Royal was very proud of the young man and the job he was doing for the Community. He just hoped he could continue keeping Lon away from the reality of what was required to make the Majesty empire successful. Royal made many promises to Lon's mother, Betty Shell, long ago. He promised Betty as well as himself that Lonnie Shell would become and stay a decent and upright citizen. He made sure his Deputy's actions were driven by the right side of the law. So far, Lon was one of Royal's proudest accomplishments. He was determined this would never change.

Royal had two aces in the hole for situations like he was facing. The first was his Driver, Farrell. The man was very gifted in his abilities both behind the wheel or in the midst of a fight. Ferrell had been Royal's man ever since the Sheriff pulled him out of a stinking cell in Catawba Correctional Prison. Ferrell was still a young man at the time. He was a young man with a hard and bloody past. Facing a lifetime imprisonment for killing the husband of his mistress, Ferrell's future looked dim. The deceased had been a man of some note in his community. He was a small-time politician who had managed to make the majority of his constituency dislike him. Royal pulled a few strings, called in favors, and paid the appropriate money to the appropriate people. Ferrell had been his man ever since.

The other ace he carried was his brother, Ezra. The man was surprisingly dangerous himself. However, his two bodyguards, Bob 1 and Bob 2, brought both muscle and fighting savvy into the mix. The two Bobs handled weapons needed for a firefight and were not hesitant to mix it up. Ezra would only join in if he was in danger or made to. His men, however, would come in very handy. Royal knew this DiPoli thing put Ezra in a tight place too. Like it or not, Ezra really had little choice. As far as Royal was concerned, his brother would have to bite on a hard nut till this was over.

Royal found himself satisfied with his firepower and the fact that he and his men knew this area as well as anybody…especially New York gangsters. He'd let them walk right into his trap. This might not be so hard after all.

~At the Seeley Lodge~

Vincent had a little sit-down with his forces. He had no intention of running around the mountains to chase his targets. He decided he'd give both Rawlings and Majesty a reason to come to him.

The first step was to abduct either Mara or J.J. and hold them at the lodge until Ford showed to either give himself up or try and rescue them. It might be a little harder to find the couple since Drago's men shot up their house earlier.

If they couldn't find either of the Rawlings, then they'd look for the girl they called Holly. She was mixed up in this someway. Probably was a girlfriend to the kid. He figured he only needed one of the three to cause the boy to come to them. Dino and his guys would take care of this phase. In fact, two of his men were already on their way to the father's garage to see if they could snatch him right away.

Vincent planned on keeping Drago and his men to guard the lodge and prepare for the hostages. It would be a place easily defended if they were attacked. He could almost see Majesty and the

Rawlings kid walking up to the lodge, surrendering and begging for mercy.

He didn't know how well the Majesty house was guarded. His lookouts said Majesty's brother would be easy to take. There were only two bodyguards and two women. He'd send Drago and a few men. That should be enough to bring Royal to the lodge. If he had to, he'd go after Majesty's wife and kids. He'd wait on that, though. Kids were such a big pain when it came to hostage situations. It would all depend on the brother and how helpful he turned out to be.

Vincent doubted the Sheriff would call in reinforcements from another County or the State. He was sure the Sheriff was hiding all sort of corruption to risk outside eyes showing up.

When the hostages were brought in and Ford and Royal surrendered there would be no survivors left to tell who did what. Maybe the blame would fall on both Majesty and Rawlings for letting their issues escalating into a feud. It wouldn't matter if all that was left was a bunch of dead bodies.

After a time, when things settled down, Vincent believed he could come back and show the bosses what kind of money could be made here. Whoever replaced Majesty could surely be made to see reason in a partnership.

The members of the gang were methodically checking their weapons and ammunition. They looked ready to go to war. Dino and Drago had moved behind Drago's car. They were examining a pair of Thompson machine guns Drago pulled from the trunk. Dino looked at the weapons hungrily. Drago was amused at Dino's reaction. "Tell you what, Dino. Let's mend fences. I'm going to do you a personnel favor. You want to use one of these babies, today?" He grinned. "Of course, you do."

Dino looked up. "What's your angle Drago? I mean, when have you ever done me a favor?"

Drago laid the machine gun back into the trunk. A crooked smile crossed his face. "Tell you what, Dino. I'll let you use my little toy today to show you we can do business. Consider it a small favor…this toy of mine. Now, when we get back to the City, I may need you to back me up on anything that gets reported to the bosses.

And when I say, "back me up", I mean whatever I say about this drama, you'll agree with me. Anything negative that gets laid on me you're going to take my side. I need you on my side of the story." He watched for Dino's reaction.

Dino squinted at Drago. "What are you thinking, Drago? Are you in trouble?" He waited as Drago lit a cigarette.

"Not me. Vincent has made some people unhappy though. He still has a couple of friends, but he's on thin ice. I don't know how this is going to shake out today. All I do know is that when we get back, there's going to be a sit-down with Vincent. Right now, it's kinda iffy whether Vincent will be walking away from that meeting. So, if you'd like to walk away too, then just back me up...*Capesh?*"

Dino smiled as he picked up one of the Thompson's. "This has a real nice feel, Drago."

Meanwhile, Vincent sat looking over a County map as he sat in a rocker on the front porch. The men looked ready to go. DiPoli's mind passed over the battle ahead. He was already thinking of being on the road tonight. In fact, he was contemplating which of his favorite restaurants he would enjoy first when back in New York. Outside of the Grove Park Inn's restaurant, it had been a long time since he'd enjoyed a meal. As he sat there on the front porch, a mountain breeze picked up causing Vincent to breathe in the cool, crisp air of early Autumn.

At the Jubal Rawlings Compound

The early morning had been a beehive of activity around Jubal Rawlings' compound. He let his folks know that the whole moonshine enterprise as well as everything else needed to come to a halt for a few days. In fact, he recruited a few of his own trustworthy men to pitch in as they all prepared for battle.

Another thing that Jubal did was get in touch with the man called "Lightning" Charlie. Charlie Nabors got his nickname from his expertise in explosives. Charlie's head was covered with a shock of long, white hair. He attributed the color to working with different chemicals for so many years. He learned his basic skills in the Army a long time ago. Then, he honed them in and around the mines of

Western North Carolina.

As if working with explosives was not dangerous enough, Charlie became involved in making moonshine after his semi-retirement from the mines. Charlie said explosives and moonshine production weren't all that different. He credited his expertise in making moonshine to some of the ingredients he used in mixing up explosive charges. Whether that was true or not was never an issue as long as people wanted to drink his 'shine and savor its unique kick.

Some people felt Charlie's moonshine compared favorably with Jubal Rawlings' recipe. Jubal took that as a compliment since he helped Charlie get into the business, teaching him the finer points of production.

Theirs was a long friendship bordering on a type of brotherhood. As teenage boys, they'd worked logging and mining together, forming a close bond that only dangerous enterprises can forge. Charlie went into the Army and Jubal to the Navy. They reunited as soon as both got home from service. Charlie and Jubal had plenty of stories about saving each other's life when they were young and doing dangerous and foolish things together. So, Charlie was easily persuaded to help Jubal and his family deal with the threats they were facing.

The strategy that appeared to make the most sense to everyone on the Rawlings side of things was to make themselves look vulnerable. It could be a dangerous tact to take, but it might cause both of the other sides to overplay their hand. Maybe, if fortune smiled on them, Royal's men and the mobsters would get in the other's way, doing damage to each other.

Ford and J.J. understood that both Royal Majesty and Vincent DiPoli were at odds over whatever they'd discussed. It was up to the Rawlings to see if they could find a way to put them in front of each other as quickly as possible. That should work to their benefit as long as the Rawlings weren't in the middle.

Possibilities were kicked around when it was finally decided they'd just have to stick their necks out and lure either the gangsters or Majesty's men into a trap. The hope was they could bring the numbers against them down to more manageable totals.

Theirs was not an elaborate or elegant plan but sometimes

fine details just got in the way. After all, war was not an exact science…especially this type of war.

During the discussions, Mara remained mostly quiet. She was present, but her mind was already on her own battlefield. J.J. worried because he knew her unpredictability and understood her hatred for Royal Majesty. Ford kept an eye on Mara as he knew how easily she could become a wild and loose cannon…using a sudden urge to cut to the heart of the matter regardless of consequences.

Holly was scared for her friend. She'd seen firsthand how hard she could go after something. There was a warrior-like fierceness in her soul. She needed to talk with her privately. Maybe she could be persuaded to pull back her rage so as not to do anything impulsively. Sadly, Holly knew in her heart that it was too late for Mara to be dissuaded from the path she'd already begun.

Before they all left Jubal's compound, plans were made to protect the families staying at home. They would not be surprised here…at least not without a severe cost to those foolish enough to try.

"Lightning" Charlie approached Jubal with a last-minute change of plan. He swore it would change the odds drastically if it worked. Jubal smiled. "I knew you'd find a way to blow something up, Charlie. Let's shake the mountains!"

~

So, the scheming was done and the plans were in place. The war was primed to begin. Each party seemed anxious to get it started. It was evident that anything, even something as small as the crack of a firecracker would set the whole conflagration in motion. The peacefulness of this mountain community was about to blow up in a single day. There was no reason to even think that compromise or peaceful surrender would ever be considered. This was a day with only one possible outcome…fight to the death, let those still standing claim their victory.

Chapter Seventy-Three

"As he struggled, he heard a low, menacing growl."

The black Buick Roadmaster pulled slowly into the gravel parking area of J.J.'s Motor Pool. Two men were inside the car, scanning the building closely through the dirty windshield. The only movement on this early morning was on the small front porch of the building. Seated in three weathered, wooden chairs sat a trio of ancient-looking Black men. One appeared to be telling a story while the other two looked to be almost asleep in the early morning sun.

They pulled in front of the building. The driver, Rico, got out of the car and positioned himself so that the vehicle gave him some immediate cover if needed. He kept a close watch on the large, open doorway to the garage bays.

The other fellow, Santo, appeared to have a need to adjust his coat, trousers, and shirt collar as soon as he stood outside the car. Cautiously, he walked up to the three Black fellows. As he walked, he slipped his right hand inside his jacket, resting it on the holstered .45 caliber Colt.

Climbing the single step, he paused, listening for any sudden movement from the garage office. The sound of, "Fine morning, wouldn't you say, Mister?" gained Santo's attention as his gaze returned to the three old fellows.

Before he could answer, one of them pointed to the Buick, asking, "Would you be needing some work on that fine piece of machinery today?"

Santo surveyed each one of the trio known to many as the Three Wise Men. "Naw, car's okay. We was just wondering if you might have seen someone we're looking for. We need to find him. We got to talk to him about a job."

The trio made a show of looking at each other as Harv said, "Now, who you need to finding today mister? We've been parked here on this front porch all the morning."

"I'm looking for a Rawlings fellow. You guys know him, I bet."

Wallace spoke, "Well, if you mean J.J. Rawlings, he's the man who owns this fine establishment…but I don't think he'd be looking for another job."

Santo's eyes darted back and forth from the men to the open garage door. Rico moved from behind the car, his body tense, ready for action.

Santo spoke to the trio in general. "No, we don't have a job for J.J. Rawlings. The job is for er…what is it, Elvis Rawlings. You probably know him."

Rico spoke up for the first time as he edged closer to the porch. "Yeah, if Elvis isn't here we'd like to talk to J.J. Rawlings. We'd like to speak with him about his boy." He looked hard into the garage but could see no movement.

Wallace spoke up, "Well, Sir…J.J. left for a bit. Gone to pick up a car that needs some work. I expect him to be back real soon. But now, if you need to see Elvis…why he's just right there in the office. Go on in…you may have to give him a holler so he'll know you're looking for him. Elvis will be glad to speak to you, I'm sure."

The two gangsters looked at each other quizzically. Each man slowly walked by the *Three Wise Men* who stared up at the two men, smiles on their faces.

Santo slipped inside the door while Rico found a position only half way in the door, keeping an eye the three men on the porch. The office was not very large. There was a counter with what appeared to be some office furniture on the other side. They were both bothered by the darkness of the office and the air filled with smells of motor oil and ages old grime. The large front window was so dirty that sunlight barely penetrated.

Santo called out. "Hello! Anybody here? We're looking for Elvis Rawlings. Is Elvis in here?"

They heard a shuffling from across the counter. Both pulled their pistols as they squinted to see exactly who was in the room and where they stood.

An unusual sounding voice called out causing both men to jump. *"Elvis is here! Welcome to the motor pool! Elvis needs a nut!"*

Santo moved forward. "What the hell did you say? Where are you? Why ya sound so funny?" He moved around the counter to search for the smart-aleck spouting off at them. He tripped over a stack of old parts catalogues which sent him sprawling into an old desk. He caught himself by grabbing the desk top. Just then he heard the voice.

"Hey baby! Elvis is all shook up! Awk! Kiss me baby!"

Rico stepped inside the door, his gun leveled across the counter. He was trying to understand who was talking to them in such a way. Santo noticed the bird cage for the first time. He pulled a chain on a desk lamp and gazed into the bird cage at the white bird inside. The bird cocked his head to the side as he stared at Santo. He squawked, *"Elvis loves you baby!"*

Just then a movement was sensed from a darkened corner. J.J appeared, swinging a short length of lead pipe. Santo's head exploded as he collapsed to the floor. Rico leveled his pistol at the sudden appearance of the shadow behind Santo.

He got off one wild shot just as he was yanked backwards, back into the sunlight. His eyes fell towards the now empty chairs where the three Negro men had been sitting. Before he knew it, his hand holding pistol was jerked backwards at such a severe angle, he dropped his gun. As he spun around, a hard fist slammed into his face with great force. He staggered off the porch, falling to one knee. Just as he looked back at his assailant, he sensed movement to his right. Glancing up into the morning sun, he realized one of the Negro men stood looking down at him. Before he could react, the fellow swung a baseball bat across Rico's skull.

Rico ended up laid out on the graveled ground. Wallace stood over the gangster, a big smile on his face. "I've used that old bat on relatives, sneak thieves, husbands and ex-husbands, boyfriends past and present. Even used it once on one of my previous wives…at least I think she was my wife." Wallace looked off into the distance. "Yeah, I think she was my wife…probably had something to with why she divorced me...but I was only defending myself. Think she had a knife she was going to use on me." He looked back at the collapsed form of Rico. "But, I got to say this…you're the first gangster I've ever got to slam…felt pretty good, too!"

J.J. came through the office door dragging the limp body of Santo. He laid him out beside this companion. Elvis could be heard still squawking due to the loud gunshot. Phil walked up, rubbing the knuckles on his right hand. He was carrying a roll of sturdy rope.

Santo was the first to regain consciousness some time later. He realized immediately he was outside. He also realized both his hands and legs were bound. He began squirming to see if his bindings would loosen. As he struggled, he heard a low, menacing growl. Looking to his right he saw three very large dogs looking at him with malice.

As he slowly looked around he could see that he was surrounded by a heavy, wire fence on three sides. The fourth side of the enclosure was the back of the garage. He, and the still unconscious Rico were tied to a large shady tree in what appeared to be a dog lot. The three dogs inside were sitting, watching over the bound men in a serious vigil. Santo could see for certain, neither he or Rico would be going anywhere anytime soon.

Chapter Seventy-Four

"Don't think I can make it today, Deputy."

Mara would not be denied. After all, it was her house and she better not find anything damaged inside. If even one thing was broken or missing there would be somebody's head on a stick.

Mara rode between two of Jubal Rawlings' men on the bench seat of a 1951 Chevy pickup. The two men, Roark and Lam, were some of Jubal's moonshine cooking crew. Mara gauged them to both be in their mid-forties. They were not dirty in their looks or dress but carried a light odor of stale sweat. If it had not been for the open windows, the men's aroma might have driven Mara to the bed of the pickup. Instead she toughed it out, appreciative that they were putting their lives on the line for her.

Roark slowly pulled up the Rawlings' driveway. He didn't stop until he had the truck nosed back out toward the County road. Lam, short for Lambert, opened the door and stepped down before the truck fully stopped. He was holding a .410gauge shotgun with a Smith and Wesson revolver in a holster. Both men had been casual on the way over, talking with Mara about some of her recipes. Now, they were different men. Their bodies were tensed, their eyes squinted in a hard focus seeking any danger.

Mara immediately started to exit the car but stopped on Roark's command. "Just wait a minute, Miss Mara, we don't need to rush into this thing. Let's let the air out of the bottle slowly. Don't need any surprises."

For the first time, Mara felt a small surge of anxiety run through her veins. She reached inside her shoulder bag to feel the comfortable grip of her own Smith and Wesson Model 39. Lam steadily advanced on the house, stopping just at the door. He waited a heart-beat and slipped inside the nearly open front door.

Mara found herself forgetting to breathe. She lightly gasped as she realized the front door had been locked when they left the previous night. Minutes passed as they waited for Lam to reappear. Mara, who rarely was bothered with sweating, felt a trickle roll down the side of her face. The tiny hairs on her neck seemed to stand on end. Finally, she could take it no longer. The cab of the truck seemed to be out of oxygen to breathe. She jumped from the cab just as Roark turned to tell her to wait. She gave him a hard look which was all it took to satisfy the man. Their attention turned back toward the house to see Lam walk out shaking his head.

Roark held his ground while Mara walked quickly to the porch. Lam met her at the steps, holding her back with the look on his face. "You may not want to go inside Mrs. Rawlings. Somebody's been here and shot up the bedrooms. It's a pretty bad mess up there."

Mara's eyes opened wide as her face flushed considerably. She found herself cursing under her breath. She blew by Lam and headed directly upstairs. Half way up the steps she stopped. There was a moment when she suddenly felt herself to be a stranger in her own house. Her home had been violated which meant she was in turn violated. Standing on the step, she felt her anger turn into a burning rage.

She bounded up the remaining steps, stopping at her bedroom door. The destruction was everywhere. She knew that whoever did this fully expected her and J.J. to be lying in their bed. Walking to the side of the bed, she knelt, picking up a shattered picture frame. It had been a gift from J.J.'s parents. The destroyed frame held a favorite picture of her, J.J., and baby Ford. She remembered it being an Easter Sunday morning so long ago.

Lam's shout alerted Mara at once. She dropped the destroyed picture frame and hurried to the steps. Just then she heard the sounds of gunshots from the front of the house. She heard Lam call out, "Come on Mrs. Rawlings! They're here! Hurry!"

Mara flew down the steps to see Lam crouched by the door firing toward the front yard. Through the window, she could see Roark trying to fire back from behind the truck. One body sprawled behind a tree, a dark stain on the left side of his shirt. Another body was close by, crawling for cover because of a leg wound. Neither wore uniforms and did not look to be Royal Majesty's men.

Lam shouted to her amid the rapid sound of countless bullets being fired in their direction. "They've got us pinned down in front. Roark took a shot in his side. He's trying to get inside the truck and drive by the front here. If he can, we might be able to jump in the truck bed so he can drive us out of here." It didn't appear to be a sound plan concerning Roark's bleeding side.

Just then they heard the engine of the truck fire up. Roark was backing the truck toward the house. A burst of fire blew out the windshield killing Roark. Dino stood across the yard with a smoking machine gun. The truck continued until it crashed into the front porch. Roark was slumped against the steering wheel showing no signs of life. Lam was firing as best he could. He shouted, "See if you can get out the back. I'll do my best to hold them off."

Mara raced to the back door just as a hulking man kicked the door in and entered. Without thought, Mara went down into a kneeling firing position. She fired three times, hitting the hulking figure in the chest with two shots. He lunged forward, but fell lifeless in front of Mara.

Without thought, she kicked the back door closed and ran to the side of the house that faced J.J.'s workshop and garage. Slipping out the window, she raced to the building without being seen. There was still gunfire to the front of the house. Reaching the door, she realized there was a heavy lock on it. Two shots later the door was opened and she rushed inside, closing the door behind her. She quickly reloaded the Smith and Wesson from bullets in her pocket. She suddenly remembered something. Secreted away in a compartment by the workbench was a Remington *Wingmaster* pump shotgun. Mara grabbed it and began loading it as quickly as she could from the box of shells in a drawer. She dropped the remaining shells inside her shoulder bag and headed to the attached garage.

Inside the door was her prized 1932 Ford Convertible. She started it and hurried over to the garage door. The gunfire stopped which meant poor Lam had probably joined Roark. She eased the door open at first, then pushed it the rest of the way as quickly as she could. Running back to the car she almost made it inside when a voice called out.

"Hey! Stop right there. Drop your pistol!" She looked over at the rugged looking fellow and then smiled nervously. Her voice sounded shaky and scared, "Yes! Yes sir! I'm putting the pistol down. Please don't shoot, Mister. I can see you mean business."

The smile threw him a bit as he watched her take her

shoulder bag and sit it on the seat of the Roadster. Then, in a flash, she pulled the shotgun from the car and pulled the trigger. The first blast caught his shoulder, spinning him around. She chambered another shell and fired. The second blast hit him square in the back and blew him back out the door.

In a flash, she was inside the Ford, throwing it into gear and blasting through the open door. She felt a thumping sound as the tires on the right side ran over the dead body. A thought flashed across her mind as she cut across the yard, away from the front of the house. *"That fellow...and the one who burst into the kitchen didn't look like anybody who'd work for Royal. It had to be some of the Mob boys! Was this about Ford or was it..."*

Before she could finish her thought, she heard the blast of a shotgun followed by additional gunfire. Mara downshifted and cut further away from the house. She heard a few rounds make contact with the back of the car which angered her further. A crazy thought filled her mind, *"I should just turn this car around and run over the whole lot of them."*

That thought was quickly dismissed as the rapid fire of a machine gun was heard from behind her. Her foot immediately slammed onto the accelerator as she headed to the paved road.

Behind her, Dino Bellini stood in the middle of Mara's flower garden, his Thompson machine gun smoking from spent shells. He shouted to the men gathering in the yard, "Get the cars! Run her down if you have to! Now! Somebody help get Santo in a car. Let's go!"

Mara took a long, much needed breath. She'd escaped but she wasn't sure she'd gotten away. All she could say for sure was that it would take a hell of a driver to catch up with her.

She sped down the highway, her eyes glancing from the road to her rearview mirror. Suddenly, a dark car came onto the highway from a small side road that wound back into the woods. She knew immediately it was in pursuit of her. A red, flashing light caught her attention in the rearview mirror. The cars roared down the highway with the dark car, a Plymouth, pulling alongside Mara.

She glanced over at the driver as they raced along. He was wearing a Deputies uniform and appeared content to ride along side of her. *"Now...I know who you work for!"*

He looked over at Mara who responded by flipping him a bird and smiling. He returned the smile and feinted as if he was going to bump her. She dodged and returned the favor. They went a half a mile going back and forth. Mara was getting angrier at the man as each second passed. He seemed to be having fun.

The two cars came out of a winding stretch of road and Mara realized what the Deputy had been doing. He had her squeezed to the right side of the road, almost entirely on the wide shoulder. He had kept her from turning onto two intersecting roads they passed on their left. Up ahead, she saw what amounted to a roadblock. There were two pickups across the road and another rusty looking pickup sitting behind them.

The Deputy fell behind her now, pushing her toward the roadblock. Mara watched the Deputy in her rearview mirror and made a quick decision.

She slammed her foot on the brake pedal and pulled hard on the hand brake. At the same time, she started spinning the steering wheel. The Deputy went flying by, trying to miss her and stop his car. Mara held on to the steering wheel, fighting to keep the car under control. The tires caught as she fought to bring the car around. She double-clutched, throwing the car into a lower gear as she peeled out in the opposite direction.

The Deputy came to a sliding stop by running up against one of the trucks. He fought to get his car back in the chase. The three pickups joined in the chase. Everyone involved in the chase, except Mara, was startled as they looked ahead.

Coming down the road at full speed was a convoy made up of Dino Bellini and the remainder of his crew. Mara was weaving on the road keeping everyone guessing as to where she was going next. She bore down on the front vehicle as they sped towards each other. At the same time, Deputy Benny Goins and the boys from the Haddish clan drove toward the oncoming vehicles. The whole scene turned chaotic at once.

Before the lead driver knew what was happening, Mara was on top of him. He cut hard right to miss her which made him clip the car beside him. Dino was in the next group of cars, leaning out the window with the machine gun. He started to shoot at Mara when gunfire from the on-coming vehicles came his way. He turned the machine gun at the coming vehicles and fired in short bursts.

Mara, was weaving between the oncoming cars whose occupants were now more interested in dodging bullets from the on-coming vehicles. Brakes began squealing as both groups were suddenly at each other's grills.

Mara somehow managed to avoid an accident as well as the gunfire. She continued up the highway noticing that only one vehicle was following her. She rounded a sharp curve and then took a sharp right onto a dirt road she believed would take her around the mountain into Treemont.

Deputy Goins knew these back roads just as well as Mara, maybe better. He continued in his pursuit, not thinking about the clash between the Haddish men and the gangsters. He thought, *"Now, this old girl is good, but I've been driving these roads longer than she has."*

Mara was letting off her accelerator going into each curve and accelerating out of it. She could tell there was only one car following her and he was matching her move by move.

Deputy Goins looked cool and calm, but he was seething inside. *"Run as hard as you want Mara, I'm going to run you off this mountain."*

The chase continued along the curvy dirt and gravel mountain road. Mara's Ford was quicker through the curves and handled superbly due to J.J.'s mechanical expertise. In fact, if this wasn't a life or death matter, Mara would be having a blast.

The Plymouth was more powerful but was heavier. The suspension was nowhere close to the Ford's, causing it to fall behind little by little. Deputy Goins was a stubborn man and he felt all he needed was one little advantage to fall his way.

That advantage came in the form of a recently fallen tree beside the road. The tree had long, thick limbs that extended onto the road. Mara came on it just as she slid through a sharp curve. She tried to dodge the mass of tree limbs by adjusting her slide. However, the right tire slammed into the thick limbs causing the car to jump off the road. As the car landed, Mara tried to adjust quickly but the road was slick, with little or no gravel to help catch the tires.

Before she could correct the path of her car, it slid completely off the shoulder of the road, the right front tire making hard contact with a sizable rock jutting out of the ditch. The sound of crunching metal underneath the carriage made Mara sick to her stomach. Without looking, she knew the car was not drivable. She jumped out of the car as she heard the Plymouth approaching. Unconsciously, she rubbed her nose to find a streak of rich, red blood on her hand.

She could see the Plymouth now and knew the driver was coming for her. Before plunging into the woods, she grabbed her shoulder bag but didn't see her shotgun. She headed for cover behind a cluster of trees just as Deputy Goins came out of his car. He took time to fire two shots, hitting just above Mara's head causing tree bark to fly.

"Mrs. Rawlings! Hey now, this is Deputy Benny Goins. I need you to come out of the trees. There's no need for you making this so hard. I've got to take you in for questioning. It's just routine. Your husband and son are already at the Sheriff's Office."

Mara gasped at his words but immediately knew it was a ploy. "Don't think I can make it in today, Deputy. Tell your Sheriff I'll be along to see him shortly. Got a few questions to ask him when we're alone."

"I can't see that happening, Mrs. Rawlings. Why don't you just come on out so you can get back to your family." Deputy Goins slipped around to Mara's right and cautiously approached the other side of the cluster of trees. He paused just a second, then jumped clear of the bushes and fired into the spot he felt Mara was hiding.

Mara had been aware of what the Deputy was attempting. She'd already changed her position and hoped she'd guess correctly as to which direction Goins was approaching. As Goins jumped out and began firing, Mara bent low and began running back towards the road. She heard the Deputy holler out at her causing her to half-turn as she ran, firing her pistol in his direction.

Goins was three steps into a dead run when he heard the pistol shots. He planted his foot to stop but only found soft ground, causing him to pitch sideways. He hit the ground hard as his rib cage bounced off the trunk of an old fallen tree. He swore he heard at least one rib make a cracking sound. The resulting pain exploded throughout his body. His screams were permeated with curses as he struggled to his feet.

Mara heard the scream just as her foot caught an exposed root as she tried crossing the ditch to the shoulder of the road. She pitched forward, losing her pistol as she bounced on the dirt road. Scrambling to her feet, she started toward the pistol only to hear a gunshot and feel the bullet zip past her shoulder. Her only recourse was to find cover behind her car. For the first time, she believed she was about to die.

The Deputy's footsteps were coming closer. He was limping due to the pain from his fall. He walked over to Mara's pistol, picked it up and checked the remaining ammunition. Smiling, he called out, "Just so you know Mrs. Rawlings…I'm going to shoot you with your own gun." He walked forward, glad this mess was soon to be over.

Mara could see him coming now. The passenger side door of the Ford had sprung open during the crash, giving her a good look through the interior of the car. Through the driver side window, she could see the cocky look on Deputy Goin's face. Noticing the limp, she smiled to herself as she called out. "See you've got a bad limp, Deputy. Might want to get off your feet and rest a bit over there."

She heard him laugh in response so she called out, "Okay, Deputy. You might wish you'd listen to me. These things can be worse than you think."

The Deputy stopped. "Come on out from behind the car, Mrs. Rawlings. That'd save me some steps."

"Now Deputy! I just don't think it fair for you to ask me to make it easy for you to murder me. Makes you come across as not much of a man, much less a gentleman."

The thought of dying didn't bother her as much as the thought of dying before she could kill Royal Majesty. In her mind's eye, she thought she saw a flash, a glimpse of a bright, moving light. It was an illusion, she knew. It had to be a vision of the lights she'd seen on Brown Mountain twice before. Maybe the vision was meant to give her peace as she entered the afterlife. All she knew was, it meant she'd be all right. It would only be another minute.

Deputy Goins stepped around the back of the Ford to find Mara, her back propped against the open door of the Ford as she leaned into the interior. Her body seemed to be trembling as she awaited her death. He spoke softly to her. "Mrs. Rawlings? It's okay.

I'll make this quick. I'm sorry to have to do this but the Sheriff just can't have you digging into the past any longer. I really don't believe he meant for that girl to get killed. Even the Sheriff admitted he shouldn't have let that DePaul fellow handle it. He was just a sorry little worm anyway."

With that, Deputy Goins raised the pistol. In the same instant, Mara suddenly raised up from inside the Ford. She swung her shotgun toward the Deputy and fired, all in one motion. Firing at point blank range, the Deputy was blown backwards before he had a chance to blink. The charge sent him sprawling backwards to the ground. Lying on his back, he would have been looking into the treetops had he still had a face remaining.

Mara collapsed to the ground herself. She was exhausted, her mouth dry as a cotton ball. Sweat covered her body causing chills to run across her skin in the cool, misty air. She hugged herself as she looked over at the remains of the Deputy. The only thing she could think of at the moment sounded strange as she spoke it out loud. "My lord Mara…you're getting too damn good at this killing people."

She sat there, propped up against the Ford allowing the cool air of the peaceful woods rejuvenate her body and mind. Closing her eyes, a new thought crossed her mind. She opened her eyes and slammed a fist against the car as she shouted into the woods, "I'm still coming for you Royal! I'll kill anybody you put in my way." Then she added in a quiet voice, "You've gotten away with too much for too long. You're going to die you son of a bitch…and I hope it's by my hand.

Chapter Seventy-Five

"That's why they call me "Lightning", I guess."

The peace along the highway was finally restored. No one came along and stopped the two groups from shooting at each other. Neither group annihilated the other and one didn't turn tail and run. It ended because both parties seemed to lose interest.

Dino was interested in where Mara was headed with a Deputy in hot pursuit. The Haddish's, on the hand, weren't so sure they needed to do battle from moving vehicles with these strangers. It was not the type of fighting they were accustomed to. The machine gun fire made them more than a little skittish. They were hardened ground fighters but this was not their element. With Deputy Goins gone chasing after the fleeing woman, they figured it was time to go back to find the Sheriff and regroup. There were also their wounded that needed attention. Noah Haddish did not like the idea of running gun-battles against men firing machine guns. He would speak to Solomon and he would be heard…at least if he was still alive.

Considering the amount of gunshots fired, there was a small amount of blood to show for their combined efforts.

Dino was having difficulty firing reliably with the submachine gun from a moving vehicle. He'd sprayed a lot of bullets only to have most of them go high. He blamed the bumpy road for fouling his aim.

Three of the Haddish clan were wounded, one of those severely. Dino and his men somehow escaped further injuries from the wild fuselage. Still, the gangsters had received heavy casualties at the Rawlings home. Two were presumed dead since they didn't make the run after the Rawlings woman. Two more were wounded. A shoulder wound and a leg wound. Both joined in the running battle but now looked weak, their faces ashen.

One of the Haddish's had taken part of a shotgun blast to the shoulder and side of the head as his truck passed one of the gangster's cars. He was angry the battle ended so suddenly. His blood was heated up from the pain and the fact his cousins were leaving the battle scene.

A second Haddish was lying in the back of one of the pickups, bleeding from a bullet wound that shattered his wrist and an ugly graze across the side of his head. He was breathing but moving very little.

The third wounded Haddish had a gunshot wound in his side. The bullet traveled through the pickup door and struck a rib. He looked to still be bleeding and his breathing was labored. The trucks were hit with gunshots multiple times, but they still ran.

Dino and his crew drove away in the direction of Mara's escape. It didn't take long to figure out he was not going to find the woman. He needed to decide where to go next. They may have missed the Mother but there was still the Father and the kid himself to be found. There was no need to return to the Rawlings home. He might just swing by the Father's garage instead. Earlier, he'd sent a couple of good men by the garage to pick up the elder Rawlings.

By now they should have the Daddy and maybe even his son. Still, it wouldn't hurt to have a look just in case. If no one was there, he'd head back to the lodge to prepare to go after Majesty. Dino wanted Ford Rawlings badly, but now he was looking forward to putting the arrogant Sheriff down just as much.

Noah Haddish was behind the wheel of one of their trucks. As he led his clan members away from the highway battle site, his anger grew concerning this vendetta. It didn't make any sense to him anyway. He knew the mighty Sheriff would pay the family well and even grant a favor or two if needed.

Still, he didn't like the idea of meddling into other people's troubles. However, it wasn't his place to be contrary to his elders. All he knew was that there'd come a day when he would be one of the elders who made decisions. He was determined to live long enough to be placed in that position.

Noah had no idea where the Deputy went. Last time he saw him, he was chasing after the woman in the yellow car. He laughed at the thoughts of her trying to outrun that old boy. He knew Goins to be a "runner" on these mountain roads since his younger days. He'd even run more than a few loads of moonshine out of these mountains. By now, he guessed the woman was a part of some wreckage on the side of a mountain.

So, for now, he'd forget about the Yankee boys and try to find Sheriff Majesty. He'd see what the "big" man had in mind for him to do next. Whether or not he would do it was another thing. He really wished he had a chance to tell Solomon exactly what he thought of the situation. Maybe he'd just take a chance and go speak to Solomon before he saw the Sheriff. After all, his three wounded cousins could do little more fighting at present. It seemed a prudent plan and the wounded needed attention.

As he drove along, Noah could only think of two things that would make him happy. One was to get this job finished and get home. The other thing that would please him would be for his cousin Eli, who lay wounded in the bed of his truck, to stop screaming and cursing. His anger was brought about in part because they didn't stay and fight with the Yankee boys. Of course, the bloodied shoulder and head could have accounted for a lot of his anger. He was most fortunate he only caught a small splattering of the buckshot as the two vehicles passed each other.

As Dino and the Haddish clan went their separate ways, Jubal and "Lightning" Charlie were busy. Jubal had two of his men, Wyle and Vernon, helping put together what he hoped would be a way to improve the odds for the Rawlings' family.

Jubal watched as Charlie and the boys worked away. He noticed how fast and fluid Charlie worked. The nickname "Lightning" was usually thought to refer to the powerful explosions he could create. He enhanced that reputation by making a powerful moonshine potion that could set you on your butt.

Either one of those things added to Charlie's reputation, but the nickname was originally acquired by the quickness in which he worked. Jubal and J.J. watched as Charlie quickly laid out his line of explosives. They decided that whether or not this plan worked, there was about to be one hell of an explosion on Brown Mountain.

Charlie walked over to Jubal, handing him a box with wires dangling from connectors. "You'll have to position yourself over there, just where the road curves. That's where all the wires come to a junction. You can set it off just as soon as the last car comes out of the curve. I just hope they're traveling tight. You'll have to make that call."

Jubal shook his head as he took the box. "This is going to be one mighty blast. Can't believe you came up with that much explosive so quickly."

Charlie chuckled, "That's why they call me "Lightning", I guess."

Chapter Seventy-Six

"Come on boys, we're doing us some rabbit hunting today!"

Ford and Holly were desperately trying to find Mara. They'd been by the house where they found four dead bodies. Two were Jubal's men, Roark and Lam. Both good, reliable men. Signs of gunfire peppered the house, both inside and out. The two bedrooms were particularly destroyed. Holly looked ready to cry at the destruction to the Rawlings house. She brought a couple of blankets from the house to put over Roark and Lam's bodies.

Ford found two bodies out back that he figured to be DiPoli's men. Mara's Ford convertible was missing which he took as a good sign. There were tire marks from the small garage through the yard tracking Mara's get-away. The tire tracks tore up sod all the way to the lower portion of the driveway. He was sure she had made it to the County road. How far down the road she progressed was another thing? He couldn't be certain of which way she traveled when she hit the pavement…that is, until he saw the black tire marks left by her car.

Holly was filled with fear as well as a bit of anger as she thought of Mara. She was originally supposed to be with Mara but was left behind. Knowing Mara, she knew that was no accident.

Ford needed to head toward Brown Mountain where his father and Uncle Jubal were waiting. They were putting together a trap which should even up the odds some. He wanted to find Mara but he needed to find some of the gangsters and lead them into the trap. His Mother was important, but at this point he knew it was all about adjusting the odds.

The idea was to let them chase him so he could lead them into the deadly trap set up by Lightning Charlie. Any survivors would be handled by his father, Jubal, and Jubal's men.

The small mountain road would be blocked after the trap was engaged. The good thing was that it wound through the mountain until a cut-back road would bring them out on the County highway. At least that's what Ford and Jubal remembered. Ford realized there was always a chance the road may have been grown over, blocked by fallen trees, or just washed away since the last time he traveled it. He'd just deal with that when the time came.

Ford didn't want Holly along with him but she wouldn't stay with Billie. She was already upset that Mara had left her behind and Ford wouldn't be the second person to let her down today. He guessed she was as safe with him as she would be anywhere.

Ford's Chevy hit the paved road leaving tracks of burned rubber for a good distance. Holly sat back enjoying the rush of power. After a minute she turned to Ford, "Tell me Ford, why is it you didn't want me with you today. I know there's danger everywhere we go today and you want me to be safe. Is it because I'm Julia's little sister? I can appreciate that to a degree, but I don't think that's the whole of it."

She hung on as they blew through a curve. She could hear the tires protesting mightily. Ford reached over, turning the radio on. They heard the last verse of Elvis Pressley singing, *All Shook Up.* He quickly turned the radio off and hit the steering wheel with his fist. "I don't know which I hate most, that singer or Royal Majesty.

Holly scooted closer to the door as she said, "What do you like, Ford? I'm not sure you're much fond of anything or anyone anymore. You said we could be friends…a sister you said. I don't think you have any more feelings about me that you do Mara's bird! I've reached out to you. I want to help…even be close if you'll let me. You may not care for me, but I really do care about you!"

Holly became even smaller as she said in a quiet voice, "Always have, always will."

Ford continued to roar down the highway for almost a mile before he slowed a bit and spoke. "Holly, honey… I don't know the words to say. I've had two women in my life that I deeply cared for. Through no fault of theirs, one ended up in a dirty field…run down and killed."

He allowed the car to slow a bit more as his voice lowered. "The second one ended up with a bullet shot through her face…her beautiful, perfect face. The last time I saw her was in a hospital, covered in bandages with tubes coming out of that face."

By now, he was gripping the steering wheel so tightly his knuckles were bone white. "I keep telling myself that I didn't put them there. The thing is, if they'd never gotten mixed up with me they would still be alive…unhurt, living their lives. I couldn't protect them. I have to take the blame because I was the one thing they had in common!"

Ford took a deep breath. "Look, here is the thing. I just can't lose you, too. If you get hurt in all of this, I may just as well die myself. I can barely carry the guilt I have now. I can't have you on my conscious too. I do care for you…and it scares me."

He began speeding up again, "From that first moment I saw you in the store window…I knew. I tried fighting it, but I just knew that I would fall for you. Not because of anything to do with Julia, either! It was just I saw you and I saw home. Not a place but a state of being. I've been half-way around the world and back since I left here. Felisa was more than I ever deserved. We became close, but she only felt like a place I could call home. Holly…I think of you, I think of my home...you're…"

Before Ford could continue, a bullet smashed into the left front headlight. Ford's attention focused back to the road ahead only to see several vehicles headed his way, all with someone pointing a lethal weapon in their direction.

Dino Bellini spotted the '57 Chevy coming toward him as soon as it topped a hill. The car just stood out anywhere it went. Angelo was driving as Dino leaned out the car window, waving frantically at his men. He managed to get the machine gun out the window and began firing wildly. Other men were firing too, some not even sure why.

Dino and his men raced toward Ford and Holly. Ford reached over, pushing Holly's head down below the dash. She shouted at Ford, then screamed as several bullets made contact with the car. One slug found the windshield creating havoc inside the car.

Ford shouted for Holly to stay down as he began to swing the car back and forth. Any normal person would try and turn away from the oncoming fuselage. Instead, Ford changed gears and bore down on the lead car.

Two things happened simultaneously. The driver reacted by swerving away from Ford's roaring car, side-swiping another car which slid off the road. The other thing was a sudden explosion inside the car.

Ford looked over to find Holly trying to aim his heavy S&W Model 29 at one of the passing cars. Before he could say anything, she pulled the trigger two more times. The sound inside the car was deafening. It was all Holly could do to hold the pistol steady when she fired. The other thing Ford noticed was that Dino Bellini was last seen ducking down in his car as the Holly's two bullets crashed through the glass behind him.

The two vehicles passed quickly. Dino was trying to get the Thompson back out the window to fire but Ford was already weaving around another skidding car.

Within another two seconds Ford was through the gauntlet. Ford had a trickle of blood on his cheek from flying glass while Holly had a small bump on her head from impact with the dash…possibly when Ford first pushed her head down.

The Chevy was the one to suffer the most. The beautiful car had taken several hits in the body and through the glass. Thankfully, no one or nothing of importance had been hit. This was mostly due to the quickness of Ford getting into close quarters with the gangsters.

The rearview mirror…or the part that was left, hung askew. Ford looked in his side mirror to see the enemy turning around for pursuit. For the first time today, Ford felt like smiling.

Without looking at Holly, he shouted. "I told you to stay down! What are you doing with my gun anyway?"

"Hey! They were shooting at us. I was just returning the favor. How do you ever hit anything with this thing? It just about kicked right out of my hands. It's pretty loud isn't it! Surprised that fellow with the machine gun! Thought he was going to drop it out the window."

"Well, he didn't. And you better stay down this time because they're coming back."Ford pushed the Chevy and it responded with a roar. He knew there wasn't a car within a hundred miles that could keep up with this powerhouse. In fact, he needed to pay attention to his pursuers so as not to gain too big a lead. He needed to stay just far enough ahead to keep them coming but not let them get so close they could do actual damage with their guns.

Looking over at Holly, he found her reloading the pistol with bullets from the glove box. She had a look of determination on her face that was unmistakable. "Holly! Please stay down!"

Instead of getting down, she turned around in the seat so she could look out the back window. "Do you think I could shoot the glass out without messing with your driving?"

Her voice was surprisingly calm…almost distant. She cocked the hammer and prepared to fire when Ford grabbed her hand. "You're going to deafen me, girl! Save your bullets till you need them, okay? What has gotten into you?"

Holly looked disappointed, then almost angry. "I can't just sit here, Ford. I've got to do something!"

She began fidgeting with the gun. Ford was distracted trying to watch her, the road, and the gangsters behind him. A minute passed and he could no longer take it. Ford nearly shouted, "Holly! Leave that gun alone. You're going to shoot me…or yourself. Just watch our backs. I'm trying to keep those fellows interested and not lose them."

Holly laughed. "Now, that's funny. They're chasing us and you're afraid we're going to lose them. This is the craziest chase I've ever seen. Do you ever do anything normal?"

Ford couldn't help but smile. "We're almost ready to turn off the highway. J.J. and Jubal's waiting on us. Do you understand what's about to happen?"

Holly didn't answer. She braced herself as Ford took a hard right onto a dirt road. The flat ridge of Brown Mountain loomed above them as they drove up the winding, uneven road. The road became darker due to the increased density of trees as well a sun beginning to sink in the western sky.

Occasionally, Ford could hear a random gunshot rattle through the trees. As he drove deeper into the mountain he began to slow down a bit, allowing the gangsters to get closer.

By now, Dino was about to explode. He was sick and tired of chasing this hillbilly. He had to give him credit though…this boy could drive. He made driving these sorry roads look so easy.

They were driving single file. Dino's driver, Angelo, was actually beginning to catch up with Rawlings. He checked the Thompson again. He couldn't wait to use it on Ford Rawlings. He looked greedily ahead as he thought to himself, *"Who names their kid, Ford? Had to have been his mechanic daddy's idea."*

Dino didn't know where this road was leading but he knew it had to end somewhere. He suddenly didn't care for the idea of going deeper into the woods. He leaned forward as if doing so would allow him a better view into the Chevy ahead of them. Something didn't seem so right any more. Maybe this was a bad idea.

"Angelo, let's get this thing over with. I don't want to go so far into this mountain we can't find our way out. Catch that hillbilly. We've got other business to attend to."

By now, the sun was getting exceptionally low. Other mountains were shielding Brown Mountain from the sun's sinking rays. They were running in and out of patches of vague light and semi-darkness.

The Chevy suddenly turned off onto another road just as Dino was leaning out the window to fire a burst at the fleeing car. Angelo whipped their car onto the road just in time. Up ahead, Dino heard a loud noise filtering back toward them. It only took another second when he knew what was about to happen. It was a trap…he had no doubt!

Ford was hitting the horn in two long bursts followed by two short bursts. They had made it. Now, all he had to do was get passed the danger zone and hope each and every car following him would be caught in the trap.

Dino screamed at Angelo, "Floor it man! We're about to be hit. It's a set-up!"

Angelo punched the accelerator and the big car responded. Dino leaned out the window, waving frantically for the cars to follow suit. The Mobster didn't know if he was doing the right thing or not. All he knew was he needed to stop Rawlings here and now. He hoped by rushing ahead they could beat any trap that was set.

The burst of increased speed caught Jubal and J.J. by surprise. J.J hollered for Jubal to blow the charges just as the last car rounded the curve. There was a long gap between the first two cars and the remaining vehicles.

Ford was watching in is side mirror as he slowed. Holly was on her knees in the front seat looking backwards. Suddenly, there were several very loud explosions that occurred in quick succession.

The dark woods lit up as a sudden inferno raised up behind Ford. Trees fell in front of the gangster's cars, along-side the cars, behind the cars, and even on a couple of cars.

There was a low cloud of smoke and dust that materialized to hang under the wooded canopy. The first two cars managed to escape the trap. The next one lay under a large tree. It was wholly crushed with smoke seeping from under what was left of the hood. There were no signs of anyone trying to get out of the vehicle.

The next two cars were only damaged slightly from sliding into each other as they tried to stop. The last car had a tree across the back end. The rear tires were flattened as well as the trunk. Gasoline was running from the ruptured tank and the occupant was pulling himself away from the wreckage. It was evident there was no escape from the maze of fallen trees. The survivors found cover so they could decide what to do and figure out who was hiding in these woods.

Before long, shots began to be heard. There was still smoke and dust in the air. Flames were dancing in various spots creating odd shadows and adding to the confusion inside the blast area. Dino's men began firing, but saw no actual targets. They managed to huddle together trying to decide if they should make a run for it to get out of the tight spot they were in. The big question was, which way was out?

Ford was rolling to a stop. He could hear sporadic gunfire being exchanged between the mobsters and whoever was back there to fight them. He knew mercy would be given only if they were to surrender immediately. He doubted the gangsters had enough sense to know how to surrender.

Ford could hear another sound above the gunfire. Holly screamed, "Get out of here Ford. The blast didn't get all of them!"

Just then, a black Buick rolled out of the smoke followed by another one. Bullets began kicking up the dirt, hitting the tree trunks and occasionally striking the body of the car. Ford did not hesitate but jumped back into the car and roared away like a bat out of hell.

Holly was firing the S&W revolver as fast as she could manage. She wasn't sure if she was hitting anything or anybody…but it felt good just to let them know they were facing someone armed and dangerous.

Ford headed up the small mountain road as he realized they were terribly exposed at the moment. Holly began reloading again. She shouted, "Did the trap fail? How'd those guys get through?"

Ford replied as he kept focused on the dirt road ahead, "Just didn't get them all. How many have we got behind us?"

Holly stuck her head out the window and began firing again. "There's two cars behind us is all. I think we can take them!"

Ford looked over to see her hanging out of the car as she emptied the pistol again. He pulled her back inside just as the car hit a rough, uneven spot in the road. She bounced hard against the dash, dropping the pistol to the floorboard. Just then the rat-a-tat-tat of the machine gun was heard from behind them.

"Can you just please stay inside the car and keep your head down. That guy is going to get lucky with that Thompson and blow your head off!"

Holly was in the floorboard to retrieve the pistol. She sat there reloading and shouting at Ford. "What's the matter Ford? I guess you're afraid to have the blood of another girl on your conscious. We can't have you feeling any more guilt…no, not Ford Rawlings! I mean, it couldn't be that you care that much for me…it's about how you feel…about you! You don't really care for me do you, Ford? Which is it?

Ford gave her a hard look, seeing for the first time how angry she'd become. He looked back at the road and shouted back, "Both…it's both Holly. Dear God…please help me, it's both! Can we just focus on one thing at a time!"

Holly sat there, an amazed look crossing her face first and then a cloud of uncertainty. She fumbled with the bullet she was trying to load, dropping one shell to the floor. Neither said anything for a moment. Then Ford shouted, "Hold on!" The Chevy lunged across a "wet-water" creek that crossed the road. The car actually left the ground for an instant before landing hard and side-swiping a large tree by the road.

Ford fought the steering wheel just as bullets from Dino's machine gun luckily found one of the rear tires putting the Chevy into a tail spin.

Before Ford could recover, the Chevy crashed into a deep, ragged ditch on the other side of the road. Ford heard the first car hit the same ditch in the road that began his wreck. The heavy car hit and landed with a solid thud, sliding to a stop. The second car hit the wet-water ditch hard, sliding off the road on the other side. No one was hurt and the gangsters immediately got out of the vehicles.

The engine of the Chevy was still running but the depth of the ditch had one of the rear tires in the air while the other was a ragged mess of rubber. The Chevy wasn't going anywhere.

Ford grabbed Holly and pulled her out the driver's side door he forced open. She reached back, grabbing the pistol and the box with the remainder of the ammunition.

She landed in the dirty ditch and was pushed further down by Ford's hand. Immediately, bullets tore into the Chevy and surrounding landscape. Ford reached back inside, retrieving a hunting rifle and an ammunition belt. He told Holly to crawl along the ditch toward the rotting carcass of a long-ago fallen tree. He followed, stopping every few seconds to check to see if the gangsters were following.

Fortunately, Holly's earlier shots kept the men from immediately attacking them. They cautiously held back, waiting to see if they were going to be fired on.

This enabled Ford and Holly to reach the large tree trunk and settle in. Neither side called out to the other. The engine of the Chevy was still running and was the only sound in the deep and darkening forest. Ford looked over at his beautiful car and the damage that befell it from one end to the other. He then looked back at the wide-eyed woman beside him. He couldn't tell if she either wasn't breathing or was just holding her breath from the excitement and danger.

"You know, country girls look just as pretty covered in dirt and mud as they do when they're squeaky clean."

Holly looked up to see the twinkle in Ford's eyes. "My lord Ford, this ain't much of a time to act the fool."

Ford caught the first hint of fear in Holly's eyes. To be truthful, he was scared to death as he considered their impending fate. He smiled as warmly and confidently at her as he could. "I'm not kidding Holly. Even a mud bath doesn't change the fact you are a beautiful woman."

Holly blushed a little through the mud on her face. She

unconsciously ran her fingers through her waterfall curls. As she did that, she pulled from her tangled, muddy hair a clump of something wet and slimy. She looked at her hand to find some form of a wormy slug rolled up in her hand. She squealed as she tossed the unwanted clump toward the woods.

Ford's laugh was interrupted by the explosion of an automatic weapon raking destruction across the log. As soon as the firing stopped, Ford grabbed Holly, pulling her along as they ran further into the woods.

A heavily accented voice called into the woods. "Run away little rabbits. Come on boys, we're doing us some rabbit hunting today! I've got some payback for you, Elvis. You've sung your last song!"

Ford pulled up, a flash of anger replaced the fear in his face. He shouted back towards the road. "You can't kill me Dino…you can't even remember my name you *muto dago!* I'm going to leave you up here for the bears to eat. By tomorrow you'll be nothing more than *un mucchio di schifo d'orso!*

Gunfire exploded into the trees from the road. More shouts came their way, but they were so muffled they couldn't be understood.

They made their way toward a small cut in the mountainside that offered a few large rocks for cover. By this time, both Holly and Ford were winded. They fell behind the rocks to catch their breaths. Holly sat with her back against a rock while Ford did lookout duty. He was looking for an escape route for Holly while he held the gangsters at bay.

"I understood the "dumb dago" part back there. Guess that's just a normal insult. What was the other thing you said?"

A grin crossed Ford's sweaty, dirt-smeared face. "I told him I was going to leave him up here for the bears to eat and that by tomorrow he was going to be "a pile of bear crap". Don't think he cared for the visual.

Ford noticed Holly staring at him intently. "What? You're looking at me…strangely."

Holly smiled, "I guess I'm a little worried for you…you've thought about it, I'm sure?"

He gave her a puzzled look. She giggled, "I mean, dying

having only the dumb first name of a second-rate car to be remembered by!"

Ford was utterly dumbfounded. This girl was in the most desperate situation of her life and all of a sudden, she decides to make corny jokes. He looked a little closer and realized the utter fear behind her eyes.

"You're one to talk, Holly. Dying with the name of a prickly bush to be put on your tombstone!"

She laughed out loud before she could stop herself. Then she whispered, "Just remember Ford, I'll always be the last girl to love you."

Chapter Seventy-Seven

"Jubal and his two boys began screaming rebel yells, running back and forth along the edge of the woods."

Jubal and J.J. were both swearing enough to silence a rowboat filled with sailors. They were angry that the first car slipped through their trap. That could always happen. For a second car to get through, well that was unthinkable. Now they were trapped themselves, so to speak.

Their vehicles were hidden off the small road, away from the direction they needed to go to help Ford. The multiple fallen trees made chasing after Ford and the mobsters impossible.

Jubal fired a shotgun blast at the hunkered down gangsters as he spat tobacco juice at a nearby rock. "Dammit J.J.! How'd those two cars get through? Now it's getting dark and we're stuck here trying to pick off these Yankee SOB's! Couldn't go help Ford even if we didn't have these yay-whoes to mind. We'd have to move four…maybe five trees just to get up the road."

Charlie was considering the situation as he spoke. "I could clear this road in a hurry if somebody hadn't insisted on using pretty much every dad-blasted bit of explosives I brought!" He held up one last stick of dynamite. "Oh, yeah…I saved this to stick to put up your butt if this didn't work. You want to light it, or should I?"

Jubal fired another shotgun blast at the car sitting in the middle of the fallen trees just to keep the mobster's heads down. Spitting more tobacco juice, he murmured, "Wouldn't have hurt to have had those charges set to where they'd gone off quicker. But what do I know? I mean, you're "Lightning" Charlie, lord of the explosives."

He spat again as he reloaded the double barrel shotgun. "Two damn cars! Two! Chasing Ford through these mountains." He looked down at the shotgun in his hands. I should have been standing in the middle of the road and stopped them SOB's." He cocked both barrels and fired in the direction of the mobsters.

"Dammit, I hope Ford's all right. He had that Harmon girl with him. She was supposed to be with Mara…wherever the hell she is."

J.J. had been mostly quiet during Jubal's last tirade. He was more than a little worried. Ford was on his own for now, but he'd been on his own for a long time now. The road eventually crossed back and would come out on a County road about five miles from where they stood. Ford was as good a driver as anyone had ever seen in these mountains. Leading those wise guys a merry chase shouldn't be that difficult for him. You just never knew what you'd find on these rough mountain roads, though.

J.J. looked around the woods and frowned. "We can't let those boys sit there till it gets completely dark and the fires die out. They'll be thinking they can slip away back down to the main road. It'll just tie us up here that much longer."

Charlie was agreeing with J.J. when Jubal snatched the stick of dynamite from him. "You got a fuse I can stick in this to light? How about we make it a little interesting for them boys. I think this whole situation needs to be a little more festive. I'll be on the other side after I speak to Wiley and Vernon. Get ready, in about ten minutes it's going to get a lot livelier…so be ready."

With that, he was gone, blending into the woods to J.J.'s right. J.J. watched the darkening area where DiPoli's men were hiding. He wondered what was going on in their minds. Just to see what might happen, he called out. "You men behind the car. Come on out! Surrender and we'll keep you safe. You don't want to spend the night in these woods!"

A couple of shots were fired in his direction. J.J. thought, *"Well, that's two less bullets that can do anybody harm. I wonder if they're more afraid of what we'll do to them or what their bosses might do to them for surrendering. May just be a long night."*

About ten unnerving minutes passed after Jubal left J.J. The darkness was growing quicker now as the mountain shadows began to fall across the wooded contours. Finally, it was Jubal's voice that broke the eerie silence of the moment.

"You boys hiding behind the cars. Listen up, now. I'm going to make you a deal. Code of the mountains, now. We don't go back on our word. Something sworn to is sacred unless the other fellow breaks the pact. Are you ready to listen to my offer?"

An accented voice answered after nearly fifteen seconds passed. “What *youse* got to say? You got our attention.”

J.J. could almost hear a laugh in Jubal’s voice as he called out. “We’ve got you surrounded! Our whole clan is here now. We’ve been talking about what to do with you. Most everybody wants to get home to supper so they just want to kill you and be done with it. Maybe throw you over in the pig’s sty. Those damn pigs have got one big appetite. As far as I’m concerned, I don’t think that sounds right…ain’t exactly human, you know. Come on out and I’ll personally keep you safe. We’ll keep you safe till the rest of your men are caught and then we’ll send you back North. Just come on out with your hands on your head. Walk toward my voice. Better do it now before something bad starts.”

A long minute passed when a shout was heard from inside the parameter. “We ain’t trusting any of youse hillbillies. We got more men coming! They’ll be along soon. Dino’s probably killed that Elvis fellow by now so he’ll be back with more men. You’re the ones that better leave! They’re not going to like what you done here!”

Jubal didn’t say a word in answer. Instead, two jars of white lightning were lobbed at the last car…the one with the tree lying across its backside. Both jars were capped and tied with a flaming tail of cotton secured to the lid. They hit the rear of the last car and shattered. Immediately a hot flame shot up around the car. Within a few seconds a loud whoosh was heard followed by a great flame jumping toward the sky. An explosion of fire erupted toward the sky as the gasoline soaked ground burst into flame. Another explosion occurred as the flames followed the gas fumes right into the car’s fuel tank. The car jumped a bit even with the fallen tree still in place. Flames began consuming the area around it.

As the sound of the explosion began to diminish, Jubal took the stick of dynamite he’d taken from Charlie, lit it, and threw it as high as he could in the air over the burning car. The fuse was short resulting in a huge explosion just above DiPoli’s men.

Vernon and Wiley began firing into the carnage. Jubal, Charlie, and the two boys began screaming rebel yells, running back and forth along the edge of the woods. They sounded as if a group of twenty mad men were about to descend on the gangsters.

J.J. was surprised to see three men running in his direction with their hands in the air. Their eyes were so wide-open they appeared to be some wild creatures running from a forest fire.

He jumped up, keeping his rifle leveled at them as he motioned for them to stay together. He put them on the ground lying on their bellies. In just a moment, Jubal and his boys came up bringing a couple coils of rope. The prisoner's arms and legs were bound and they were carted off to a pickup.

The shadows from the flames and smoke danced around the woods giving the appearance there were living spirits all about. Jubal walked over to J.J. "There's two in that crushed Buick. Don't guess they'll be going home. The others are banged up some but they'll live. I'll have the boys blindfold them and take them up by the house till we know what to do with them."

There was a long silence between the two men. Their minds were grinding away on what was going on with both Ford and Mara. Jubal kicked one of the fallen trees and let out a litany of curse words.

J.J. walked away toward his pickup. "I'm going to find Mara!", he called over his shoulder. I'm not sure where she'll be but I'd bet the Sheriff will be nearby…maybe even that DiPoli fellow, too. Look for me when you and Charlie get this mess cleaned up. You've got a good size campfire to get under control I'd recon."

Chapter Seventy-Eight

"...then I'll have lived and died with the man I've loved the most in this world."

Holly finished reloading the revolver with all but the last three bullets. Ford was doing the same thing with his rifle. He was grim since he'd just realized about half of the ammunition on the belt had been for another weapon. The rifle felt heavy in his hands. It offered him little assurance, since he was left with only two extra rounds. He mumbled, "*Things just keep getting better and better!*"

He scooted over closer to Holly who seemed to appreciate the closeness. They both peered over the rocks to see what Dino and his boys were doing. "I think there's only three of them…those odds aren't so bad." Holly was trying to sound hopeful.

"Only thing is, one of those guys is firing a Thompson and they don't seem to lack in the ammunition department." Ford's voice had a hard edge to it which would make most people think twice before speaking again.

"I guess some people are just better at planning. Probably has something to do with their vocation…I mean, we're not exactly planning to murder people on a daily basis."

Ford did not know of any words he could use to respond to what Holly said. He looked at her only to notice she had a calm, distant expression on her face now, as if they were talking about anybody's regular day job.

Holly let out a deep sigh as she looked over at Ford. "Ford honey, tell me what you meant in the car when you were talking about how you cared for me. You said both…you didn't want me hurt but you cared for me too. I know this is an awkward time but could you just clear that up for me."

Ford looked at Holly with a most incredulous look on his face. "You know Holly, you have been spending entirely too much time with my Mother. She's the world's worst at trying to have an awkward conversation at the worst time. Look, I don't think I can quite talk to you about this at the moment. Sort of got a few other things on my mind."

Holly shifted her position to see better to her left. "You're probably right about spending time with Mara. But I like her. She's really interesting and smart."

She paused, "Of course, killing a man together sort of helped us bond. Once you do something like that…well, it kind of stifles some of your more normal emotions or hesitancies. I didn't mean to make this situation seem a small thing, Ford. I just wanted to have an answer before one or both of us dies. You think we're going to die today, Ford?"

Ford noticed the young woman was as composed as anyone he'd ever seen in a stressful situation. If he hadn't been so stressed at the circumstances he would have grabbed her and held her as tightly as he possible could.

"I don't know about dying today, Holly. I'm just going to say that I'll be damned if it will be because of Dino Bellini!"

Ford sensed movement to his right. Holly was following a shadow that appeared to be moving up on their left. Ford was thankful that there was some open ground in front of the rocks that gave them a chance at a shot or two if they were rushed. He was mostly concerned about their flanks. There was absolutely nothing they could do to prevent a man from sneaking around their flanks in order to get a clearer shot.

On the count of three, Ford and Holly took two quick shots to their closest flank to slow down the gangsters. One of the men was heard to fall down followed by a loud burst of Italian curses about the slick footing.

They searched behind them but the ground rose up sharply, giving them no escape route. That also meant that no one was going to come up directly behind them for a "kill" shot. Ford's mind raced trying to find a solution. It was so frustrating. Ford knew they were trapped, pinned down. There wouldn't be any J.J. or Jubal arriving at the last minute to save them. Unless Dino made some grave error, there was just going to be a short, bloody battle on this spot...very, very soon.

Ford's mind flashed to Julia and Felisa. He looked at Holly and was shocked to see the shadows of the trees falling across her body. The shadows made her look as if she was covered in blood. His mind screamed as he almost lost it, ready to jump up and take the battle to Dino and his boys. It was Holly's voice that caught him.

"I'm sorry Ford. I shouldn't be talking about things like that. Not now and maybe not ever. I just want to say this and then I'll shut up." Her voice caught so it took a second for her to continue.

"I was so happy you were with Julia. I really was. And she was so happy…so complete. I thought you were the greatest, most manly man I'd ever known. You were funny, smart, both strong and gentile. I was so happy for Julia. I had the biggest crush on you…in a good way. I just wanted you to be my big brother."

Her voice caught again but she continued. "When we lost Julia, I lost you. At least that's what I thought. But my heart wouldn't let go of you. When you left, I felt the emptiness of losing both of you. I wasn't very good for a long time, you know."

She sniffled loudly followed by a small giggle. "Sorry! It was Mara that helped me get myself back together. Mom and Dad were great, but Mara made life real again. When I was around her and your Dad, it was like I was still around you. At first, I thought I was just going through a grieving process. But as time went on I finally realized I cared for you…I loved you."

She looked at Ford with eyes that glistened, even in the fading light. "Ford, I never thought for one moment that you could ever feel the same way about me. I never even expected to see you again. Goodness knows I knew if I ever saw you again I'd never tell you about my feelings or try to act on them. I was just so happy to know you were okay. I realized I was fine with only that."

Ford was listening to Holly but was aware there was only silence surrounding them. He wondered where Dino could be and what he was planning.

"When Mara came to me about Harris DePaul I didn't know what to do. I'll admit I was scared…oh my goodness, I was terrified. I got so scared that I knew I had to help her. I was afraid for her to go alone, I was determined to do it for Julia, I had to do it for me and my family, and I had to do it for you, Ford. You had lost as much as anyone. Julia lost her life but you lost a life that should have been."

It was obvious that tears were rolling down her face. Her voice trembled as she finished. "If I die here today…if I die with Ford Rawlings by my side…then I'll have lived and died with the man I've loved the most in this world. I love you, Ford! Thank God,

I love you."

Ford wanted to reach out to Holly but knew he had to stay alert. Dino wouldn't wait much longer. As if to quell any doubts, shots suddenly rang out.

The bullets were coming in from both sides. The chatter of the Thompson machine gun began chipping away at the rocks from the front. Bullets were hitting the rocks at multiple angles causing sharp pieces of rocky shrapnel to fly all around Holly and Ford.

Ford tried firing blindly to his right. He fired a few rounds toward the direction of the machine gun fire. The sound of gunfire was terrible, as if it would never let up. Holly emptied the revolver toward her flank. She slid down between two rocks in order to load her last three bullets. Ford fired his last round and prepared to use the rifle as a club.

There was a sudden silence as Dino realized he held the advantage. Angelo and the other hood, Raffi, came out of their flanking positions. They all walked forward, stopping about ten yards from the rocks. The acrid smell of gunfire hung in the dank forest. Dino was grinning at his victory.

"Come on out, Ford. I'll make it a clean head shot…quick. See, I even got your name right. Don't make me come over there and get you. I'll do the girl quick, too. It don't need to be messy. I'm tired of all this so let's get it over with. Besides, I've got a date with a Sheriff."

Ford slowly stood up, still holding the rifle. He actually had it leveled at Dino which made the man a little nervous. Dino's eyes began blinking as he wondered if Ford had one or more rounds in the rifle. Holly was still scrunched down behind the rocks frantically trying to get the last shell in the revolver.

"Drop the rifle, Ford. I mean it. Drop it now!"

Dino pulled the Thompson up to a firing position and was about to pull the trigger when a brilliant light swept in front of him and his men. The light seemed to pull all of the air out of the area around the rocks. Angelo and Raffi tried to shield their eyes, crying out as if they had been painfully blinded.

Dino was forced to tightly close his eyes as the brilliant light bore into his very brain. He pulled the trigger on the Thompson but had no idea as to where he was firing. The rat-a-tat-tat of the gun was almost lost in the swirling whirlwind that surrounded him.

Holly looked up at Ford who was shielding his eyes with his hand. Unlike Dino, Angelo, and Raffi, he was standing his ground. There was a look of amazement on his face. Holly shouted at Ford who looked over at her almost calmly. She showed him the revolver and tossed it to him. Ford caught it and in the same motion turned and shot Raffi. The brilliant swirling light continued but was bothering Dino and Angelo much more than Ford.

Ford hopped down from the rocks and pointed the pistol at Dino. Angelo was able to see Ford's position and cried out as he tried to point his pistol toward him. His arms seemed deadened and slowed. Ford turned his pistol on Angelo and shot him in the chest.

Then, just as suddenly as the light appeared, it was gone. Dino was kneeling, his face toward the ground as he leaned on the Thompson to keep himself partially upright. He looked up to see Ford standing above him, only four feet away. A movement to his right caught his eye. It was Holly who was coming out of the rocks.

Dino looked at Ford in amazement. "What in the hell was that?"

Ford was still in a bit of shock but he managed "They call them the Brown Mountain Lights. Some say they're ghost lights…my Mother says they're angels getting ready to return to Heaven after doing their work on earth. I think they just may be God's grace."

He looked over at Holly who was bending down beside the body of Angelo, her hand checking for a pulse. Ford shook his head, "I don't know…Mara just may be right!"

Dino blinked a couple of times and tried to stand up quickly. He caught Ford off guard as he pointed the Thompson saying, "Well, here's a taste of the devil!"

The side of Dino's head seemed to explode as Holly fired Angelo's pistol at Dino from only a few feet away. His fingered twitched on the Thompson's trigger but there was no eruption of gunfire. The Thompson was as empty as Dino Bellini's eyes.

Ford looked at his half-raised revolver and then at Holly who had collapsed to the ground after shooting Dino. She could not find words as Ford fell to her side. They wrapped themselves in each other as their minds tried to understand what had just happened.

A minute passed when Ford stood, pulling Holly along with him. "We need to go! We've got to find Mara! Wherever she is will probably be the end of this thing. They looked back at the bloodied ground containing the three mobsters.

"What is God's good name happened, Holly?"

Ford walked over to the Chevy and turned the ignition off. He walked on to the black car. Holly stumbled along with him towards Dino's Buick. She had a wide-eyed look of shock on her face. "I think…it's like you said…Mara's angels."

Chapter Seventy-Nine

"Complications, she thought."

Mara felt very conspicuous driving the Deputy's car. She was upset about her Ford convertible, so much so, that she found herself wondering what it would take to get it fixed. Outside of her family and friends, that Ford was about as dear to her as any human. Somebody was going to pay for hurting her car.

She stopped herself when she thought of Deputy Benny Goins, lying on a mountain road, his head mostly blown away. She almost smiled, *"I guess somebody already did!"*

One part of Mara thought she should feel bad in some way for taking a life. The other part reminded her that he was about to kill her and that bad people like that should die. It was about their actions, not hers. Then, Mara's mind reflected a glimpse of Julia in her coffin and any remorse dissolved.

Mara didn't want to venture too close to the Sheriff's office for fear of the car being recognized. She wondered about the old mine office but couldn't think of a reason for Royal to be there unless he was dumping a body. That thought made her shudder as she thought of Ford and Holly.

J.J.'s garage seemed like as good a place as any to land for the moment. She'd have to be careful though. There could be men hidden around the place waiting for someone to blunder into a trap.

It was beginning to get dark as Mara parked down the road from the garage. She had the same terrible feeling approaching the garage as she did earlier at her home. The apprehension brought a rise of anger and bitter bile from the pit of her stomach. She wondered if she'd ever feel really safe again. After year's away from New Jersey and the crippling fears she left there, this place had become her safe haven. Now the fears had returned along with the many bad memories.

The shadows were getting longer as she slipped around the back of the garage. She hoped that Gene, Roy, or Tom wouldn't get excited and give her away. She needed to check to see if the boys had been left enough food and water. J.J. was very good to take care of the dogs, but this was an unusual day. She wondered again, for the hundredth time, what was going on with J.J. and Ford.

Mara gasped when she came to the fenced in dog lot. One whole side of the fence was destroyed. There were no signs of the dogs, but there were plenty signs of destruction. It appeared a vehicle had rammed one side of the fence until it was destroyed. Mara's senses went on high alert as she shrunk back into the shadows.

Sliding back around the other side of the garage, she kept trying to push her fears away. She moved to the front of the building looking for any sign of light inside or more damage. By now, her heart was in her throat as she feared the worse.

She noticed the door to the office was slightly ajar which was not as startling as seeing a body crumpled on the ground between the old chairs used by the *Wise Men* and the door.

Mara rushed to the body, fearing the worst. It wasn't J.J. or Ford though. As she turned the body over, cradling the head in her lap, she could see it was Harv Coleridge. He was breathing, but his breaths were shallow. One side of his head was crusted with dried blood around a good-sized knot.

Mara began speaking Harv's name, first softly, then in a louder, more demanding voice. She gently shook him, then began stroking the side of his face. Suddenly, Harv's eyes fluttered and he tried to get up from his prone position.

Mara held him down and began softly speaking so as to reassure and calm the old gentleman. "Harv, you're okay. It's Mara Rawlings. I've got you…you're okay. Lie still a minute…just try and be calm. I've got you!"

Harv's eyes began to focus on Mara's face. He moved his head which resulted in a shock of pain. Mara held on to him a little tighter. "Harv, you've been hit on the head. I think you'll be okay. Try and be still. Can you tell me what's happened to you…what happened around here?"

The old man closed his eyes, letting his body fully relax. He then told Mara about the capture of the two gangsters and tying them to the tree in the dog lot. After telling Mara more details, Harv asked if he could sit up and lean against the wall. He did so with minimum pain and only a slight feeling of nausea. Catching his breath, he told Mara the remainder of the story.

"You see Miz Mara, J.J. left to meet his brother. Phil Sizemore left to pull Miz Mary Sorrels car out of a ditch and then check on those gangsters. Said he'd swing back by in a bit unless he ran into problems. Wallace and Trace had to leave, so it was just me left to watch after the prisoners. I walked into Mr. J.J.'s office to use the restroom facilities. When I came back outside there was a man standing there with a gun pointed in my face. He wanted me to get his men out of the dog lot. He was right cautious about them dogs of yours. Wanted me to tell him how to get them out, he did. Said he'd shoot them through the fence if I couldn't get rid of them."

Harv's head began hurting worse so he stretched back out on the porch before continuing. "Well, mam, I told him I wasn't sure about what to do about his problem. He was not happy with my answer. First, he punched me in the stomach, then he pushed his gun into my neck. Said he'd be glad to shoot me and dump my body for the dogs to eat."

Harv smiled up at Mara. "I sort of managed a grin 'cause I knew that neither Tom, Roy, or Gene would ever eat me. Well sir, he spotted the dog door going into the building and asked me if it could be shut from the inside. I looked at him like he should know that's what the door was for.

Harv pulled a plug of tobacco out of his pocket, bit off a piece and began chewing. "Aw now, that's the stuff. Well, that ruffian took me inside and began making a lot of loud noise which brought the dogs inside to see what was up. Stood me by the dog door in case they came in angry. Ole Roy, Gene, and Tom came in sniffing around. They saw me and I guess recognized me, so I wasn't bothered none. I heard him say, keep them dogs in here or I'll kill every one of them and you too. I went over and shut the dog's door so they couldn't get out. By that time, I heard an engine roaring and that man ran right through the fence to the dog lot. Next thing I knew, he was cutting the men's ropes loose and had them in the car."

Mara was puzzled. "How did you get your head mashed in?"

Harv chuckled, "Oh, I walked out the front door to see which way they went. Little did I know one of the fellows we had tied up was still around. He was looking for something on the ground…something I guess he dropped when Wallace clubbed him with his baseball bat. Probably his gun, I'd say. Anyways, I saw him and he saw me. I tried to get back in the office…was going to shut the door and lock it so he couldn't get inside. Guess he caught me before I got in the door. Don't know what he hit me with but I can tell you…it put my lights out."

By now Harv was rubbing the side of his head. "I'm pretty sure the first fellow pulled back around to see why the man wasn't in his car yet. I wasn't fully unconscious I guess. I heard him say to go back to the lodge. Then he said something about the Sheriff's house. Didn't hear all he said because I was fading and the fellow made an awful racket pulling out. Guess I'm lucky they didn't shoot me. Last I remember I tried to get to the office to call for help. Guess I passed out instead."

Mara sat beside Harv. She didn't know what to do. Waiting for J.J. or Ford did not feel like a good option. If she was going to get to Royal before anything else happened, she needed to go now. No gangster was going to deprive her of dealing with Sheriff Royal Majesty. He was hers and hers alone.

A thought crossed Mara's mind when she thought of Royal being at his house. *What about Angelica Grace and the kids. Maybe Florence, the Nanny, would be there too. Complications she thought."*

She jumped up and ran inside. Bringing Harv a wet cloth and a cool cup of water, she told him to stay put. "If you see J.J. or Ford, tell them they can find me at the Majesty house. Tell them to come as soon as they can!"

Harv was trying to protest her leaving but had no way of restraining her. She ran to the Deputy's car just as a pair of headlights turned off the highway. Mara pulled her pistol off the seat and prepared herself. She also had the shotgun and Deputy Benny Goins's pistol. She thought, *"The war's already begun…I can do battle here and now."* She brought up the pistol and cocked the hammer.

Phil Sizemore stepped out of his wrecker with his hands in the air. "Mara! Mara, that is you! It's Phil Sizemore! I've got news!"

Mara slowly lowered her weapon, a release of tension

rushing through her body. "You scared me to death Phil! I was about ready to shoot you!"

Phil walked over cautiously, then to her great surprise, grabbed Mara and hugged her tightly. "Boy howdy, I'm so glad to see you safe. I first saw that Sheriff's Department car sitting here and didn't know what to think. Are you okay? There's been some bad things going on around here today."

Mara grabbed Phil's arm, "What's happened Phil? Do you know anything about J.J. or Ford?"

Phil took both of Mara's hands. "Look Mara, there's probably more I don't know than I do. Let me tell you what I do know. I was told by Monty Black that there was a big chase out on the highway going toward Brown Mountain. Sounded like those gangster guys were chasing what appeared to be Ford down the highway towards Brown Mountain. The all went flying by Monty's property. There was gunfire. In fact, one of his beef cattle was shot. Anyways, the last Monty saw was that Ford was leading them towards Brown Mountain. I know J.J. and Jubal were setting a trap for whoever Ford could lead that way. I guess that's what was happening. I was going out there as soon as I came by here and checked on the prisoners."

Mara pulled away from Phil. "You go check on J.J. and Ford. The prisoners escaped. One of their kind came by and managed to get past the dogs. Busted Harv on the head."

She hesitated. "Wait! Take Harv to the Doc Phillips' first. Tell him we'll pay for Harv. Don't let Harv say no. Then go after J.J. Tell him I'm on my way to Royal Majesty's house."

Phil grabbed Mara's arm as she turned to go away. "You really shouldn't do that Mara. At least wait on J.J. or Ford to go with you. I haven't told you everything. Those gangsters also kidnapped Ezra Majesty and his wife. Don't know about the sister. But they've got them and trying to get Royal to parlay with them. I know this to be true because Lon Shell told me. Seems someone called into the Sheriff's Office looking for Royal. Left a message instead. Brazen of them, huh!'

Phil looked over to Harv as he continued. "I'll take care of Harv, but you should know, you're going to have some company over at the Majesty place."

Mara asked as she thought this through, "What about Ezra's two bodyguards…the two Bobs?"

"From what Lon told me, Royal had them over at his place. Left his brother without protection. Great brother, huh!"

Mara didn't answer but jumped in the Deputy's car and started it with a roar. She shouted at Phil, "My Ford is wrecked up on the mountain. I forget which road. When we get a chance, we'll go find it so you can bring it to the garage. Afraid J.J.'s going to have a good bit of work on the old girl." She looked at Harv. "Take care of Harv and I'll see you later. I'm still going to the Majesty's. If nothing else, Angelica Grace my need some help. Royal can burn in hell as far as I'm concerned!"

With that, Mara roared off leaving Phil standing in a cloud of dust and grit. He walked over to Harv to give him the news he was going to see the Doctor. He heard Harv speaking in a solemn, prayerful tone as he walked up.

"Lord, be with that child. She's going straight into the devil's home. She'll be needing all the help you can spare, Lord. Amen."

Chapter Eighty

"The Family's business wasn't changing, but the style certainly was."

Ezra Majesty did not come along without a fight. For that matter, neither did Raven or Serafina. Drago and three men went to find Ezra. They expected some type of fight since the brother supposedly had two bodyguards around him at all times. Someone had called them the "Bob-see" twins for some reason. They were supposed to be more than adequately trained and equipped for a fight.

When they arrived, there was no sign of anyone guarding the house. They simply went to the front door and knocked.

A dark, strange woman answered the door and they burst inside forcing her aside. Ezra met them in the foyer and tried to pull a pistol. Aldo was on him before he could clear the weapon, knocking him to the side as he pulled the pistol from his hand. A woman screamed behind Ezra which distracted Drago and his men.

In another instance, Ezra pulled a long blade from the sheath masquerading as a cane. Ezra sliced at Aldo, cutting him deeply across the arm he threw up to shield himself. Drago was already moving, slugging Ezra on the head with the butt of his pistol.

As Ezra crumpled, a scream was heard from behind them. The strange, dark woman jumped on the back of the one called Dante. Serafina was already slicing Dante's throat with a long, deadly knife blade. Aldo turned and shot the woman in the back before Dante could hit the floor. Dante and Serafina's blood flooded over the fine piece of rug as the other woman screamed, "Serafina! You killed my sister!"

Drago grabbed Raven as she rushed forward. Everyone's eyes stared at the two bodies on the floor, their blood mixing in one horrific scene. Raven went limp in Drago's arms, passing out from the sudden rush of terrible loss.

Drago tied Ezra and Raven's hands for their trip back to the lodge. Aldo's arm continued to bleed from the deep cut. He would need a Doctor or at least find a way to stop the bleeding or he would surly die.

Drago pulled a sheet off a bed and fashioned a heavy bandage and tourniquet. Some of Ezra's fine whiskey was poured on the gash before it was bound. Aldo held on to the whiskey bottle, taking sips regularly. He wanted to shoot Ezra but knew Drago would not allow it. They needed him alive at present. He swore to be the one to kill Ezra when the time came as he took another long swallow of the whiskey.

Drago had the third member of the crew, Pepe, to drive Aldo and the Majesty's back to the lodge. He had one more thing to check on.

Earlier, two of the men, Rico and Santo had gone to the garage owned by the father. They were to bring back the father or any other family member they could find. They hadn't shown up when he left the lodge. He did not have a very good feeling about them or their whereabouts. Another problem, even more troubling, was where Dino and his men had disappeared to. They had gone to the Rawlings home and hadn't been heard from again. Drago could only wonder if this whole thing was falling apart already.

Drago arrived at the garage to find his two men tied up in the dog lot behind the building. After rescuing Rico and Santo from the garage, Drago headed back to the lodge. Maybe Dino would be back with more prisoners. This was taking much too long and had become very messy.

In his mind, Vincent was digging himself a deep grave. The *Family* did not consider long conflicts and bloody results made public to be good for their business. Drago was ready to get this mess cleared up, so they could go home.

Thoughts of Vincent made Drago think, *"He might be better off dying here than doing so at the hands of one of the Family's executioners. It seemed lately, those guys were fond of meting out the most severe types of death. Bloody and very painful. The Family's business wasn't changing, but the style certainly was."*

Drago and Rico arrived only a few minutes before Santo pulled in. They went directly into the lodge, speaking quietly to the guards outside. Dino had not returned.

Inside, Ezra and Raven were both tied and gagged, sitting in separate chairs. Ezra's face sported a cut and some ugly bruising. His wife sat slunk over in the chair. Tears filled her eyes as she continued to morn her sister by mumbling her name over and over. Drago did not expect any further trouble from either one of them.

Vincent came into the great room from his bedroom. "Well! We have us one Majesty. What we do not have is the Majesty I want nor any of the Rawlings bunch. I sent Beppe over to give Royal a message that if he didn't give up, I'd cut his brother's heart out. Do you know what that stupid hillbilly told me?"

Vincent was grandstanding now. "He sent word back saying, "Good luck finding a heart in Ezra Majesty!" He says if we harm Ezra or his wife in any way he will see to it that we all pay a terrible price. The other part of his message stated we had till midnight to clear out of Burke County or we'd never be seen again! That arrogant *stanna maybaych*!"

Vincent walked over and stood by Ezra. He looked at Drago and shouted, "Where in the hell is Dino! Has anyone heard from him? Drago? If he doesn't show up in the next hour we're leaving without him. That dumb little *maddiul'*. He'd better show up soon and have a good reason to be this late!"

And so, it continued for the next hour. Vincent raving, Vincent arguing with Drago, and Vincent planning the demise of every citizen of Burke County. Drago was ready to shoot him on the spot.

Chapter Eighty-One

"Mara softly closed the door behind her as she crept into a dreadful darkness."

J.J. was torn between finding Mara or taking another road back up the mountain to look for Ford. He knew either Ford made it safely back to the highway or he and Holly were stuck on the mountain, fighting for their lives. He was about to turn back to the mountain when a vehicle passed him going the other way. The vehicle, a wrecker, came to a skidding halt in the road and turned around. He knew exactly who it was.

Phil Sizemore pulled his wrecker over as J.J. turned around and stopped in front of him on the grassy shoulder. Phil quickly told J.J. about everything that had happened including the prisoner's escape. The night was getting uglier by the minute. Both men knew Mara was headed right into the middle of the worst of it and Ford was still unaccounted for. It was as hard a decision as J.J. had ever had to make.

Finally, he sent Phil to look for Ford. Asked if he was armed, Phil pointed to a Marlin hunting rifle fitted with a scope resting on a rack and a Colt .45 automatic he held up. Phil smiled at J.J., "Believe I'm good. I've got plenty of firepower. I've even got my little sawed-off shotgun under the seat if it gets dicey."

J.J. headed to the Majesty place as Phil went to find Ford. The wrecker driver hadn't experienced this type of excitement since he shot at Nazi's in the war. He almost wished he would run into a few gangsters so he could show them how good a shot a North Carolina boy could be.

Both men headed their separate ways, wondering what was ahead of them. The one thing they both knew for certain was that more blood would be shed tonight.

~

Meanwhile, Mara arrived at the lower gate to the Majesty home. She parked the Deputy's car where it could be seen just to make anyone coming by wonder what was going on. She knew the property fairly well. J.J. would bring her up this way on occasion as Royal was building the estate. The parameter of the property was secured with either a wall of stone or a tall, heavy wrought arm fence.

Mara knew one area where a few ancient oak trees grew near enough to the wall that some of their sturdy limbs reached across. Hopefully, a limb would allow her to swing over the wall and drop to the other side. She hoped that Royal had not added guard dogs or had the trees cut down. She also prayed that climbing out on a limb would not result in it breaking and sending her crashing down.

So far, Mara spotted no guards. She knew they were around, though. Royal's compliment of Deputies was made up of both honest cops for law enforcement and thugs to do his dirty work. So far, she was on the fence concerning which side Lon Shell was on. It was hard to image Lon would be a part of Royals illegal deeds but the young man was very close to Royal and his family. She guessed she'd find the truth about Lon tonight, along with many other secrets Royal was hiding.

She'd armed herself with her pistol, Deputy Goins pistol, and a heavy hunting knife of J.J.'s. At first if felt like plenty. The closer to the wall she got the less formable it seemed.

The tree closest was still about six feet from the vertical surface of the wall. The giant tree soared upwards. There was a good, thick limb that reached out over the wall. However, it looked to be at least fifteen feet from the ground. That was going to be a risky drop.

Mara managed climbing the tree with little effort. Climbing trees was something she loved to do as a girl even though there weren't many good climbing trees in her New Jersey neighborhood. J.J. used to laugh at her climbing trees around the Rawlings home when she first moved to North Carolina. Now it was a skill that would get her close to Royal Majesty.

Mara scooted out on the limb until she was just past the wall underneath. The hearty limb began to sway with her weight. She took the hunting knife and using all her might, buried the blade into the limb just above the wall. Taking the heavy Deputy's pistol, she pounded the hilt of the knife, driving the blade deeper into the wood.

With one deep breath, she held onto the hilt of the knife and dropped off the limb. The knife held long enough to allow her to drop onto the top of the wall. She nearly toppled over the wall. The knife fell from the limb, bouncing on the wall and over to the wrong side. The top of the wall was narrow but Mara managed to get her body under control long enough to grab the edge and drop over the side.

She skinned her fingers, hand, and chin but landed safely on the ground without any major damage. It was worth the pain and effort just to get to Royal Albert Majesty.

Mara hated that name as much as she hated the man. It sounded pompous, arrogant, privileged, and entitled…it was everything Royal stood to be. Mara felt that by the end of the night all that name would represent would be a line on a tombstone.

She stayed in the shadows, moving quietly toward the house.

The night was clear with the full moon shining brightly. All Mara wanted to do was get as close to Royal as could, while staying safe from detection.

She figured there'd be plenty of distraction when DiPoli and his men arrived. That was when she planned on striking. She'd deal with Royal first, then, if possible, take out DiPoli too. Her plans covered everything but escape. She'd deal with that when the time came. She hoped J.J. and Ford would arrive before the battle became too heated.

Mara checked the two pistols she carried. There was no way she could have brought the shotgun with her over the wall. It would have been nice to have held that kind of firepower in Royal's face.

She had to steel herself from thinking of Ford and J.J. She would only think of them being safe. An awful dread kept trying to creep into her thoughts. And what about Holly. She knew that dear girl had dealt with too much heartache already. She couldn't have let her come with her even though she knew she would have been steady. *"She'll help protect Ford. It will be no different than me being at his side. She won't disappoint...she's as brave as any of us."*

Mara kept these thoughts going over and over in her mind as she crept closer to the house. A movement caught her attention causing Mara to freeze. It was one of Ezra's bodyguards, Bob one or the other. Why in the world would Ezra hire bodyguards with the same name? She hadn't considered Ezra being in the middle of this. *"Oh well, if Ezra gets in the way, I've got two guns...he can go to hell with his brother."* That thought brought a cruel smile to Mara's face.

Bob moved toward the front of the house as he made his rounds. They probably didn't expect anyone coming at them from the direction Mara took.

Mara saw her opportunity. She moved quickly right up to the house to look for an opportunity to get inside. In only seconds, she'd found exactly what she was looking for. It was a small, unlocked door to the cellar. She didn't know if it would give her access to the upstairs but it was her best choice at the moment.

Mara slowly opened the door just as one of the Bob's came around the corner. She picked up a stone and threw it into the night causing Bob's attention to be distracted. Mara softly closed the door behind her as she crept into a dreadful darkness.

Chapter Eighty-Two

"What if he's already dead?"

Vincent DiPoli was filled with rage that his plan was not working. He had started blaming others, especially Dino, that it was falling apart. He had Ezra and Raven Majesty tied up as bait to bring Royal to the lodge. The only problem was, Royal wasn't coming. DiPoli's leadership had sunk to screaming…accusations, orders, and cursing. He began changing his mind as to what should be done next and contradicting his own self.

Drago was busy getting the men prepared for the assault on the Majesty estate. While Vincent was busy becoming an angrier man, Drago was trying to figure out how best to attack the estate and survive.

They knew little about the property and even less about how many men Royal had protecting him. He'd been able to get a little information from Ezra. The brother was more than a little agitated at his brother's inaction on his part. Upon hearing Royal's proclamation that his bother did not have a heart and they could kill him if they wanted, Ezra began cursing Royal. It seems this was not the first-time Ezra had been left hanging by his older brother.

Ezra wasn't giving up every detail or answering every question. What he did say was more than a little helpful. Drago learned about Royal taking Ezra's two bodyguards, Bob and Bob. He also learned of the presence of six hired guns from a clan up in the mountains.

Ezra smiled when he told Vincent about the Haddish clan. "They'll have you all skinned and mounted by this time tomorrow."

Ezra mentioned Royal would have his driver and at least six heavily armed Deputies surrounding him. He went on to speak of Royal planning to get even more men if time allowed. "You're going to be walking into a fight with a small army. I hope you know you are all going to die tonight!

Raven Majesty started shouting about the revenge that would be meted out for her sister. "I curse you! All of you! You are vipers but you will die the death of cowards poisoned by your own vileness! I will see vengeance before the night ends. Hell is coming for you all!" She continued shouting at them and cursing them in some unknown language until she had to be gagged.

Drago estimated there would be as at least fifteen men plus Royal to have to deal with tonight. He wasn't happy with the odds but he felt good about the amount of fire-power and the number of men they'd bring to the battle…that is, if Dino ever showed up.

The fact that Dino was still a no-show was very troublesome. He didn't even know where to look for the young punk. He doubted he was just lost and couldn't find his way back to the lodge. It was beginning to be apparent Dino and the men with him had met with a deadly problem.

Drago was sure by now that Dino or his men would not be coming back. Whoever they'd run into must have been plenty good enough to take out that many hard-core men that were more than adequately armed. What also mattered was that if someone took out Dino and his men, would they be joining the fight at the Majesty house.

Drago began thinking very seriously about just shooting Vincent and heading to New York. He really doubted the Bosses would be too upset with him. The only thing that kept him from doing it was at the core of his being. He really did love a good and violent fight…and this was to be that for sure.

Vincent, on the other hand still believed Dino would be showing up at any time. He was heard to be letting everyone within earshot know what he was going to tell Blinks Bellini upon his arrival.

Drago figured they were outnumbered two to one or better. Vincent seemed to have forgotten about the Rawlings kid and his family. Drago figured it was just as well since the odds of handling Majesty and his men were bad enough without adding more people to deal with. Still, he wondered about the Rawlings. If Royal was dug in at his place, then who took out Dino and his men? Drago shook his head, "*Who in the hell was this Ford Rawlings? Did he take out Dino and his crew? How could one hillbilly cause all of this damage and uproar?*"

Vincent interrupted Drago's thoughts. "I'm ready to go Drago. Let's get this show on the road. I still want to be on the road to New York tonight. What in the hell has happened to Dino? I'm going to kill that *piccolo culo.*"

Drago said under his breath, "What if he's already dead?"

Drago rounded up the men and gave them their instructions. He was planning a two-fold strategy. Part one was the attack on the Majesty estate. Part two was an exit strategy because he planned on living through this and getting home.

Vincent ordered Ezra and Raven shot and left out in the woods. He was evidently creeped out by Raven's constant chanting. She'd continued chanting even with a gag in her mouth. Her "curse" was beginning to wear on Vincent and the whole crew. Vincent laughed at her, but Drago noticed he kept watching the woman nervously. He figured Vincent still had one foot still in the old Italian heritage of curses and omens.

Drago did not plan on killing Ezra and his wife. He would leave instructions with his two guys to leave them tied and gagged in the lodge. They'd stay behind long enough to make Vincent believe the deed was done. Drago needed both men to take part of the attack. He would have liked to have someone watch over the pair so he could use them for leverage if things went badly and he needed a way to get out of this country-style hell. After all, they could always come back and kill them later.

The group headed out with Vincent becoming excited, talking rapidly and reminding everyone of their jobs. If he used the term, "No Quarter" one more time, Drago would actually go ahead and shoot the man.

The men left with grim looks on their faces and an itchiness to get it started. Three sets of eyes watched the cars go out of sight before creeping up to the building. The three people were just about to approach the building when the door opened suddenly. Two men came out and immediately left in the one remaining car.

Earlier, Phil Sizemore had once again found one of the Rawlings family in unusual circumstances. Phil passed Ford on the mountain road, only noticing it was him in the dark car as his wrecker's headlights crossed the car's windshield.

It took Ford and Phil only ten minutes to decide a plan of action. Actually, Holly first suggested they might learn more by checking out the lodge before going to Royal's house. It was that decision that brought the three of them to the shadows outside the hunting lodge.

Ford hurried over to the window on one side of the door while Phil Sizemore did the same on the opposite side. Holly was left on her own behind a pile of wood. She caught Ford looking back at her so she motioned she was going around back. Ford shook his head for her not to go, but she was already gone.

Ford nodded to Phil and they covered each other as they slipped inside. Phil made his way back through the lodge as Ford checked the kitchen and pantry. Inside the pantry, he found Ezra and Raven, both bound to a chair with a gag in their mouths.

Ford untied Raven who immediately grabbed him in a hard hug. Tears flowed as she cried out about her sister's death. Phil untied Ezra who let out a string of swear words that seemed to have no end. Outside of the cut and bruises on Ezra's face, neither one appeared to be badly harmed.

They walked out into the great room just as the front door swung open. Ford and Phil pulled their guns, pushing Ezra and Raven to the side. A silhouette froze in the doorway as time seemed to stand still. A shaky, soft voice spoke.

"Hey there fellows. The back door was locked, I sort of twisted my ankle when I tripped over an old bucket on the ground. You're not going to shoot me, are you?" Holly tried a weak smile as she limped towards the sofa. "Sorry! I didn't mean to startle everyone. Are you folks okay?"

Thirty minutes passed as Phil and Ford spoke with Ezra. Holly managed a quick pot of coffee, serving Raven as she spoke about the murder of her sister.

Ford and Phil both tried to calm Ezra who was becoming more and more angry. They tried to reason with him and get him to let Phil take them home or at least to the Sheriff's Department. Ford felt there should be someone around that would not be affiliated with Royal's nefarious dealings. Ezra reminded Ford that he had no authority over him and he would go wherever he damn well pleased.

Ford finally threw up his hands and told Ezra to go wherever he wanted…he just wasn't going to be his ride. With that, Ford,

Holly, and Phil left for Royal Majesty's house leaving Ezra and Raven standing at the front door. Ezra stood there cursing as Raven cried out her sister Serafina's name, once again swearing vengeance.

Chapter Eighty-Three

"Make your peace with God, Sheriff."

Royal stood in his foyer, staring at the wooly face of Solomon Haddish. The man, along with a younger Haddish, just seemed to appear at his doorstep in spite of the many guards around his property. The stature of the man looked greater inside a room than when he stood outdoors.

Ferrell stood just behind and to the right of the mountain clan leader. Solomon made even Ferrell look to be an ordinary man when compared in size. The clan leader stared at Royal, his normal composure missing. He took a step toward Royal, mimicked subtly by Ferrell.

"Yes, Sheriff…you heard me clearly. I am taking my men back to our home. Our contract is dissolved…I will forego your payment."

"What makes you think you can do that, Solomon? You're not someone known to go back on your word."

Solomon stood with his feet a shoulders width apart, his hands clasped in front of him. He appeared calm while Royal was obviously becoming agitated.

"You see, I never considered you a man known for keeping your word, Sheriff."

Royal moved quickly, putting his hand on his revolver. "Listen here, you smug son of a b…" Royal could not finish the sentence as Solomon smoothly produced a long bladed knife that he held to the Sheriff's mid-section. In nearly the same instance, Ferrell held a cocked .45 Colt to the back of Solomon's head ignoring the pistol Noah Haddish held pointing at him.

A very tense second passed before Royal calmly said, "I ain't got time for this bull! Why don't you and your boys run back to the mountains before the real men decide to do battle. Thought you were more than this Solemn. I won't be calling on you again…just don't be breaking any laws in my County."

All four stepped back from each other, the tension still hanging in the air. "I have three badly wounded men already, Sheriff. They were offered no medical attention from you. You are much more concerned about your safety than any of your charges…and that, Sheriff, is my concern. You plan only for your own survival."

He slid his knife back in its sheath. "There was no mention of going against automatic weapons or running down the highway doing battle from open trucks. These gangster's you find at your doorstep are most likely there because of your own actions. You and your brother are not the type of people the Haddish wish to be found in partnership. You deceive in small tokens, but you still deceive. For that insolence, you will one day meet your maker…possibly before this night ends."

Majesty snarled at Solemn, "Get out of here! I got no use for a bunch of cowards who don't know anything about fighting."

He turned away from Solemn until the man spoke one last time. "Sheriff…come see us sometime. Bring all the men you can muster…if there are any left to follow you after tonight. Somehow…I don't think there will be. Make your peace with God, Sheriff. You'll be speaking to him very soon, I think."

Solomon and Noah Haddish slipped away as quickly as they came. Ferrell followed him to the door and watched him blend into the darkness. Solomon made his way down to the bottom of the hill, near the gate. He walked up to a truck and gave his remaining men instruction.

J.J. walked over to Solomon and asked about his wounded. "They're all stable now. Our people are well versed in healing. Israel was hurt the worst but he is being attended to. We will watch for infection. He is tough and will be fine, God willing."

J.J. watched Solomon closely. "What did Majesty say…don't imagine he took it too well."

Solomon studied J.J. before he answered. "Mr. Rawlings, I allowed Royal to spin a tale of outsiders coming into the mountains to do terrible things. I appreciate you opening my eyes to the whole truth. I trust you because you have proven to be our friend for many years. So, allow me to thank you again for the many services you have fairly provided. We do well repairing our vehicles, but we can find ourselves at a disadvantage at times. You've made affordable parts available to us as well as given us your wisdom and advise. I would offer to stay with you but I'm afraid we need to go home and see to our wounded."

"Thank you for your words, Solomon. I hope what I told you tonight would be considered…wisdom. Royal Majesty is good for no one. I think he will have a bad night, tonight."

"Mr. Rawlings, we know who Royal Majesty is. We allowed ourselves to be deceived in taking this job, but that is on us. We had no idea he was planning on having your family murdered."

"However, my family being harmed in such a careless way is on me. That which was about to happen tonight would have cost my family dearly, of that I am sure. We will be on our way, but we will not forget the service you provided tonight." With that, the Haddishes drove away to the security of their mountain home.

J.J watched them out of sight, then turned and began his trip up to Majesty Manor. He felt he could slip through the gate and manage to skirt the driveway all the way to the house while avoiding Royal's men. All his years of stealthy hunting in the mountains were good practice for tonight. As he started he had a thought that he might be leaving his so-called wisdom at the bottom of the hill.

On up the hillside, Ferrell prowled the darkness in front of the house. He wanted the men to be especially alert now that they no longer had the Haddish boys to add to the security. Ferrell felt a kinship with the darkness. That was when he did his best work before he went to prison. The truth was, it was still when he was at his best. One of the Bobs stepped out of the shadows as Ferrell approached. He paused when Ferrell held up his hand for him to stop. Ferrell found that when he wore his killing face, even some of the biggest men stepped aside.

Walking a little further he held up a fist as he passed two of the Sheriff's Deputies at their posts. He continued to a stone ledge that bordered Angelica Grace's flower garden. He stood there a moment before taking in a deep breath and slowly releasing it.

Ferrell turned quickly, re-tracing his steps back towards the house. As he passed each guard, he said the same thing to them in a low, menacing voice. "Get ready! They're here!"

Chapter Eighty-Four

"I'm a Majesty and my Wife's sister has been murdered."

Deputy Sheriff Lon Shell pulled cautiously in front of Ed Seeley's hunting lodge. There were no cars in front or around the building. There also was no one to be seen. He was wondering if he should have gone directly to Sheriff Majesty's house. Just then, a shadow move quickly across one of the windows.

Lon positioned the car so he could get out, keeping it between him and the house. He carefully walked to the porch as he watched for any signs of danger or deception. The door opened easily which was not usually a good sign. Holding his revolver in ready position, Lon quickly slipped into the house, ready to fire.

Ezra Majesty came out of the kitchen holding an ax from the woodpile just outside. Raven materialized behind him, holding a butcher knife in each hand. They looked ready to attack.

Lon held up both hands and called out to Ezra, breaking their urge to rush the Deputy. Fifteen hectic minutes passed as Ezra and Raven told their stories to Lon. Ezra was as angry at his brother as he was at the gangsters. Raven was distraught to the point of hysteria. She wanted to go to her sister to see that her body would be taken care of properly. Just as importantly, she was hell-bent on going after the gangsters to bring vengeance on their black hearts.

Lon had about given up trying to reason with either of them. The Sheriff already had more than half the force with him. He was surprised Royal had commandeered Ezra's bodyguards leaving his brother and sister-in-law exposed.

Lon couldn't pull any more Deputy's into what he knew for sure was going to be a fight. He wondered if the battle had already begun. He had to have two Deputies at the station because there were prisoners in the lockup and someone needed to take calls and operate the two-way base radio. A car wreck on the other end of the County had another Deputy tied up. The last Deputy, not with the Sheriff, was chasing around the Brown Mountain area looking into a great explosion that was heard earlier. The same Deputy had earlier discovered the results of a battle at the Rawlings home.

It was Francis Potter who had dropped by to see Mara and found the house shot up with two dead bodies at the front of the house. There was another one at the back door and one more by the garage. Francis had to be taken to the hospital, complaining with her heart after seeing the aftermath of what looked to have been a terrible battle. Lon had planned on swinging by the Rawlings home after leaving the lodge on his way to Sheriff Majesty's home. The evening seemed to have exploded with violence. It appeared his plans were about to change once again.

The two Majesty's were insisting on him taking them to Royal's. He'd already radioed into the Office and had someone send an ambulance over to Ezra's to collect Serafina LeClair's body. That satisfied Raven for the moment concerning her sister. Now, she was even more insistent on going to Royal's.

He was telling her for the third time, he could not do what she wanted when she lifted one the knives against his chin. Ezra responded immediately by taking Lon's service revolver.

"Deputy, this is something we didn't want to do. I take your point that it would not be a good idea for you to bring two civilians, witnesses to boot, to what will be a dangerous place. I understand this…but you see, I'm a Majesty and my Wife's sister has been murdered. Please…go with us to Royal's and we will give you your pistol back and let you do your job."

Lon started to argue as Ezra cut him off. "Deputy, we are going to my brother's house tonight. You will go with us or you will stay here tied to a chair. Don't worry about what my brother might have to say to you when we arrive. Trust me, I doubt he will have any time to speak to you at all. He and I are going to have a serious conversation however…that is if he's still alive by that time."

Chapter Eighty-Five

"If he spotted Vincent right now, he'd shoot him without hesitation."

Beppe Carbone was having a hard time making his way through the property. This was not what he was built to do. Besides, he did not have on the right kind of shoes to traverse over the damp, dewy ground.

He was making his way toward the house from the right side. Two other men followed along, on either side of him. Drago had taken out the guard closest to the gate. He was on him, slicing his throat before the man had a chance to react. He had a great distaste for Drago but he would have to say he was both talented and efficient in his deadly skills.

He and his two comrades had taken out another man along the way. It was not as quiet as Drago's kill, but Majesty had to know they were coming by now.

The left side of their flank was not going to be dealt with at this time. Beppe figured his position in the attack was to draw fire once their presence was discovered. Vincent, Drago, Aldo, Parido, and Gianni would be roaring up the driveway at any time now. Once they made it to the house, Beppe, Ermete, and Jacopo would rush the house from their side. The idea would be for them to gain control of the parameters of the house while taking out any guards hiding in the shadows. The men in the cars should draw the Sheriff's attention out front.

Actually, Drago would be ducking out of the car he was in just before reaching the house. He would attack the house from the other side, slipping inside and killing anyone he saw…except the Sheriff. Vincent wanted him for himself.

Beppe hesitated beside a tree to catch his breath when a series of shots rang out. Jacopo went down, crying out in pain. He was still alive but was not getting up on his own.

Beppe bent low and ran as best he could to the right of the gunshots. Ermete was cutting back and forth, making his way just to Beppe's left. Beppe was glad he was wearing dark clothing. He was sweating profusely and breathing like his lungs might explode. If he spotted Vincent right now, he'd shoot him without hesitation.

Walking parallel to Beppe, on the other side of the driveway, was another party that really didn't need to be there. J.J. knew he should wait on any help that might show up. He had slipped past the guard near the gate and was making his way toward the house avoiding Majesty's men. J.J. knew his biggest weakness had always been his impatience, especially when things got tough. Shots were heard and J.J. knew the battle was only starting. He moved closer to the driveway so that he could move more quickly up the hill.

No sooner had he moved closer to the driveway when the roar of oncoming cars came his way. He tried to dive into some nearby bushes when a powerful bee stung him in the back of the leg. J.J. rolled, biting down on his lip so as not to cry out in pain. A bullet sprayed from a machine gun caught J.J. in the hamstring. The cars roared on by as J.J. was already removing his belt to make a tourniquet. He knew that if he was going to be in this fight, it was most likely going to have to come to him. Right now, he wasn't sure if he could even make it back to the driveway.

The roar of the cars made their way toward the house as more shots rang out. The distinctive fire of a Thompson machine gun peppered the night from one of the cars. The three cars screeched to a stop in front of the house forming a rough triangle. There was gunfire coming from around the house as well as two front windows.

Beppe took off running, leaving Ermete to deal with the men left guarding that path to the house. After twenty laborious steps, Beppe heard a man scream from off in the darkness. Either Ermete found a target or a target had found him. The gunfire was getting intense as Beppe approached the right side of the house. He rushed toward some deep shadows only to run into the large bulk of another man.

Beppe collided with one of the Bob's as the man was reloading his shotgun. The two large men hit the ground hard, a loud grunt coming from both. Beppe rolled away from the other man just as Bob lunged in his direction. He'd produced a hunting knife that he slammed into the ground, just missing Beppe's calf. Still, he grabbed Beppe's leg and started twisting and pulling it as he tried to get the knife out of the dirt.

Beppe screamed out in pain as his leg felt like it might come out of his hip socket. He pointed his pistol at Bob's head and fired.

Bob's head exploded into the dark shadows, leaving Beppe's pants legs covered in warm, mushy bone and matter. Beppe immediately became sick and threw up.

On the other side of the house, Drago found the other Bob. The big man turned on Drago just as he slid his killing knife into Bob's side. Still, the big man grabbed at Drago, grasping him by the throat and shoving him toward the ground. Instead of falling, Drago spun around, pulling his knife from Bob's side and plunging it into the back of the man's neck, just where it met the shoulders. Bob was dead before his body found rest on the ground.

Drago then moved to the house to find access and more victims.

Chapter Eighty-Six

"After all, it had been a wonderful lifetime."

Before the attack began, Mara had made her way through the cellar, finding the steps more by feel than anything else. Even if she'd found a light switch, she would have been hesitant to turn it on. Waiting at the top of the steps, she made sure the door would open when she was ready. As soon as she opened the door ever slightly, she heard voices. They were anxious and angry. She could hear Vincent and one other voice she did not recognize. The person had an unusual accent that fell on the ear with a unique mountain twang. Mara closed the door and waited.

The voices became muffled with the door closed. The darkness seemed to lay heavily on Mara and she found herself breathing with greater effort. Images came to her mind as she sat there, waiting.

A sudden image caused Mara to gasp, too loudly. More images rushed at her as a cold sweat covered her body. She felt sick and weak…light-headed. Suddenly, she could smell the man's cologne. That stinky, sweet fragrance put on too heavily over a body that needed washing. He had the stink of dried sweat and a heavy garlic smell on his breath that Mara could almost taste. Mara found herself sliding down the wall, ending up sitting on a step.

Mara tried to push the images back but they would not leave. She could feel his hands on her body, roughly pulling and tearing at her clothing. Then, there was his voice. It came to her as if he was really there. A boyish sounding voice bellowing as if he were a man.

She stood up only to find her legs too weak to hold her. She slumped back to the step. Whispering, she pleaded, "Why now! Dear God, why now! Oh God! Make it stop. Don't let this happen…please! I've got to do this for J.J. I've got to protect Ford! He's my son…you gave him to me. Please God, please!"

Tears were running down her face so fast she couldn't wipe them away fast enough. Her breaths were coming in waves of panicked heaving. It was too much she thought.

The face of Sabato Ferrari laughed out at her, mocking her. It was still just as cruel as it had been that night. He was telling her he could do anything he wanted to do to her. His Father was a connected man, a powerful man. She should be proud he was going to mount her and share his body with her. He raised his head back and drained the last drop of whiskey from the bottle he'd been carrying when he attacked her. Dropping it beside her, he reached down to tear her panties off.

That was when Mara grabbed the bottle and broke it on the floor. He looked at her and began to laugh again. That was when she forced her knee to his groin. As he reacted, she slammed the broken bottle into his face. He screamed out…such an awful, animal-like scream. His hands were holding his face as she squirmed out from under him.

Mara saw her younger self standing over Sabato as he cried out holding his bloodied face. He cursed her as he looked at his bloodied hands. Mara could see the bloodied and battered woman that resembled her younger self as she stood, looking cruelly at the boy. Suddenly, she kicked him in the groin again. As his hands grabbed his crotch, the young Mara took the remainder of the shattered whiskey bottle and stabbed the boy's face again, not once, but twice more.

Mara was horribly sick by now. She slowly moved down the steps, throwing up a terrible bile from her very core. It had been years since all these memories had come back with such realness. She had always been able to force them back into the dark recesses of her mind when they tried to rise up. It had become so much easier once she met J.J. Her life had become so happy through all these years…ever since the day J.J. returned from the Army with her the brand-new Ford convertible. Seeing him get out of that car cemented her ever-lasting feeling of hope and safety. But now, the primal fear she once knew was trying to return.

Mara tried to recover from the debilitating images from her past. She told herself for the millionth time that Sabato got what he deserved. It cost him an eye and left him with a heavily scared face. It cost Mara her life along the New Jersey shoreline. That was when she fled to Mercerville, going into hiding and wondering when his father, Anatolio Ferrari, would find her and send his men to end her life.

She wondered, *"Did the memories come back because of what she planned on doing to Royal? Could it be that Vincent DiPoli and his Italian Mob connections brought these memories to return?"* She sat on the floor, wondering if she would somehow be found out and Sabato Ferrari would again be coming for her."

This had always been her secret…her secret alone. J.J. knew only that she had troubles in New Jersey. She told him it had to do with the son of a man connected to the Mob. She never told him details and he loved and trusted her enough to respect her desire to keep it to herself. That was J.J. Rawlings, a man worth everything…a man worth protecting even with her own life. After all, it had been a wonderful lifetime.

Mara stood up, wiping her mouth on her sleeve. She felt for the stair rail and walked straight to the top, opening the door just as the sound of gunfire erupted at the front of the house.

She walked into the lighted room, her mind roaring, *"Where are you Royal? It's your day of reckoning. You're going to pay for Julia Harmon and all your other sins."*

Chapter Eighty-Seven

"It's all there, Royal. All of your sins."

It appeared DiPoli and his men had put themselves into a position that left them surrounded. Actually, they were positioned between the remaining Deputies and the house. This would allow the doorway to the house to be attacked and entered.

One heavy car sat parallel to the front of the house. The other two sat in something that resembled legs of a triangle, the point facing away from the house. The sound of gunfire came in bursts from both sides of the fight. Even with a full moon, it was difficult to assume how many casualties there were on either side.

Vincent was carrying Drago's machine gun. He continued to spray the front of the house. In another moment, he would be ready to charge up the steps. He just needed someone to be his wing man. That someone turned out to be found in the massive form of Beppe Carbone.

Beppe appeared from the side of the house. He looked a little unstable. Vincent at first thought he was wounded. Beppe surprised him by making his way to the car that was offering protection. Vincent asked Beppe what was wrong and received an unexpected answer.

Beppe had a handkerchief out trying to wipe something off his shoes and pants leg. Even in the moonlight, Beppe was disheveled, his clothes showing signs of wet grass as well as dark stains of dirt and blood. Beppe's face and head were covered in sweat. He spoke in a detached voice. "Me and another guy was rolling on the ground, fighting. He grabbed my leg and was twisting it. I blew his head off. Made a mess…a bad mess."

"Listen Beppe, I need you to focus…listen!"

Beppe looked up at Vincent. "I'm hearing you Vincent. You ready to go in?"

Vincent was surprised that Beppe knew what needed to be done. His mind was clearer than Vincent expected. Just then another shot came from an upstairs window, resulting in the man across from Vincent crying out. He fell against the car, a fatal wound clearly visible between his shoulders. The sniper on the second floor was their biggest obstacle to getting inside.

Vincent cursed. “Where’s Drago. We’re getting picked off out here. It’s that upstairs window.” With that, Vincent sent a burst of bullets into the window.

Vincent reloaded the Thompson as Beppe watched. As soon as he finished, Beppe calmly said, “Let’s go Vincent. We got to end this.”

Beppe stood up firing his .45 while Vincent moved forward firing the Thompson. They both made it to the porch and slipped inside the house.

At that moment, Drago was making his way down an upstairs hallway. He could hear gunfire coming from a bedroom on the front of the house. Quietly opening one door, he found the room empty. That’s when he heard gunfire in the room on the other side. He cautiously opened the door to hear another gunshot fired, followed by a volley from the Thompson hitting the room.

Drago ducked just in time to see Ferrell turn his gun on him. The bullet flew by his head, missing only by inches. He ducked and rolled into the room, firing toward a space Ferrell had already vacated.

Ferrell moved to his right and fired again, this time using his Ruger pistol. Drago came up from his crouch and lunged at Ferrell. They collided with fierce impact. Their bodies crashed around the room as each one tried to gain advantage. Both men ended up losing their pistols as the room furniture was being destroyed by their struggles. They were both powerfully built men who knew how to fight in close quarters. They became entangled in a fierce life and death struggle.

As the two men struggled upstairs, Vincent and Beppe began creeping through the downstairs. The gunfire outside had fallen away to only occasional single shots. The two gangsters left at the cars were responsible in keeping any of the Sheriff’s men from coming up to the house.

Beppe led the way into the house. They carefully crept along, getting the lay of the house. Both were aware Royal or his men could be setting a trap for them. Neither one believed Royal to be dead…yet.

~

Mara came out of the dark cellar into the kitchen. The overhead light was still on which surprised her since the sounds of gunfire demonstrated a battle had begun. She was startled when she realized a man was standing across from her at the kitchen door.

Fortunately, he was not aware of her presence as he stared outside. She noticed he'd barricaded the door and was the lone sentinel in the room. As she stared at him she recognized him to be Deputy Arvil Smeltzer.

He started to reach over and turn out the kitchen light when he froze, his back still toward her. Mara had her pistol ready in case he turned around as she crept toward him.

She stopped at a hanging ceiling rack. It took only a second to pull something down. A small noise was made as one pot moved just enough to touch another pan. Arvil swung around, lifting his rifle only to be met by a large skillet to the head. Arvil's legs collapsed from under him. Mara tried to catch him and failed miserably.

Mara laughed, "I think ole "Skillet" Rawlings would be proud of me!" The action seemed to quieten her mind and send the bad memories elsewhere, allowing her to focus on what she had to do.

Mara took the time to drag Arvil to the cellar door and rolled him onto the steps. Quietly closing the door, she heard Arvil's unconscious body drop down another step or two.

Mara was trying to remember the layout of the house from a visit she and J.J. made during Sheriff Royal Majesty's grand opening party. J.J. didn't want to come, fussed all the way there, then spoke on and on about how overdone he found every part of the house as they traveled home.

She stopped when she heard Royal's voice shouting. "Keep the front covered! No one comes in here…No One! Ferrell, go upstairs and take out anybody who moves. Arvil! Arvil! Keep an eye on that back door!"

He was walking down the hall, mumbling about how Arvil better be in his position when he walked directly into a face to face encounter with Mara's two pistols.

He started to say something only to have Mara push a gun harder into his face. His arm started to move upwards only to feel her other pistol pushed hard into his ribs. "You don't want to disagree with me right now, Royal. How about we find your office and talk a minute?"

Royal actually chuckled a bit as Mara turned him around. He felt her check him for weapons. She stuck one of her pistols in her belt and relieved Royal of his Python. She hefted the big pistol, "My lord, Royal. Is this the biggest pistol you could find? Not making up for any shortcomings, are you?"

"Mara, you certainly have no idea of what you speak. I am, after all, a Majesty."

For his remark, he received a stiff shot across the back of the head with his own Python. She shoved him through the door into his office. "Sit down Royal, this won't take long. We're about to solve a murder case of yours." Royal sat down hard in his chair. He immediately reached for his desk drawer, out of habit and desperation.

The gunshot sounded as if the room exploded. Royal jumped back so quickly he almost fell out of his chair. "How in the hell do you shoot this canon, Royal. It almost jerked my arm off. My goodness, that's a huge chunk out of your desk. What is that, mahogany?"

"What the hell do you want, Mara? We've got a lot going on here. In case you don't know, there's some men coming here to kill me."

Mara smiled, "Sorry…I got here first."

"What did you say? What do you want Mara? I know you love your son, but you don't need to become a killer like him."

Mara pulled the pistol up and Royal became quiet. "Don't try and antagonize me, Royal. You tried to intimidate Ford when Julia was killed. We all know the game you were trying to play to get Jubal to come around…so don't mess with me!"

He sat back, holding is hands up. "What do you want, Mara. Make it quick! I'm not so sure my guys are winning out there." As he said that, the sound of gunfire increased.

Mara turned the desk lamp on and the room light off. “Don’t get any ideas, Royal. I just want you to know, I’m here to make you pay for the death of Julia Harmon.”

Royal’s mouth opened but Mara would not let him speak. “You don’t get to talk yet, Royal. You see, I’ve got all the evidence…I know you were responsible…I’ve got proof.”

Again, Royal tried to speak. This time, he forgot to close his mouth. “Harris DePaul.” The name fell like a rock.

“What about Harris DePaul? How did you know we found his body?”

“Because, Royal…I killed him and put him in the back seat of his car...and then put the car in that dirty stink-hole. Gave him the company of an old rabid dog that happened along. Wish it had been you instead.”

Royal looked at Mara, almost a recognition of respect on his face. “Did you just confess to a murder, Mrs. Rawlings?”

Mara cocked the hammer of her pistol, pointing it at Royals head. “You should watch your mouth, Royal. I may just confess to another murder right here in this room.” Royal twitched at this and sunk further into his chair.

“I had a talk with Harris before I put him in that car. He told me about being coerced to kidnap Julia…take her into the mountains to rough her up and scare her. He did all of this under your direction. He did it because you are too big a coward to do your own messy work. You are one pompous coward, Royal. In fact, I think your daddy was too! Why else would he give you such a ridiculous name?”

Royal’s look went from resentful to rage. “You’ll regret that! I’m going to nail you to the wall.

Mara smiled at Royal. Her voice as cold as a grave. “I have the pistol you gave Harris. The one you told him to kill me with. The pistol that killed Jeff Martin. It’s got your fingerprints on it, too. Oh, and I’ve also got that surveillance report Arvil Smeltzer did on me…and one that you had done for Julia, too.” There’s also a letter Harris left with a very detailed description of your dirty work. It’s all there, Royal. All of your sins.”

Royal fidgeted, looking for the first time like a guilty man. "How did…you don't have any of that stuff…how could you?"

Mara spent a quick two minutes explaining the hotel security box and Ellis Banks. At the mention of Ellis' name, Mara noticed a change in Royal's expression. The loud sound of gunfire caught both their attention. Then the sound of gunfire became much lighter. They both knew that it was almost time for a final reckoning.

"It won't hold up in Court, Mara. I can afford the best lawyers in the State…if it even would get to court. Then, after all of your hard work my dear…I'll arrest you for murder."

Mara laughed loudly. "Oh my, Royal! You still don't understand, do you. I'm not trying to get you arrested. I just wanted to let you know that I knew you were guilty before I killed you."

"What do you think you are? Some kind of cold-blooded killer?" Royal smiled at Mara, a very cocky type of smile. That is until she spoke.

"I killed your Deputy, Benny Goins, today. You know, after you sent him to kill me. I blew half his head off. He's lying up in the mountains, at least what the animals haven't been at yet. Smile all you want, Royal, but I'm going to kill you…now." Mara raised the gun, her finger on the trigger.

The voice was soft. Neither Royal or Mara heard the door slide open. "Mara. I would really appreciate it if you would lower your gun. I do understand what you want to…no, need to do. I don't think you need to be his executioner. You've been through too much. This will hurt you…more than you're already hurt, I'm afraid. He needs to be punished, he needs to be stopped. You just shouldn't have to do it."

Mara backed away from Royal, keeping herself positioned to where she could see both Royal and the intruder. She was shocked to see the person standing in front of her. The look on her face mirrored the look on Royal's.

Standing in the doorway stood Angelica Grace Majesty, a rifle held purposively in her hands.

Chapter Eighty-Eight

"Give me the gun Ezra and we'll leave this very minute."

Deputy Sheriff Lon Shell wanted to be furious. After all, he was being forced to drive two civilians to an active crime scene at gunpoint…his gun, being the point. Yet, he understood the positions of Ezra and Raven Majesty. A brother under attack and a sister murdered. He wondered if Ezra was more concerned about the Majesty wealth than he was his brother. Either way, here he was, headed into what could only be a catastrophic situation.

Lon was surprised to see a Deputy's car parked just over from the main gate. As he pulled up beside it, he recognized it being the unit Benny Goins drove. Ezra and Raven began protesting as soon as he stopped and turned the engine off. "You all go ahead and shoot me if you want. I'm going to check this out." Lon pocketed his car keys as he exited the car.

Using his heavy flashlight, he carefully examined first the interior of the car and then the surrounding ground. Ezra and Raven were out of the car by the time he finished looking around. They were all startled when a voice called out to them.

"Lonnie Shell! We have you covered. Don't make any sudden moves. That goes for Mr. and Mrs. Majesty, too. We aren't going to harm you."

Lon pointed his flashlight toward the voice just as Ezra held the pistol in the same direction. Raven pulled a shotgun out of the back of Lon's car. She had no idea if it was loaded but was prepared to defend herself.

Ford Rawlings walked out of the shadows, holding a weapon of his own. Lon heard a footfall behind him which turned out to be Phil Sizemore. He was holding a rifle in a non-threatening position.

Lon told Ezra to lower the weapon and did the same for Raven. The shotgun wasn't loaded, but he didn't want her doing anything stupid given the circumstances. Raven reluctantly lowered the weapon but did not put it down.

Lon walked over to Ford so he could speak lowly to him. "What's going on, Ford? Have you been up to the house?"

Before Ford could answer, gunshots were heard from the direction of the house.

"That's been going on ever since we arrived just a little while ago. There were quite a few shots at first but it's gotten more sporadic lately. We were just getting ready to go up to the house when we spotted your headlights. Phil's wrecker is hidden across the road and I've gotten one of DePoli's cars inside the gate, just out of sight. I found my Dad's pickup hidden just over that direction. And then there's a dead Deputy just over in those trees. I'd venture there's more along the way."

Lon noticed movement just inside the gate and was surprised to see Holly Harmon walk out into the moonlight. She also was holding a weapon. Lon could see she had been in a scrape of some sort as she was covered in fresh grime, her curly hair even more tangled.

Ezra walked over to Lon and Ford as Holly caught Raven's eye. She moved over to the dark woman. Ford was surprised when Holly wrapped her arms around Raven as the woman began crying lowly. He realized from what he'd just heard that they both shared the grief of losing a sister to violence.

Quickly, Ford told Lon Shell the many events of the day. Ezra was fidgeting as the Ford spoke. He finally exploded. "Enough! We need to get up to my Brother's! If you want to wait then give me the keys!"

Lon turned to see is own gun pointing at his head. Ezra was favoring his club foot, looking as if he could barely stand. Lon held out his hand, "Give me the gun Ezra and we'll leave this very minute."

Ezra looked at Ford who nodded. "We'll go too, Ezra. We need to get this thing finished, okay."

Ezra handed the pistol to Lon. "Thank you! Can we go now!"

Ezra rode in the car with Lon. Ford followed in the big Buick, that Dino used. Behind him, Phil Sizemore drove the other Deputy's car with Holly and Raven in the back seat. The idea was to confuse anyone still on the grounds. The Sheriff's men might hold their fire seeing two Deputy's cars. DiPoli's men would see the Buick and at least hesitate to see what was going on.

The ploy was working as the three cars made it to the front of the house, a few yards from DiPoli's remaining men hiding behind the tri-angle of cars. There was hesitancy by the two remaining Deputies and the two gangsters behind the Buicks. Suddenly, DiPoli's men opened fire at Lon's car. The Deputy's began firing at the Buick.

Ezra cried out as Lon gunned the engine and plowed directly into the barricade of cars. One of the gangsters was thrown into the car behind him, crushed between the two vehicles. The other one retreated up the steps and fell inside.

One of Royal's dishonest Deputies charged the house, thinking the men inside were allies. Phil and Ford came out of their cars causing the Deputy to come to a halt and try to fire at them. Phil knocked him out before he had a chance to fire.

The second Deputy approached from the other side. He had a rifle leveled at Ford and Phil. A loud blast was heard causing the men to duck into a defensive stance. The Deputy was thrown backwards from the blast of the shotgun held by Raven Majesty. She had found a box of shells in the car.

For the first time in the last hour, there was quiet on the grounds of the Majesty Manor.

Chapter Eighty-Nine

"...his bloodied hand shook as he held on to the knife."

The fight between Ferrell and Drago had reverted to the most basic animal instincts of survival. The men were pounding each other's bodies with their bare fists. Neither one could conceive of backing down, quitting, or losing.

Ferrell grabbed a heavy, broken table leg, sweeping it upward, hitting Drago on the side of the head sending him sprawling up against the broken bed. Drago's vision was blurred, especially in the darkened room. Ferrell managed to get to his feet turning on Drago as he lay up against the bed. Drago's hand found the hilt of the knife he'd dropped early in the fight. He turned on Ferrell just as the man brought the table leg down toward Drago's head.

Instead of crushing Drago's skull, the club made contact with the tilted bed post which deflected the blow. Drago lashed out with the knife, slicing deeply across Ferrell's left leg, just where the thigh and the knee connected. Ferrell screamed and fell toward his left. Drago struck again with the knife, this time slashing deeply across the man's right leg just where the Achilles tied into the calf muscle. The man screamed out again, falling partially on top of Drago.

Drago rolled over onto Ferrell, pinning him to the floor. He grabbed the man's head and shoved it hard against the floor with one hand while slamming the knife through his upper chest, just below the shoulder. The knife penetrated Ferrell's torso, sticking into the wooden floorboard underneath. Ferrell was pinned to the floor but was not giving up the fight. Using his free hand, he grabbed Drago by the throat in a crushing grip.

He didn't try to knock Ferrell's grip loose. Instead, Drago grabbed the man's throat and began squeezing as hard as he could. Both men struggled to tighten their neck muscles, willing themselves to continue squeezing. Ferrell's eyes began to bulge and his grip weaken. He was losing blood profusely from the wounds in his shoulder and legs.

Ferrell's sticky lifeblood began pooling on the floor. His eyes flickered until they settled into a dead stillness. Drago stood, placed his foot on Ferrell's chest and pulled the knife blade from the floor and through the dead man's chest.

Without hesitation, Drago made his way to the staircase. His head spun, his eyes blurred, and his bloodied hand shook as he held on to the knife. He didn't bother looking for his gun…there would be plenty of them downstairs.

Chapter Ninety

"He's guilty, Angelica!"

Angelica Grace waited patiently as Mara considered her options. Mara lowered the guns she held, her eyes fixed on Royal. "I can't stop, Angelica. He's your husband…father to your children. But you gotta see, I can't stop now. He's such an evil man…he's done so many evil things."

She turned to Angelica. "He's the cause of Julia's death…he sent the man to take her. He was going to kill me…and even J.J. and Ford. I've got proof!"

Mara had a wild look in her eyes. She knew DiPoli's men…the mob, were coming for them. Any minute now…she knew it! She cried out, "He's guilty, Angelica!"

Angelica Grace's eyes were sad as she quietly said, "I know."

Royal started to stand, reaching for his pistol that had been set down at the end of the desk. "No!" Angelica raised her voice for the first time! Royal looked at her, stunned that the rifle was now pointed at him.

"Gracie! What are you doing? We've got to get ready. DiPoli and his men are coming! Shoot this woman so we can defend ourselves!"

Angelica Grace moved from the doorway. "I think you've done enough evil in this world, Royal. I can't bare you any longer. Florence has taken the children away for their safety. You would have left them in this house even though you knew it would be a battlefield. You don't love them and you don't love me! You brought me to a beautiful land but you and your brother have made it all ugly to me. You are so blind you can't even see how evil you are. I'm sorry Royal, I wanted you to change…I prayed for it."

Mara un-expectantly found herself in the middle of a domestic battle of serious proportions. She was within a trigger squeeze of killing Royal. She didn't know how Angelica Grace would respond. For all Mara knew, Angelica was also within a trigger pull of killing her husband…or maybe her.

Royal looked at Angelica, shaking his head. "To hell with this, Gracie." He leaned over and grabbed the pistol. Before he could raise the weapon toward Mara, Angelica fired the rifle.

Royal screamed out as the bullet passed through is forearm. The pistol fell to the ground and Mara kicked it over towards the wall. Everything fell apart at that moment. Royal was cursing his wife as she chambered another round and moved across the room. Mara pointed her pistol at Royal and was about ready to put another bullet in the evil man when a voice rose above the rest.

Vincent DiPoli was standing in the doorway, the Thompson machine gun ready to cut down anyone who moved. Beppe Carbone stood behind him, covering the hallway.

"Looks to be as bloody in here as it is outdoors." Royal's face froze as he saw Vincent holding the machine gun. The large, mountain of a man, Vincent's bodyguard, stood just behind him, glancing over his shoulder beyond Vincent.

The whole room stilled. Royal was frozen as he held onto his damaged arm. Vincent had a very satisfied look on his face. "I can see we all brought some fine weaponry to the party. Let me just say that I think my gun trumps all the rest of you. How about everyone drop your weapons of choice and give me the room?"

Vincent waited a second, but no one responded. He tried again, "Sit down Royal, you're not going anywhere." His words were fresh on everyone's ears when he took a few quick steps toward Royal, pushing the barrel of the Thompson into is neck. He shouted to the room. "Do what I say or I'll take his head off!"

Mara spoke, "Why don't you go ahead…that's why we're all here, it seems."

Royal fell backwards in his chair as Vincent laughed. "No friends left Sheriff Majesty? That must tear at your gut when even your wife wants to kill you."

Royal knew he had a .32 caliber pistol in the drawer, only inches away from his hands. He just needed to pick the right moment.

Vincent suddenly let loose a short volley into the wall bringing panic to all. Mara started to shoot DiPoli but the big bodyguard was too quick. He knocked the pistol out of her hand, grabbing her so roughly that the other pistol fell to the floor.

Mara tried to struggle but the man was so strong. She was surprised when he whispered in her ear, "Be still. Stay back and you'll be okay."

Mara relaxed and the man released her, gently guiding her back against the wall. In the flurry of commotion, Angelica Grace moved back into the doorway. She held the rifle so it was pointed at Vincent's head.

"You drop your weapon Mr. DiPoli…I'll not ask again."

Vincent did not even look at Angelica. Instead, he spat, "Kill that whore, Beppe. I'm tired and we need to get on the road."

Before Beppe could even say a word, Drago appeared behind Angelica Grace placing his knife at her throat. Her neck began to ooze blood as he pushed the blade into her porcelain skin. Mara didn't know if Angelica was bleeding or the blood was coming off the very bloodied hand that held the knife.

Royal jumped up, a loud, "Nooo!" falling from his lips. Vincent reached across the desk and smacked Royal with the butt of the Thompson. Adding to the immediate drama and confusion came gunfire from the front of the house. A terrible crashing sound as metal contacted metal was hard. This noise was followed by a shotgun blast.

The table lamp was knocked to the floor when Vincent slammed Royal with his Thompson, leaving the room dark except for the moonlight coming from the window.

A voice cried out from the front foyer. "They're coming Mr. DiPoli. They're killing everybody. I'm the last one left!"

More gunfire was heard and then silence. Mara crawled to a more neutral corner, picking up Royal's Colt Python from the floor.

As soon as the firing started, Angelica Grace stomped her high heel into the shin of Drago and pushed away from him as he cried out in pain. Beppe went into a crouch and Royal ducked behind the desk. Drago recovered and grabbed Angelica's dropped rifle, running toward the front door.

He chambered a shell and fired as he ran, just missing Ford as he came through the door in a low, running crouch. Ford went into a roll, ending up against a staircase. He started to fire but a body fell on top of him from the staircase. Aldo was wounded and out of ammunition but he still wanted to fight.

Lon feinted twice before rolling through the door. He would have been shot by Drago had not the man turned his rifle on the struggling Ford. He fired directly at Ford, just as Aldo swung him to the floor. An "ooph" sounded as one or both of the men felt the impact of the bullet.

Lon started to rise when a burst of gunfire sailed down the hallway past Drago. Vincent ran into the hallway, fearing he was about to be shot if he stayed in Royal's office. He put his back against the wall just outside the door and fired a burst toward the foyer. He started to fire a burst back through the door into the office when he heard Drago curse loudly. The rifle was out of ammunition keeping him from shooting Lon.

Drago took hold of the rifle barrel as he ran toward the prone Lon Shell. He was about to club the Deputy Sheriff with the rifle butt when he caught movement in the front door. A chorus of gunfire blew the man into oblivion. Standing in the doorway was Raven holding a smoking shotgun. Standing on either side of her was Ezra and Holly, both with smoking pistols.

Vincent couldn't believe he was seeing Drago fall. He put a fresh clip in Thompson and took a deep breath. After a second's hesitation, he quickly stepped inside, pointing the deadly weapon into the room with the intent of killing everyone inside.

Before he could pull the trigger, Beppe Carbone stepped up to Vincent from the darkened room and shot the gangster through the side of the head. Beppe caught the Thompson only to lay it and his pistol gently on the floor. He turned around to face the hallway and raised his massive arms in the air.

Back in the foyer, there was a groaning that caught Holly's attention. She had not been able to find Ford immediately. Realizing he was one of the men tangled up on the floor, she rushed over to him calling his name.

He was addled, but alive. The bullet had struck Aldo, passing through the gangster's shoulder and nicking Ford's chest. As the two men fell to the floor, Ford's head had landed hard on the marble tile.

Holly fell beside him, pulling him to a sitting position as she tried to get him to speak to her. She almost jumped out of her skin when a penetrating scream filled the room.

Aldo was not dead from his wound. He picked up Ford's pistol and was getting ready to fire it at the semi-conscious man. He would have killed him and probably Holly too had not Raven leaped across the two and landed heavily onto Aldo. He fired upon her impact, grazing her thigh. In an instance, Raven used one of the sharp knives she'd brought from the hunting lodge. She rammed it into Aldo's throat, screaming, "This is for Serafina! Vengeance for my sister!" She stabbed him twice more and tried to pull Aldo's head from his body. When she couldn't do so, she collapsed, wailing and crying in a pool of Aldo's blood.

Royal was able to see Beppe shoot Vincent from his position behind the desk. He opened the draw and slid out the .32 pistol. He stood, pointing the pistol, not at Beppe but at Mara. "This is all your fault, damn you!"

It was not Royal's gun that fired, though. Angelica Grace had pulled the .38 Police Special she kept in a holster around her thigh. She fired it twice, directly at her husband. Royal spun around, grabbing the desk to keep from falling. He looked up to find himself looking directly at Mara. His grip on the desk was very shaky as he looked at the woman.

Royal looked down at his wounds. He was amazed at the blood oozing into the material of his finely fitted shirt. Words slipped out of his bleeding mouth as he looked at Mara. "Please…tell Lon, I'm sorry. Tell him I'm proud of him…always have been. I want…no, please tell Betty she did a fine job raising Lon. Tell her I'm grateful."

Royal slipped a little on the desk as his own blood pooled around his hand. His look held Mara's gaze. "Help me…have mercy."

Mara looked into his fading eyes. "There's no mercy for you Royal…hell has no mercy!" With that she fired Royal's 357. caliber Python directly into his heart. The bullet ripped through him and tore through a plaque on the wall noting his community service as Sheriff.

Mara and Angelica Grace's eyes met. "Angelica, I had to do that. I'm sorry."

Angelica wearily shook her head. "You had every reason. We all have to learn to live with what we do and what we don't. That's just how it always works isn't it, Mara? Life goes on. We can live for the future or die marred in the past." With that, Angelica Grace Majesty walked to Mara and hugged her in a warm embrace.

Mara's mind flashed a snapshot of Sabato Ferrari lying on the ground, his face a bloody pulp. "Yeah, I guess you're right."

Mara was uneasy, but she had to ask. She pulled away from Angelica a bit, still holding onto her arms. "Why was Royal going on about Lon and Betty? I would have thought he would have said something about his children."

Angelica took a deep breath. "That's the thing…Lon is one of his children. He coerced Betty when she was very young. To her credit, she would never marry Royal and made him promise not to let Lon know he was his father. Royal has been Lon's benefactor in many ways over the years. I only knew about it because I started finding bits and pieces of papers showing things he provided for Lon. I guess he made sure he got into the Law Enforcement Academy. All in all, Lon's done well. He's a good Deputy Sheriff…one of the few that stayed away from Royal's illegal enterprise. I couldn't tell you for sure if Lon was aware of things Royal has done, but I really doubt it. I really don't think Royal would allow it."

There was an awkward silence. They gave each other an understanding hug and headed to the foyer to see what had transpired. Walking past Beppe, they stopped. Mara stood on tip-toes and gave him a light kiss on the cheek while Angelica reached up and squeezed his shoulder affectionately. "What's your name, sir?", Angelica asked.

"Beppe Carbone, mam. I'm sorry for all of this. It seems I've found myself with too many crazy men recently. I'm truly sorry!"

Mara pulled his arms down. "Go home, Beppe. Go back to New York. Go see your family and leave these crazy men alone."

Angelica reached up and cupped his chin in her soft hand. "Yes…do that Beppe. Have beautiful children or raise beautiful children. Our time is too short for this type of life."

With that, the two walked past him and down the hallway to the foyer. Mara hurried over to Holly and Ford. He was about to get his senses back. She noted the bloodied pile of what was once a man lying to the side.

Mara looked over when she heard Angelica exclaim, “Oh no, Raven. I’m so sorry! Has anyone called an ambulance? He may live if we can get help.”

Raven was sitting on the floor holding a decorative table runner to her husband’s abdomen. Aldo’s shot that grazed Raven’s leg had hit Ezra. He was breathing, but very shallow. Rich red blood was soaking into the cloth as Raven tried to staunch the bleeding.

Lon came running back into the house with first aid supplies. “I raised the Office on the radio! They’re sending an ambulance. He bent down and began trying to help Raven with Ezra.

Phil came inside for the first time. He walked over to Ford, Holly, and Mara. “Mara, Holly…you guys okay? How’s Ford doing? You all right, buddy?”

As Ford nodded his head, Phil began telling him about cleaning up the grounds. “Mostly dead guys out there. I’ve rounded up three wounded. They’re out front…won’t be going anywhere. I got into a scrape with one of the gun thugs. He was wounded but wouldn’t surrender. I don’t think he could walk but decided it a good idea to shoot at me. Didn’t last long. All that’s left alive is two Deputies and a Mob guy. All the rest are dead…at least the ones I was able to find in the dark. A damn bloody night…terrible waste I’d reckon.”

Mara started to walk to the door when she thought of something. “Oh…and Phil, there’s another fellow down in the cellar from the kitchen. It’s Arvil Smeltzer. He’s probably got a concussion. I hit him over the head with an iron skillet.” She looked at Ford and smiled.

He smiled back. “Uncle Jubal would be proud of you, Mother!” She grinned at Ford and saw a big grin flash on Holly’s face.

Mara turned back to the door. There was a terrible pain in her stomach. She wasn’t wounded but she was feeling a growing, gnawing pain. She scanned the immediate grounds looking for one face. It wasn't to be seen and she was scared to death to think just what that might mean.

Phil had Ford sitting up against a wall. Holly was looking at the bullet crease on his chest. Phil was examining the knot of Ford's head. "One thing I don't understand. There's no sign of any of the Haddish clan. They're nowhere to be found…dead or alive. Guess they could see what was coming."

Ford's eyes widened. "You need to look for Dad. He's here somewhere! I found his truck down at the highway. Find him, Phil!"

As everyone took care of each other, the sound of sirens became increasingly louder. Raven was heard saying, "Stay with me baby. Just a few more minutes. Help is coming. Ezra! Ezra, stay with me!"

Angelica Grace Majesty met the two ambulances as well the two remaining Deputy cars that arrived. She ushered them into the house as if she was graciously greeting guests for a social function. Mara walked in beside Angelica, giving her another sympathetic hug. The two women stood together, helping direct rescue personnel as well as other people who continued to show up at the Majesty Manor.

Mara saw Phil walk into the darkness. He called back, I'm going to find J.J. Ford says he's here. Don't worry Mara, I'll find him." The wrecker driver walked away, dreading what he would find.

Beppe Carbone was already walking in the shadows along the driveway. Getting away from the Majesty house was his number one concern at the moment. He'd have to figure out the rest once he did that. Going down the driveway in custom leather shoes was easier than his recent climb to the top of the hill. It was also much better since no one was shooting at him.

A groan off to his right caught his attention. He didn't have his gun, but he had his hands. It could be one of Vincent's men or it may just as easily be one of Royal's men. Beppe eased over, hovering above the man he found behind a large piece of shrubbery.

It wasn't one of Vincent's and it wasn't a Deputy. Beppe bent down for a closer look when a hard fist struck his jaw. Beppe was more surprised than hurt even though the punch rattled him a little. He grabbed the man, not wanting to hurt him as he was already in obvious pain.

Recognition suddenly came to Beppe. "Mr. Rawlings! I'm not going to hurt you. It's Beppe Carbone! You repaired my car…you fix your coffee just like my old man."

J.J. didn't know what to expect when the big man grabbed him. He decided he couldn't do anything to the man so he decided to greet him. "Hey Beppe. Seems I got myself shot in the leg. Lost my gun and couldn't get up to the house. Hell, couldn't even get back to the road. Sounds like there was quite a party up at the big house. Anybody left alive?"

J.J. suddenly became serious. "Did you happen to see my wife? Her name is Mara…is she okay? Did you see Ford?" J.J. became very quiet as he waited for an answer. He needed to know but was scared to death to hear the answer.

Beppe used his strong hands, pulling J.J. to his feet. "Let's get you over here. You're right, Mr. Rawlings, there was some bad business up there. Your wife's okay, though. She's a tough one. Your son and that girl are both okay, too. I don't know about the others, but it's over."

Beppe helped J.J. move over to a large, purposeful rock that sat right by the driveway. "Somebody will be along soon and get you. Probably be a lot of traffic coming and going soon. Ambulances are already up at the house. They'll get you fixed up. Like I told your wife, I'm sorry for all these troubles. Just don't worry, nobody else will be coming. I'll guarantee it.

Beppe checked J.J.'s leg, adjusting the tourniquet and checking for blood leakage. He patted J.J. on the shoulder, saying, "You take care Mr. Rawlings. You and your family have a safe life." He shook his head and started down the driveway.

Turning back, he spoke, "It was nice to meet you Mr. Rawlings. You were very nice to me when you fixed my car. I hope you understand I was never going to hurt your family. He paused, "Excuse me for asking, but is your son's name really Elvis?"

J.J. laughed, "That's the birds name!"

Beppe threw up his hands. "No wonder he gets so mad when you call him that."

With that, he started to walk away. J.J. called after him,

"Don't look like you have a ride home Mr. Carbone. It's a long way to New York."

Beppe shrugged, "Guess I'll figure it out."

J.J. reached in his pocket, pulling out his truck keys. He tossed them to Beppe who managed to catch them in his meaty hand. "My trucks at the bottom of the hill, over behind some rhododendron bushes. Take it and safe travels."

Beppe was surprised…completely shocked. "But how do I get it back to you?"

J.J. laughed. "You'll figure it out!"

In only a few minutes, Beppe Carbone was headed down the highway in J.J.'s pickup. He was still shocked at the man's generous offer. He didn't understand it but he knew what he was going to do when he got home. He was going to hug and kiss his wife and daughters like he'd never done before, then he was going to eat and eat the wonderful food his wife would prepare, and then, he was going to sleep as if he'd never wake up again.

Epilogue

Early Fall, 1958

Mara Rawlings hung up her telephone. The call had brought back so many memories. Her eyes were misty at the thoughts of time past. She still could not grasp all the events that had taken place a year ago. It was even hard to consider everything that had happened since then.

The call she'd received was from an old friend of Ford's, a Mr. Joseph Moretti. He was a charming man, making her think of so many older Italian-American gentlemen she'd known so long ago. The man could not say enough good things about Ford and his lifetime in New Jersey not so long ago.

Mr. Moretti shared with Mara some of the details of the terrible circumstances that led to Ford returning to North Carolina. He was happy to share with Mara that Felisa and her mother, Dorotea, were both improving. "They're living in Italy now. I made arrangements through some friends to transport them there when their health allowed them to travel. They are safe and continuing to heal. Felisa's wounds will take longer, but the warm Italian days will restore her. She is able to speak a little now."

Dorotea was feeling well enough now to operate a small bakery. The business was located just below their apartment. Joseph spoke again of having friends that found them a place to live and a business to own in their new home.

Joseph's voice was filled with emotion as he spoke further about the Gervasè women. "There is a wonderful hospital nearby. The best surgeons in Italy will continue to work with Felisa until she is as good as new. They are going to be fine. They have people who already love them and care for them. They will be more than fine…they will flourish!"

Before Mara could ask, he added. "I don't think they will ever come back to New Jersey. It will be for the best. They have some cousins in Italy, I believe. Plus, my friends there will make sure they are happy and safe. They are both very dear to my heart. They will always be all right. I hope to see them again. Lately I have become melancholy. I would love to see my homeland again."

Mara could only imagine who the “friends” of Joseph Moretti were. She knew how these things worked. If she was sure of anything, she knew Felisa and her mother would most certainly be all right.

Joseph Moretti did not call just to speak of Felisa and Dorotea Gervasè or of the time Ford spent in New Jersey. Instead, he had very good news for Mara. The news left her as stunned as the day Ford showed up out of the blue, one Fall day a year ago.

“Mrs. Rawlings…Mara…I have something to tell you. I must confess I was interested when I learned that you, Ford’s mother, was once a New Jersey native. And, a woman of Italian heritage as well. You see, there was a familiar ring to your last name. I hear a lot of things, and so, I know a lot of things. Thank God I have been blessed with a mind that is rarely forgetful.”

He paused as he took an extra breath. “I thought on the name, “DeVoti”. Then I made a few calls. I was not trying to be intrusive, but I was curious. You see, I remember hearing of some troubles having to do with a petty gangster, Anatolio Ferrari’s son, Sabato. It all happened years ago. The troubles had to do with a young Italian girl by the name of DeVoti. Anatolio was crazy with anger and had his men looking for her even in Chambersburg.”

“I made calls and other people made more calls. That is how I finally learned that Sabato tried to rape and savage this young girl whose last name was DeVoti. It seems she fought to keep her honor and did much more than that. In fact, this deviate paid a price for the many sins he’d previously committed on a number of innocent girls.”

By now, Mara’s heart was beating so rapidly she could hear the sound of it in her ears. Joseph went on. “My friends tell me she broke a liquor bottle he was drinking from and used it to lacerate his face for his transgressions. In fact, he lost an eye and was left with a face filled with scars. He was never the same again which left his father crying out for vengeance.”

Now Mara’s breathing was uneven and it took both hands to hold the receiver still enough to use. “Mara, let me tell you something that I hope will be of comfort to you. Some of my friends made a point to visit the home of the Ferrari’s. These *anamali* were still no more than two-bit hoods, using their evils to prey on the old, weak, and scared. But I must tell you…they do this no more. It seems the evil old man died a year ago. His reprobate of a son took over his father's business but he cannot be found now…and he will not be ever heard of again. Trust me in this matter. This means that the innocent girl that fought for her virtue and fled her home will never have to worry again about any reprisals from the Ferrari's. The past has been forever buried and will never be revisited.

All Mara could manage was a whispered, "Thank you!"

"Well, Mrs. Rawlings, I have even more good news. I believe Mr. Jovanni Visconti and his lovely Bride, Natale, had a magnificent wedding. As you know, they wanted to have some Justice of the Peace do a quick ceremony last year but neither family allowed them to go through with such nonsense. Ford and Holly had a wonderful time at the wedding. He was a very handsome Best Man.

Holly is a beautiful and lovely girl. I believe she will make you a wonderful Daughter-in-Law in the Spring. I'm sure you are very happy for her to become a part of your family. I just hope my health allows me to come to North Carolina for the blessed event."

Mara recovered enough to say, "Oh yes! You must come. I understand you are a wonderful cook. Come down and we will share recipes. You must come. My lord, bring anybody who'll come along."

Joseph laughed until he began coughing. "We'll see. I'll make sure Ford and Holly get back to you safely. I think the many troubles you and your family have known are behind you. I hope you all have a most happy life and that it will soon be filled with many grandchildren!"

They spoke only a few more minutes as Joseph's coughing became worse. She hung up and spoke out loud to only herself. "A most happy life would be so wonderful. I hope it is Mr. Moretti. We've lived too many lifetimes that haven't been that way. I hope this one stays for a long time."

Just then J.J. came in from his shop. "I just heard the news on the radio. Interim Sheriff Lonny Shell has been elected as the new High Sheriff of Burke County. I guess with Ezra dying back in April, the Majesty dynasty is played out."

The State Police, F.B.I. and other Agencies had been investigating the bloody night for the last nine months. Lon stayed on as Interim Sheriff and was found to be innocent of being involved in anything illegal. Some friends of Royal Majesty made sure a plaque celebrating the deceased Sheriff was hung at the courthouse. In the end, it became something Angelica Grace could point to and tell her children it was for their Daddy's memory.

Mara smiled at the news of Lon's win. She called to J.J., "Oh, and I got a letter from Angelica Grace today. Her and the children have found them a home in Baton Rouge and are already moved in. She's been introducing the children to a few of her kin and getting them settled into life in Louisiana."

"I asked about Raven. She hasn't seen her yet. All she knows is that she got settled in New Orleans. Angelica said she doubted Raven would ever contact her again. She's carrying Ezra's death in a dark way. Angelica believes Raven will disappear into her old occult roots. She thinks she's having her sister's coffin moved to the property she bought. I tell you, those two sisters were scary people."

J.J. smiled. "Well, I'll tell you, that Ezra was a mad toad himself! I think they all deserved each other. Remind me to never visit New Orleans!"

He started up the steps and called back over his shoulder. "Do you still want to drive over toward Brown Mountain to see if the lights show up tonight?"

Mara smiled, "I think it'll be a good night. It's going to be clear. Maybe we'll get lucky?"

"Okay. I'll only be long enough to change clothes and then we can leave. I'll even buy you dinner down at Mary's Diner before we head out to look for the lights."

Mara drew a deep breath. "You know something J.J., we just never knew how lucky we got on that mountain back in the day."

J.J. topped the steps and called back. "Honey, no truer words could be said. I'll be right back down, we'll have to see what kind of magic old Brown Mountain has to show us tonight."

Mara called to her husband. "Are we taking my Ford? I think its running just fine now. You did wonders getting the old "girl" up and going again."

J.J. returned to the top of the steps. "Let's take Ford's Chevy. I'd like to blow out the cobwebs. Finally got all the parts in and put back together. She needs a little road time…plus there's more room inside!"

Mara knew there was a grin on J.J.'s face without having to look at him. She couldn't help but grin herself. As she sat on the steps, waiting for the return of the love of her life, she gazed into the living room, her eyes falling on a photograph sitting on the small table near the door. It had been damaged once but it was still one of her favorites. Looking back at her from the new frame were the faces of a much younger Mara and J.J. They were holding their baby son at Easter…it was the luckiest time of all their lifetimes.

AUTHOR'S NOTE

Elvis, Fast Cars, and the Brown Mountain Lights is wholly a work of fiction. The characters, the town of Treemont, and the events of the story are only the fictional telling of a story. Actually, it is the mysterious Brown Mountain Lights that are the most factual aspect of this saga.

Brown Mountain is a 1.5 mile-long, low mountain ridge rising to the elevation of 2,600 feet. It is part of the Pisgah National Forest and sits along the county lines of Burke County and Caldwell Counties.

Sightings of the glowing orbs have been documented from the time of the Catawba and Cherokee Indians. The sightings continued by pioneers and explorers crossing the Western North Carolina mountains, Civil War soldiers, residents, and scientists. Many legends and lore have been told concerning the lights and their origins. Many explanations have been given over the centuries. Some of these explanations are of a whimsical or even bizarre nature. Fortunately, for those who like to romanticize such phenomena, there is still no absolutely definitive answer as to what causes the glowing *ghost* lights.

Other books of fiction have been written using the Lights as part of the story, using an explanation of the lights to fit the story. National Geographic was involved in research to discover the origin of the Lights. Staff from Appalachian State University (Boone, NC) have been involved discovering an explanation of the small, glowing orbs. Television shows such as the *X-Files* have used the phenomenon in their productions. People still travel to the locations where the view of the *ghost* lights are best seen. These areas are surrounded by the beautiful Western North Carolina mountains and valleys. Seekers of the lights may be disappointed in not seeing the orbs make an appearance, but they will still be rewarded by the beauty of the region.

While this book offers a character's unique description of what the *Lights* are, it is of course a description that holds no validity. In fact, it is most likely a description you will find in no other book…fiction or non-fiction.

I hope the reader will take time to research the *Brown Mountain Lights* by doing internet searches. You will find recordings of the *lights*, as well as best viewing points, ideal times to look for them and interesting bits of history going back to the days when only the Native American tribes lived in this land. The *Brown Mountain Lights* have been capturing man's imagination and whimsy for hundreds of years and personally, I hope they always will.

So, I encourage you to partake in a little whimsy on your own. Try and catch a look at the lights when you are in the area. Explore Western North Carolina if you aren't already a resident. Who knows, you might run into a little mountain magic yourself.

~

One other note concerning this work. Over the years, there have been Authors who have produced outstanding works referred to as a *Saga.* The original meaning comes from Icelandic prose narratives composed in the 12th and 13th centuries. The term came to be used in a looser way of definition into the 20th century. It finally became accepted as a long, detailed account; a work of heroic deeds that may travel across a lengthy amount of time. It could also be applied to a series of stories running consecutively. James Michener was one who served up this type of novel with great results.

Not to compare myself to the great writers who have used this format, I would like to say that this is my attempt at creating my own version of a *Saga.* I hope you found it entertaining as you followed the characters though their journeys. It proved to be a story not made for brevity.

Please note my other novels listed at the front of this book. I hope you will invest your time again with one of my works.

ABOUT THE AUTHOR

Gary Street has lived around the East Tennessee / North Carolina mountains all of his life. He worked as an outside salesman for almost four decades, traveling through this amazing area. The natural beauty and the amazing people coupled with the deep cultural and historic roots of the area have always played a part of this Author's life.

Growing up in a family who enjoyed a good story told well certainly had an effect on this writer. Setting out to see if he could actually write a book, he determined four things. A good story needs to be told well, a writer should always be considerate of his potential readers, the characters deserve to written in the best version of themselves, and a writer needs to stay true to his story…make it theirs.

Writing quickly became a passion, something to enjoy and look forward to doing. The first story was penned in 2014 and published the next year. *Elvis, Fast Cars, and the Brown Mountain Lights* is my fifth novel in five years. As a writer, I am very blessed to have these five unique stories to tell.

Gary's wife, Nancy, is the creator of his cover artwork. A talented, self-trained artist, Nancy excels in architectural artwork. They live in Johnson City, Tennessee. They have two sons, Ryan and Chris who reside in the great State of Texas.

With the completion of this work, Gary plans on following his passion with another good story, well told.

Made in the USA
Columbia, SC
01 July 2020